The Medicine Girl

by

Deidra Whitt Lovegren

ISBN: 979-8-9862976-1-3 (Hardcover)
ISBN: 979-8-9862976-0-6 (Paperback)
ISBN: 979-8-9862976-2-0 (eBook)

Any references to historical events, real people, or real places are used fictitiously. Names, characters, and places are products of the author's imagination.

Book design by Blue Marble Publishing LLC
Illustrations by Russell Norman

First printed edition 2022.
Blue Marble Publishing LLC

deidrawhittlovegren.com
bmpublish.com

Dedicated to my mother, Eva Ann

Richmond
Old Virginia
Shirley Plantation
Saltville
Abingdon
Witt
Nashville
Tennessee
Memphis
Carolinas
Tupelo
Arkansippi
The Crimson Republic
Tuscaloosa
The Kingdom of Georgia
Booth
Montgomery
Savannah
Lucy
Brainbridge
Thomasville
Tallahassee
The Florida Penal Colony

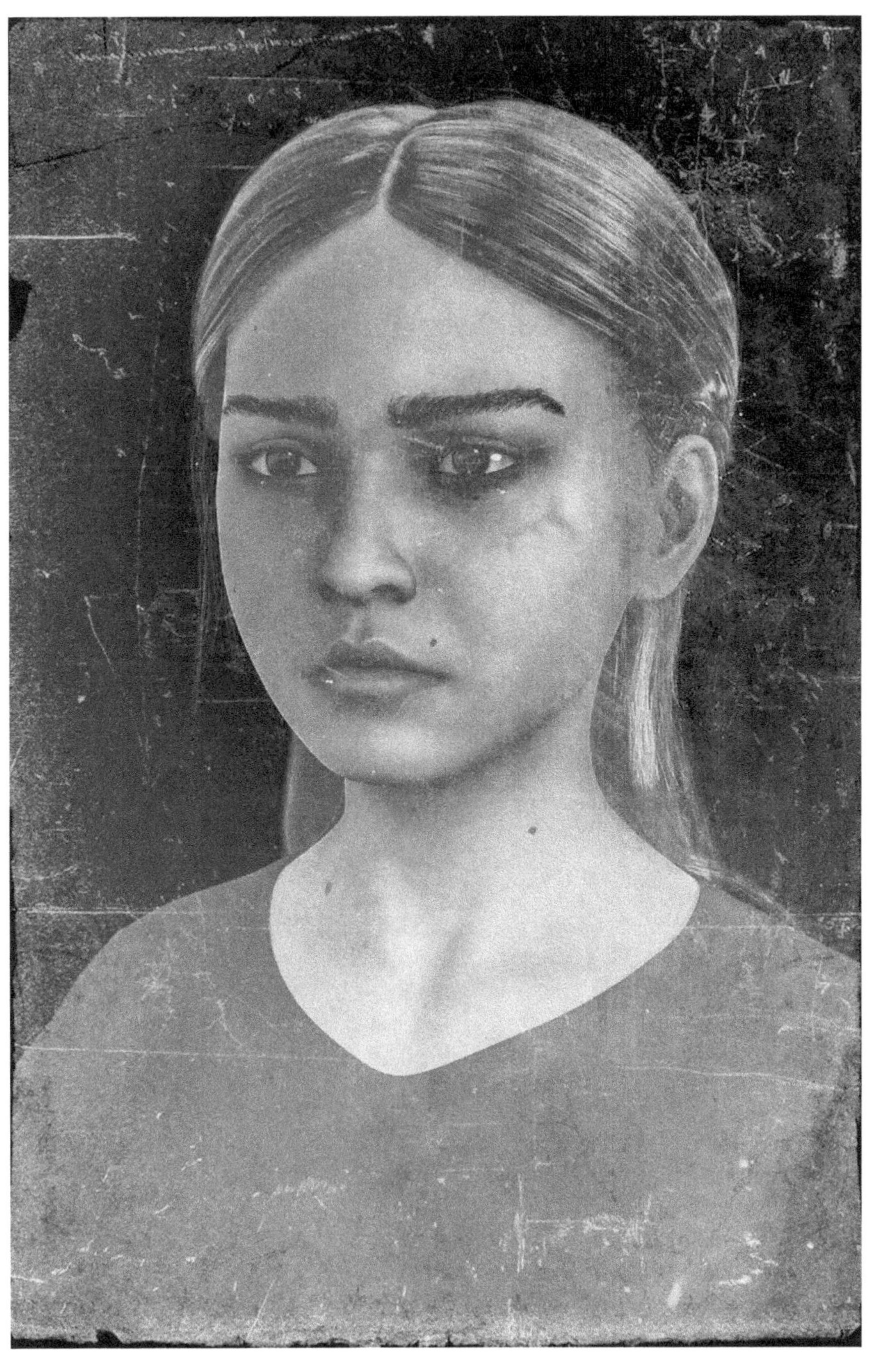

The Medicine Girl

Chapter 1

Tallahassee, The Florida Penal Colony

When the Medicine Girl's father slapped her for the first time, she cried out. Her cries weren't from pain, as her upbringing had been hard—harder than the calluses on her bare feet. They weren't from fear either, since she knew that if he wanted her dead, she'd be dead. She decided her tears sprang from outrage, the sheer surprise of an unwarranted blow. For her father, cruelty was always the point. There was no lesson to be learned except that her father had power and she had none.

She never made that mistake again, crying in his presence, as she noted his sunken eyes glittered at the sound of her sobs.

So she did what all weak things do.

She watched and waited.

Ever since the State of Florida had been cordoned off as a free range penal colony, the Medicine Girl had planned her escape. Especially after the United Authority began crucifying recalcitrant warlords and their families outside of the old State Capitol building, yet federal power had waned over the last three decades—at least to hear her father tell of it.

The Medicine Girl awoke, hungry as always.

As she stole across the marshlands at daylight, she carried her small machete, looking for sabal palmetto. If she were lucky enough to find one along the ravaged landscape, she would feast. The flowers of the "cabbage palm" were edible, its purplish-black berries thinly fleshed, but sweet. Above all, the Medicine Girl craved the heart of palm, located deep in the sabal palmetto's center.

When you feel weak in your body, you need protein, her mother had instructed her. *If you cannot find any meat, find nuts. Find beans. If necessary, kill the palm and take its heart.*

With her sharp gray eyes, the Medicine Girl spotted the familiar fronds, jutting out from an unfamiliar copse. She scanned the area, looking for anything or anyone who meant her harm. After she was sure it was safe, she strode over to the plant, trusty machete by her side. Cutting the tops off the thickest palm, she hacked at the woody base and removed the outer leaf stems. Finally reaching the tender, creamy white core, she extracted the leek-like cylinder.

Heart of palm. Her taking it would cause the death of the plant, yet sometimes, sacrifices had to be made. Cutting the heart into paper-thin slices, the Medicine Girl popped one right after another into her mouth.

Chewing the palm slices thoughtfully, the Medicine Girl considered there were not many places for her to go.

Should she leave Tallahassee and head to Orlando, the farthest point south, the Medicine Girl would face enormous storms from the warming seas that battered the peninsula's coastlines throughout the year.

Even in Tallahassee, her clan often felt the effects of the erratic weather. Her father and his men grew skillful in watching the winds and in studying the movements of mercury in the old glass barometers. They could predict with some accuracy when a storm threatened, becoming proficient in many things since the last wars.

Still, she had once traveled southward to Orlando as a little girl and remembered it as a mystical place. She puzzled over the colorful ruins that lay before her. Mountains of metal. Husks of buildings. Statues of mythological creatures. Her mother told her what she knew, about a time before the end of electricity. Lights that flickered. Boxes that kept food cold. Cars, trains, buses, airplanes.

The Medicine Girl discounted most of those tales. Frankly, all of it was irrelevant now.

She did not care about what happened before.

Propped up by the United Authority, her father ruled his portion of outer Tallahassee from the remains of a small cinder block structure, constructed nearly a century earlier. Inner Tallahassee was far too dangerous to control, and her father let chaos reign while he reinforced his position and alliance with what remained of the federal government.

All of her life, the Medicine Girl had watched strange men come and go about her father's dwelling. She heard her father laugh with them, drinking fermented honey together like KinsMen. She watched many of them punished as well. Sometimes she was ordered to attend to their injuries afterwards. Sometimes she was ordered not to.

As the sea levels steadily rose around the peninsula, infiltrating groundwater aquifers, the Medicine Girl's father came to power commandeering a desalination facility. Those who controlled the water supply held considerable sway in the penal colony, as trade had mostly replaced the United Authority's federal currency.

Her mother had told her about coins and paper money and plastic cards with numbers on them. So much had happened decades before the Medicine Girl had been born to one of her father's least-favored concubines. She would listen to her mother's tales, but when the older ones spoke of the days before the end of electricity, she grew bored. *There was enough trouble in the present to make borrowing from the past a fool's errand.*

The Medicine Girl found herself amazed at the relative ease in providing clean water on a small scale. She mulled over the viciousness of the skirmishes over something so elemental, but in the penal colony, it seemed to her that the warring clans enjoyed war for war's sake. Ensuring a consistent water supply was another excuse to squabble.

So much expended energy, the Medicine Girl concluded. Nature was far simpler than men with their frustrated desires. Everything in nature had a definitive purpose. The balance was delicate, each factor crucial. Vast cycles depended on things filling the measure of their creation.

Her mother's teachings. Her mother taking time to show her the minutiae of life and how beautiful things were. Her mother's explanations making things all right for a time.

The Medicine Girl ached for her.

Evaporation is part of the water cycle, her mother explained, instructing the Medicine Girl on how to find just the right plastic container among the scores that littered the shores.

Take your knife and pare off the end of a bottle. Roll the bottom inward to make a gutter. This will catch the condensation on the sides. Place it over a smaller container full of seawater.

Be patient. Let the sun extract the water and leave the salt.

Above all, Medicine Girl, be patient.

Due to the absence of a permanent police presence in the penal colony, the United Authority relied on government-backed warlords to maintain a semblance of order. Routinely, the Medicine Girl saw federal men enter her father's compound, arriving by caravans pulled by haggard men in chains.

High-level visitors from the United Authority often wore sunglasses, precious items made before the last wars. The Medicine Girl trusted no one who hid his or her eyes. She'd stare at them as they arrived, trying to divine their purpose. Then she'd disappear into the foliage behind the house and listen.

Being marginalized had its advantages, as no one—especially her father—noted her comings and goings.

When the United Authority first informed her father that Florida would become a free-range prison, he was given a choice to relocate. The United Authority had use for a man of his abilities in other parts of the fractured country. *A good warlord was hard to find.* But her father refused to leave Tallahassee. He trusted the land, knowing the remaining ecosystem well enough to survive, to keep his clan unified, to find nubile concubines to bear his children. For over five decades, the hilly terrain had been his home, even in the time before the end of electricity.

In Florida, it wasn't hard to find fish, sometimes three-eyed and gasping in the yellow nights. It wasn't hard to find water, though not fit to drink until properly treated. It wasn't hard to find firewood, even when the demand for it increased when waves of diphtheria, tetanus, and pertussis hit, and bodies needed to be burned. It wasn't hard to defend his clan, his women and his children, especially himself. He was a beast of a man, who wielded a knife or a length of motorcycle chain with ease, often fighting with both at the same time.

But he was getting older, and the Medicine Girl was getting prettier.

Her father called the Medicine Girl into his cinder block hovel. Being summoned was not unusual, as few had her expansive knowledge of healing or hurting the human body. Ever since her mother's abrupt departure two years prior, he'd used the Medicine Girl's skills as he saw fit.

But of late, he noted the pursing of her lips and slight rolling of her eyes at some of the things he asked her to do. He found her moving too quickly or too slowly, never feeling satisfied with her performance. Her mother had known how to behave, being deferential and subordinate at all times. Her mother kept her head down and answered him clearly. The Medicine Girl often just nodded, her gray eyes saying all the things she wouldn't dare.

Recently, the Medicine Girl had disobeyed him, tending to a subordinate's broken jaw when he had told her just to staunch the bleeding from his ears.

She needed reining in.

The Medicine Girl entered his presence, paring slices and munching on her heart of palm. It bothered him that she appeared so much at ease; his other children looked down at their dirty feet whenever he deigned to speak to them.

"I need to show you something on the border," he stated.

She nodded.

"Pack a day bag. Return here. We will leave immediately."

She nodded again, backing out of the unadorned room. None of his people were permitted to turn their back on him. Not even his daughter.

It was a four colony-hour walk to the border. She noted her father's long confident strides through the brush, as powerful and determined as a man half his age.

He doesn't think he is old, she thought.

From childhood, the Medicine Girl had learned to observe the terrain, stopping on occasion to pick up a flower or a leaf or fragrant berry or ugly mushroom, secreting it on her person. She gripped her rucksack. She carried her small machete in her hand.

As the small retinue approached the border, the Medicine Girl saw double rows of razor wire and anti-personnel landmines planted as indiscriminately as dandelions. Rumor had it that mines peppered the penal colony's borderline from Jax to Pensacola, doing an effective job in keeping undesirables where the United Authority wanted them to be.

The Medicine Girl's father stood by her, close to the reinforced barrier to the Kingdom of Georgia, alongside two old men, both war-torn and weary. One of the men grimaced, in obvious physical pain. The other man looked stoic, resigned to his predicament.

She paid little attention to either, focusing on her father. Although he'd never been kind to her, she had felt his animus grow with every step as they approached the border. She absentmindedly fingered the handle of her machete.

"If I were to tell you to escape, how long could you last on your own?" he asked, interrupting her thoughts.

"Until I died."

He slapped her.

"Tell me true, Medicine Girl. How long could you last on your own out there? A day? A week?"

The Medicine Girl resisted the urge to rub her cheek. She blinked back hot tears, forbidding them to fall.

"With what I have, a month or so."

"A month," he spat. "You are arrogant and unteachable. What did you pack in your rucksack? Gold?" he demanded to know, grabbing it from her.

"Dried fish, a flask of water, sunflower seeds, may-haw berries. A flint. A cooking tin." She looked him straight in the eye while he rummaged through her things.

"What do you have to heal you?"

"Honey, thyme, Neo." At the last, the Medicine Girl held up a little yellow tube, always to be found in her right pocket.

Before the Medicine Girl, her mother had been the keeper of the yellow tubes. The ointment was fought over. The Medicine Girl had the scars to show for it, keeping her remaining stock safely concealed outside the lean-to. Those who tried to take it from her got her machete instead.

In the Medicine Girl's hands, Neo cured oozing wounds and purulent infections that left untreated often led to raging fevers, necrotic limbs, or, on occasion, death. Neo had been one of the clan's treasured possessions, as was the Medicine Girl's medical prowess.

"If I were to banish you, where would you go? What would you do?"

She stared at him, her gray eyes narrowing.

He slapped her harder, causing her to fall to her knees. Eventually, she stood up and looked at him calmly.

"I would sleep during the day. Travel at night. Go north on the Nine Five. Go west on Two Six at Central Carolina. Walk along the Seven Seven until I reached the ruins at Charlotte Banks. The Carolingians don't ask a lot of questions, and I'd avoid anyone in a uniform."

"Good," he nodded, with a smile that did not reach his eyes. "Always avoid uniforms. Declare your allegiance to no one."

The Medicine Girl nodded back.

"Except to me," he murmured low. "You will always be loyal to me, unlike your mother—"

The Medicine Girl slowed her breathing. *He was baiting her. Trying to get her to do something rash and stupid. But why all the theater? If he wanted her dead, why didn't he just kill her outright?*

"Charlotte would be a good route to take," he muttered, looking at her suspiciously. The Charlotte Banks had held a great deal of cryptocurrency, in a world of 1's and 0's, before the financial markets imploded after the EMP bombs fell. Any gold or hard currency in the banks' reserves, long ago looted, proved as useless as the communication devices found on so many of the corpses.

"I have people in Old North Carolina," her father continued, looking past the barbed wire. "I am still known in those places."

She didn't know what she should do with that information. Her father's face darkened as he turned to face her, coming towards her, putting his pockmarked face inches from her own.

"But I am *very* well known here. I am the Warlord of Tallahassee."

With that, he commanded the two old men to run onto the rows of razor wire. The ill man landed first, his thin body quickly shredded. The second man crawled over his bloody body and landed squarely on the second coil. He writhed and moaned in pain, but not for very long.

The small group stood in silence until both impaled men stopped moving. The Medicine Girl closed her eyes, her fists clenched.

"If you don't want to do what I command you, every jot and tittle, then feel free to climb over these men to your freedom," he whispered, close to her, his foul breath turning her stomach. "But trust me. You won't last a day. And MilitiaMen know what to do with little girls who don't obey."

She stepped back from him, her head bowed low.

It was never a good idea to loiter on the border between nation-states. Her father and his men had already turned around to walk homeward.

She followed behind them at a fair distance.

Her mother taught her what history she knew, decades since the wastelands of China and Russia coordinated cyberattacks, crippling America's power grids, water treatment plants, and financial sectors in all 53 states and territories.

North Texas was especially hit hard by a series of high altitude nuclear electromagnetic pulse bursts. The resulting EMP detonations destroyed electrical circuitry from South Oregon to Classical Massachusetts.

Even if there were functioning power plants, the transformers as well as the transmission and distribution lines had become incapable of relaying power, much like the federal, state, and local governments.

That was all the Medicine Girl had heard the older ones clamor and argue about: what had happened in the past and what would never happen again in the future. She found herself rolling her eyes at their lamentations.

Any effort expended on anything other than surviving the day seemed pointless to her. The past lay in the past.

Growing up, the Medicine Girl had never felt at home inside buildings for very long, preferring to wander through the thickets and fields and woods in the North Florida wilds.

Away from her father's cinder block lair, her mother raised her in a wooden lean-to, thick palm fronds thatching the roof. A quiet place, her mother instructed her only child in all things, especially how to glean treasures from the earth. The Medicine Girl learned at her mother's side before her mother was betrayed.

We are civilized as long as we are comfortable, her mother had often said, showing the Medicine Girl the plants that healed in time and the plants that killed in minutes. Her mother made her recite the names of poisonous mushrooms over and over again and made her explain what a certain root could or could not do. She'd test her daughter's knowledge by asking if a certain berry was a purgative or how to make a powder from dried leaves or what bark could be used as an elixir or which gland held a serpent's venom.

The Medicine Girl never failed to answer correctly.

In the days after they returned from the border, the Medicine Girl watched her father's cinder block hovel. From a safe distance, the Medicine Girl saw strangers from the south approach, heard their bartering and bawdy laughter, sealing their agreement with fermented honey.

Like her mother, she had been sold.

Did her father think she didn't understand his furtive glances and thinly-veiled remarks to his men? Just because she was quiet didn't mean she was an idiot.

She knew her father, a feckless man, would barter for anything that kept him in relative comfort. And for whatever reason, she knew he felt threatened by her, his gray-eyed daughter, a slip of a girl who rarely blinked in his presence, standing cross-armed and in judgment.

Late into the night, she packed her rucksack and left the lean-to for the final time.

The black cherry flatbread she'd left for her father and his men in the kitchen contained a sufficient quantity of powdered black cherry tree leaves. The Medicine Girl hoped her father would break bread with his men in the morning, perhaps even those to whomever he sold her.

All who partook of the bread would soon find themselves staggering and convulsing. She hoped they'd be dead within an hour of eating her final offering.

She'd be across the border before anyone missed her.

The corpses of the two old men still hung from the razor wire, aiding her crossing over. She glanced down to see their bloated bodies, black bloody foam frothing from their mouths and noses. Seeing their pitiful state after baking in the sun for days, she steeled herself, converting her sympathy for the corpses into unadulterated hatred for her father.

I should bury these men, she thought. Her mother would have taken the time to find a shady spot under a watchful tree. But the Medicine Girl did not have the time or her mother's compassion. Her head start was minimal, and if her father lived after eating the poisoned bread, he'd send men to come after her.

But where to go?

From the information she had gathered from recent inmates consigned to the Florida Penal Colony, the Westland all the way to South Mexico was barren. The State of United Dakota sounded promising. At least there was talk of clean water and fertile fields. She had even heard some prisoners remark on bumblebee sightings in that clime.

After crossing the razor wire, the Medicine Girl shook a handful of sunflower seeds into her mouth.

Now all she needed to worry about were the landmines.

Pack a day bag. Return here. We will leave immediately.

Chapter 2

Attapulgus, The Kingdom of Georgia

The Kingdom of Georgia's oppressive heat made stripping stiffened corpses all the more difficult. However, most of the dead men's blood had pooled in their lower extremities, making any necessary cutting much easier.

The Medicine Girl wiped her brow with a MilitiaMan's kerchief. *He wouldn't be needing it anymore.*

She'd walked far in the night, keeping off the main roads and byways. By dawn, her previous life in the Florida Penal Colony became unimportant, and she fixated on what she needed to survive the day. Yet, if the Medicine Girl had been accurate in her self-reflection, she'd have remembered being wholly detached from her community ever since her mother's betrayal.

The Medicine Girl severed herself from all she had known and cared for in Tallahassee the moment she watched her mother tied behind a cart, skillful hands bound and useless in front of her. Mother and daughter had stared at one another, paralyzed by grief.

Until that day, she and her mother had never been apart. Now, all she knew of her mother was that she had been taken north. She'd heard her father drunkenly joke that her mother was dead, but like most of his lies, the Medicine Girl chose not to believe it.

She wondered what chaos her own departure had caused—who survived the poisoning, who was blamed, who was killed in her father's fit of rage. If her father was dead, there were others who would fill his place. He wasn't special.

Regardless, the Medicine Girl was here now, proceeding with great caution, as The Kingdom of Georgia had, out of necessity, forged ties to her father's clan. No doubt he'd send men after her or at least post a bounty.

She decided simply not to care, yet hoped all of the black cherry flatbread had been consumed in his filthy cinder block lair by as many of his men as possible.

Somehow the Georgian sun felt hotter than the Floridian one.

At least these carcasses aren't bloated yet, the Medicine Girl noted. She would never get used to the feel of deadmen's skin slippage or the smell of purge fluid. Watching the blackish liquid drip from putrefying cadavers disconcerted her, she who seldom flinched under the grimmest of circumstances.

She inspected the dead men's eyes. *Cloudy, opaque. The potassium build up was evident.* Her mother had explained what the silent dead could not. By the Medicine Girl's calculation, the battle between these unfortunates had occurred the day prior to her arrival.

The obscure field where a forgettable skirmish fought by unnamed men had neither advanced nor retarded anyone's cause. However, the battle did leave things behind that would aid the Medicine Girl. For that fact alone, she was grateful.

As usual, no female corpses were to be found on the scrapping field, typical of the militias who kept their women and girls behind walls, fully veiled, and out of sight.

Running into the United Authority worried the Medicine Girl far less than the militias, as their individual ways of doing business varied considerably. At least with the United Authority, there was some semblance of civility.

She made quick work of appropriating anything of value, sizing up a dead body before moving on to the next one. A pair of black leather boots hung over her shoulder, tied together by thick laces.

The gleaners had been there earlier. She'd watched them from the woods outside of Attapulgus, just before the United Authority ran them off, catching very few alive.

It was a capital crime to pilfer from the dead; extrajudicial sentencing was summary and swift. The United Authority made public executions for scofflaws purposeful, painful and gory, celebrated on the scrapping fields by a local militia's distinct battle cry.

Each to their own, she decided. In her twelve years of life, she found there was often little logic in reasoning why people did the things they did. On dark nights, the Medicine Girl remembered her father's ClansMen cheering on the torture and executions of gleaners in the Florida Penal Colony. Their gleeful shrieks gave her goosebumps.

She never understood the prejudice against the gleaners, who served a purpose like the crows and buzzards. *Why should the dead's things be wasted?*

After witnessing her first public execution, the Medicine Girl kept powdered black cherry leaves on her person at all times in case she was arrested. She had heard too many stories. The Medicine Girl was prepared to die in as little pain as possible. She had seen the many ways her father knew how to prolong someone's torment.

She needed to get to the Crimson Republic as quickly as possible.

Before she was sold, the Medicine Girl's mother explained how the human body knew what to do with itself, whether birthing a new life or meeting its death. She showed her daughter how a tea or a broth or a piece of bark helped the body do what it must do: breathe, eat, excrete, copulate, birth, heal, sicken, die.

All we can do is alleviate suffering, her mother often said, while helping a warlord's concubine give birth or hastening the death of an old one. She demonstrated how to crush dried leaves or cull seedlings or extract oils with her deft hands.

The Medicine Girl needed to be shown only once before becoming proficient at a task. She learned quickly, mainly to garner one of her mother's rare smiles.

The Medicine Girl still had her mind set on walking to the State of United Dakota. More than 1500 colony-miles from Tallahassee, fleeing that far north meant dangerous months of walking, cutting up the midsection of the United Authority. She would have to cross through territories protected by the Militia of the White Crosses, the one militia to which her father had pledged his loyalty, such as it was.

She didn't mind the long walk, as walking comforted her, especially when the summer nights cooled, enlivening her senses. She could live off the land, she imagined. If not, she would die. She was not so fond of the world to regret leaving it.

Generally, militias were easy to spot from afar. They were not subtle, their young men boisterously leading and little boys following behind, pulling handcarts full of weapons and provisions. The older men brought up the rear, calling out commands and making raucous remarks, starting chants and singing bawdy songs.

It was all so tedious, she sighed, chewing on a few wild sunchoke roots. *A parade of fools going nowhere.*

Watching the procession, the Medicine Girl remembered her dead maternal grandfather who had studied history, back when those things mattered. He talked of endless war—wars and rumors of wars—and the old lie: "Dulce et decorum est pro patria mori." *It is sweet and fitting to die for one's country.* The Medicine Girl had seen enough of war and death to know it was neither.

Sometimes when one of the older militia members walked off the trail to relieve himself, the Medicine Girl would use twenty colony-inches of fishing line to garrote him. She'd count to fifty in Latin, like her grandfather taught her, until the MilitiaMan's eyes bulged out and his loins loosened.

She'd count to fifty again just to make sure.

Nihil. Ūnus. Duo. Trēs.

She'd purloined a leather satchel and several knives that way—even a pistol with two bullets. *Her father did not possess a loaded gun!*

On the outskirts of Bainbridge, she stopped to study her makeshift map on a piece of corrugated cardboard. The charcoal markings made by a grateful Floridian convict were barely perceptible, but his knowledge of southern topography had been accurate so far. It proved to be more than adequate payment for an eye salve made out of garlic and onions.

Perhaps she could skirt Lake Seminole and head north on the Eight Four to Dothan? Would paying for passage on a boat heading upriver be a viable option? She could join a caravan north, but there would be too many questions for a girl traveling alone.

She rearranged the items in her leather satchel, lost in her thoughts. She drank from a flask and retrieved a strip of dried squirrel, taken off one of the dead MilitiaMen. Chewing on the tough meat, she walked until midday without stopping.

She crossed another Georgian scrapping field covered with bodies, choked with dislodged viscera, assorted gore, the remnants of painful deaths.

With a practiced eye, she saw that the gleaners had left precious little. As was her custom, she waited, observing the abandoned area, far and wide. It was quiet, especially in the years since most of the frogs had died.

A low moaning came from the perimeter of the woods, just at the edge of the clearing. She lowered herself to the ground, making her way through the overgrowth. After waiting a considerable time until she was sure there was no danger, she rose to her full height. A small movement came from the same direction as the despairing sounds.

Alleviate suffering, Medicine Girl.

It was a young man, not much older than she, dressed in the robes of the Militia of the White Crosses. Sprawled flat on his back, the man held his right leg, impaled by a crude weapon made from rebar.

The young man had managed to tie a tourniquet around his upper thigh to stanch the bleeding.

She approached him.

"Drink this," the Medicine Girl ordered, holding out her flask of water, laced with crushed mint she'd found growing in a wet thicket.

He took the flask, draining it entirely.

"Thank you," he replied, handing it back to her. He lay back down, exhausted by the effort.

"How old are you?" she inquired.

"Fourteen."

"Your leg is putrefying. It needs to come off," she said matter-of-factly.

"Gangrenous?"

"Yes. It needs to come off," she repeated. "If not, by this time tomorrow, you will be dead."

"Can you do it?"

"Of course."

She stood and looked at him, taking full inventory of his condition. His dirty blonde hair appeared to be full of lice. His dark blue eyes were haggard, but full of intelligent curiosity, blazing with ferocity. *If he could strangle the gangrene in his leg, he would.*

"The Illuminati Pagans seemed to have known what we were transporting. Our regiment took casualties and were forced to retreat. These men have been left for dead," he stated, almost as if reporting to a superior officer.

"These men are dead and none of that matters," she replied, wondering why he was wasting what little strength he had left. First, she needed to disarm him. "I need your dagger."

He reached into his shirt pocket, felt for the sheath and tossed the knife to the Medicine Girl who caught it with one hand.

She gave him the remaining squirrel jerky and watched him attempt to eat it far too quickly. He threw it up.

If he survives, I will make him tea with thyme in it, she decided. If he did not live, the thyme would be wasted.

She busied herself in making fire. To hide the smoke and concentrate the heat, she dug a hole in the soil with her machete, tunneling the dirt out to create a small chimney. Using a few small twigs and short branches, she lit the underground fire in the larger hole. Soon, she sterilized her knives in the flickering flames. Satisfied, she extinguished the fire when the job was done. After tearing rags from another dead man's shirt, she prayed over her tools and for the guidance and direction to use them properly.

Who do we pray to, she once asked, seeing her mother do the exact same thing over her own tools before helping someone out of their misery. *Which gods, mother?*

All of them, the Medicine Girl's mother replied.

After all was prepared, the Medicine Girl handed the young man a thick stick to bite on while she worked.

"I don't need it." He looked her full in the face.

The Medicine Girl shrugged and began.

He jolted awake, grabbing her by the throat. When he realized it was just the girl who cared for him, he released his grip on her and melted back to the ground in a pool of sour sweat.

"What's your name?" he whispered, weakened by the removal of his leg.

"I don't have a name."

"I'm J-Jasper," he stammered, stuttering from a wave of pain. "Jasper Crimson-Atlanta."

"Atlanta was burned to the ground immediately after the wars. Your people have been dead for a long time."

He ignored her.

"You fainted," she informed him.

"Did I cry out?"

"You were as silent as these others," the Medicine Girl said, motioning to the dead all about them.

"Thank you," he said, a bit louder.

She ate wild raspberries that she'd found by the lake. They were small and bitter, but edible nonetheless.

"You will heal well. I used Neo," she bragged, surprising herself that she boasted a bit. It was unlike her and she blushed. "Neo will help you heal," she added quickly.

"Thank you, again," he groaned with the effort of sitting up. "Neo is precious. I appreciate your generosity—and your swiftness in, uh, helping me." He looked about to see what she had done with his leg.

She responded by giving him a handful of the tiny fruit.

"Do you have people to care for you?" she asked. The time to leave was long past and delaying her departure was dangerous.

"I belong to the Militia of the White Crosses."

"Will they come to collect you?" she asked, looking around, on guard now. She arose, preparing to gather her few things.

"Yes, they will come back," he said, reaching out to touch her arm, wanting to steady himself as he sat up.

"I cannot be here."

"Agreed. You must go."

"Lay back down. You won't be strong enough to move for a time. I will leave you some provisions until your people return."

"I cannot pay you."

"I didn't heal you for pay," she snapped at him, angry for some reason she didn't understand. She continued to shove what she could into her leather satchel.

"Wait! I carry a Universal Pass. Take it with you," he implored in a firm voice.

"You will be killed if you do not have the pass in your possession," she warned.

"I may be killed taking a piss tomorrow," he replied with a grin. She didn't return the smile.

"I cannot," she protested, shaking her head. She finished assembling her things. "Goodbye, Jasper Crimson-Atlanta."

"You must take my Universal Pass. It will give you free passage to any part of the United Authority," he reassured her, reaching deep into his pants pocket to retrieve it.

He felt nothing. Frantically, he began to feel his other pockets. He looked up just in time to see the remnants of the Medicine Girl's small smile.

He laughed.

"Travel well," he said, watching her walk away.

She slung her satchel over her shoulder, gave him a slight wave, and disappeared into the brush.

Only then did Jasper look down to see a new black boot on his remaining foot, perfectly laced into a bow.

"Travel well," he said, watching her walk away.

Chapter 3

By the Riverside at Lucy, The Crimson Republic

Although the synthetic ropes cut into her wrists, it was the loss of the Medicine Girl's leather satchel that hurt her more. She watched, immobile and powerless, as the RiverMen opened it up, pulling out her belongings with reckless abandon.

They poured out her powdered herbs, tossed aside curative leaves and berries, ate the hardtack and dried meat she'd taken off the Georgian corpses, more dead men moldering in the hot sun on the scrapping fields.

She watched the RiverMen with blank gray eyes, revealing nothing, not even the intensity of the hatred she felt for them. Yet some of her hatred she reserved for herself. She'd been too reckless, exhausted after walking through the night. Although determined to leave The Kingdom of Georgia behind her at all costs, her capture by stupid men seemed a high a price to pay.

The RiverMen laughed when they discovered her flint stone, fishing line, and small machete. But they whooped and hollered like only southern MilitiaMen can when they discovered the gun, holding it up for all to see. *A gun with two bullets!*

The RiverMen took turns holding it, pointing it at her, pointing it at each other, making comments about her they felt she was too young to understand.

On her person, she'd secreted the Universal Pass and the Neo. Although the things in her leather satchel were precious, the medallion and the antibiotic were irreplaceable. Though violent thieves, the RiverMen apparently were not deviants or they would have found those things on her.

They will not molest me, she thought. From what she overheard from the prisoners and ClansMen back in her father's cinder block hovel, that type of abuse seemed more fitting to a NorthMan's predilections.

The RiverMen had captured the Medicine Girl outside of the Lucy outpost, once she crossed the Nine Five Bridge into the Crimson Republic. Their eyes glittered when the Medicine Girl attempted to pay them off with hard colony-currency, not militia script that lost its value outside the protectorate realm.

In her attempt to secure passage up the Chattahoochee River to Columbia, the RiverMen disbelieved her story about being a vanguard for one of the Crimson militias. *Who would send a little girl to make arrangements for troop movements?* However, the RiverMen weren't entirely sure, as the girl was clever and insistent, and the implausibility of her backstory seemed typical of MilitiaMen's tactics. *They were tricky bastards.*

"We should sell her," the one who appeared to be the leader said. The Medicine Girl looked at him with disinterest.

"Ransom! Let's send her clan a ransom demand," a toothless man suggested.

"You don't even know her clan," another countered.

The RiverMen squabbled until one man assaulted another, a roundhouse punch to the head. A melee ensued, amusing the Medicine Girl by its wild brutality. She lifted her feet when a younger boy collapsed before her, his nose bleeding in great spurts.

After the fisticuffs, the men uniformly agreed to take her back to their camp until they could figure out how to best monetize the situation.

Tied up, she rolled her eyes. She was now a prize for stupid men who breathed through their mouths, the poisoned river water having infected their sinus passages. *Her mother would be so disappointed in her.*

Truth be told, it had been her fault. She had been anxious to put as many colony-miles between herself and her father. *Declare your allegiance to no one*, the warlord had often quipped. The Medicine Girl repeated those words often—his last piece of advice. Why she had trusted a go-between to arrange Midwest passage with the RiverMen made the Medicine Girl even angrier with herself. *She knew better.* That her personal Judas had been a boy of six or seven years was particularly galling. *Had she been just as duplicitous as he was at that age?*

Seething under the RiverMen's tarp that acted as an inadequate shelter by the fetid river, she decided to kill them all.

As they toyed with her possessions, she watched the half dozen men with her clear, gray eyes, missing nothing.

She was patient.

"Can you cook?" one of the RiverMen asked her.

"Of course," the Medicine Girl replied.

"There is no meat to be found along the bankside," he complained.

The RiverMen had not fished for years, even before the electrical grids went down, as fish die-offs had choked the Chattahoochee for months at a time.

"There is meat near the bankside," she corrected him. "We passed several water moccasins." She pointed at the nearly invisible ripples in the water. "Net as many as you can. Keep them alive until I prepare them. If you haven't thrown everything away, I will need the salt and wild onions from my satchel. I need a fire and a pot of water. There are black walnuts in a grove a half a klick back on the western side of the road."

The men looked at one another, made assignments, and disbursed. They hadn't eaten well in days.

Still tied up, the Medicine Girl looked over the campsite while they were gone, noting where each of the items from her leather satchel had been placed. Before she left, she would retrieve all of her things, as well as anything else of value in the RiverMen's camp.

In time, the RiverMen returned with a bounty of water moccasins, fattened up on lizards and blind birds that floundered on the lower limbs of riverside trees.

"I'm going to untie you, but if you run—you are going to wish you hadn't," the leader said, mocking her by laughing. "I kind of wish you would run. You would be fun to track."

She understood his meaning.

When the synthetic ropes were removed, she massaged her forearms, wrists, and fingers—restoring proper circulation as her mother had taught her when caring for bound victims.

There was much to learn about curing or ailing the body, and her mother appeared to know all about life and death. She even seemed to know that their time together would be short, causing her to redouble her efforts in educating her daughter.

The Medicine Girl watched one of the RiverMen make a fire, placing a battered cooking pot full of murky water over it. She wandered over to stoke the fire, encouraging the pot to a raging boil. She needed to purify the water. From the look of the RiverMen's skin and the color of their eyes, they were not boiling their water long enough.

While working, she surreptitiously kicked a thin piece of shale, its edge landing in the fire's edge. Perhaps the jagged rock would retain enough heat to melt through the synthetic ropes, a useful weapon to have if she were tied up again. However, she didn't think the men would do much after the supper she would prepare for them.

"Hand me one of my knives," she ordered one of the younger RiverMen with such authority that her request was granted. On a flat rock, she cracked open the black walnuts, extracting the rich nutmeat, dicing it into a glistening, oily paste. She chopped up wild onions and radishes, even a few mushrooms and chanterelles that she'd found growing in a mossy patch under a conifer tree. She threw all into the boiling pot, creating an aroma that made even her mouth water.

"When do we eat," the RiverMen's leader asked, having watched her closely, mesmerized by Medicine Girl's knife.

"Less than a colony-hour," she replied. "Bring me the snakes."

Two of the RiverMen carried over an industrial plastic barrel full of river water and water moccasins. She fished one out with a forked stick, quickly grabbed the snake by its tail, then smashed its head against a rock. After she ensured it was dead, the Medicine Girl cut off four colony-inches from the tail, hung it over a low tree branch, and let the snake bleed out.

Next, she took her machete and split the entire length of the snake's belly, starting from its shortened tail, peeling the skin off from the meat. With her nimble fingers, she gutted its entrails and tossed selected parts into the pot to thicken the stew. The bones detached nicely, as she inspected the meat for fragments. She took out a few of the smaller snake bones and placed them in the crucible to grind for later. It was good for treating infections, especially gangrene. But for this meal, she had another purpose for the bones.

The RiverMen splayed out on the ground to watch the Medicine Girl prepare their sumptuous meal, making offensive comments, enjoying her heavy labors on their behalf.

You must first cut off a water moccasin's head, her mother explained, showing the Medicine Girl how to prepare a water moccasin for them to eat. *If you do not cut off the head first, then the entirety of the meat will be poisoned.*

The Medicine Girl observed her mother's careful handling of the snake, stifling involuntary shudders.

I don't like snakes, Mother.

Snakes are beneficial to us. They eat rats and rodents and other carriers of plague and disease. Snakes are also delicious to eat, especially fried, assuming you can find enough nut oil.

Then why do people hate snakes? The Medicine Girl asked, repulsed by the dying snake's gaping maw, its glassy eyes, its still-flickering tongue. Her mother buried snakeheads, as they could bite even after being severed from their bodies for a time. *Why do people hate snakes,* she repeated.

Why do people hate anything? Fear and superstition, her mother replied. *Both are detrimental to people like us. Where you have fear and superstition, you have cruelty. And women and children take the brunt of men's cruelty. It has been that way since the beginning.*

The Medicine Girl remembered looking at the snake's severed head until it stopped moving.

Be careful of dangerous things, her mother added. *You must be aware of them long after you think they aren't dangerous anymore.*

The RiverMen were growing restless.

"Is it time now?" the leader asked, sharp and petulant. His eyes were yellowed, his skin was mottled and unhealthy. The river he lived on and drank from had affected his liver and kidneys. *He would not live out the year*, she concluded. *Then again, he'd not see another day either.*

"The stew will be ready soon."

The men began to fumble with their bowls, rustic tureens, large cups—any receptacle they could find to receive their portion of the aromatic stew the Medicine Girl had concocted.

"I say it is ready," the leader declared, approaching the cooking pot. "We eat now." *It was not a suggestion.* The Medicine Girl eyed the thin piece of shale within reach, just on the fire's perimeter.

"Then the time is now," the Medicine Girl replied, moving out of the way while each man elbowed one another to fill his bowl with as much as he could.

She stood by with her hands at her side, watching the RiverMen consume her snake stew with great relish. Soon, they were face down in their meal, slurping the thick gravy, chewing chunks of snake meat flavored by the plants that grew without complaint under their filthy feet.

Had the men not been stupid, they would have noticed that the Medicine Girl had failed to remove the venom sacs before she killed and skinned the snakes. It was easy enough to do. The sacs were located just behind their arrow-shaped heads.

Had the men not been stupid, they would have noticed that the Medicine Girl had, instead, cut off the snakes' tails to bleed them.

Her mother once explained how the hemotoxin in snake venom worked, how it effectively broke down its victim's blood cells, and how it resulted in painful hemorrhaging. Human blood infected with water moccasin venom could not clot, especially when crushed snake bones were added to the stew, making minor tears in a WaterMan's mouth and esophagus and stomach. The venom had so many entry points to choose from, so much of the bloodstream to infect.

Calmly, the Medicine Girl watched the RiverMen eat their fill, laying down on the riverbank after glutting themselves.

When she saw them touch their mouths, feeling the initial numbness and tingling of the poison, she backed towards the fire, picking up the thin shale rock with a rag. It glowed white hot, and she held it in a defensive posture, waiting for an attack.

But most curled up on the ground, hand to chest, laboring to breathe, spitting to get the metallic taste out of their mouths. She saw a few try to stand, weak and lightheaded, confused and fearful.

The snake meat had been effective, she thought, pleased with the results. She hardly needed to add so many poisonous mushrooms to her stew, yet the resulting nausea, vomiting, cramping, and diarrhea appeared to debilitate the RiverMen even further. She watched them for hours, dying in their own filth.

Above all, Medicine Girl, be patient.

She continued to stand in quiet repose, the RiverMen writhing around her, superstitiously calling down curses on her from their own particular WaterGods. Fear showed in their glassy eyes as their prayers went unanswered.

If they could have been able to stand, she reasoned, *they would have been exceedingly cruel to her.* She prepared to leave the encampment, the first thing she did was retrieve her leather satchel. She walked among the dying men, finding most of her things, adding a few more. She found the gun with its two bullets on the leader's body. He also had a good leather belt that she removed and fastened about her own waist. She tucked the gun into the waistband of her trousers.

The Medicine Girl considered taking the cooking pot, peering inside to inspect her handiwork. The snake stew did smell very good, and she stifled a smile, pleased with herself.

She looked at the stone knife in her hand and walked over to one of the dead RiverMen, his face and body contorted in agony. She'd always wondered about blood that could not clot.

And unlike the water moccasins, this time the Medicine Girl started with the heads.

After looting the RiverMen, the Medicine Girl finished the remaining black walnuts, finding them creamy and rich and filling. They were a welcome treat after such a laborious day.

The RiverMen's encampment yielded little more of value, but she found a proper canteen, a small frying pan, two flint stones, several knives, more synthetic rope, and several pairs of cotton socks. She swapped out her raggedy boots for an overly large pair, taking time to tend to her blisters. The new dry socks felt heavenly.

After securing her belongings into her bulging leather satchel, the Medicine Girl made her way to the river and appropriated one of the RiverMen's smaller logboats. The watercraft was light and efficient, perfect for her size. Finding a makeshift paddle, she launched the craft from the riverbank.

Ever since the dams had blown during the wars, the water level on the Chattahoochee River had been diminished. The decade-long drought in the southeast didn't help the river's vitality, but it did make paddling upstream all the more easier. For that, she was thankful.

Although dusk had fallen, there was a full harvest moon illuminating all of the ripples of the creatures that still swam in the river, a river that gave off a faint phosphorescent glow.

*Had the men not been stupid, they would have noticed that the Medicine Girl
had, instead, cut off the snakes' tails to bleed them.*

Chapter 4

Montgomery, The Crimson Republic

The Adjutant General of the Crimson Republic State Defense Force gave one last heave before dismounting. Then he stood, putting on his regulation undershirt, his back scarred from the scrapping fields as well as from the nights away from his permanent wife. He had specific tastes and found very few temporary wives who could satiate him.

Of all the temporary wives he'd been with, his most recent favorite—Jalen—seemed to know instinctively what he needed from her to find release. Jalen was, indeed, very talented, with her long lacquered nails. He mulled over buying her for his own personal use, yet he knew in time he'd tire of her just as he had grown bored with all of the others.

For now, though, she distracted him.

Although the United Authority paid in advance for his temporary marriages, the general left Jalen a little extra militia script on the sideboard, money accepted throughout Montgomery. He also left her a pair of earrings he'd come across, earrings fashioned from colorful mil-spec wire. Jalen had seemed pleased with them, but temporary wives were all accomplished liars.

Their time together over, the general gathered up his personal items and strode into the communal bathroom of the United Authority - Comfort Station #22. An old hotel had been repurposed for the community's use, one that had been posh in prior decades. Wood rot and peeling, yellowed wallpaper bespoke of better days. But the rooms were large, the doors latched, and the women were relatively clean, unlike many of the diseased skags his men fraternized with in Arkansippi and Louisiana.

Since the wars, there had been no running water in the Crimson Republic's capital city, but the station's novice attendants scurried about the general, offering him and the other patrons clean rags and chipped ceramic bowls of hot water to refresh themselves.

Jalen lay very still in her bed, hoping no one would notice her temporary husband was finished. *Certainly she must have fulfilled her quota for the day.* She begged Mama Mae for the rest of the night off, Mae who knew firsthand how taxing the general could be.

She luxuriated in the momentary stillness.

"No joy is unalloyed," Jalen murmured to herself, lolling on her back on a mattress stuffed with moss and sweet-smelling hay. Her mother often used that expression, but Jalen wasn't sure she knew what it meant. *Something about disappointment? If so, then that squared,* she thought. *Her mother was the most miserable woman who walked the wreckage of the world. She epitomized no joy.*

The week had been exceptionally busy.

Jalen hated when the various militias arrived to parley with the United Authority. Foreign girls from as far away as Old North Carolina showed up, looking to earn some colony-currency. Yet as many as came in, most girls left empty-handed and broke, both in body and in spirit.

Although the United Authority ran respectable Comfort Stations, other CatHousers and PimpMen in the city did not. Jalen couldn't walk down the streets anymore without some much-abused free range temporary wife in her way, their homemade lipstick smeared from ear to ear. They dyed their hair blue from boiled blueberries, an advertisement of their cut-rate fees.

Jalen rolled over and called out for her novice attendant.

"Catalina!"

"Yes, ma'am?" A small wisp of a girl scurried into her room, afraid of getting a pinch or a swat for dawdling. But Catalina counted herself lucky. The other temporary wives who worked in the United Authority - Comfort Station #22 were not half as kind as Jalen.

"Catalina, I am starving. Find me a scrap of something to eat, will you? Maybe a piece of meat or cheese. I haven't had a bite to eat all day."

Neither had Catalina, but that was expected. The servants ate late at night, after finishing the laundry.

"Yes, ma'am."

There goes a good girl, Jalen smiled. But as she watched Catalina leave on her errand, Jalen's heart grew heavy. *How long did little Catalina have until she was on her back, providing a release for some doughy bureaucrat? How long until she labored under a MilitiaMan, earning a pittance for his pleasure? How long before the light went out of her eyes?*

Jalen couldn't even touch her own wages until she retired at 26. She frowned. *Most temporary wives died well before then.*

Like Catalina, Jalen herself had been eleven or twelve years old when her father sold her to the Comfort Station as a novice attendant. The first year had horrified her, as she learned what men and women did to each other. She remembered crying every day during her first year in service, but after a while, Jalen never shed a tear, even when Mama Mae beat her.

It wasn't bad considering the alternatives, she decided. There weren't many other things she could do to keep herself fed.

Mama Mae often talked about the times before the wars, but whenever she did, Jalen and the other girls rolled their eyes behind her back. Mama Mae's stories of air conditioning that cooled with a flick of a switch and smart phones that played music and showed moving pictures—it all seemed ridiculous and far-fetched. According to Mama Mae, everyone had those devices on their person at all times.

It must have been a very busy, noisy world, Jalen concluded.

Her stomach growling, Jalen grew impatient with Catalina's absence. She should have returned far more quickly with her meal.

Jalen knew that being a novice attendant and serving those in the station proved to be the best way to learn how to become a temporary wife. One needed to recognize and understand the different needs of the men and women they served, how to discern if a temporary spouse was going to be a physical threat, and how to survive the inevitable beating without losing a tooth or fracturing a jaw.

After the wars, the United Authority had established Comfort Stations in all of the remaining state's capitals. True, states that had seceded from the federal government had their own rules about such matters. From what Jalen heard, some stations allowed girls to keep half of their temporary marital fees. She'd also heard some of the stations allowed temporary wives to be beaten to death for an enhanced fee. All and all, she was pleased where she was. *One couldn't believe every story some bedraggled Crimson MilitiaMan told, trying to impress someone, even a temporary wife.*

Jalen once counted how much she earned over the years, if she had been able to keep her full fees without the United Authority taking its cut. Shocked at the number, she threw a basin across the foyer, shattering a glass window. Mama Mae had reprimanded her for that; her quota of temporary husbands had doubled for a while.

Jalen got up from the bed and paced the worn carpeting.

Finally, Catalina entered with a small covered plate, a basin full of warm water and apple cider vinegar, a thin bathing cloth, and a small jar of plumeria oil.

Jalen grabbed the plate of food, removed the burlap covering, and greedily ate pieces of warm goat cheese, hazelnut bread, and pickled onions. *Maybe the general would keep his ugly earrings and bring her a chicken next time*, she mused. After her feast and somewhat contented, she smiled, reclined, and let Catalina attend to her.

First, Catalina washed her face as the general liked her face made up, and Jalen's makeup was smeared beyond repair. As both United Authority military and MilitiaMen's wives were not allowed to wear makeup, Jalen found many of her temporary husbands had a fetish for thick white talc face powder, smeary red rouge, and charcoal blackened eyes.

Next, Catalina handed Jalen a warm cloth to clean herself with while Catalina stripped the top sheet off the mattress to launder. Finally, Catalina rubbed plumeria oil where Jalen needed it most, to ease her muscles and to calm her nerves, especially when one of her temporary husbands was demanding or difficult or cruel.

Catalina had been shown how to find plumeria blooms, to pluck off their petals, to crush them in a crucible to release their fragrant oils. It was her favorite task, and she hummed a wordless tune while she worked.

Attending the temporary husbands as they prepared to leave was her least favorite thing to do. The men, and occasionally women, made comments to her that she did not understand, but they shamed her nonetheless. She just smiled and let them pat her.

"You have another husband tonight," Catalina said, replacing the items onto the tray to take back down to the main floor.

"What does he look like," Jalen muttered aloud, not expecting a reply. *What did it matter?*

Catalina shrugged her nonanswer.

"United Authority or MilitiaMan?"

"MilitiaMan," Catalina replied.

"Shit."

Catalina returned to the main floor just as the MilitiaMan was being shown to Jalen's room.

As she entered, Catalina saw Mama Mae standing behind a filthy, stone faced girl about her own age. She had startling wide gray eyes. Whether she was the smartest or most ignorant girl that Catalina had ever met remained a mystery. *The girl's face was inscrutable.*

"Cat, I have a new novice attendant for you to instruct."

"Yes, ma'am."

"The girl will train with you for a week, watching you take care of Jalen. Then she'll be ready for Hephzibah...it seems Hep needs a new novice."

Catalina tried hard not to but flinched at the sound of Hephzibah's name. *Hep needs a new girl because she tortured the last one.* Regaining her composure, the only way to survive at the Station, Catalina replied, "Yes, ma'am."

"I don't know this child's name." Mama Mae put both of her meaty hands on the Medicine Girl's thin shoulders, as if to squeeze the information out of her. "United Authority pulled her off the river, stuck her with a battalion coming to town for the week. I picked her up cheap at the Family Trading Station. Now, she's ours."

The new girl's mouth flattened further into a tight thin line as Mama Mae spoke.

"Go on, now. Go with Cat."

Deciding the new girl was disposable because she was simple, Mama Mae let the two girls be. Let Catalina train the idiot for a few days before Hep chewed her up.

"Welcome to hell," Cat informed the girl. "What's your name?"

The Medicine Girl did not answer. Cat wondered if she was mute—as so many traumatized girls were for a time.

But Cat felt the new girl was neither emotionally disturbed nor witless. *Quite the opposite.* The new girl seemed like she would gladly murder everyone on the premises.

"Make this easier on both of us, will ya? What's your name?" Catalina asked.

"I don't have a name."

"What do people call you?"

"I don't have people."

"I am going to have to call you something," Catalina sighed, already exasperated with her new charge.

"Then you decide," responded the Medicine Girl, arms hanging at her sides. Catalina watched the new girl's eyes scan her immediate area, as if determining what she could use for a weapon.

Catalina lugged Jalen's tray down the stairs to the first floor with the Medicine Girl following behind. They entered a large room of the former hotel, a reception area of sorts. A few dirty glasses sat on a table next to various bottles and jars full of amber liquid. Catalina picked up the glasses and trash left by thoughtless MilitiaMen.

"I will call you a name from the Christian Holy Bible," Catalina decided. "How about Eve?"

The Medicine Girl shrugged, not caring in the slightest.

"When was the last time you ate?"

"Union Springs," came the terse reply. "I need water."

Catalina motioned for her to follow. They walked into the makeshift service area, just off the main reception area. She put down Jalen's tray next to others, then walked over to a five-colony-gallon carboy filled with boiled water. Finding a well worn plastic glass, she poured a generous quantity of water and handed it to her apprentice.

The Medicine Girl inspected the glass, smelled the water, and held it up to the remaining light.

"I boiled it myself," Catalina snapped at her. "I boiled it for at least four colony-minutes."

Partially satisfied, the Medicine Girl drained the contents of the container.

"More water," the Medicine Girl demanded. Catalina refilled the plastic container and watched her drink her fill several more times.

While the Medicine Girl quenched her thirst, Catalina prepared remains from the food trays that the Comfort Station's temporary husbands had not eaten. She trimmed up the remnants, cobbling them together to look as pleasing as possible. She then presented the food to the Medicine Girl.

"Thank you," The Medicine Girl said, starting to eat a crust of cornbread, shards of goat cheese, and a half-eaten plum. She ate the burnt ends of dried meat, heavily coated with salt used to preserve it.

"Would you like to bathe, Eve? I can find you some clothes that will fit you," Catalina asked politely, but it wasn't a question. The girl needed to bathe. She smelled like raw sewage. Her clothes were layered in filth; they would need to be burned.

A brief look of concern passed over the Medicine Girl's face, eyes troubled.

"Eve," asked Catalina. "There is a tub out back. It's private. It's safe."

The Medicine Girl nodded.

Catalina walked her out back behind the station. An empty metal tub, just large enough for a small child, lay behind a panel of solid fencing. With another carboy full of water nearby, both girls worked to empty the entirety of clean water into the tub.

"I got some soap, too. Stole it from Jalen. This is made out of lye from shagbark hickory ashes." Catalina handed a small sliver of soap to the Medicine Girl.

"Shagbarks have the best nuts. I like to eat them raw," the Medicine Girl confided.

"I usually toasted mine in the embers," replied Catalina, smiling at a distant memory. "I guess I'll leave you to your bath."

Catalina turned to leave.

"Wait."

"What do you need?" Catalina paused, looking over her shoulder.

"Would you watch out for me?" the Medicine Girl asked.

Catalina stopped, surprised at the request.

"Just for a little while," the Medicine Girl qualified her request, firming up her voice. "I just want not to worry, for a little while."

"All we have is a little while. Those bitches always seem to want something," Catalina griped and spat on the ground. "I'll watch out for you. Don't you worry."

She turned away to give the Medicine Girl her privacy.

"Thank you," came a weary voice. Catalina heard the Medicine Girl scrub the grit and lice and blood off her. She was certain the water in the tub would run black with filth.

"I heard they got you on the river. Did any of the United Authority men hurt you?"

"One tried." The Medicine Girl did not elaborate.

"What happened, Eve? Can you tell me about it?"

"I had a machete on me. And he's not much of a man anymore."

Cat laughed.

"So why aren't you dead? They should have crucified you for injuring a United Authority soldier."

"Oh, they won't find his body," mumbled the Medicine Girl. "But the badgers and foxes will. He's in tiny bite size pieces."

Catalina shivered as her smile melted away.

Eve was going to get her in trouble.

The MilitiaMan was done with Jalen, and, thankfully, he did not take too long.

She called out for Catalina.

The Medicine Girl, dressed in a heavy print floral that was far too big for her, clomped along after Catalina in a pair of dirty high heels.

"I don't like these clothes," the Medicine Girl said.

"Sorry. That's what these people like," explained Catalina. "It reminds them of the time before the end of electricity."

"The station boys don't have to wear dresses," the Medicine Girl complained. "Why do we? Where are their clothes kept?"

"On the other side of the station in the boy's cupboard. We can sneak over there later and get you some pants, but while you are on the floor, you gotta wear a dress."

Catalina heard her name hollered again. *Jalen.*

"We gotta see what Jalen wants—right now before we get in trouble!"

The Medicine Girl gamely tried to follow along after Catalina in the impractical shoes. *She would get herself a good pair of pants from the boy's cupboard. And some thick boots.*

"Who's this?"

"Eve. She's new. A novice attendant from the Family Trading Station. Mama Mae says I'm supposed to train her."

"For whom?"

"Hep."

"Good lord in his merciful heavens, Cat. Not that monster. Not Hep."

"Yes, ma'am."

Annoyed with the chattering young girls, the MilitiaMan took his time getting dressed. Catalina averted her gaze. The Medicine Girl stared at him with her impenetrable gray eyes until his face flushed. He pulled up his pants, grabbed his tunic, and stomped his feet into his boots.

"Catalina, see that this man has what he needs, then come right back."

"Yes, ma'am."

Catalina followed the MilitiaMan into the communal washroom. Jalen sat up in the bed to take a better look at the new girl.

"So, you are Eve?"

"Apparently," replied the Medicine Girl.

"Did you bring me vinegar?"

"Vinegar? For what purpose?" asked the Medicine Girl.

"For what purpose? To prevent me from having any babies," explained Jalen. "I don't need any more carved out of me."

The Medicine Girl snickered.

"What are you laughing at?" Jalen demanded.

"Vinegar? Water would be just as useful as vinegar! And what a waste of vinegar. If you want to be infertile, drink thistle tea three times a day. Vinegar isn't going to do anything but give you an infection."

"We use vinegar here," Jalen clapped back. "What do you know about any of this business, anyway?" Jalen pulled her robe tight.

"I know that one of these men will impregnate you or give you the pox or take you as their second permanent wife. After that, you might be sold or killed. Most likely you'll be beaten until you are useless and spend your days cleaning out public toilets. In the long run, it won't matter much if you use vinegar to clean out your private parts or shove poison sumac up them."

Jalen looked at the Medicine Girl in utter disgust.

"Why are you talking to me this way?"

The Medicine Girl ignored her and walked around the perimeter of the room.

"Excuse me!" Jalen yelled, waving her arms to catch the Medicine

Girl's attention. "You cannot talk to temporary wives this way. Try that with Hep. Hep will—"

"What do you have to protect yourself with in this room?"

"Protect me, from what?"

"From what? That man who just left slapped your face. Very hard."

Jalen snapped her mouth shut and touched her own cheek. It was inflamed.

"There's swelling under your right eye. If he'd punched you, he would have damaged far fewer nerves." The Medicine Girl walked over and pulled down Jalen's lower right eyelid. "Your face should feel numb, but it will be painful later once the shock wears off. Bruising will start in a day or two. You need a cool compress to lessen the swelling."

"I-I don't know what you are saying."

"Do you know what swelling is?"

"Yes, of course I know what swelling is."

"If that man had clapped your ears that hard, your eardrums would have burst. You need a weapon in this room. Hide one in your bed, under the pillow. I suggest a jar of giant hogweed sap. Smear that in their eyes when they get too rough. It will blind them."

"You're mad."

"I'm not."

"Yes, you are. You're crazy."

"Perhaps," conceded the Medicine Girl. The thought had crossed her mind as she paddled upstream on the stinking river. For a moment, she felt as if the harder she paddled, the closer she would get to her mother. *Her mother was north, and she just needed to get there to be safe in her arms.*

Instead? She was hauled out of the water like a sack of garbage, beaten when she resisted the men in uniforms. She soon learned to not resist. It was much better to watch, to lay in wait, to choose the moment to fight or flee.

Above all, Medicine Girl, be patient.

She wandered over to the man's dinner tray, picking up and eating remnants of the MilitiaMan's meal. *Some kind of boiled meat. A few tender root vegetables, nicely salted.*

"You can't eat that," Jalen whined.

The Medicine Girl looked at her, then slowly ate an entire dinner roll without breaking her gaze.

Catalina returned to find Jalen with her mouth open and the Medicine Girl with her mouth full.

She looked at them both, one to the other, then back again.

"What did I miss?"

"This place feels wrong. I need to leave," the Medicine Girl declared, pacing around the room.

"Ridiculous," Jalen replied in a huff, styling her hair with a comb, one missing several teeth. "You can't just get up and leave. You were purchased. Mama Mae owns you. In any event, where would you go? You'd be hunted down by dawn. You simply do not quit working at a Comfort Station."

Catalina sat on the edge of the bed, shoulders hunched.

"This is a bad place." The Medicine Girl gestured towards the door. "I am not serving slaves, and I am not going to be groomed to be one."

"What are you going to do?" Catalina whispered.

"I am going to leave in a few hours. You should leave, too. If you stay, you will both die unexpectedly and in pain," the Medicine Girl stated. "More MilitiaMen are coming. Another war has started on the Crimson Tide border, close to where they pulled me off the river. I've seen them."

Catalina listened intently, her heart beating, eyes flashing. *She could leave, too.*

"Another war? Good God, what is left to fight over," Jalen mumbled, looking at her fingernails, picking up a scrap of sandpaper to file them.

"They think the Kingdom of Georgia is weak," the Medicine Girl explained. "I heard them say as much."

"Well, are they attacking or aren't they?" Catalina asked, perturbed with the endless nonsense of war. Men came to her dressed in every kind of uniform, yet they were all the same underneath.

"The scrapping fields are full of dead men from here to the Florida Penal Colony," the Medicine Girl added. "It's worse here."

"There's always been fighting and talk of fighting," Jalen groused, rolling her eyes, waving off the Medicine Girl's gloom. "You don't think the men don't tell me what's really going on out there?"

"If they talk to you, you don't listen," the Medicine Girl concluded.

Jalen looked stung.

"What else have you overheard? What else have the men been talking about?" Catalina pressed, beginning to make a mental list of what she needed to get if she left with the Medicine Girl. *An impossibility, yet still...*

"The MilitiaMen talk about the United Authority. Taking it down one way or another." The Medicine Girl grew very somber. "Dark times are coming, and I'm not dying at a Comfort Station under a man."

"Which of the MilitiaMen are conspiring? White Crosses? NorthMen? Sylvanians?" Catalina talked low, looking about as if Mama Mae herself was going to appear.

At this, the Medicine Girl quit talking. *She had said too much to these girls she didn't know.* Her solitary trek had made her too trusting.

"She doesn't know anything," Jalen scoffed. "Catalina, go get me my vinegar."

"I know what I know," the Medicine Girl answered Catalina, her voice a warning. "And I feel it here." She placed her right hand on her heart. "And here," she put her left hand on the side of her forehead. "When both my head and heart tell me something, my mother said I should believe it."

"Where is your mother now?" inquired Jalen.

"North," The Medicine Girl muttered, more to herself. She tilted her head up.

"North is a big place. You want to narrow it down?" Jalen teased her, but not in a mean-spirited way. "Where will you go, Eve, assuming you can escape?"

"I don't know," the Medicine Girl said truthfully. "But I'm going to leave this place. I'm going to find my mother in the north, and we will find safety somewhere."

Safety. Jalen laughed. She put a protective arm around Catalina's shoulder.

"We should leave, too, Jalen," Catalina implored. "You've been a good mistress to me. We can just leave."

Jalen turned Catalina to face her.

"Cat. Listen to me. If we leave, we will get caught. The United Authority will kill us. Slowly."

"We are already dead," Catalina replied. "I want to go with Eve."

Catalina's eyes were expectant, waiting for Jalen's approval. *Eyes still so full of life,* Jalen sighed. As for herself? Jalen was tired. Dead or alive, either way was fine with her. She just wanted peace.

"I will stay here," Jalen decided. "I don't know how to be outside of this room."

For a time, the three girls sat together, deep in their own thoughts.

The Medicine Girl finally stood. "I am getting boy's clothes from the cupboard and whatever else I can steal. And I'm not wearing these useless shoes!" She kicked off the much-hated high heels.

Jalen reached out, taking one of the Medicine Girl's calloused hands, the girl's grubby nails were raggedy and split. She squeezed her hand.

"When you leave tonight, Eve," Jalen said, voice strained, "Take Catalina. Take her far from here. I will help you both the best I can."

Catalina gasped.

"Will you take her, Eve?"

The Medicine Girl nodded.

Catalina returned to find Jalen with her mouth open and the Medicine Girl with her mouth full.

Chapter 5

Outside of Booth, The Crimson Republic

Of all the things Jalen helped the girls acquire, the Medicine Girl treasured the firesteel the most. The small piece of iron alloy sparked magnificently, blazing any tinder that lay before it, dried moss, pine needles, yellowed leaves.

About 25 colony-miles outside of Montgomery, the Medicine Girl spotted an abandoned church. A thin creek ran behind the dilapidated structure. *A good place,* she thought. They needed to replenish their water supply. *They needed to rest.* She prayed to her mother's gods that the church was vacant.

"My feet hurt," Catalina complained, pulling off an overly small pair of dirty tennis shoes. She scrunched her freed toes and wriggled them to work out all the kinks. "I don't think I can walk another step, Eve. Ever again."

"You'll get used to it," the Medicine Girl replied, focusing more on the fire she was building than on the status of Catalina's feet.

"I guess they would hurt worse if Mama Mae cut 'em off," Catalina added, knowing that planning an escape from a Comfort Station would result in her ankle bones being crushed. The threat of becoming a cripple, lying in the streets, usually proved to be a good deterrent for those thinking about leaving. An actual escape warranted death, a much preferable outcome.

Catalina took their sole knife and began to pry the toe cap off of the offending shoes, hoping that would provide more comfort to her cramped feet when they began to move again.

The girls had walked most of the night, Montgomery receding behind them with every footfall. Heads down, they moved fast and purposeful, holding onto their few belongings with a firm grip. Catalina followed behind the Medicine Girl who often looked at the skies to determine the right direction. *North, always north.*

After a time, Catalina remarked about the increased number of

United Authority soldiers and MilitiaMen encamped about the city, clogging the main and secondary roads. It was a fortunate time to leave as the men's arrival caused chaos in Montgomery. As more men created a boon for Mama Mae and the Comfort Station, no one minded two servant girls scuttling about the dark streets, even late at night. In any event, the MilitiaMen seemed distracted by something more important.

Predictably, there would be a bounty for the two runaways by morning, but payable in militia-script. It was a paltry amount, yet enough for desperate men to consider.

Even in ruins, the church felt peaceful at dawn. *It wasn't hard to imagine people sitting in the nave, the large vaulted ceiling collecting the prayers to their Christian god*, the Medicine Girl thought. The remains of the stained glass windows reminded passersby of better days, when people had time for such beautiful things.

"When do you think they'll send a tracker?" Catalina asked. She rubbed her aching calves now.

"I don't know," the Medicine Girl responded, assembling a tiny mound of kindling in a corner of the large room. She flicked the firesteel, which flashed off a satisfying shower of sparks.

After she had a small blaze going, the Medicine Girl arranged some wire hangers she'd found in the closet as a de facto grill, putting their small cooking pot of water on the fire to boil.

"I hope Jalen is all right," Catalina fretted, sprawling out on the floor behind the altar.

The Medicine Girl looked grim.

"When do you think they'll come for us?" Catalina inquired again, eyes clouded with worry.

"Maybe we won't be missed for a few more hours. Maybe they won't miss us at all? Maybe Mamma Mae thinks some foreign MilitiaMen took us? If anything, we are replaceable."

"True," Catalina conceded, feeling a bit better.

"And when the warring starts? They'll forget all about us. There are always women and girls who do what they need to do to survive. Boys, too, for that matter."

"Oh."

"I don't know if we're worth the trouble of paying a tracker," the Medicine Girl muttered.

Catalina fell silent.

"We need to leave the Crimson Republic."

"Where are we heading, Eve? Is anywhere safe?"

"Maybe the north," she replied. "Anywhere is safer than here."

Catalina didn't need to ask why. Busy with Jalen and the endless chores at the Station, she hadn't realized how much the capital city of the Crimson Republic bristled with tension. The Crimson Republic had warred with the Kingdom of Georgia for years, especially over the water and marijuana trade. The skirmishes had escalated to the United Authority level.

She wondered about Mama Mae and the other station administrators. She thought about the other novice attendants and serving boys, now more at risk from their actions. She worried about Jalen and the discovery of her aiding and abetting their escape. *Perhaps Jalen was dead already?*

Soon, the water boiled, bubbling noisily. As a rule, the Medicine Girl waited three colony-minutes—it was what her mother always advised. *There isn't a healthy body of water in this land anymore, from sea to sea. No matter how blue or how clear water appears, don't be tempted. No matter how much you thirst. Protozoa and bacteria and parasites want to feed on your body. Kill them before they kill you.*

The Medicine Girl knew when her mouth was dry and her tongue was swollen that she'd waited too long to prepare water to drink. At the end of their long journey out of Montgomery, she noted Catalina was breathing hard, her speech slurred.

Catalina had just mentioned the painful shoes, but the Medicine Girl knew she was hurting. *She'd pushed them both too far.* Catalina wasn't used to living rough.

As the water cooled, Catalina listlessly watched as the Medicine Girl took inventory of their possessions. It didn't take long. There weren't many of them.

The night before they left the Comfort Station, Jalen managed to gather things for the girls' departure. She found a small package of sailmaker's needles, a bar of soap, several bills of hard colony-currency, a plastic container, a small cooking tin, a rough spun wool blanket, and a Bowie knife. She shoved all into a soldier's canvas bag. Inexplicably, Jalen tossed in a jar of rouge and a vial of perfumed citrus oil.

As Jalen gathered what she could, the Medicine Girl crept over to the far side of the decrepit hotel to pillage the boy's cupboard for more appropriate clothing. A few pairs of curious eyes stared at her, but boy servants knew better than to get involved in matters that did not concern them.

She extricated two pairs of filthy athletic shoes, gray woolen socks, thick homespun trousers, and a couple of threadbare jerseys from sports teams that hadn't existed since the time before the end of electricity. Shedding her floral dress in the hallway, she began to clothe herself in layers.

Catalina rummaged in the kitchen and pantry, filling a knapsack with as many nuts, dried berries, opossum jerky, goat cheese, and flatbread that she could get her hands on. The larder held little in reserve, but she'd gathered enough food to sustain them for a few days.

As they reunited in Jalen's room, Jalen tried to advise them the best she could, offering the latest gossip from her fellow temporary wives. The Medicine Girl found none of it useful, but Catalina hung on her every word.

"And don't fight a man if he wants you," Jalen said. "Sometimes it's better just to give in."

"Or you can skin him alive," the Medicine Girl offered. "That's always an option."

Jalen ignored the Medicine Girl, putting her arms around Catalina. They both talked in low voices, as tears rolled down Catalina's face.

"We don't have time for this," the Medicine Girl huffed.

"You're right," Jalen said, kissing the top of Catalina's head. "Take these things. Go far and go fast."

"Come with us?" Catalina asked, one more time, hoping Jalen would change her mind.

"No," Jalen replied. "I'll cover for you as long as I can."

On the way out of the back door of the United Authority - Comfort Station #22, Catalina pilfered a bottle of barley gin from Mama Mae's own personal stash.

"How long can we stay here?" Catalina asked, lying on the chipped slate floor. Her voice echoed in the church. The pews had long been torn out for kindling, but an impressive metal cross still hung on the main wall, reigning over the general wreckage.

"Not long."

"I like it here."

"I do, too."

The Medicine Girl tested the boiled water, then extinguished the small fire she'd made inside the church. Although the water was still very warm, it was drinkable.

She poured the water into their plastic container, giving Catalina the first swig. Catalina drank steadily, handing the container back to the Medicine Girl. She drained it entirely. The Medicine Girl filled the plastic container from the pot, again and again, until all of the water was finished.

Catalina measured out a modest portion of their food stores. *How long would this meager amount last?* Munching on the nuts and goat cheese, Catalina wondered aloud what Mama Mae would say after discovering her food and liquor supplies had been plundered by two of her novice attendants.

"*Not the goat cha-heeze!*" Catalina imitated Mama Mae's southern drawl. The Medicine Girl snickered. Catalina stood up and continued. "*Oh my lawd, those little beetches have absconded with mah fine whiskey!*"

"*Ah picked her up cheap at the Family Trading Station. Now, she's ours,*" said the Medicine Girl, doing her best southern drawl.

"Miserable hag," Catalina laughed bitterly. While exploring the back section of the church, she imitated Mama Mae's distinctive walk. The Medicine Girl giggled, continuing to eat her share of the food, very slowly.

"I should have stolen her red wigs and falsies, too. I'm sure they'd kindle up a fire quite well."

"If we hadn't been in such a hurry, we could have torched the entire station," the Medicine Girl stated, as if that had been the preferable course of action. "Catalina. We need to sleep."

"Hey, look over here. This must be the choir room," Catalina explained. "Check out this closet! Maybe we should move in here for a bit? At least we could close the doors. If we tie the door handles together from the inside, that might give us a little more protection."

The Medicine Girl wanted to object. *Enough time to be terrorized before the final blow.* She hated confined spaces, preferring to take her chances in the open chamber where she could jump through any number of broken doors or windows. Hearing a distant rumble of thunder, she wondered who else might come into the church, looking for shelter.

But Catalina had a point. Perhaps it would be better to remain secure and hidden for a time. Perhaps the gods of this place would take mercy on them, just for the night.

In relative comfort, the two girls slept like the dead in a closet. Catalina did not miss being roused before dawn to prepare Jalen or assist her temporary husbands with their needs, and the Medicine Girl did not miss sleeping with one eye open, awaiting a painful death at the hands of her father's men.

The Medicine Girl jolted awake, feeling for the knife by her side.

"What's wrong?" Catalina whispered, any trace of sleep gone from her voice.

The Medicine Girl motioned for Catalina to be quiet.

Catalina half-arose from the cozy nest she'd made from Jalen's blanket in the choir room's closet. The Medicine Girl listened intently, until convinced all seemed well. She untied the door handles of their refuge and cautiously stepped out.

The torrential rains had arrived the previous evening, lasting long into the night, neatly filling their plastic container to the brim. The Medicine Girl had left it and the pot out under a section of the sanctuary where the roof was gone. Inordinately pleased she didn't have to boil water to drink, she put her hands on her hips and smiled. Good water lay everywhere: in the plastic container, in the pot, in the heavy dew on the thick blades of grass.

She remembered dew-collecting with her mother. They would tie clean rags to their ankles and walk amidst the long, wet grass, stopping to twist out the dew from the rags into basins, dripping clean dew water straight into their mouths.

"I'm hungry," Catalina announced. "What should we eat this morning?"

"Grasshoppers," the Medicine Girl replied.

Catalina would have protested, but in the end, catching the grasshoppers proved to be great fun.

She watched as the Medicine Girl laid the blanket near a log in the grassy field near the creek that ran behind the church. She would then make a great commotion, clapping her hands and barking, causing the bugs to scatter wildly. In the early morning hours, grasshoppers moved more slowly. As they hopped on the blanket in an attempt to get away from the noise, their feet caught in the blanket's thick fibers.

Both girls competed to scoop up the most wriggling creatures.

"I got three!" called Catalina.

"Six," grinned the Medicine Girl. They added the newly caught insects to their cooking pot, covering it with a flat piece of rock which worked as a makeshift lid.

"Let's try it over by the peach trees," the Medicine Girl said, spotting a small grove. As it was mid-summer, the trees should have been full of fruit; however, it was clear they'd been harvested for some time, picked over by roving bands. A few rotted peaches lay on the ground, providing a banquet for all sorts of insects, but especially a delight for grasshoppers.

The blanket unfurled again. Both girls clapped and barked. The insects attempted to escape their assault, floundering in the blanket's fabric.

"Nine!" Catalina called.

"Eight!" laughed the Medicine Girl. "You beat me!"

"It was only a matter of time," Catalina replied.

"You pick up things quickly."

"I'm sure if I'd stayed at the station, I'd have picked up lots of things—the pox, head lice, the clap, the clam..."

"Then you'd have to pick up rosemary and eucalyptus oil to treat your sores," the Medicine Girl added.

"Hah! I'd have Mama Mae send me the clean lot. I'd have been the best temporary wife there. Better than Jalen."

"That's not a hard job," the Medicine Girl replied, falling on her back, feet and hands in the air. She mimicked Jalen's voice. "Oh, you're so big, corporal! Oh, you big strong man. Take me! Oh! Oh!"

Both girls dissolved into laughter.

The grasshoppers pinged in the pot, frantic to escape. The rock lid, though, did its job well, keeping them in their place.

The Medicine Girl grabbed a fat one from the pot, showing Catalina how to pull off its head so the entrails came out with it—in one firm pull. She then snapped off the grasshopper's wings and legs. Using a sailmaker's needle with a length of thread, the Medicine Girl pierced the center of the bug, stringing them together like popcorn on a garland.

After making a small fire, The Medicine Girl dry roasted strands of them, laying the cooked ones on the thin blanket, which had proven to be almost as good as a net in capturing the small creatures.

The Medicine Girl gathered red berry fruits from the wild rose bushes near the front of the church. She crushed the berries with a stick, tied the remnants up in a piece of a choir robe, and boiled the packets in water for a few minutes.

"It's rose hip tea," she explained to Catalina. "It'll help heal your sores."

Both of the girls' legs and arms were scratched by brambles, bitten by insects, and cut by various impediments along the way. The Medicine Girl wished she had her Neo. None of their wounds appeared to be suppurating, but she always hated to find an infection the hard way.

Both girls continued to eat their fill, adding goat cheese and a few of the nuts from the station's pantry to complete their meal.

"How long can we stay?" asked Catalina again, her eyes showing contentment in the fire's light.

"We should have left earlier today. We should leave now."

Catalina frowned a bit. "I like it here. It reminds me of..." Of what she couldn't say. Something ephemeral, like a memory she didn't have.

The two sat contented, the Medicine Girl whittling toothpicks out of pine for them both.

"Maybe we could stay another day," suggested Catalina.

"There are men looking for me," said the Medicine Girl.

"They're looking for me, too."

"Not from Montgomery."

"Where are you from?" Catalina asked.

"The Penal Colony of Florida."

Catalina's sharp intake of breath startled even the Medicine Girl. "It's death if I'm discovered with you..."

"It's death to run away from a Comfort Station. It's death to steal liquor from your employer. What does it matter if I'm the devil herself from hell? We both need to head north. No one will know us up there, and they don't honor the law from here."

Catalina stood up, moved back to the choir room's closet and began to sort through their things.

Was Catalina leaving her? Is this where they'd split up? The Medicine Girl felt a weight on her chest. *She remembered her mother walking behind a cart, hands tied in front of her. She'd never felt more alone.*

Catalina returned with the bottle of barley gin.

"Let's get drunk, felon."

The Medicine Girl gave Catalina a puzzled look.

"Let's get jaw-droppingly, grasshopper-crunchingly, church choir-singingly drunk." Catalina unscrewed the top and took a long pull. *It burned her throat.*

"We shouldn't waste it. Alcohol is good for disinfecting wounds," the Medicine Girl warned.

Catalina took another drink.

"Gin is a good footwash," the Medicine Girl suggested. "Mixed with some ashes, it makes a good strong soap."

Catalina took a longer drink, then handed the Medicine Girl the bottle.

The Medicine Girl shook her head.

"You're going to make me drink alone?"

Silently, the Medicine Girl cleaned up the remnants of the fire and their meal, adding, "I'm not making you do anything."

She heard Catalina tip the bottle again. When she turned, she saw tears running down Catalina's face. She attempted to stifle a tiny sob.

"Cat, whatever is making you cry, doesn't matter," said the Medicine Girl, quoting her mother. "The past lay in the past."

"Well, sometimes it hurts," Catalina said, screwing the top back on the bottle. "Sometimes it feels like it's all happening again, you know?"

"I don't know what to say," the Medicine Girl mumbled awkwardly. "I'm sorry you are sad."

"Me, too, Eve," Catalina replied. "Don't you ever get sad, sometimes?"

"No."

"Not ever?"

"No, I don't get sad," clarified the Medicine Girl. "I get angry."

Without another word, they both gathered up their things, retreating back to the choir room's closet. The Medicine Girl deftly tied a thick knot, yoking the two inside door handles together.

In a few hours, the closet doors were violently wedged open.

"That's her," called out a gruff voice.

"Take them both."

The Medicine Girl grabbed a fat one from the pot, showing Catalina how to pull off its head so the entrails came out with it.

Chapter 6

Tupelo, Arkansippi

The Tracker almost felt guilty for taking Mama Mae's money. Finding two little girls holed up in a church closet, one clasping an empty bottle of gin, didn't take much effort.

The skinny girl flew at him like a bobcat when they first pried open the closet's doors, leaving a deep impression of her teeth on his forearm. He punched her as hard as he could in her stomach. *That took the wind out of her sails.* She collapsed at their feet like a sack of potatoes, gasping for breath.

The one with murderous gray eyes was who they'd come for. She sat as silent as a statue, hands laced behind her head. *Was she giving up this easily?* He'd been warned about her.

While Catalina moaned in pain, coughing and wheezing to catch her breath, his partner shoved their few possessions into a canvas bag. The Tracker and the Medicine Girl balefully glared at one other. He lunged for her, hoping she would flinch or recoil, but she did not blink an eyelash.

Each man took one of the Comfort Station's novices out of the choir room closet, dragging them down the aisle to a handcart, just outside the narthex. Their instructions were to capture the Medicine Girl alive, if possible. But accidents happened on the highways; their client would understand if things went awry.

The fouler man held Catalina by the throat, forcing her into a wooden crate, anchored atop the handcart. The Tracker then shoved the Medicine Girl in the crate after her, deep splinters ripping into her skin from the rough hewn slats. He tied the makeshift door shut with a length of rope.

In all, the Medicine Girl did not resist. Instead, she slowed her breathing.

She watched and listened.

The handcart was unforgiving, as the two raggedy men pulled it up the Eight Two from Booth to Tuscaloosa. The crate was ill-fitted for its use in the back of the wagon. It slid about wildly, causing the Medicine Girl and Catalina to hang on to the frame, bloodying their fingers in the process. They jostled about like loose melons.

"I need water," Catalina whispered.

"Maybe they have some gin," the Medicine Girl remarked wryly, attempting to cheer her up. Catalina offered her a short laugh, not noticing the Medicine Girl's increasing concern for her. *Catalina was not well.*

The day after their capture, the Medicine Girl watched Catalina hold on to her stomach with one arm, curled up tightly into a fetal position. Her skin grew paler each hour, cold and clammy in the mid-summer heat. The little Catalina spoke was through a grimace, her lips drawn tight, teeth clenched. Oftentimes the Medicine Girl watched Catalina bite her own lip until it bled, refusing to cry out.

The Medicine Girl wished for chamomile and ginger. She elevated Catalina's legs the best she could in their tight quarters, but that did little to alleviate Catalina's suffering. A growing rage threatened to blind her. She hated not being able to help her friend. She hated being confined. She hated the men who treated them like animals. More than anything, the Medicine Girl hated feeling helpless.

When the men stopped by the side of the highway to let the girls relieve themselves, the Medicine Girl noticed a tinge of blood in Catalina's urine. She also saw a purplish discoloration in her loins, where Catalina took the Tracker's gut punch.

The Medicine Girl asked Catalina if she could feel the injured area. *Ask for consent before treating a patient,* her mother had advised. *Some people don't want your assistance. They have their own reasons.*

"I'm good." Catalina waved her off.

The Medicine Girl didn't press the matter. Neither girl had much dignity left, so the Medicine Girl let it be. Getting back into the crate, Catalina grit her teeth, attempting to project a strength she did not have. The men stood close by, tormenting them, making vile remarks.

She could ask the men for help. *What good would it do, thought the Medicine Girl.* The men did not seem to care about Catalina. They had their prize.

"We need water," the Medicine Girl called out to the men. After several more minutes, the men stopped to drink from their canteens, shoving handfuls of hardtack and ham into their gobs.

"We could use some food, too," she added.

"You can shut up," the Tracker said, still angry about Catalina's bite. His companion ignored the girls. *His share of the payment wasn't enough to deal with the girls' constant complaints.*

"My friend is sick. I need the canvas bag," the Medicine Girl demanded.

In truth, Catalina had died in her arms a few miles earlier. Her breath had become slow and labored; the Medicine Girl had nothing to ease her suffering. She held her close until Catalina passed.

"I'm sure you could sell her if she was well. No one is going to buy a sick girl." The Medicine Girl attempted to reason with the men.

The men considered her point.

"All right then," the Tracker relented. He fumbled through the items they'd shoved into the cart alongside the crate. Pulling out the canvas bag, he rummaged through its contents. "You have your weird little witch potions in here?"

The Medicine Girl crossed her arms, surreptitiously retrieving the firesteel sewn into the armpit of her undershirt, ignored by the men who had just checked her pockets.

After the Tracker ensured nothing dangerous was in the canvas bag, he tossed it to her. The Medicine Girl caught it with one hand.

"I'm here, Catalina, I'm right here," the Medicine Girl called out, never taking her eyes off the men. She took out Jalen's rouge and perfumed oil. She took out the sailmaker's needles.

"You going to get her dolly'd up?" asked the Tracker's companion. "I think I'd like that..."

The Medicine Girl worked fast.

She flung the perfumed oil at the Tracker's partner. *Citrus oil. Highly flammable.* As he spluttered in outrage, she flicked the firesteel which ignited the oil, engulfing him in flames in an instant. As he dropped to his knees on the asphalt, he attempted to bat down the blaze, only managing to spread the oily firestorm farther.

From the front of the handcart, the Tracker watched in horror, his eyes rounding in shock. In seconds, he collected himself, setting off towards the Medicine Girl, speeding around the burning hulk of his partner.

In the interim, the Medicine Girl pulled out a half dozen of the long, thick sailmaker's needles, banded them together in her little fist and ran towards the Tracker. As the Tracker pulled his arm back for a roundhouse punch, she blocked it with her left hand. Jabbing the needles deep into his neck with her right hand, the Tracker froze, stunned by the frontal assault.

In an attempt to grab her right wrist, he was shocked she held on so fast—even more surprised when she ripped open a deep trench from the side of his neck down to his throat, severing the jugular vein in the process.

His mouth moved, soundlessly cursing her and her mother. He fell face forward onto his stomach. As great gouts of blood sprayed, the Tracker's hands reached for his neck, trying to staunch the bleeding, to no avail.

With one look, the Medicine Girl knew he would be dead in less than ten colony-seconds.

The other man required mercy-killing, as he was burned terribly, but not quite dead. She toyed with the idea of prolonging his pain, but the Medicine Girl remembered her mother's way and obliged him with a quicker end. With a rag, she covered his charred mouth and nose until he stopped moving. Then she kicked his corpse in the face.

Normally, she would have left everything behind and started walking north. She debated with herself what to do, what she had time to do.

No good would come from her standing alone on the highway

surrounded by three corpses. One by one, she dragged the men's bodies off the highway, tossing them unceremoniously into a shallow ditch, knowing the animals and insects would make short work of them.

She then pulled the handcart, still containing the crate with Catalina's body deeper into the woods.

Catalina deserved more than rotting under a hot summer sun in a cage.

She pulled the handcart deep into the forest, until she found a quiet clearing, idyllic, green, peaceful as a prayer. The Medicine Girl took everything off the handcart, unfurled the blanket on the soft moss, then gently laid Catalina's body on it. She wrapped her body in Jalen's blanket.

Returning to the handcart, she rifled through the men's belongings, finding a small covered cooking pot. Unlatching the pot's lid, she used it to dig a proper grave. With dogged determination, she paced out a trench about five colony-feet wide and measured six colony-feet deep, removing rocks and roots as she went.

After she had excavated Catalina's grave, she carried her friend's body, tucking it into the freshly dug pit. The Medicine Girl felt for Jalen's rouge tin in the canvas bag. Opening the lid, she patted out a little of the reddish balm, rubbing color on Catalina's cheeks and lips, making her face look as if she only slept.

This girl had been her friend. Would she ever have another?

Silently, the Medicine Girl used the cooking pot's lid to fill in the soil. Now the animals wouldn't desecrate her body as it decayed, returning to the earth in its entirety.

After her labors, the Medicine Girl sat back on her heels and considered the mound of earth.

For the first time in the Medicine Girl's life, loneliness bruised her heart. Even when her mother was taken, she hadn't felt so bereft. The Medicine Girl covered her eyes with her dirty fists. Breathing rapidly, a sickening, sinking sense of dread threatened to overwhelm her. Deep inside of her, a childlike voice cried out.

Where did Catalina go?

Angrily, she looked up at an indifferent sky, blue and serene in the twilight. She remembered Catalina drinking gin and catching grasshoppers. She grinned remembering how Catalina tried to teach her how to walk in high heels. She laughed thinking about her imitation of Mama Mae.

A sole tear stole down the Medicine Girl's cheek. She wiped it away. Before the Medicine Girl left the grove, she laid down by the gravesite and chose to feel gratitude for someone who had cared for her, if only for a little while.

At the Comfort Station, Catalina had watched over. Like a mother. *Like her mother.*

Sitting up, filled with grim determination, the Medicine Girl decided what she would do in her remaining days.

Two things.

First, she would go north. She would find her mother. She would know if she still lived.

Second, she would kill her father.

Other than those two things, nothing mattered.

The United Authority didn't recognize slavery, per se. Although among its remaining states and territories, it sanctioned Family Trading Stations. Records were kept on every transaction, primarily so the federal government could extract taxes from its citizenry. The business provided the government a significant source of revenue, necessary in such trying times. The government didn't run on star spangled dreams, and someone needed to provide for the common defense.

Maintaining any semblance of law and order was an expensive proposition in the fractured realm.

In the south, anyone engaging in the sale or trade of family members was required to report said transaction to the Memphis Station. Failure to report, record, or pay taxes on the sale of family members resulted in death. As usual, in cases where the United Authority lost out on the proceeds, transgressors' deaths were particularly unpleasant and gruesome.

After years of unrest, Family Trading Stations became a fixture in state capitals, at least those capitals which were still functioning under the United Authority. Family Trading Stations were initially proposed as a legal way to help displaced persons find unity and purpose among the societal wreckage, common after the end of electricity. Whoever desired and could afford to purchase a second wife or a first son or an eighth daughter could attend the auctions, open to all who could pay. This included those looking for a new family member to carry on the family name, tend the fields, boil water, catch game, filet fish, or bear children, as each family's situation required.

There was no requirement or regulation that guaranteed new family members had to be treated in any certain way. That was for the patriarch or head of household to determine. Should a family member have an accident or be worked to death, the United Authority did not intervene. The United Authority knew when to mind its own business, and as its most profitable subsidiary, the Family Trading Stations enjoyed great latitude in making a business of creating families.

From the maps the Tracker carried, the Medicine Girl determined that following the Two Two would take her to Memphis. Ever since the entire state of Louisiana had been declared environmentally unsound, its bayous hopelessly poisoned, most governmental enterprises had moved north to Memphis. If she were right, all of the records for the southern Family Trading Stations were kept in repositories there.

With the Carolinas perpetually at war with itself, Tennessee seemed to have the most stability to foster industry and commerce. For Tennessee, Memphis remained the most viable city, as roads were still in good repair and its water treatment and sewage plants were well-maintained by nonviolent convicts who hadn't been shuttled off to the Florida Penal Colony.

A decade or so prior, the capital city moved to Memphis as Nashville split between militia factions. Knoxville and Chattanooga still reeled from increasing outbreaks of the Mountain View Plague. Tick populations surged in the summer, worse than what afflicted parts of Old Virginia.

The United Authority allowed the Illuminati Pagans to maintain order in Memphis, its chief warlord holed up in the library on the campus of its former university. Rumor had it, Xerxes surrounded himself with as many books as he could appropriate, acquired by any stratagem as required.

The Medicine Girl's father often made fun of the Memphis warlord, arrogantly naming himself after an ancient king—one purported to be eight colony-feet tall. *Maybe I should call myself Alexander the Great or Julius Caesar,* her father had said only half in jest. His sycophants laughed. *You can never trust a Tennessee warlord,* he added. *Everyone knew they were shills for the United Authority. They were warlords in name only.*

Before beginning her trek on the Two Two to Memphis, the Medicine Girl inventoried her accumulated possessions, culling through the Tracker's and his henchman's belongings. She placed what she wanted into the canvas bag, slinging the strap across her thin body. Every five colony-miles or so, she'd change shoulders, stretching the way her mother had demonstrated to avoid strains and circulation problems. *The body needs to move,* she often said. *All of it. Don't tax one area at the expense of another.*

The Tracker's maps were the most useful items; the food provisions were the most welcomed. But she was delighted to find a small cache of seaweed iodine crystals. It would be a relief not to have to boil water for a few days. *Perhaps she wouldn't have to boil water until she finished her business in Memphis?* This was assuming she was successful, assuming she wasn't sold off herself. This was not an impossibility as she was alone and underage. *Actually, it was more of a probability,* she admitted to herself.

She sipped water from the Tracker's canteen, grateful to be able to reserve her strength instead of building yet another fire. She needed to think as she walked. Though the Family Trading Station would have a record of her mother's sale, conjuring up a plan to make a Memphis bureaucrat tell her where her mother was would be taxing enough.

It was easy to determine from the old maps where the wealthy areas had been before the wars. They were normally just outside the city, away from the river. The Medicine Girl surveyed the landscape, looking for expanses of green that once had been golf courses. The wealthier areas had roads named after trees and flowers, with nearby remains that had once been hospital complexes.

From her map, she found Windyke, Tennessee, a dozen colony-miles from the Library of Xerxes, a place that would hopefully yield what she needed to bargain with.

After the end of electricity when the cities burned, CityDwellers waited for assistance from the United Authority that never came. The subsequent carnage and bloodshed as resources dwindled spawned tales of horror that the OldOnes still whispered about. After pantries and storehouses were emptied, household pets began to disappear. Then other mammals went missing, sometimes two-legged ones.

Those in the suburbs formed or strengthened existing militias to protect themselves from desperate refugees fleeing the smoking chaos and escalating depravity of the urban areas. Inevitably, the suburbs dissolved into turmoil, too, as people became more desperate and violent. Although not all of the Bill of Rights were in effect, the 2nd Amendment still held firm, especially in Tennessee.

Tennessean homes had enough weaponry and firepower to fend off a small army of would-be assailants. However, in most cases, guns were used to obtain things a family or tribe or militia needed. Bodies littered the streets. Stores were burned. Homes were pillaged.

Those who lived in the exurbs had been somewhat safer during the early days, holding out until the United Authority brutally restored order.

Now, the cities seemed safer, as infighting between powerful suburban clans led to wholesale murder. When the militias became involved, full scale warfare occurred on the scrapping fields over county control. As the cities began to stabilize, the suburbs lay in charred ruins, homes gutted. People resettled in more hospitable climes.

The Medicine Girl prayed to her mother's gods that she would find what she needed, something a starving populace might overlook in their singular desire to feed their bellies.

After a few days of salvaging through the palatial remains of single family homes in abandoned cul-de-sac after cul-de-sac, the Medicine Girl finally found what she was looking for. She gathered up a half dozen of the treasured items, placing them in the canvas bag. For the rest of her trove, she dug a hole in an overgrown backyard near an empty shell of an inground pool. Here, she buried a cache, secured in layers of plastic and wrapped in heavy living room curtains that she hoped would keep the moisture at bay.

In the ransacked homes she wandered through, she found remnants of things she couldn't imagine anyone needing, all rotting in the mud and dust. Plastic—in all forms—was everywhere, in the kitchens, in the cabinets, in the bedrooms. There were plastic toys and plastic containers and plastic furniture and plastic objects for which she could not fathom the purpose.

In the thirteenth home she entered, she found a locked closet behind a partially-burnt out garage. Militia symbols were painted on the house, which she ignored. *Let them die crazy*, she spat. *Endless fighting, for what? It was hard enough to feed oneself.*

Using a knife to pry off the closet's rusty lock, she finally popped it off entirely, opening the door to discover a treasure that her mother had mentioned to her only once.

I have told you about cars, her mother said. *You have seen their useless metal husks around the penal colony. They are only good for shelter now. During the wars, there wasn't any lead-shielding around car batteries to protect them from EMP bombs. The only car that might work would have a diesel engine, one from long ago. But there is no petroleum. One day you might find other transportation outside the colony, like a bicycle or scooter. These are man-powered machines with tires, built for one person to go far and fast.*

The bicycle squeaked in protest as she wheeled it out of the forgotten closet. She felt the firm tires, made of a hard plastic foam, not ones of air tubing that her mother described.

She wheeled the bicycle into the garage, still out of sight from the side road. Rummaging in the canvas bag, she came across a plastic jar of rendered tallow. Using her fingers, she lubricated the bike's moving parts as best she could, rotating the pedals to ensure the bike was sound.

How am I supposed to ride this contraption?

Placing her belongings down, she straddled the metal structure. Walking the bicycle out to the remaining fragments of sidewalk, she chanced being out in the open. She started pedaling while awkwardly sitting on the bicycle seat. *How fast it was!*

A smile stole across her face until she realized she didn't know how to stop the machine. In a panic, she closed her eyes as her speed increased down a slight incline in what remained of a driveway.

The bike clattered against an unforgiving red maple tree; the Medicine Girl's knees skidded on the concrete, leaving two bloody streaks on the pavement. Tangled in the bike with her hands still grasping the handlebars, she squeezed them as she stood up, understanding too late that the grips on the handlebars stopped the bike. She noted how grasping them activated tiny breaks on the wheels.

She gingerly walked the bike back to the garage, deciding to stay with it in the forgotten closet for the night. *It was a good thing the jar of tallow was still relatively full,* she thought, rubbing the balm on her aching knees. It had been just the thing for both her and the bicycle.

She planned to leave in the morning, but the Medicine Girl still had many preparations to make around the wreckage of the house where she had buried important things. There were sharpened sticks to whittle and holes to dig. There were fish hooks and rope and knives to hide about the property.

Exhausted by her efforts, she laid down, placing the canvas bag under her head, nestling in a torn shower curtain that adequately covered her in the night.

Fear crept into her thoughts as she considered her plans for Memphis. But she remembered what her mother would ask her, when she was feeling overwhelmed: *How do you eat an alligator?* The Medicine Girl would reply: *One bite at a time.*

She calmed herself by making a mental list of things she must do before stepping one foot north. She would master the power of the bicycle, she would tend to her knees, and she would eat more of the Tracker's provisions.

After ensuring she had taken the necessary precautions, the Medicine girl fell into a black sleep, her hand resting lightly on the bicycle.

From the front of the handcart, the Tracker watched in horror, his eyes rounding in shock.

Chapter 7

Memphis, Tennessee

The Medicine Girl awoke early in the morning, out of sorts, stiff from sleeping on the concrete slab floor. Shrouded in a dark mood accompanied by an overcast sky, she felt disheartened to find herself still alive. She missed Catalina, envied her a bit, her small body resting underneath a few feet of comforting loam. It seemed a preferable state.

The Medicine Girl's knees ached, the memory of her first attempt at riding the bicycle making her feel foolish and inept. Rarely did she fail when she tried her best. *Perhaps this was a harbinger of sorts, a warning that going to Memphis would be a fatal mistake? Perhaps the gloomy day meant she would be captured yet again or worse?* She shook her head, attempting to dispel the troubling thoughts. Her mother had cautioned her against looking for signs and portents and trying to make meaning out of unrelated events. *Things would be what they would be.*

She laid back down, watching a beetle skitter across the floor, oblivious to her presence. She doubted the insect was concerned with either its past or future. The bug just was. Along with Catalina, she envied the bug, too.

Misgivings aside, she stretched, increasing the blood flow through all her limbs, flexing and bending just as her mother had done every morning before she boiled their water for herbal tea. The Medicine Girl took her time twisting into various positions, all the while breathing in and out. Anxiety seemed to leave her body with each exhale; clarity increased with every inhale. *She wished her mother was there to sing to her.*

It would take a couple hours to bike to Memphis.

She packed the canvas bag with a few essentials. If she planned correctly, she would return to Windyke by early afternoon. If she miscalculated, nothing else would matter.

Xerxes leaned back in a cracked leather wingback chair, situated by one of the few remaining mahogany reading tables. Footsteps of guards and random assistants echoed in the rotunda of the former University of Memphis. He looked around at the stacks of books he'd stored into his sanctum, wondering which one to reread again.

The sun streamed through an intact bay window, its warm beams of light falling on his desk. Xerxes got up, milled about the bookshelves, touched their spines, pulled one out, and leafed through it. He knew the text by heart. He snapped the book shut, replacing it lovingly on the shelf.

He brooded. Xerxes was bored.

His chief consul, Darius, had just finished an exhaustive report of all the things that threatened his tenuous hold on the Family Trading Station. Darius, with his slicked back hair and powerful voice, read through the latest financial tallies, a small abacus on his belt clicking and clacking as he fumbled with the wooden beads. The only other ornament Darius wore on his person was a decorative sheath about his waist. Appropriated from a Boston museum's antiquities wing, Darius had looted a dagger, its finely cut jewels forming floral forms on its hilt.

Darius calculated figures as Xerxes requested, competently recalling statistics from over a prior decade, ever since he started in service with the warlord of the Illuminati Pagans.

"The net sales of able-bodied children dropped last quarter. Typhoid fever outbreak," Darius pursed his lips and rolled his eyes. *Children and disease. What can you do?*

"Does that grand total reflect the United Authority's bonus and incentives?"

"And your discounts and returns, generous as you are," Darius purred. "There's just no pleasing some people."

"Are we prepared for the United Authority audit?"

"As always," Darius smiled, in his fawning, oleaginous way. Secretly, he was offended, his competence being questioned in the slightest. Darius made an effort to ensure the hardness in his heart did not show itself in his eyes. The charcoal he used to outline his eyes smudged a bit due to the South's damp, humid weather, giving him a haunted look. His roughspun tunics were perpetually stained under the armpits.

Xerxes mulled over the figures Darius reported while eating dried fruits, one by one, from a chipped crystal bowl. Finally he sighed, shooing Darius away. He didn't want to be bothered with any more lackluster reports or general complaints about his business.

The truth of it was, he was more than worried. The United Authority replaced those who did not consistently meet their quotas; even though Xerxes had served the United Authority for many years, job security rested on one's present performance. With the United Authority, loyalty was one-sided, and the Illuminati Pagan's numbers were off.

"Give me the room," Xerxes ordered, as factotums and other subordinates quickly followed Darius out of the library's rotunda. After all had left, Xerxes walked to the wings of the building, towards another stack of books, a few relics of the past who, like himself, had survived so much.

Xerxes touched the book's hardcovers, heaving a deep dramatic sigh, one so indulgent and full of self-pity that his eyes watered. After he wiped his petulant tears, he returned to the rotunda to find a young girl standing in front of his desk.

Her hair was a long wave of glossy black, eyes gray and piercing. Dressed in a pair of boy's trousers, oversized tennis shoes, and a filthy t-shirt, she sat a dirty canvas bag on top of his desk.

Xerxes should have called for the guards. He should have pulled out the small loaded revolver he kept strapped to his ankle, day and night. The gun was covered by the heavy fabric of his robes, robes richly embroidered by women at the Family Trading Station.

He had options. With one word, she would be captured, tortured, and killed. *Preferably all three.*

However, Xerxes was intrigued. He sat back down in his cracked leather wingback chair, facing the little stoic figure, one eyebrow arched, waiting for her to speak.

She said nothing.

"Do I know you?" He addressed her, failing to suppress a small grin.

She did not return the smile or the greeting.

"Do you wish to die?"

Again, nothing.

"Do you wish to be sold to the NorthMen? They like little girls like you." He smiled, broadly, malevolently.

The girl stood, hands by her side.

"Well, what do you want, child?" he inquired, using his left hand to straighten his oily hair. "Have you come here to kill me?"

"I come here to make you an offering," she replied evenly.

"A what?"

"An offering. A token of appreciation for the favor you will grant me."

She had Xerxes' complete attention.

"I am doing *you* a favor?" *Impertinent little thing,* he thought. "How magnanimous of me. Well? Show me your offering."

The Medicine Girl took out a book from the canvas bag and placed it in front of him.

"This is *The Art of War.* It was written by an ancient Chinese general who never lost a battle," she recounted. "It holds the secrets of military strategy from the past."

Xerxes eyes lit up. The few hundred books he had managed to gather in his collection had been read and reread until they almost crumbled in his hands. A new book—especially one that might strengthen his rule—sparked his interest.

"I've heard of this book," he lied. She noted his body language to reference his duplicity in future discussions. "Do you have more books for me?" Xerxes added, almost too quickly.

She nodded. She withdrew a heavier volume from the canvas bag. Watching him figuratively salivate over her offerings, the Medicine Girl calculated her next moves.

"This is the first volume of *The Story of Civilization.* It was written by a renowned historian and his wife. It explains the nature of mankind and the repetition of history."

"There is nothing new under the sun. History does, indeed, repeat itself," Xerxes agreed. He walked over to her and took the tome in his hands. "I will read this."

"Inside that book recounts the story of the first Xerxes, the one from Ancient Greece," she explained, seeing his eyes widen, his hands slightly trembling.

"I will read this one *first*."

She waited as he felt the book's heft, opened to the table of contents, perused the endnotes.

"There are ten more volumes," she informed him, matter-of-factly.

"Can I have them all?"

"You may," she promised.

Xerxes giddily flipped through the pages of both books.

"Do you have more books?"

"I do," she pulled out the last book and handed it to him. A thin paperback.

He read the title out loud. "*How To Win Friends and Influence People.* Does this man know how to do this?" Xerxes seemed incredulous.

The Medicine Girl shrugged her shoulders.

"Where are the other books?"

"Only I know," the Medicine Girl said, remaining motionless.

"Give them to me now," Xerxes ordered.

"No."

"No?" Xerxes put the book he'd been thumbing facedown on his desk. "What do you mean, telling me *no*? You are an awful little child."

"Call your consul. You will need him to research a trade for me."

"Not only have you told me *no*, but you have also told me what to do." Xerxes frowned at her, walking the length of the hallway and back. He sat at the desk again, picking up Dale Carnegie's book. He put it down and sighed in frustration. "I suppose you know how to influence me. Heh, girl? This must be a good book," he mused, reading the torn back cover.

"I need your consul to tell me who bought the Warlord of Tallahassee's consort last fall."

Xerxes looked at her pointedly.

"Who are you?" he inquired.

"It does not matter," she replied. "I have a cache of books that will help you better rule your militia and your stations. If you read them, you will rise higher in the United Authority and achieve greatness."

Now it was his turn to remain silent.

"One name," she demanded. "And then I will give you enough books to line those shelves."

"It's against the United Authority's Family Trading law to divulge party names in official transactions. The penalty is—"

"Death," she interrupted him. "I know this. The penalty is always death. It's ceased to shock anyone."

She had a point, Xerxes surmised, rubbing his chin. *And who obeyed the laws these days, anyway?*

"I need a name," she repeated. "You need books. A fair trade. Afterwards, you will never see me again."

"You have a deal," Xerxes conceded. "But you will be told the name of the buyer after you show my men where you have hidden my new books. When you deliver what you promised, I will give you the name you want."

The Medicine Girl nodded her assent.

And as soon as you show me where they are, my men will kill you, Xerxes thought. Her offering proved to be very enticing, whetting his appetite before the main feast. He might let her live just because she brought him an interesting diversion on such a tedious morning.

"Attendants!" he bellowed, doors swinging open almost before he finished calling out.

"Send me Darius. Prepare a vanguard for a search and recovery."

The warlord's attendants saluted, looking sheepishly at the young girl by the warlord's desk. She appeared to be harmless, her hands by her side, palms facing towards them, but someone would pay for this little girl's unannounced presence—*in the heart of the Illuminati Pagan compound!* Xerxes appeared too distracted with the book in his hands to think of punishing them at the time. It would, undoubtedly, occur to him later.

The rain started in earnest just outside of the city, soaking the Medicine Girl and MilitiaMen as they began their four colony-hour walk to Windyke to retrieve the rest of Xerxes' promised books. But the rain didn't last long. A few miles outside of the city, the suburbs looked parched and wilted, as the rainbands didn't seem to evenly disperse precipitation. That was expected now, flood or drought, as biomes changed from year to year.

Before the Medicine Girl departed, Xerxes served a lavish luncheon, brought into the rotunda for her, a gesture of grandeur that fell flat. In her silent way, she set upon the delicate fare as if she were eating pine bark.

"Limeade sweetened with Vermontonian maple syrup," Xerxes gushed, downing a large glass. The Medicine Girl's glass remained untouched. "You don't like limeade?" he added, a little disappointed. "You should try it."

The Medicine Girl reached past her own glass and took his, upended it, drinking all of the sweetened liquid down in one large gulp. She sat his empty glass back by his plate.

When it was time, Xerxes would kill her himself, he vowed. *Preferably with his bare hands.*

As blank faced as the Medicine Girl appeared, the sheer amount of food awed her. Even when her father held banquets with United Authority men and other warlords, there was not such a diversity of cuisine or voluminous quantities. *And there were just the two of them.*

"I have eaten my fill," she declared. Already she had filled her pockets full of morsels to eat later. She had hoped to leave with Xerxes' guards earlier in the day, to conclude her business and get on with things, good or ill. "I am ready to leave. Tell Darius we will return in a half colony-day. He should have the name I need by then."

"Of course." Xerxes' reply dripped with sarcasm. *This slip of a girl giving him orders.* He wiped his mouth on the sleeves of his robe. He wouldn't press any more delicacies on her. As usual, the remnants would go to the Family Trading Station. The matron there could do with the foodstuffs as she liked. From what he'd seen of her of late, he guessed the corpulent matron ate all of his table scraps herself.

While Xerxes called for an attendant to send in Darius, the Medicine Girl retrieved the empty canvas bag. She worried a bit about where she'd hidden the bike, hoping she'd return to Memphis in time to retrieve it before it was stolen or used for scrap metal. Now proficient at riding it, she marveled at how much it reduced her travel time by at least a half, even more if the roads were adequately paved.

But she was getting too far ahead of herself; she did not have the name of the man her mother had been sold to. She did not know if she'd even survive the day.

"Darius, enter please," Xerxes greeted his consul. "This is my new little friend. She has a request for you."

Darius looked at the urchin in front of him in disgust, unimpressed until he locked eyes with her. Her gray-eyed gaze held, unnerving him.

"Who is it that you seek again, my dear?" Xerxes pretended to forget. *He forgot nothing.* "Tell Darius what you wish, girl. He is the keeper of records for the Memphis Family Trading Station. I'm sure he will have the information for you when you return—when you come back with the rest of my books."

She stared straight at Darius, but addressed Xerxes. "I need your consul to tell me who bought the consort of the Warlord of Tallahassee last fall."

"Did you get that, Darius?" Xerxes smiled.

"Yes, Xerxes. I will check the records."

"Good." Xerxes clasped his hands together, very pleased with himself. "Now little girl, go bring me my books."

The Medicine Girl led the small group through the dusty suburban streets, houses in all states of disrepair, more street signs missing than not. A stray dog barked unhappily at the strangers. A few eyes peeked out of broken windows and behind brick walls as Illuminati Pagan MilitiaMen followed behind a young girl. Odd as it was, no one would intervene.

As they approached the house where the Medicine Girl found the bike, she noticed that the four MilitiaMen paired off, no longer a group. The hairs on the back of her neck stood up, and she wondered how long she had.

"Where are the books?" barked the largest of the men. He looked angry, irritated with this unnecessary excursion, demeaned by having to babysit a waif while picking up fripperies for a warlord, one who was becoming increasingly unpopular.

The Medicine Girl remained quiet. She sized up the men, noting what weapons each man carried. She opened her canvas bag, pulled out a large pair of floral gardening gloves, putting them on, one finger at a time.

"Where are the books?" the man repeated, louder this time. His thinner, scrappier companion grabbed her by the throat and squeezed. She gasped for air.

"C'mon now, girl. It's a long walk back. The sooner we're done here, the better."

The other pair clustered around them, itching to return to the city.

"Let go of her throat," another ordered.

The Medicine Girl coughed and spat until she caught her breath.

"Tell us now or next time I won't let go."

"The books are in two places," the Medicine Girl said, pointing to the locations to separate the men. "There is a pile of books inside the far upstairs closet by the bathroom. The second pile is on the side of the house, buried by the pool. You will see the mound."

One of the men slapped her, knocking her to the ground. Ignoring the Medicine Girl, they discussed how to best collect the trove of books.

But she listened to their plans.

Just because she was quiet didn't mean she was an idiot.

Two MilitiaMen headed for the far side of the backyard, retrieving United Authority-issue shovels from their packs as they went. It was easy to see the fresh mound. They set about digging.

The other two traipsed into the home, heading to the second floor, taking the stairs—two at a time. Near the top of the staircase, the Medicine Girl had hollowed out several floorboards, covering the holes with a thin layer of ragged carpet. As they approached the landing on the second floor, both men punched through the thin fabric, sharpened sticks impaling their feet through their shoddy boots.

As they attempted to pull out their legs from the false stairs, both men skewered their ankles and shins on sharpened downward facing spikes on the sides, immobilizing their feet on all sides.

As the men writhed in pain and swore horrible oaths, they noticed the smell of white birch tree oil, which permeated the staircase. From the bottom, the Medicine Girl flashed sparks off her flint to ignite the flammable sap she had laid, creating an inferno. The trapped men were consumed before their screams carried too far.

The Medicine Girl didn't have much time. She retreated to the kitchen, opening the back door, where a double strand of fishing line lay across its entrance, ankle height, as noticeable as spider silk.

"Fire!" she cried, "Fire!" She wrapped a cloth over her nose and mouth as the burning men's shrieks added verisimilitude to the ruse of her distress call.

One of the men looked up, threw down his shovel, rushing to respond as smoke billowed from the upper floor. The other man, the youngest of the four, returned to steadily digging.

As the first man ran into the home, the fishing line tripped him. The Medicine Girl looped another length of fishing line around his neck, holding fast to the line with her knee in his back. Her flowered gardening gloves prevented the thin line from cutting into her own hands.

The man struggled, thrashing about, clawing at his neck. *This was unfortunate for him*, the Medicine Girl thought. *Had he been trained properly, he would have spent his effort attacking her, not the fishing line.*

Nihil. Ūnus. Duo. Trēs. She finished counting, holding the line tight until all movement ceased. Patiently, she counted to fifty again as the black smoke began filling the kitchen, making her eyes water.

Satisfied that the man was dead, the Medicine Girl dropped to her knees below the smoke and scuttled out the front door, circling back to the pool area.

Where was the fourth man?

A tall southern red oak grew in what she assumed had been the neighbor's yard. As the shambles of the house burned and fell in on itself behind her, the Medicine Girl made her way along the perimeter of the yard, canvassing the area from the ground. When she got to the tree, she climbed it, hand over hand, as high up as she could go.

Where was the fourth man?

She checked the grounds again, looking for any movement. She expanded her view, squinting off into the distance.

She saw him, running at a breakneck pace in the wrong direction, away from Memphis. Wild eyed, the man seemed confused, following the curving roads in the cul-de-sac that looped around, endlessly rejoining each other.

Good, she thought, climbing down from the oak, feeling for her knife. *Let him wear himself down. He'd be far easier to track that way.*

"I come here to make you an offering," she replied evenly.

Chapter 8

Windyke, Tennessee

The Medicine Girl had a four colony-hour walk ahead of her back to Memphis, but she felt clear headed and, thanks to Xerxes, well-fed. She hoped her ruse had bought her enough time—enough time for Darius to search his records, enough time for Xerxes to let his guard down, enough time for her to gather her courage for what she had to do.

Before leaving Windyke, she'd poked around the remains of the burnt out structure. The fire had spread to two other vacant homes before dwindling into nothing. She located the remains of the three corpses and attempted to find anything salvageable on them, to no avail. The fire burned all. She considered burying the men's charred remains, but decided to conserve her time and energy. *Let them mingle with the ash.* As for the fourth man? The animals would feast where she left him.

There was much to do before she returned to Memphis.

She moved the books to another vacant home for safekeeping, finding the remains of a wine cellar in the basement, long since looted. She wrapped each book in pieces of an old plastic tarp to protect them from further damage. In a more peaceful time, she imagined returning to the books, lying down on a grassy patch, and leisurely turning each page, reading the voices from ages past. She frowned at the hundreds of pages she would have to forego for now, but all that mattered was learning the name of the man who had her mother.

Once again, she packed her canvas bag so she could travel faster. She calculated the odds of her surviving a second trip to the capital city and meeting Xerxes, face to face.

They were significantly worse.

Xerxes opened one eye and groaned. He'd fallen asleep reading *The Story of Civilization.* On each page, the Durants, astute historians that they were, flung pearls of wisdom by the handfuls, explaining the intricacies of the human condition from its earliest origins.

Although Xerxes possessed just the second volume, a gift from the strange girl, he'd soon have the entire series upon the return of his men. He grew impatient. He could wait, though. In the meantime, Xerxes had over 800 pages of Greek history to savor. He was loath to get up. He rolled on his stomach and continued where he left off.

Soon, his obsequious personal attendants would come up to the library's 4th floor, his living quarters, and roust him from his late afternoon nap for more bureaucratic headaches.

Reaching for the jug on the end table, he poured a splash of limeade from an old plastic container into a dented metal cup. As he drank his fill, he stewed on the problems that awaited him in the rotunda.

Trouble brewed amongst the Illuminati Pagans, mainly from smaller factions unhappy with Xerxes and his leadership, more so in recent days. The fact that his militia was becoming an arm of the United Authority upset the Tennessee Elders. The fact that the militia didn't innovate and capitalize on their cozy relationship with the United Authority angered the younger MilitiaMen.

Nothing lasts forever, he brooded. Xerxes seldom left his library anymore; it seemed no quarter was safe and his long experience in running the Illuminati Pagans now failed him at every turn. *Or perhaps he just didn't care anymore*. Xerxes snuggled down into his chair with his book, disappearing into ages past. *Let the present take care of the future.*

The United Authority had clamped down on his efficient, albeit brutal, management of the Family Trading Station, demanding better treatment for the women and children in his care. His handlers wanted to know why so many died under his watch and in such barbaric ways.

Every family member who was lost or injured or died under Xerxes' care cost the United Authority tax revenue, resulting in more-than-routine audits of his records and egregious penalties for trumped up charges. Yes, it was assumed Xerxes was skimming off the top. However, even he knew he took more than was commonly acceptable. The United Authority attempted to rein him in, even mandating he no longer engage in the warlord's "right of first night" and the sampling of the women for sale. *Ridiculous.*

Besieged from all sides, Xerxes retreated more and more into his lair, finding himself walking the near-empty library shelves at all hours, isolating himself from problems that seemed to triple at sunrise. He was so tired of it all.

Barbarity didn't seem to quell his problems. He'd crucified and gibbeted scores of people. Spies from other militia groups—especially the hated Militia of the White Crosses—still turned up, galling him, knowing he caught a fraction of them. The religious militias bedeviled him the most, their rancor increasing as Armageddonists began to take over most of Tennessee.

Having the gray-eyed little girl appear before him, bribing him with her canvas bag of books, attempting to extort information, tied him into knots. Was he so weak that random *children* could just show up in his intimate chambers? Or was it a sign that he needed different tactics? Perhaps Sun-Tzu would teach him better warfare strategies, thousands of years from the grave.

Xerxes needed council. He needed wisdom. He'd sent search parties in the areas under his control to find him more books, more light and knowledge, but every year fewer and fewer writings were discovered. In recent months, his men had just brought him faded copies of newsmagazines and an occasional newspaper. There was nothing to be gained from reading them.

He reached for the Durants' tome, opening it where he'd left off, a passage on Xerxes from the 5th century BCE. *When Greek spies were caught in the camp, and a general ordered their execution, Xerxes countermanded the order, spared the men, had them conducted through his forces, and then set them free, trusting that when they had reported to Athens and Sparta the extent of his preparations, the remainder of Greece would hasten to surrender.*

Perhaps that was a tactic he could use? He'd reclaim prominence in the region by reminding all about the might and grandeur of the Illuminati Pagans.

He'd set the White Crosses and Armageddonists straight.

He'd set all the defectors in his own militia straight, as well, even if he had to crucify them himself.

As Darius was Xerxes' most trusted confidant and respected counselor, his personal residence was located on the 2nd floor of the library. *But that trust and confidence went only one way*, Darius mused. Darius didn't rise to his current level of prominence from a child bought-and-sold at the Classical Massachusetts Family Trading Station simply by being a sycophant. He kept his options wide, varied, and open.

More than anyone else, Darius knew that Xerxes' days were numbered. Though Darius dutifully and accurately reported the militia's finances and selected gossip to the warlord, he neglected to inform Xerxes about how much he took for himself. It was a significant amount. *How else could he survive the inevitable schism?* Even now, prominent captains and lieutenants were jockeying for position, instinctively knowing Xerxes' reign was in its death throes. With regard to successors, Darius planned to wait and see which horse to bet on—and to finance.

As it was almost time to meet Xerxes in the rotunda for his evening briefing, Darius finished preening in front of a shard of mirror, combing a pomade made from animal tallow through his hair and outlining his eyes in charcoal.

He, too, drank limeade from a container, refreshing himself before a late supper, a meal served nightly to the two men in the rotunda as they previewed the next day's schedule.

Darius didn't know how long the Medicine Girl stood there before he felt her presence.

"I thought you'd come by to see me," he smiled, blotting his eyeliner a bit. He turned and gave her a wide, welcoming grin.

She remained silent, standing with her arms down by her sides, palms facing towards him.

"I know what you want, little girl," he mocked her. She looked at him, gray eyes revealing nothing. "What price will you pay for that specific piece of information?"

"Tell me who bought the consort of the Warlord of Tallahassee last fall," the Medicine Girl asked evenly.

"That is very valuable information," he commented, making a

disappointed clucking sound. "Forbidden information, even. It's a federal crime, a capital crime, to discuss either party of a family trade. However, I am sure you are prepared to pay for the information."

"Tell me, and I will ensure that you live for a few more hours. If not, I will cut your heart out now."

Darius threw his head back and laughed. *How much he liked this little girl!* If the Illuminati Pagans were half as bold, they'd have overthrown the United Authority and ruled the entire southern region by now.

"Your mother was sold to the Richmond warlord in Old Virginia for two thousand hard colony-currency. Whether she lives or not, I have no idea. Now, may *I* live? For just a few more hours?" He laughed at her again, returning to the mirror to inspect himself. He smoothed an eyebrow, perfectly arched.

As he straightened his robe and finished adorning himself, he clipped his prized abacus to his belt, preparing to loop his jeweled dagger and sheath about his waist.

He noticed the floral dagger was missing from its case.

"Where is it, you little bitch," he muttered, in a low and lethal voice. "Where is my dagger?"

She remained silent.

"I will ask you again, little girl. If you do not tell me the truth, I will call for the attendants to flay the skin off your thin bones, then gut you like a fish. This is the last time I will ask you. Where is my dagger?"

"In Xerxes' chest."

Darius stared at her in disbelief. Her gaze expressed her boredom with him and his petty concerns.

"Well, go and get it. Bring it to me."

"No, I don't think so," the Medicine Girl replied.

"Xerxes cannot be dead," he concluded, as if trying to convince himself. "But if I call for the attendants, you will be dead in moments. Or maybe I will make a special case out of you and your insolence. A death more interesting and elaborate..."

"Your attendants are unable to help you."

"You've killed them all?"

"No," she replied off-handedly. "Not yet."

The Medicine Girl opened her canvas bag and perused Darius' bedroom chamber. She pulled things out of his chest of drawers, hefting items on his desk to see what objects of value she would take.

Darius attempted to move towards her, but he staggered, legs unable to follow his simple commands. "What have you done, little girl," he asked, a note of fear in his voice.

"The suburbs of Memphis have a bounty of jimson weed. By this point, your attendants are unable to move as well. They're probably hallucinating, unable to reason, incapable of following orders. Like bringing you more limeade or killing a girl."

"Am I drugged as well?"

"Yes," she said truthfully. "You will most likely survive, though. You'll see frightening illusions and become hysterical. Your heart will race. It'll feel like it's beating out of your chest." The Medicine Girl continued to scout the room for anything useful. "I don't think you'll end up in a coma, but I'm not sure how much limeade you drank. Regardless, you won't die from jimson weed. More likely, you'll be killed on the spot for treason. I would imagine most people in this city can recognize Darius' jeweled dagger."

Darius peered at his face in the mirror. Already psychedelic distortions twisted his perception, as the hallucinogenic substance began to take effect. *He seemed to have grown horns and fangs, his face a shade of ghastly green.*

"Your eyes are dilated. Soon your vision will blur and you will have trouble speaking, even breathing. You may rage. You might jump to your death."

"How long will I be under the drug's influence?" Darius asked, genuinely curious, as the walls seemed to both breathe and melt around him.

"Hard to gauge. Maybe a day or two?"

Darius' face blanched, noticeable under his heavy makeup.

"Take me with you," Darius begged, legs wobbly, the black seeds of the white-flowering plant working quickly. His last lucid thought concerned the outcome after the discovery of his dagger in the Memphis warlord's chest. *His execution would be merciless, an example for all usurpers.*

Even with Xerxes dead, his own life would be worthless. No rising warlord trusted another warlord's consul, unless he could finance a revolution. Darius' best possible outcome would be selling himself at the same Family Trading Station he'd overseen with so much cruelty. *He wouldn't last the night.*

"Please take me with you," repeated Darius, now imploring the Medicine Girl, a flash of panic in his dark eyes.

"No, I will not, but I will take this." She snapped the abacus off his belt and tossed it into her canvas bag. It would be a novelty for her since Darius would not be needing it any further.

Without turning back to look at the man dissolving into fits and tears, the Medicine Girl left.

There was little time to do one last thing.

Of all the invisible people in the world, the ones who aren't watched or taken very seriously are usually young girls and old men.

The Medicine Girl walked the short distance to the Family Trading Station while pandemonium broke loose in the library, attendants vomiting, bureaucrats screaming about phantasms, guards passed out from erratic heart palpitations. As she shouldered her canvas bag, she walked, head lowered, making her way down the staircases of the library.

Once on the ground level, she proceeded to the main receiving area of the Family Trading Station, walking right through the front door.

It was a vast building, an old art museum, still too quiet for as many people were crowded into filthy cells, cordoned off by age and sex. The women's wing appeared to be on the right side, the younger children housed down the far hallway. Perhaps twenty-five females, red-eyed and weak, all having seen unspeakable things, were locked in small cells and fed in troughs like pack animals.

"May I help you?" asked an attendant, confused why a young girl managed to walk around unescorted at that time of night. The attendant appeared nineteen or perhaps twenty colony-years.

"I need the keys to the family cells."

The attendant instinctively put his hands over the key ring on his belt, suspiciously looking at her.

"Whose permission—"

She balled up her fist, striking him in the right temple, knowing she'd caused his brain to violently career against his skull's lining. Instantaneously blacking out, he dropped like a boulder, a thin trickle of blood running out of his ear.

The Medicine Girl relieved him of his heavy key ring, walking resolutely to the first cell. She didn't fumble with the lock, just handed the entire lot of jangling keys over to the first intelligent-eyed woman she saw.

"Unlock your door. Pass the keys along."

A quick nod of understanding.

The Medicine Girl sprinted down the long hallways, ignoring the frantic calls from the other cells, looking for a rear exit out of the old art museum, now loud with doors clanging open and the hurried movement of feet.

Determining the proper path through the labyrinthine corridors, the Medicine Girl paused in front of a small red metal cabinet hanging on the wall next to an exit door. *In Case of Emergency* read the white lettering on the front panel. Curious, she opened it to find a useless circuitry panel; underneath, though, was a small ball peen hammer and a short-handled ax. She retrieved both, tucking them into her waistband.

Sounds were louder now, as MilitiaMen's threats and screams were met with heavy resistance in the lobby of the Memphis Family Trading Station. There were guttural curses and shrill, high-pitched screams, children's screams.

Silent as a shade, the Medicine Girl slipped out the back.

Before she had left with the MilitiaMen to retrieve Xerxes' books in Windyke, she had hidden the bike under a raggedy burlap tarp in a scrub brush pile near the sewage pits. *She prayed to her mother's gods that it was still there.*

"Girl!" yelled an old woman splayed out on the crumbling sidewalk, her leg clearly broken, her voice fierce and determined.

The Medicine Girl paused.

"Hand me a sharp rock to kill a MilitiaMan with when they come for me," she demanded, blue bloodshot eyes locking on her gray ones. *There was no denying her anything.*

The Medicine Girl removed the ball peen hammer from her waistband. "Do more than that," she said, handing the old woman the lightweight, potent weapon. "I'm sure you can take out two or three of those wastrels."

The old woman hefted the tool. A broad smile spread across her lined face, a face marred by blisters and welts. *This old woman's life has not been easy*, the Medicine Girl thought.

"I will kill at least two, my dear. Easily."

The Medicine Girl reached into her canvas bag, pulled out an old plastic water bottle and gave it to the old woman. The powder from dozens of ground black seeds caked around the bottom. Carefully, the Medicine Girl added water from her canteen. She capped it and swirled it around until the seed powder dissolved.

"Datura?" the old woman smiled, reaching out a thin arm to take the bottle, bringing it to her eyes to view it more closely.

"Yes," the Medicine Girl answered, "Jimson weed. To end your suffering when you are ready."

"Now I understand all the commotion," she cackled. "Good girl, good girl."

The Medicine Girl failed to suppress a grin. She handed the old woman her canteen, watching her drink her fill of good clean water.

"I must go," the Medicine Girl said reluctantly. *She had wished to sit and talk to the old woman longer.*

"Little girl, you know there is war coming, yes?"

"There is always war."

"No, my dear. This is a bigger one than the last. Where are you heading?"

"Richmond."

"Travel at night. Take the Four Oh to Eight One. If you live, find the Goatman of Witt, east of Knoxville. He will repay your kindness to me. Give him this." She untied a thin piece of brown rope around her neck which held a signet ring. Removing it, she curled the ring up in the Medicine Girl's hand. "The Goatman of Witt, yes?"

"I will give this to him. Who shall I say sent me?"

"Give him the ring. He will know," her voice quavered a bit, eyes watering.

"Take care, mother." The Medicine Girl knelt down and hugged the Old Woman. "I could stay and splint your leg—"

Horrific sounds came from the alleys surrounding the Family Trading Station. Assorted shrieks and gut-wrenching groans edged closer to them.

"No, girl. You must go. You must run."

"I will," the Medicine Girl said, standing to leave.

"God bless you," the old woman added, before raising the ball peen hammer over her head like a saber. In her other hand, she held tightly onto the bottle full of powdered jimson weed mixed with water. "God bless you!" she called out again.

"Which god?" the Medicine Girl called over her shoulder.

"Any one of them. The gods all respond in the same way—in silence!" The old woman unscrewed the water bottle and drained its contents.

Darius attempted to move towards her, but he staggered, legs unable to follow his simple commands.

Chapter 9

Nashville, Tennessee

"And this is your room," Mama Belle said, showing the latest girl in, an old piece of trash from Montgomery. Foisted on her by the United Authority, the new temporary wife was a tangle of bleached blonde hair, smeary charcoal eyeliner, and a surly expression on her face which belied her age. *Maybe 21 or 22 years old?* Mama Belle didn't think she would last much longer, as her eyes were dead, not a single spark left.

Good clean girls were getting harder and harder to find, Mama Belle complained to herself. Just last week a half dozen of her girls had to be put down, covered with syphilitic lesions from top to bottom. The United Authority was none too pleased to lose that revenue stream; lost product was a problem. And Mama Belle did not need another audit or worse—a federal compliance expert telling her how to run her business.

"And girlie, I don't know who you pissed off in Montgomery, but welcome to Nashville's United Authority - Comfort Station #39." Her words were cold. "Watch yourself here. I'd be as happy to kill you dead than put up with your bullshit."

Jalen gave the new madam a smirk, hoping it passed off as an acceptable smile. She limped to the mattress, smaller and filthier than the one she had in Montgomery. She sat down on its edge.

Taking full stock of her accommodations, Jalen noted the Comfort Station itself had been converted from a cheap motor lodge. The place had never been luxurious or grand; no remnants of beauty remained. What paint was left flaked off the walls. The stained ceilings were low and the crumbling bathroom held a small basin and a few dirty rags.

"Do I at least have a novice attendant?" Jalen asked Mama Belle. "Or do I clean up as well as service?"

Mama Belle paused before answering, straightening her black wig in the curtainless window's reflection. The madam turned to the side, checked out her rear end, sucked in her stomach, and pushed up her tits until her ample cleavage became more pronounced. Jalen bit her lip to keep from laughing.

"You will have two novice attendants," Mama Belle checked her lacquered eye makeup in an old, cloudy hand mirror. "I trust you can keep them from running off this time?"

"Two full time novices?"

"Yes, two. You'll need two. This is a busy Comfort Station. Not only do you need them, but we need them trained as soon as possible for the life."

"What are their names?"

"Well, Abigail is thirteen. We've been shorthanded this month—so much so that the United Authority lowered the age for temporary wives to fifteen."

"Fifteen!" Jalen recoiled. She, herself, had started as a novice attendant at twelve, working six years before entertaining her own temporary husbands. *Fifteen seemed far too young.*

"Yes, fifteen. That's the law. Demand is up. You'll be busy."

"How busy—"

"You'll turn about four temporary husbands in an hour."

"*Four?*"

"All right," Mama Belle replied. "For you? Five. You'll turn *five* an hour. And if you roll your eyes like that again at me, I'll unload an entire phalanx of White Crosses up here. They'll be happy to lame your other leg." Without another word, Mama Belle spun on her heels and left.

Jalen shut her mouth. *Four or five men an hour?* She rubbed her temples, a vicious migraine threatening.

In hindsight, she was lucky to be alive after Catalina and Eve escaped, but Jalen was, if anything, a remarkable actress. Her years as a temporary wife had made her so. It was paramount to know when to cry on cue or laugh on demand.

After Catalina and Eve's escape in Montgomery, Mama Mae had come into Jalen's room, spitting hellfire and damnation. Jalen played the much aggrieved victim, blaming her black eye on the insolent girls, claiming her personal things were pillaged and dear possessions stolen.

As a result? Simply a thrashing for carelessness and a transfer to what other temporary wives called "The Train Station." *Nashville.*

Nashville itself was known for its Red Quarter, a place full of Comfort Stations—catering to the most peculiar of tastes, a hodgepodge of former hotels clustered together near the downtown area. As Nashville acted as a major crossroads for the United Authority, sparring militias, merchants, and assorted warlords, commerce in the Red Quarter was robust. Both weapons and people were bought and sold at the Family Trading Station. Gambling thrived alongside a brisk business of unsanctioned alternative medicines, hallucinogenic drugs, and pleasures and perversions.

Deathcarts routinely made their stops within the Red Quarter, picking up corpses at regular intervals and tossing them into the Cumberland River. Occasionally, a temporary wife would jump into the river as well, to save herself from the trouble of keeping up with a hectic marital schedule.

Jalen sighed, attempting to acclimate to her sudden come down in circumstance. In Montgomery, she had been something akin to Comfort Station royalty; she was asked for, preferred, almost doted on. Now? She shuddered to think of what sort of person would visit the cut-rate dump to which she had been transferred.

Tears of self-pity welled up.

The two-week wagon ride from Montgomery to Nashville was physically and emotionally painful, the food and water scarce, the treatment curt and rude. She and a half dozen other girls survived the journey by catching rainwater in plastic containers and working off book hookups en route, exchanging temporary marital services for hardtack or jerky from the rare ploughboy or lost MilitiaMan.

A little girl with red ringlets and wide green eyes slowly walked into her austere room, carrying a few stained, threadbare towels, diluted vinegar, and a plate with a torn hunk of bread, goat cheese, and some sort of nut butter.

"I'm Abigail, Miss."

"How many husbands do I have waiting for me?"

"Right now? I'd say two or three, Miss."

Jalen let out a disgusted groan, one so full of bitterness that Abigail jumped.

"This is not enough food. See if you can find me some ginger root tea or cherries."

"No, Miss. This is all you get until evening."

"What?! This is dog food."

"No, Miss. They use dogs for the stew, and stew is served on Thursdays."

"Dog stew," Jalen clarified, incredulously.

"It's delicious, Miss."

"Water, then. How about you fetch me some water?"

"I can get you water."

"Good. Go get me water."

"You want clean water?"

"Abigail, I am going to drink it. Yes. Please bring me a large glass of drinking water."

"Okay, I'm going to have to boil it though."

"Are you telling me a Comfort Station of this size doesn't have sufficient purified water for its temporary wives?"

"Sometimes they do. Sometimes they don't. I'll go ask in the back house. I'm not sure if today is a good day."

"Who is the steward of this Station? He and his idiotic staff must be incompetent."

"No, Miss. They all try the best they can. Just depends on supply lines."

"The federal lines or the MilitiaMen's lines?"

"Can't say. From what I hear, more and more federal supplies end up in the Armageddonists' hands. They are hella tricky."

"I don't follow politics," Jalen waved her off. "I just do my job. And I expect you to do yours. Get me some clean drinking water."

"Yes, Miss."

"Somehow get me some more food, too. I'm hungry."

"Yes, Miss."

"Where is the other girl helping you? Mama Belle says I'm supposed to have two of you. God help me if I have two girls just like you."

"I'm trying my best," Abigail flinched, as if waiting for a blow. "I'll do better. Please just give me a chance." The novice attendant left in tears, holding her head in her hands.

Jalen felt bad for the girl, but saved the rest of her sympathy for herself. While she had a moment of relative peace, Jalen laid down and massaged the back of her knee where Mama Mae had hit it with a wooden bat.

All told, Jalen would have stayed in Montgomery and taken a daily beating than toil under whatever horror show awaited her here in Nashville.

She looked out of the grimy window towards the Cumberland River, thinking of her next possible moves, wondering if she had any left.

The ninth man of the day was kind to her. Afterwards, he handed her crumpled gardenia blossoms from the bottom of his pockets. She rewarded him with an authentic smile.

Jalen cupped the petals close to her nostrils, her eyes closed, lost in the depth and sweetness of their rich fragrance. It revived her like one of Abigail's cool vinegar baths.

"Where is the other novice attendant?" Jalen asked, as Abigail had been run ragged with boiling water, changing sheets, serving food and drink, and escorting men about the Comfort Station.

"Tamara aged out. She's in the life now," Abigail explained.

"Does she work here?"

"No, Miss. She's too pretty to work here," Abigail replied, oblivious to Jalen's shocked expression. "She's a temporary wife down at The Heritage Comfort Station." Abigail mentioned the former hotel's name with great reverence.

"So...it's just you and me?"

"No, Miss. New novices just arrived this morning. Mama Belle is showing them around. I expect we'll both meet them around your dinner break," Abigail figured.

"How many more husbands for me this afternoon, do you think?"

"It's slow today," Abigail mused. "So maybe ten? Would you like me to bring you some more water?"

Jalen nodded curtly, continuing to rub her knee.

The dinner rations were about half the portion of what she received in Montgomery. No meat. Mostly just coarse bread served with a thick oatmeal gravy. Jalen was so hungry, she couldn't remember chewing any of it. She shoved it down her gob so fast it burned her throat. Jalen stared at her empty plate. She picked it up and licked it.

"Miss?"

"What now. What can you possibly want from me?"

"I found some crackers. You want them?"

Jalen turned to see Abigail holding a small plastic plate with assorted pieces of crackers. Then she looked at Abigail, thin, sunken-eyed, already missing several permanent teeth at her young age.

"Thank you, Abigail. I think maybe you should eat those, all right?"

"Novices don't eat until closing."

"Eat them now, Abigail. I won't tell anyone."

Abigail looked to see if Jalen was poking fun at her.

"It's all right." Jalen laid back in her foul, sweaty bed as unwanted tears streamed down her cheeks. "Eat your crackers."

Abigail retreated to the far corner of the room and ate bits of cracker after cracker until they were gone.

Jalen dozed off after her paltry dinner, falling into a dreamless sleep. When she was jostled awake, a familiar face materialized into view.

Eve.

She heard Abigail's cheerful voice introducing her.

"Miss? Miss? The new novice attendant is here. Mama Belle says I'm going to train her." Abigail smiled, revealing brown broken teeth.

The Medicine Girl stood as indifferent as ever, dressed in a burgundy velvet dress with a prim collar that had once been white.

"Eve?"

"Jalen," the Medicine Girl replied, calmly looking around the confines of the room. "This place is much worse."

"Don't I know it," Jalen whispered aloud and sat up. She looked at the Medicine Girl's arms, battered and bruised, and her scabby legs. A long fresh cut appeared to be healing well on her right shin. Purple handprints encircled her thin neck like a necklace.

"You have husbands waiting," Abigail whispered.

"Then go get one of them bastards, Abigail. Eve will stay here until you return."

"Okay, but Mama Belle says I'm supposed to train her," Abigail replied, hesitantly moving towards the door.

"Just leave us be for now, all right?"

Abigail looked unsettled. After she departed, Jalen stood up and threw her arms around the Medicine Girl, hugging her gently, avoiding her injuries. She pushed back to get a closer look at her.

"What happened to you, Eve?"

"I had a little trouble in Bellevue."

"Someone turn you over to the Family Trading Station?" Jalen handed the Medicine Girl a tumbler full of water.

"Something like that." She drank it all.

"How's Catalina?"

The Medicine Girl replied in stoic silence, her gray eyes despairing at her question. *What words could she say?* Jalen exhaled sharply, tears springing to her eyes.

"Tell me she didn't suffer," Jalen begged.

"Not long," the Medicine Girl muttered. They stood in companionable silence for a time.

Wiping her eyes, Jalen walked back to the bed, looking at the Medicine Girl sideways. "That dress is an abomination. It's three sizes too big. And how did you get assigned to me, anyway?"

"I switched with another girl. I told her you were loud and bratty and willful."

"You lied to be assigned to me?"

"I told her the truth to get you out of here."

Jalen laughed. "No—no, not this time. There's no escaping this hellhole for either of us. Besides, Nashville is an armed camp, and I can hardly walk after the beating I took for you."

"We are going to get out of here," the Medicine Girl repeated emphatically. "This is a bad place to be. War is coming."

"War is always coming. Who gives a shit?"

"It's different this time, Jalen."

"The more things change, Eve, the more they stay the same."

"That doesn't make any sense."

Jalen sighed. *She was still so young.* "I'll try to help you out, Eve." Jalen's voice faded as she wasn't even sure she could help herself. "And I hate it here," she added. "You're right. This is a very bad place."

"I hate these shoes," the Medicine Girl complained. "Why do comfort stations make us wear these ugly shoes? They serve no purpose." She took off the raggedy white high heels without unbuckling the straps and threw them against the wall.

Abigail and an older man, dressed in Illuminati Pagan uniform, stood at the door's entrance, witnessing the Medicine Girl's tantrum.

"Ahem, Miss. Your temporary husband is here."

The Medicine Girl walked up to him. "I need your machete."

"Pardon me?" the MilitiaMan answered, puzzled by the novice attendant's impertinence. He put his hand on the long knife sheathed at his side.

"Let her borrow it," Jalen goaded him, as if handing over a dangerous weapon to a Comfort Station girl occured in the normal course of events.

Curious, the man unsheathed his machete and handed the butt of the knife over to the gray eyed little wench, dressed in a swath of velvet.

Without another word, the Medicine Girl knelt down by the despised shoes and hacked off the high heel in one whack, first one and then the other. She tossed the knife behind her back, watching it flip and twist in the air, just before catching it with her other hand. She proffered the machete to the man before walking out of the door.

Stunned, Abigail looked at both the man and Jalen before following after her, closing the door behind them both.

The Medicine Girl felt as if she had just fallen asleep when Abigail shook her shoulder.

"We need to get up, Eve."

"It's still night," the Medicine Girl groused, rolling on to her back, stretching her limbs, rotating her hands and feet.

As usual, she followed her mother's morning routine of deep breathing and slow movements to enliven her body.

While Abigail fretted, the Medicine Girl took her time applying crushed pipsissewa leaves to her sores and cuts. She chewed on a few leaves to calm her mind.

"Fine, now I'm ready. What's first?"

Abigail led her to the communal washroom where the yardboys had delivered lukewarm water for their morning baths. Afterwards, they went to the back room for a morning meal of cornmeal mush and black raspberries.

Around daybreak, the Medicine Girl boiled ashes from a hardwood fire to make lye. Abigail mixed in a portion of rendered meat fat from the previous evening's dinner to make a good hearty soap. They commenced washing Jalen's linens and personal items, a day's work in itself.

Burdened by the heavy dress, the Medicine Girl wiped rivulets of perspiration from her face. The long sleeves got in the way, making her work all the more tedious. Aghast, Abigail watched as the Medicine Girl ripped off both sleeves at the seams.

"Mama Belle will be furious! Eve—what happened to your shoes?!"

The Medicine Girl looked at her feet, now clad in United Authority military-issued boots.

"What's wrong with them?" asked the Medicine Girl. "I found these by the latrines. Brand new boots! Just sitting there."

Abigail threw up her hands, exasperated with her trainee. Men were lining up in the lobby, documentation in hand, ready for their allotted time with their temporary wives. At this rate, Jalen wouldn't be ready. If Jalen wasn't ready, then the Comfort Station wouldn't make its quota for the day. If the quota wasn't met, then Mama Belle would be furious. And when Mama Belle was upset? Sometimes the deathcarts had to make an unscheduled pickup.

Abigail feared for them both.

Mama Belle's office was no more elegant than her girls' hovels. She sat on an uneven wooden chair behind a rickety desk, using the nub of a pencil to scratch out and tally disappointing numbers on reclaimed paper. Her wig sat askew, her lips painted with chunky rose-colored beeswax.

Disease was decimating the Comfort Station's bottom line.

"The girl is here," a mincing attendant announced, knowing how the madam hated to be interrupted while figuring numbers.

"Send her in," Mama Belle yelled. *The last thing she needed was to deal with a recalcitrant novice.*

The Medicine Girl walked in, boots thudding across the floor. Dressed in the modified velvet frock, she stood bare armed directly in front of the desk, her expression blank.

"Do you know why I called you in?" Mama Belle drawled. The menace in her voice was enough for most novice attendants to beg for mercy.

"Do you know at least half of your wives are riddled with the pox?" came the Medicine Girl's sharp reply. "And do you know your attendant girls are starving?"

"You little bitch," Mama Belle gasped, shocked at the complete disregard for authority.

"Neither of your problems are hard to fix," the Medicine Girl continued, ignoring the slight. "You could skim more off the top if you ran this place a little bit better or if your reputation improved."

The madam had half a mind to call for her attendants to beat this insolent shitstain on the spot, but something gave her pause.

"Explain."

"Your kitchen is wasteful, run by a head cook who sells off most of the supply for his personal gain. Have him arrested. He is cruel and stupid. Promote his assistant, the one who makes the bread. She is trustworthy and has a keen eye."

"And?"

"I can't imagine the United Authority is pleased with your wives infecting their soldiers and allied MilitiaMen. That's going to make them look more closely at your entire operation," she argued, walking towards the desk. "And I don't think you will hold up under scrutiny."

"Go on."

"I need to make colloidal silver to cure your temporary wives of gonorrhea, syphilis, and chlamydia—and whatever else is afflicting them. If there is a competent doctor in this town, you should call one to look at each of them before the end stages."

"What do you need to make colloidal silver?"

"Silver jewelry, electric wire, salt, a glass bowl. Ask the United Authority commissary if they have any 9-volt batteries. I've heard they've found a way to recharge them. If not, I'll need copper, aluminum, and bleach."

"Those things are possible. I might be able to get you 9-volts. Anything else?"

"I need dried oregano, as much as you can buy. I'll do a steam distillation—to extract the oil. Oregano oil will cure your wives' chronic yeast infections, among other things."

"Oregano leaves..." Mama Belle finished scratching out a list with her pencil nub. "How soon can you get started?"

"How soon can you get me what I need?"

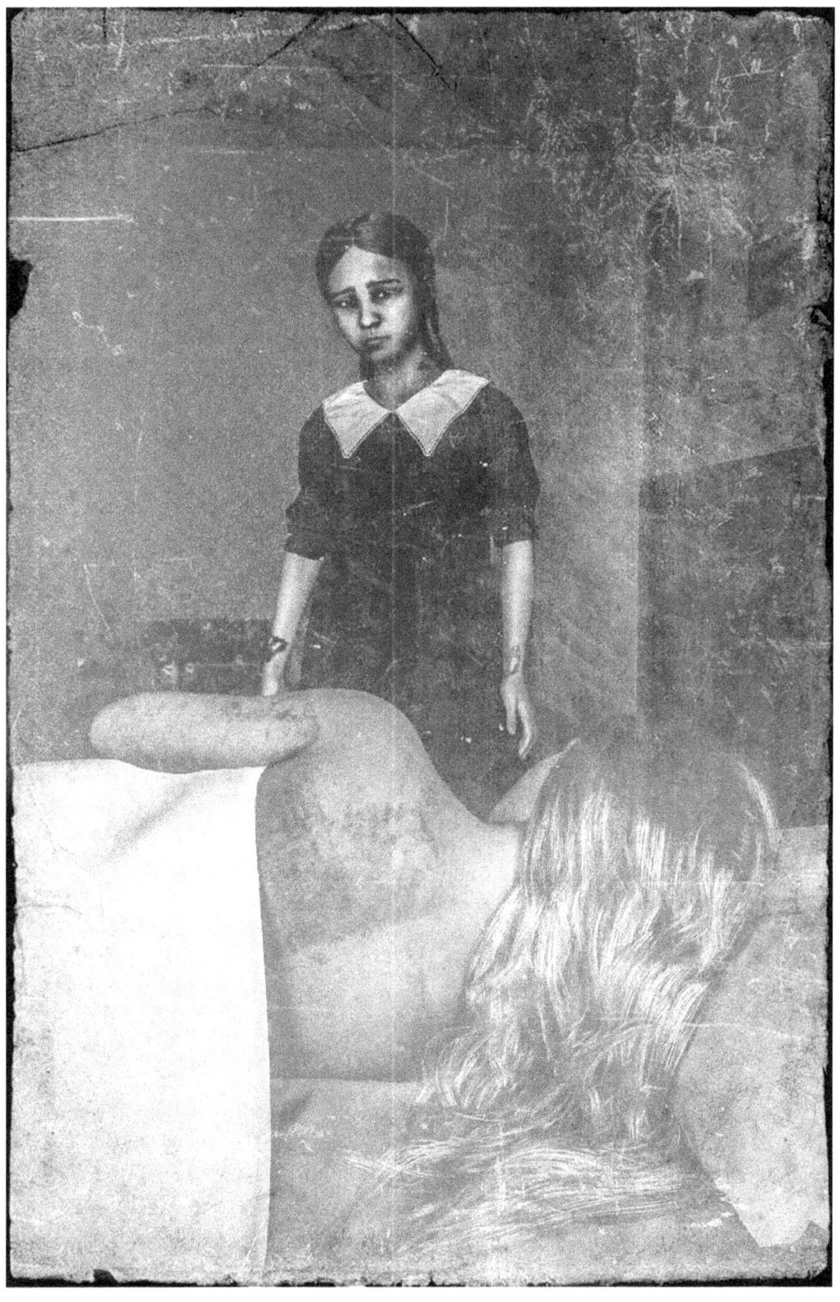

Jalen dozed off after her paltry dinner, falling into a dreamless sleep. When she was jostled awake, a familiar face materialized into view.

Chapter 10

Knoxville, Tennessee

When Lieutenant General Chapman worried, he chewed on his bottom lip. After his intel briefing on the Armageddonists, his entire mouth was abraded and raw.

He asked for the room to be cleared so he could think.

A map of what remained of the southern portion of the United Authority lay before him. Decades prior, the capital had been moved to Richmond in Old Virginia. Scores of dirty bombs had rendered Washington, D.C., Philadelphia, and New York City uninhabitable, necessitating all military personnel to carry potassium iodide tablets on their person at all times.

Prior to the Russian and Chinese coordinated attacks, criminal enterprises were successful in ransoming billions in hard colony-currency, detonating radiological dispersal devices, and traumatizing the United Authority's armed forces. However, rogue cyberterrorists won pyrrhic victories. Their internet empire dissolved the moment hundreds of EMP bombs exploded, ushering in the end of electricity, negating the world's cryptocurrency market.

All that was history, Lieutenant General Chapman mused, biting his lip again until he tasted coppery blood. What concerned him more than past geopolitics was the consolidation of anti-government militias, forming a substantial threat against the United Authority, whose fragility of the ruling power seemed to erode day by day.

The State Defense forces and their militia-subsidiaries, especially the Illuminati Pagans, were loyal. For now. *But for how much longer?* Other than managing the Family Trading Stations and Comfort Stations, citizens wondered what the United Authority did with its tax revenue. In truth, Lieutenant General Chapman wondered, too. The roads were unsafe. There were chronic food shortages, little medical care, no system of education. At best, the United Authority kept up an illusion of order.

The general's grandmother had been a Baptist preacher's wife, reading to him as a child from the Book of Revelations—usually right before bed. He had loved the bizarre biblical imagery she brought to life; the apostle John's shocking symbols and numerology fired his imagination. *The Great Red Dragon. Michael the Archangel. Fire mingled with a sea of glass. Twelve. Six six six.* But the most compelling archetypes, his grandmother explained, were the Four Horsemen of the Apocalypse. She taught him how the Horsemen always traveled together—War, Famine, Pestilence, and Death. *Where one rode, the others followed.*

In Lieutenant General Chapman's many years of warfare, his grandmother's words still rang in his ears. Across the land he had sworn to protect was death in every form. Plague and disease sprouted like mushrooms after a rain, disappearing then reappearing in more virulent strains. There were shortages of everything, especially potable water. *How many emaciated children had he'd seen expire from diarrhea?*

And then there was endless war and bloodshed, human life held so cheaply. *Wars and rumors of wars,* he heard his grandmother's voice warn in his young ears. She tried to comfort him at the time by reading scripture: *such things must happen, but the end is still to come.*

Sometimes the general wondered if the end of times had already come, and they had missed it. *Maybe they were phantoms skulking the earth without meaning or purpose?*

A polite knock at the door.

"Your lunch, sir? I asked the kitchen to make that beef stew you like."

Roxy, his aide-de-camp, knew him far too well. While the general continued to mull over insuperable problems, Roxy set out a substantial meal in front of him. A tureen of thick beef stew. A wedge of cornbread. A tin of lemon water.

"Roxy, what do you suppose the Armageddonists want?"

"What do you mean, sir?"

"None of the leaders we've caught have communicated any demands. What do they want? Money? Power?"

"I wouldn't know, sir," Roxy frowned. "Maybe a seat at the table?

Maybe a platform for their beliefs? Maybe respect?"

"Respect for traitors and murderers? That's a hard sell, Roxy."

"If you say so, sir."

Originally believed to be an assemblage of crackpot religious fanatics, the Armageddonists, a fringe group just a colony-decade ago, had amassed power among True Believers. Led by an obscure figure, a strict and secretive order emerged, maintained by a power the general did not understand. He'd tortured enough of their spies to see them die instead of offering even the smallest kernel of information.

More disturbing were the centrist White Crosses, now appearing to align with the Armageddonist cause. In recent days, MilitiaMen in the streets seemed to have diminished.

Lieutenant General Chapman had a sick knot in his stomach, as he felt certain assorted militias had retreated to the Great Smoky Mountains under Armageddonist leadership, undoubtedly unifying and gaining strength, even though half of the forest had been ravaged by the woolly adelgid. There, dead trees had become a hazard, starting fires during the droughts and creating debris fields during the floods. The weather, much like the citizens he aimed to protect, ranged in the extremes.

The general despised the thought of sending his men into the Smokies, as their enemies were entrenched in numerous caverns, lying in wait along the banks of winding, unmapped trails. The United Authority could not expend their scarce resources in hunting down every rogue militia group or those suspected of possible insurrection. He had enough trouble finding groups that committed acts of treason against the United Authority—let alone ghosts in the woods.

Lieutenant General Chapman sighed. He was old enough to remember how it used to be, when the land was united, from sea to shining sea. Even before the external threats and devastating international attacks, significant fissures had developed within the country, the government, and the military. Reemerging as the United Authority from the Second Civil War, a slim hope for unity remained in name only. To appease the hardliners, "Authority" showed that control would be maintained, implying consequences for those resisting the duly elected federal body.

This particular afternoon, he felt every one of his sixty-two years. *I am too old for this nonsense*, he thought. It was time for him to retire, yet that request was not granted by the armed services or a God he found it harder to believe in. The United Authority needed his expertise, especially with the troubles brewing in the rural areas. Most days, he felt a lone man on the watchtower.

He crumbled cornbread on top of his stew, waiting for it to cool enough to eat.

"May I get you anything else, sir?" Roxy asked.

"Just let me know when the girl from the Comfort Station arrives."

"Yes, sir." Roxy left the Lieutenant General to eat his lunch in peace.

Belly filled, the general dozed in his chair for a half colony-hour. *Afternoon naps were becoming more of a necessity,* he admitted to himself.

He wondered if elections were to be postponed again in November. The voting laws and registration procedures had changed so frequently, even he was unsure of what the Senate had decided. The Presidency and House of Representatives long since disbanded, Richmond's Capitol building held the Senate, the last vestiges of democracy. *Odd, that a hundred old men decided so much for so many, impacting even how old generals should think and act,* he thought. But he'd given up trying to understand politics long ago.

"Lieutenant General Chapman, the girl is here," Roxy announced.

"Oh, okay. Thank you, Roxy. Has she been attended to?"

"She is refreshing herself now, sir. The canteen reported she's eaten more than several of the men in her Nashville escort. She's asking for more rations, sir?"

The general laughed. "Good for her. Give her what she wants to eat."

"Yes, sir."

"And please bring me a flask of water."

"And a glass of mead, sir?" *Roxy did know him too well.*

"If we still have some," he replied, giving his aide a half smile. "It's about that time of day anyway."

"Lieutenant General, sir. Apparently, it took them almost eleven days—with transport—to arrive from Nashville. Skirmishes have broken out all along the Four Oh."

"How many men did we lose?"

"Less than a dozen, sir."

"White Crosses?"

The aide shook his head. "Order of the Snake Handlers. Apparently they're wearing purple and white Armageddonists colors now. All were captured. They've been dispatched, sir."

"Snake Handlers are a very small faction. They've never allied themselves with any other group."

"It is disturbing, sir."

"I'm going to draft a missive for Bingington—the General of the United Authority Allied Forces needs to know what's happening on the ground. Richmond isn't more than a three-week trek for the Armageddonists. If their numbers continue to grow—I just don't know—and I just need you to bring me a glass of mead right now."

"Yes, sir." Roxy left the Lieutenant General chewing his bottom lip.

Lieutenant General Chapman sat again in his overstuffed chair, its leather worn and stitched in places, but comforting in an old-fashioned way. For a moment he felt as if he could put his feet up, watch television, and maybe call out for a pizza.

He still remembered those days. Too fondly, sometimes.

"Yes, Roxy?"

"The girl is here, sir."

The Medicine Girl walked to the Lieutenant General's leather chair and sat down, putting her boot-clad feet up on the small table in front of her.

Her glossy black hair was still wet from being washed, tied back with a thin piece of rope. Her face was placid, gray eyes as calm as if she were at home in the United Authority's Tennessee Command Center.

She wore an ill-fitting Allied Forces uniform, crisp blue and yellow. It hung on her thin frame, making her appear even younger than she was.

It was hard to believe this child had been instructing United Authority medics all over Tennessee, the Lieutenant General mused. But after her tutelage, infection rates significantly declined among his troops, both from battle wounds and from temporary wife disease.

"What is your name, child?"

"I don't have a name, and I am not a child."

"Fine, young lady. What do people call you?"

"I don't have people."

The general drank his glass of mead. *He was a grandfather to grandsons, feeling out of his element talking to such a young girl.* He tried again.

"What did the soldiers call you in Nashville?"

"They called me the Medicine Girl."

"Is it alright if I call you the Medicine Girl?"

She shrugged.

"Jalen calls me Eve," she mumbled.

"Roxy, who's Jalen?" the general asked his aide, standing near the door.

"Sir, Jalen is a temporary wife who now oversees all of the Nashville Comfort Stations. She has known the Medicine Girl from her days in Montgomery."

"This Jalen now runs all of the Stations in Nashville? Even the training stations?"

"Yes, sir." Roxy consulted his notes. "And she's doing quite well, from all reports."

"How is the tax revenue under Jalen's leadership?" the general wondered aloud.

"Substantially better, sir." He placed a sheet of reclaimed paper in front of him. "I will bring you the rest of the numbers when I have them."

"Thank you, Roxy. You may leave."

"Are you sure, sir?" Roxy's eyes flashed, giving the Medicine Girl a sideways glance. He had heard tales about her proficiency with knives and fishing line.

"Yes, we're quite well here." The general moved a wooden chair closer to the Medicine Girl while his aide departed.

"Medicine Girl, I need your help," Lieutenant General Chapman informed her. "We're preparing for war, a war bigger than any war in your lifetime."

The Medicine Girl looked at him, boredom shading her eyes. "There is always war."

"This is different," he amended. "I need you to help me train men to care for soldiers."

"You want me to prevent their suffering while they cause others to suffer," she clarified. "The Comfort Stations care for the soldiers. I will never do that."

"Of course you would never do that. You are far too young and far too valuable." The Lieutenant General turned red, cleared his throat. He decided on another approach. "You misunderstand me. I need you to heal the men. I need you to show others how to care for wounds and burns. Sprained ankles. Respiratory infections. Head injuries. Trauma."

"Diarrhea?" she interrupted. The general felt sure she was mocking him.

"Absolutely," he replied. "Dysentery is a problem along the rivers, especially among the RiverMen communities."

"RiverMen are too stupid to boil their water and diarrhea is common this time of year," she added.

"It is," he agreed. "But the medics-in-training need to know so many things. How to suture. How to help with snake or spider bites. Hell, even how to recognize poisonous mushrooms."

He looked at her pointedly. She wondered what else he knew about her.

"I know what to teach them," she agreed, voice trailing off quietly.

"There is so much suffering out there." She looked out of the thick-paned windows of the antiquated manor house, commandeered years prior to be the United Authority's Tennessee Command Center. Family portraits of the original owners still hung in the hallways above the wainscoting.

She thought of Catalina.

"It's true, Medicine Girl. There is too much pain." The old general stood. "And I want you to help me prevent as much as possible."

"How will you pay me?"

"Pay you? You should want to serve your country."

"The United Authority is not a country. It's a business."

Lieutenant General Chapman's mouth snapped shut. He took a moment to respond. "Medicine Girl, I don't know where you are from or who your people are—"

"I don't have any people."

The general flushed red. He was not used to being interrupted. The Medicine Girl's face maintained its utter indifference.

He chewed on his lip. "What would you like—for payment?"

The Medicine Girl stood up. "One thing."

"Name it."

"Transport to Richmond."

The Medicine Girl walked into the training facility by herself, exactly at the appointed time.

The room was cramped, packed with United Authority men, both current and future medics, ranging in all levels of experience. Several secretaries stood at the ready to record her every word.

"Urinary tract infections?"

"Look for sweet joe-pye weed," answered the Medicine Girl. "Check for maroon blossoms. They are very bitter, but they will reduce any fever. Add honey to your tinctures or they won't be palatable enough to drink."

"Rashes? Eczema?"

"Witch hazel bark will heal any skin ailment. Eventually. It'll reduce the swelling in the meantime," she replied evenly.

"A tranquilizer?"

"Do you want to calm someone down or kill them? I mean, how tranquil do you want them to be?" the Medicine Girl asked in all seriousness, but the room burst out into laughter. She looked surprised she had humored them, covering her mouth with her hands.

"Just a mild sedative, please."

"St. John's Wort. Use its blooms to make a tea. Or wood nettle. If you want to encourage healing as well, use only the roots. Its hairy leaves will give you a rash...which brings us back to witch hazel."

The medics scribbled down her words, watching as she demonstrated how to extract seeds or distill oil.

At the end of each session, the Medicine Girl was tired of the medics' endless questions. She asked for double portions of food at mealtimes, which Lieutenant General Chapman heartily approved.

She often curled up and slept in the corner of his office.

The days were growing shorter as autumn turned the Tennessee foliage into vibrant reds and oranges and yellows. Soon winter would come with its accompanying joys and hardships.

Growing up in the Florida Penal Colony, she'd heard stories of ice and snow. Frankly, she was excited to see her first frost, assuming it would get cold enough. But some years, winter didn't come. Other years were glacial.

She would stay here for a season, she decided. She had been given a warm room and plentiful food. Her accommodations were behind the kitchen, an alcove with a door that could securely lock. The thick mat they gave her to sleep on was comfortable; an old mended quilt kept her warm enough throughout the night.

Still, her thoughts often returned to her mother, under a warlord's aegis in Richmond, a warlord allied with the United Authority. She hoped her mother was as warm and comfortable. *Perhaps she was left alone to care for the sick?* Certainly, her mother's many talents would prove her usefulness to the Richmond warlord, maybe useful enough to keep her alive.

The Medicine Girl furrowed her brow. She was conflicted. Should she leave sooner than later for Richmond? The need to see her mother was becoming an imperative. It seemed indulgent to stay here in relative luxury when her mother's fate was unknown.

She needed to get to her.

The Medicine Girl sat in the Lieutenant General's office during her free time, away from the lengthy training sessions. He had come to expect her there, splayed out on the floor concocting some potion, taking a nap under his desk, or reading a book she'd found on base. It didn't matter the subject, she buried her face deep into the book's spine, sitting contentedly in his leather armchair, feet hanging over an armrest. She'd pepper the Lieutenant General with questions about what she'd just read or questions that formed as she learned something new.

"I was thinking, Chapman," she said, looking up at him from her book as he entered his office, grimacing at the stack of papers in his hands. "You may want to teach civilians how to heal, too. You know, they can learn to care for themselves. Women and girls could teach the younger children. I think it would—"

"Medicine Girl—"

"There aren't many doctors in the townships, and they usually have no idea what they are doing anyway. Perhaps you could start a nursing corp to help with basic needs? Pulling rotten teeth. Pregnancies. Strep throat. Migraines. Even how to properly bury the dead to prevent disease...we could talk to them about water and sanitation, too! Like how to dig a well. Where to bury their shit. I mean, cholera outbreaks can be avoided. Why worry about solving a problem after it starts? Just avoid starting it, right? It would surprise you how little some people—"

"Medicine Girl," he stated firmly. "Be still for a moment."

Roxy came in, face pale and serious. He held yet another stack of reclaimed paper.

"Any of that good news?" Lieutenant General Chapman asked, knowing the answer before he asked.

"I'm sorry, sir." Roxy half-heartedly arranged the stacks of dispatches and reports on his desk.

The Medicine Girl remained silent, attempting to discern what was transpiring between the two men.

"The Sovereign State of Texas sent their ambassadors to Richmond. They are worried about Armaggedonists on their eastern doorstep."

"Texas has always been a pain in the ass," the general grumbled. "They can maintain their own borders."

"Intel sources report that the Armageddonists are amassing in the Carolinas in the Spring. Do you think they'd attack the capital from Raleigh? Is Richmond their primary target?" Roxy inquired, his forehead wrinkled with concern. Both men knew if Richmond fell, the United Authority would cease to exist.

"Not Richmond. My guess is Roanoke. They'll take the city quickly, then use it as a staging ground. Armageddonists have reached out to a few of the northern militias—with varying degrees of success. Still. It's all troubling."

Lieutenant General Chapman paced the room.

"Should we send a missive to Richmond, sir?" Roxy asked.

His question was met with silence.

"Damn," Lieutenant General Chapman muttered, walking over to the map of the southern portion of the United Authority. "The White Crosses hold sway in the Kingdom of Georgia and the Crimson Republic. Arkansippi might go either way—I can't imagine they won't flip. Ever since the United Authority shut down Louisiana, they've blamed us for the influx of Cajun refugees."

He slammed his fist on his desk. The Medicine Girl jumped.

"Should we send an intel team to Richmond, sir? To explain to the senators what is going on in the South?"

The general looked at the two of them, Roxy and the Medicine Girl.

It was hard to admit and a sure sign of the times, but these were the only two people whom he trusted. Roxy had been with him for years. The Medicine Girl's reputation had preceded her arrival from her public health work in Nashville. Overall, she was the hardest worker he had on base. He'd come to appreciate her direct advice and salient questions on important matters without grandstanding, and she had a guileless disposition he found refreshing.

"Roxy, send a sealed missive by courier to Richmond. Tell them the three of us will travel by transport to address the senators on the Armageddonist issue."

"Yes, sir."

"Whoever is influencing the senators has no idea what is happening on the ground. Richmond is not connecting the dots."

"Yes, sir. Do you have an estimated time of departure?"

At this, Lieutenant General Chapman turned to the Medicine Girl. "When can you be ready to leave for Richmond?"

"I'm ready now," the Medicine Girl replied offhandedly, returning to her book.

*The Medicine Girl walked to the Lieutenant General's leather chair and sat
down, putting her boot-clad feet up on the small table in front of her.*

Chapter 11

Dandridge, Tennessee

It had grown cold, autumn yielding itself to winter far earlier than expected. The morning the United Authority transport pulled out of Knoxville, the sky turned sheet metal gray, as gray as the Medicine Girl's eyes.

The transport consisted of a repurposed two-axle box truck, pulled by a colony-dozen of Nonessentials from the Florida Penal Colony. The engine, gas tanks, and exhaust system had been stripped out, lightening the weight of the truck. Still, prisoners often dropped from exhaustion or died from exposure when pulling a load. Governmental checkpoints along the major highways collected remains or "roadkill" before shackling another convict to the pull-lines.

Within the truck, provisions had been packed for the three-week trip to Richmond, more than enough for the eight United Authority attendants as well as Roxy, Lieutenant General Chapman, and the Medicine Girl.

Dispatches from all over Tennessee had been collected, as the general needed to synthesize the Armaggedonist uprising in preparation for his testimony before the Senate—a Senate not especially concerned with the unravelings of the outer western fringes of the United Authority.

Wrapped in a United Authority-issued wool blanket, the Medicine Girl shivered, not yet used to the northern clime. Over her white undershirt and pants, she'd layered blue and yellow uniforms, the smallest of which seemed to swallow up her tiny frame. Her thoughts turned to the Nonessentials, hollowed-eyed men convicted of crimes ranging from premeditated murder to misappropriating food. Both were capital offenses, but the United Authority required states to provide a certain quota of able-bodied men for transportation purposes.

"They should at least have boots. A quarter of them appear lame already."

"Some of our soldiers don't even have boots, Medicine Girl," the general replied, his voice heavy. "Some tie scrap cardboard around their bare feet." *If the Medicine Girl only knew how thinly supplies were rationed among the United Authority soldiers, she would understand why he was so temperamental.*

He wouldn't look at her whenever she brought up the condition of the men who pulled the hulking trailer, plodding along like mindless pack animals. Until the Nonessentials were ordered otherwise, the caravan moved forward, all day and all night.

"It doesn't have to be this way, Chapman."

"Well, it is the way it is," the general snapped, more forceful than he intended.

"Things can change," she muttered.

"Medicine Girl, the men pulling this rig are Nonessentials because of the laws they violated. Their current circumstances are the consequences of their actions."

"I don't care what they did. They are hungry and suffering now."

"You are too young to understand. Without penalties, there is no law. Without law, nothing would matter. It would be like the days after the end of electricity. Terrifying. Brutal. Chaotic."

"Who are you kidding? There's chaos now," she crossed her arms, pouting. She pointed a finger to the front of the pull-line. "Those men need longer water breaks. And there is plenty of food—why not increase rations? Look at this! There is enough food and fuel to run a small village for months. There is more than enough and to spare."

"You—" the general couldn't finish. *In the end, it wouldn't matter. Why not give the poor bastards a break?* The general looked at her. "Fine. Talk to Roxy and make the arrangements. Distribute whatever you think is appropriate."

The Medicine Girl began to take stock.

Within the relative luxury of the truck bed, the Medicine Girl listened to the hypnotic roll of the transport's wheels along the Four Oh. Occasionally there would be a whip crack and a cry from one of the Nonessentials.

"Chapman?"

"Yes, Medicine Girl?" he scowled, flipping through his papers again.

"Is that necessary—the whippings, the beatings?"

"When people act like animals, they get treated like animals."

"What if the reverse is more true? What if they act like animals because we treat them like animals?" she inquired, a quiet voice in the late of night.

"Medicine Girl—"

"What if we treated them better than they deserved?"

"It's too late to be philosophical," the general murmured. "And I'm tired." *I am so tired,* he sighed.

She nestled down in her blankets while the general continued reading by a large Army-issue kerosene lamp, its flickering light creating shadows along the walls of the truck. She was fascinated watching the general use a flint spark lighter, one that could be operated with one hand. *Click click.* Sparks flew. *Amazing.*

"Let me try!" she begged. The general handed her the flint spark. *Click click.* Sparks appeared, *with just one hand!*

"I want one of these."

"I'll put in a requisition order," he promised, hoping that would keep her quiet for a bit.

She wasn't sure he would order one for her, so she put the flint spark lighter in her pocket.

She watched him as he signed off on certain orders, fuming at the numbers, shaking his head at the obvious leadership deficiencies coming out of Richmond. *Did anyone have a clear idea of what the United Authority's objective was?*

Decades after the last wars, the military still operated in crisis mode. All efforts seemed sporadic, shortsighted stop-gap measures to ensure the United Authority didn't die a death from a thousand cuts. *Instead,* he thought bitterly, *it would die from a hundred.*

"Chapman. I have something to ask you."

He sighed. "Is this about the Nonessentials?"

"No."

"Then proceed with your request."

"The Richmond warlord bought my mother from the Warlord of Tallahassee."

"Are you from the Florida Penal Colony?" his eyes widened. *He had not considered where she'd come from, not sure of her heritage. Still, the law decreed the death penalty to those who harbored a fugitive from the penal colony.*

"Uh, not really..." she faltered, gauging his reaction.

"I see."

"Sir," she used the honorific to address him for the first time. "I'd like to request to see my mother. When we get to Richmond. At some point." Her voice trailed off. "Please."

The general looked at her. "How long has it been since you've last seen her?"

"About two colony-years," she replied. "She was sold off when I was eleven."

Eleven. Had she been on her own for two years? The general rubbed his eyes, exhaling. "I could arrange for you to see your mother."

The Medicine Girl smiled from ear to ear. Her eyes lit up with unfeigned joy. "I would like that so much!" She reached out to shake his hand, just like his attendants did on occasion. As the general extended his arm to her, she hugged the whole of it. "Thank you," she bowed a little, in case he changed his mind.

He stood up, addressing her formally. "It's the least the United Authority can do for you, seeing how much you've assisted our medics and nurses in the Tennessee region. Your mother would be proud of you, making this life a little less painful for all of us."

"Thank you," she replied, tears springing to her eyes. She blinked them back.

"One thing, Medicine Girl," he added. "And if you don't do it—it's a dealbreaker."

"Oh. Oh, I see. Yes, sir?" She mimicked Roxy's voice and military stance.

"You have to go to sleep."

"Now, sir?"

"Yes. Right now."

"Yes sir, sir." She saluted him, smiled, showing all of her teeth before burrowing back into the warm, scratchy blankets. In a few moments, the general heard her snoring, reminding him of a good hunting dog he had when he was young, a time before the end of electricity.

The general settled back down by the large kerosene lamp to continue to read through the stack of reports, written on reclaimed paper, challenging to read at times. He squinted, his eyes disbelieving the discouraging numbers. *The situation was far worse than he imagined.*

The Armageddonists continued to plunder United Authority Stations throughout the region. Their priests managed to convince disgruntled militias to join their cause, explaining how the coalition of the United Authority, allied militias, and the United Authority forces were agents of the devil.

With the unspeakable actions of the Illuminati Pagans, it wasn't a hard sell. Regardless, the Armageddonists were consolidating, growing more powerful, gearing up for a Holy War.

"Goddammit," Lieutenant General Chapman grumbled, burying his face in his hands.

On the second day of Chapman's transport to Richmond, the Order of the Snake Handlers lay in wait by the remnants of Douglas Lake, just south of the Four Oh. The Snake Handlers' scouts reported significant delays, as the Nonessentials were observed resting and eating meals instead of food scraps, a fact that made this particular United Authority transport suspect.

Why were they treating Nonessentials in such a way?

It had been easy to exterminate the United Authority attendants at the water source. No one had expected a squad of ten Armageddonists to emerge from the caverns, just north of the Great Smoky Mountains.

But this wasn't a battle; it was a raid.

"The sons of Reuben want every document or report or paper you find in the truck," recounted a member of the tribe of Joseph.

"Are we wearing Armageddonist colors?" asked a son of Rachel.

"No, wear your tribal prints."

The Order of the Snake Handlers had long divided themselves into the twelve tribes of Israel, an effective way to create a caste system. It mattered who your mother was, as women were often held in common by the male members of the tribe.

The United Authority transport inched its way down the highway, asphalt crumbling under its patched tires, turning to rewater at Douglas Lake.

In the late afternoon, Roxy moved into the cab, watching one of the two attendants steer the truck and deftly maneuver the crudely-fashioned handbrake.

Four more United Authority attendants sat on the top of the trailer, two with binoculars—each facing a different direction, one manning the whip to keep the Nonessentials moving and the other toward the back of the rig. The two remaining attendants positioned themselves inside the truck, protecting the general and the girl with a rifle and a handgun. To Roxy's knowledge, those were the only two attendants who had firearms.

"Gentlemen," Roxy greeted them, commenting on the driver's abilities in avoiding potholes and road debris. "When's the next checkpoint?"

"Sir?" replied the attendant, sitting in the passenger seat.

"The next checkpoint. Where is it?"

"Bulls Gap, sir. We're expected in Bulls Gap sometime tomorrow, depending if the weather holds."

"And how many more picnics are we having for the Nonessentials?" the driver joked, rolling his eyes.

Roxy joined them in their derisive laughter. They traded barbs and insults at the Medicine Girl's expense.

"How long until we stop to rewater at Dandridge?"

"I'm making the right turn to Douglas Lake in just a few minutes, sir."

"Good." Roxy watched them a bit longer, a small smile playing at the corners of his mouth.

Even before the end of electricity, the United Authority had taken over executions from the States, in a bid to carry out the death penalty in a more equitable fashion. In recent years, the deadly drugs were stockpiled in Richmond, then dispersed through governmental channels as needed. As such, vials of pancuronium bromide and potassium chloride were readily available by government requisition.

Roxy knew how to authenticate such requests, having long since mastered Lieutenant General Chapman's signature.

As the two attendants apathetically stared out the front window of the trailer, Roxy pulled out two long hypodermic needles from a leather pouch. As the truck glided to a stop for rewatering, Roxy jabbed both men in the neck, pressing the plunger in deep, their cries drowned out by the battle cries of the approaching Order of the Snake Handlers.

Ten men appeared, surrounding the truck, far more than what was needed. Four bowmen affixed their compound bows. Their efficient levering of cables and pulleys took out all four of the United Authority attendants on top of the trailer's roof, their bodies falling with a sickening thud on the pavement. Snake Handlers celebrated in their call-and-response shrieks.

"Gentlemen," Roxy called, opening the passenger door of the trailer's cabin, kicking out the two bodies of the men he had murdered. He held his hands up. "I am Roxy, friend of the Order of the Snake Handlers."

The tallest of the Snake Handlers walked towards him.

"I have delivered the transport as promised," said Roxy.

"So you have," the Snake Handler replied.

"I was told I would be received by someone in the Armageddonists' administration?"

"You are with the United Authority?"

"Technically, I *was* with the United Authority. I am looking to join the Movement. I had an arrangement with the Armageddonists."

"Did you betray these people?" the tall man motioned to the besieged truck.

"I did. I betrayed them for the Movement," Roxy explained, beads of sweat careening down the sides of his face in the cool air.

"Then you are a betrayer. There is no place for Judas in our Order." With that, the tall man nodded to one of the bowmen. The bowman affixed and released an arrow through Roxy's neck before Roxy's surprised expression faded.

Twelve Nonessentials stood up from their chains, frozen, unsure what to do.

"Brethren," the tallest of the Snake Handlers said, approaching, welcoming them. "I am Michael Joseph, from the tribe of Joseph, a son of Rachel. You can call me Mikey Joe. Don't be afraid."

The Nonessentials looked at one another, not knowing whether to unharness themselves from the pull-lines or stand at attention.

"Please, my friends. The devils are almost dead. When they are, you are free."

"May we sit down, sir?" one Nonessential asked, his feet caked in blood and dirt.

"Yes, please. This man is Caleb Joseph. He will take you to a cavern, a warm place where you will be offered water and bread. They will wash your feet. They will care for you."

A murmur of wonder passed between the dozen. *Who were these men?*

"You are no longer Nonessential men to be driven like beasts," he walked up to them, looking each one in the eye. "I call you my brothers. I ask you to join our cause, to restore this land to God's people."

A few of the Nonessentials began to weep.

"You are welcome here. Take off your restraints and join us in the land of living waters."

The twelve Nonessentials followed Caleb from the tribe of Joseph into the woods.

As the sun sunk lower in the sky, the four survivors secured the doors and sat in the back of the truck, listening to every word from Mikey Joe's mouth. The two United Authority attendants took their positions, weapons only partially loaded with ammunition, as rations had been cut in recent weeks.

"General, I'm going to need you to move to the center of the truck."

"Give me your weapon, sergeant," the general commanded.

"I have orders, sir."

"Your orders come from me."

"No, sir. My orders are from the Senate. We are to get you there safely."

"The Senate can eat shit, sergeant. Look, you are both young men. You can protect this little girl far better than I can. I'll hold them off for a while. Just make your way to the cab and slip out the driver's door."

"The girl isn't the primary directive, sir. You are."

"I'm an old man and this is a new world," he spat, cursing them under his breath. "We don't have time for your patriotism—your misplaced loyalty to a fractious group of old men who don't deserve it."

"We're going to get you out of here," the sergeant stated. "Now take the girl and move to the center of the truck. If you don't, I'll shoot you myself."

"When we get out of here," the general said through his clenched teeth, "I'm going to court martial and hang you from a rusty scaffold myself."

"I can almost guarantee both of us will be long dead before then," the attendant replied, eyes cold as he took his position.

Loud, strident banging started, on all sides of the truck, as the Snake

Handlers pounded their hands and fists on the metal panels. The cab began to rock.

War cries. Whoops and screams. Call-and-response chants. The blood-curdling noises echoed inside the truck.

"Cover your ears, Medicine Girl."

For once, she did as she was told. The general used plastic bins and metal shelving to construct a small barricade around her. He knew it wouldn't prevent the inevitable, but they might have a few more moments before the end.

"This is going to get ugly," the general informed her. "I'll try to divert them when they enter. If you can escape through the front, run northeast. Get to a United Authority checkpoint on the Four Oh. Take my universal pass." He handed her the gold medallion. She took it and jammed it deep in her pocket.

"I'm not going to let them hurt you, sir," she declared. The old general looked puzzled, then smiled at her and tousled her hair.

He unsheathed a short machete strapped to his ankle.

The Medicine Girl moved the lantern within arm's reach while extinguishing the light.

The doors were breached. Bravely, both United Authority attendants used their limited ammo, killing the first wave of six Snake Handlers.

Four men remained, including the tallest, Mikey Joe. A bowman lived, managing to fire a half dozen arrows into the expanse. Two of the arrows caught one of the attendants in the chest. He fell, dropping an empty handgun.

The last attendant affixed a bayonet to the empty rifle, gutting an enemy before being brutalized by two Snake Handlers, who gleefully gouged out his eyes, ripping him to shreds with their bare hands.

Three Snake Handlers remained, breathing heavily, taking inventory of the truck's goods.

"Look for any intelligence, brethren. The Armaggedonists want to see it all," Mikey Joe reminded his two men, both covered in gore.

The general held the Medicine Girl under the wool blanket, hidden by boxes and containers. Both were silent, breathing as shallowly as possible.

"Unload the truck," ordered Mikey Joe. "We'll sort it out on the highway. Caleb is sending the handcarts. We'll take it back to the cavern."

The bowman nodded. Both he and the other man started emptying the truck, while Mikey Joe opened each box and crate, discerning what was valuable.

The Medicine Girl looked at the general. His hands gripped his machete, knuckles white.

As the bowman tugged on the blanket, he looked puzzled at the resistance. He bent down to see what the thick wool blanket was stuck on when the general uncovered himself and the Medicine Girl, driving his machete right between the bowman's eyes.

From just outside the truck, the other man who witnessed the attack screeched a warning. Both he and Mikey Joe scrambled into the back of the truck, while the old man put a boot on the bowman's chest in an attempt to dislodge his weapon.

The two younger men grabbed the general, pummeling him with their fists. The general slunk down, curling into the fetal position, protecting his head. While the other man continued to batter and kick the general, Mikey Joe turned to dislodge the machete from the bowman's skull.

As he raised it, prepared to sever the general's head, the Medicine Girl threw herself over the general's unconscious body, unleashing a high-pitched scream.

Both men were stunned at seeing a young girl, glancing at one another in disbelief. Mikey Joe swiped the knife at her, but from her crouched position, she spun and swept his legs out from under him with her own. Before dropping the machete, he managed to slice her face, carving a crescent-shape gash under her left eye. The machete skittered across the bed of the truck.

In a rage, the Medicine Girl grabbed the large kerosene lamp and smashed it at the two men's feet, showering them in glass and flammable fluid. She click-clicked the flint spark, catching the men's pants on fire, along with a portion of the back of the truck. As the men rolled on the floor in a desperate attempt to put out the flames, she retrieved the general's machete.

Seeing that Mikey Joe was incapacitated due to severe burns to his face and torso, the Medicine Girl determined he wasn't going anywhere, making the decision of whom to kill first much easier.

The other man should have been less concerned about saving his leg and more concerned about her, but he didn't have long to regret his actions. The general's machete was very sharp.

The Medicine Girl turned around and leveled her gaze at Mikey Joe.

"Sister," Mikey Joe grimaced, forcing a smile, watching a bloody-faced girl stand over him. "Join us. Leave the devils to the fires of hell."

Without a word, she sliced his throat.

The fire was small, but it would spread to the entire truck. Others would see the flames at night and return.

The Medicine Girl had very little time.

She dragged the general, unconscious and unresponsive, out of the truck, off the road, and deep into a nearby thicket. There she attended to the general's substantial wounds, praying to her mother's gods he would awaken.

Her own face still bled, but not profusely. She applied pressure using a torn shirt, staunching the flow. *If I had some turmeric*, she thought.

She felt the general's pulse. Checked his eyes. Assessed him in the thorough way her mother had taught her.

This was a fool's errand, she cried, hot tears streaming down her face. The general would die. Other bad men would come. After a quick search, she and the general would be found and killed in some gruesome fashion.

She put her head down and wept.

At dusk, the Medicine Girl felt a warm lick on her arm. Startled, she looked up to see a goat's beige and white face, blinking at her.

Unsure if the animal was truly there, she reached out to touch its head. It nuzzled up to her, bleating. Soon other goats came into the thicket, clustering together.

A very old man with a walking stick followed, calling out to his little flock. "Isabel, you bad girl, come here. Findley, where are you, you rascal..." he grumbled.

Did all of the goats have names, she wondered.

"Who's there?" she asked.

"Oh, hello dear. I see you have met my goats." The old man laughed. "Your face is bleeding. And this poor man! Is he your grandfather?"

"Yes," she lied, but it didn't feel like a lie.

"Is he dead?"

"Not yet," she blubbered, fresh tears threatening to overwhelm her with grief.

"Why are you wearing United Authority clothing?"

"W-we found them." Another lie.

"Well, take those things off. You will get yourselves killed for just wearing those uniforms in this part of the country."

The Medicine Girl removed the heavy blue coat, revealing her thin white tee shirt. Shivering, she kept on her United Authority yellow pants, but she began camouflaging them with the cold dark mud.

"Will you help me with my grandfather? We need to leave this area."

The old man came over to look at the general, holding up his small lantern.

"He's been beaten."

"I think he will live," she replied.

"I think so, too." Another laugh. She wasn't sure if he was serious or not.

"Should I take off his jacket?"

"No, we will just cover him up with my old coat. Then we will lash four of my goats together and tie him to their backs. The goats are strong and can carry him back to Witt."

"Are we near Witt?" wondered the Medicine Girl.

"Perhaps ten colony-miles or so. The goats and I like to visit the lake on occasion, don't we, my loves?" He kissed two of them on top of their heads. "We will be home before midnight."

"In Witt, I need to see the Goatman," she said. "Do you know him?"

"My dear, who else could I be. Here I am," he smiled, his face wrinkling in delight. "I am the Goatman of Witt. How do I know you? Remind me."

Without another word, the Medicine Girl untied the old woman's thin piece of brown rope from around her neck and removed the signet ring.

"Someone asked me to give this to you."

She proffered him the ring, cupping it in both of her hands.

The old man took it, his ever present smile fading as he became lost into a memory. With a shaky hand, he placed the ring on the fourth finger of his left hand.

He paused to collect himself, putting his left hand over his heart, then covering it with the other.

"Help me lash the goats together so we can carry your grandfather. Come. Let's go to Witt."

The transport consisted of a repurposed two-axle box truck, pulled by a colony-dozen of Nonessentials from the Florida Penal Colony.

Chapter 12

Witt, Tennessee

"The moon is very large tonight," the Medicine Girl remarked, keeping an eye on the unconscious general. She held onto his coat, steadying him on the backs of the goats as they walked. She had wrapped herself in the Goatman's blanket to ward off the chill.

"It's a perigean full moon—a Supermoon—if you will. The moon is as close to the earth as it can get. Some people call it a beaver moon—a signal for the beavers to hibernate for the winter, warm and safe in their lodges."

"Are there beavers here?"

"I doubt it," the old man replied. "I haven't seen a beaver for...oh, decades. Ever since they drained the wetlands. A long time ago, many years before you were born."

The Medicine Girl and the Goatman walked along in the moonlight, just off the Eight One, the quiet bleating of the goats making for good conversation as he often responded to them.

The Goatman's pace was brisk. The Medicine Girl struggled to keep up with him.

"Findley, you just mind your own business," he groused. The black and tan goat butted his thigh in protest. The Goatman shooed him away. "Come here, Maribell. Let me see what's ailing you."

The Goatman sat down on the cold ground, holding Maribell like a child, looking at her hooves. "Oh, I see. No wonder you were complaining."

"What's the matter?" asked the Medicine Girl, her curiosity piqued.

"Her hoof walls need to be trimmed. Clean and proper. When they grow too long, they curl over on their toes."

The Medicine Girl came closer to observe. He dug out a tool from his waistband and set to work.

"I need to clean out the dirt between the sole and the hoof wall."

Working quickly, he soon alleviated the little white goat's suffering. "We'll fix you up better when we get home to Witt." Maribell nuzzled The Goatman's forehead. He whispered to her, a private language between the two which made the Medicine Girl grin.

"Why do you like goats so much?"

"Because they are my friends."

"Friends?"

"They keep me company. They are easy to please."

"Is it true that goats eat everything—"

"Only if they choose to. They actually are very picky," the Goatman added. "But they are very generous."

"Generous? How?"

"Goats provide me with milk and cheese. I can use their wool for making clothing and linens—"

"Like sheep?"

"Just like sheep's wool. I prefer goat hair, of course. All in all, I'll take a goat over a sheep any day. A sheep is a right bastard!" He laughed.

With her fingertips, the Medicine Girl felt the blanket draped around her shoulders—as soft and warm as any blanket she'd ever had.

"Goats are useful," she decided.

"Very useful, indeed." He smiled at her, as she drifted back to check the older man's vital signs.

Maribell took that moment to defecate.

"Goodness, Maribell! That's a lot of shit," the Goatman remarked, laughing again. "Let's take a look at it."

The Medicine Girl wrinkled her nose. "Why would you look at animal scat?"

"Like people, you can tell a lot about animals by their shit. You need to know what normal looks like to recognize the abnormal."

"Can't you just watch how they act?"

"Well, like people, goats are prey animals. They'll hide their sickness until it's very serious. But shit tells the tale!" He glanced down. "You're doing fine, Maribell!" He patted her and scratched her head. She bleated at him in return.

The Medicine Girl gave him a look of deep skepticism.

"You know, when goat shit is dry, it doesn't smell as bad as cow shit. I despise cows. Horses, too. Mercurial creatures. Awkwardly big. Bad tempered."

"I have heard there are still horses out in the Far West. But cows are useful. Why do you hate cows so much?" she asked, finding his dismissive statements perplexing.

"A milking cow kicked me in the head as a child," he whispered, as if to keep his secret from the goats. "And cows shit too much. I have mucked out too many stalls to have any affection for anything bovine."

"Cow manure is good for fueling fires," she added, attempting to add a bit of her own knowledge to the conversation.

"It is," he agreed. "But goat shit is preferable to all others."

When they stopped to rest, the Goatman offered her water from his goatskin.

"Do you butcher and skin your goat friends?" she asked, hefting the water container, feeling the intricate patterns of the leather.

"On occasion. Goat meat is delicious," he replied, giving her a sideways glance. "I assume you mean butchering and skinning my *animal* friends."

"It just seems cruel to name and to love your goats—then kill them," she countered, scratching one of the goats behind the ears.

"Oh my dear, like the sages used to say in the days when people pretended to have answers, *all* is suffering," the Goatman declared. "When I butcher one of my goats, I always thank my friend for his or her sacrifice. They have long provided me with companionship and sustenance. I have done the same for them."

She mulled over his response.

"How did you make this water bag?"

"I will show you when we get to Witt. It's important to have the right knife for the job! I start with two pieces of goatskin—very close-cropped goatskin. Tanned. Coated with pitch."

"It sounds like a long process."

"It is, but most things of value take time."

"I would like to learn how to make these water bags," she said.

The Goatman nodded as she handed the goatskin back to him.

The general moved, stretching his arms and legs, his torso firmly tied across the backs of four goats. The animals had patiently borne their load.

"How does your grandfather fare?"

"I will know more in the morning," she declared, with more surety than she felt. "Are we very far away from Witt?" Her voice belied how worried and bone weary she was.

"A colony-hour or so. Not long."

They continued on, a light frost descending on the blades of grass under their feet.

"Goatman, how did you know the old woman who asked me to give you the signet ring?" the Medicine Girl asked.

"Is she dead?" he inquired, afraid of the answer.

"I am not sure," the Medicine Girl replied. She did not tell him more of the old woman's unfortunate circumstances, and he didn't ask.

"Her name was Genevah. I loved her more than my life," he spoke quietly. "Not that my life is worth much now. As for Genevah? I have never loved another half as much. Not my parents. Not my children. Not even my own wife."

"Does your wife know about her?"

"My wife is safely dead. In fact, most people I know are dead." He laughed as if he were pleased with that thought. "This is a hard time to be alive. I am surrounded by the dead!"

The Medicine Girl looked at her feet, feeling uncomfortable that the man talked so much about death.

"Knowing so many dead people is good. That's one of the consequences of living so long." He laughed a little to take the sting out of his words.

The Medicine Girl did not know how to reply to him.

"Catalina died," she said in a small voice. "She was my friend."

"It's hard to lose friends," the Goatman sighed, empathizing with her. "It's hard to lose anyone you love. There's precious little love in the world these days."

"Do you know where they go? Where are the dead?"

The Goatman pondered her question, the goats bleating as if giving their own particular views.

"Little girl, no one alive knows what happens to the dead. That is the great mystery. There are endless philosophies of men and countless religions who worship a pantheon of gods—each one telling you what to believe about the afterlife. But truly, no one knows. Those who tell you they do are the worst of all liars."

"I thought as much," she mumbled to herself. Since she was a child, whenever an adult attempted to teach her about a new or old religion, she always felt disappointed in their thin discussions. It was as if half way through their explanation of the tenets of their faith, even they didn't believe what they were saying. Her further questioning either enraged or bored them.

"That said, there aren't too many options of what happens to us after death," he added. "There are only three possibilities."

The Medicine Girl walked nearer to him, wanting to hear his every word, puffs of cold night air punctuating his remarks.

"The first possibility is that our dead ones have ceased to exist. They don't go anywhere. Their corpses are here, waiting to return to the earth. They continue to exist only in our memories."

The Medicine Girl nodded. This seemed the most plausible.

"The second possibility is some inner part of themselves that we cannot see has gone somewhere we cannot know. A soul or spirit or essence...some piece goes someplace. Maybe a heaven? Valhalla. Nirvana. Or maybe a hell? Limbo. Purgatory. A place of fire and brimstone."

"At least a hell would be warmer," she murmured, rubbing her hands together. "Tell me. Which of those possibilities do you believe?"

"It does not matter, but I will find out long before you do." He gave her an impish grin.

The Medicine Girl's eyes flashed, wanting to ask him another series of questions, but she held her tongue lest he stop talking.

"The only other last possibility is that we are reborn back into this realm or another one, over and over again. Perhaps I was a goat in a former life," he said, bleating back at his goats. Dutifully, they bleated at him, too, nuzzling his legs. "I think I would have liked that life very much. Goats have a good life."

She nodded her agreement to the Goatman's statement, resting her hand on the general's blue coat.

For the rest of the way to Witt, they walked in silence under the watchful eye of the moon.

"Here it is, my children. Home sweet home," the Goatman sang, leading his small caravan. Behind him were at least two dozen goats. Four of the full-grown males carried the general, almost unrecognizable from his savage beating. Taking up the rear was the Medicine Girl, cautiously entering the fenced in compound.

"This way, ladies and gentleman..." The Goatman laughed. The goats knew the way to their enclosure, entering the small warm barn, fragrant pine bedding covering the floor. "Girl, take this pail down to the pond and fill the goats' water troughs."

"Doesn't the water need to be boiled—even for the animals?"

"It's a spring-fed pond. No need to trouble yourself. The water is good for both animals and man as is."

The Medicine Girl marveled at this news.

While the Goatman untied the general, the Medicine Girl made her way down the hill to the pond in darkness, the large moon providing enough light for her to avoid twisting her ankle on rocks and roots.

In no time she had filled and refilled the plastic pail, ensuring the thirsty goats had sufficient water for their needs. She tore a length of her tee shirt, dabbing it in the spring water to clean her face.

"Help me take the United Authority man inside," the Goatman said when she returned.

"No, he's my grandfather," she protested. "Before he was attacked, my grandfather said—"

"He is not your grandfather," the Goatman interrupted. "And you are a bad liar. If you lie to me again, you will have to leave. I hate liars more than I hate cows."

She stared at him, angry that he had caught her fabricating their backstory. She started to protest.

"I'm sure the Order of the Snake Handlers has some unfinished business with both of you."

She shut her mouth.

The Goatman hoisted the general up, grabbing him under his arms. The Medicine Girl had no choice but to follow, carrying his legs as best she could.

Together they carried Lieutenant General Chapman into a very rustic one-room cabin, one that smelled of cedarwood from the roof's hand cut shingles to the floorboards.

They lifted the man into a single bed, shoved into the far corner of the room, adjacent to an ancient cast-iron potbelly stove. A large pile of dried wood lay next to it in an orderly pile.

"Can you make a fire?"

The Medicine Girl looked at him as if he were joking.

"I'll take that as a yes. Make us a fire."

He tossed her a flint steel.

After warming water on the stovetop, the Medicine Girl dabbed the general's face with a clean cloth. Without opening his swollen eyes, the general took a few sips of water before moaning a bit, rolling onto his side, then falling back to sleep.

"Take this honey and put it on his wounds," the Goatman advised. "And dab some under your left eye as well. It'll draw out any infection. You don't want an infection near your eyes."

The Medicine Girl did as he instructed, although she would have rather used garlic or cloves. *But honey would work.*

"I think he has a concussion," the Medicine Girl fretted. "Other than that, it just looks like deep cuts and bruises. Maybe a cracked rib or two?"

"He needs to rest. So do we. There is plenty of room for you up in the loft. Don't worry about him. I'll sleep here and keep an eye on him."

"Is there a latrine?" she asked.

"The outhouse is off to your left. Clap your hands before you go in to scare off any creatures." He demonstrated, giggling a bit. She grinned back.

As the Medicine Girl walked out of the front door, the Goatman took off his signet ring and stared at it. His ever-present smile faded. His rheumy eyes flooded with tears as he handled the *vesica piscis* bishop's ring, engraved in a double pointed oval.

When he had received it at his investiture, its symbol seemed to be so clear: the creation or womb of the universe. He had planned to be a good priest, to serve God as he'd been instructed. Then, *Genevah.*

How holding this ring transported him back through time, when he was young and handsome! *Genevah.* Genevah was so beautiful. Beautiful enough to leave the Priesthood of God.

"I will see Genevah in the next world," the Goatman decided, drying his foolish tears.

The door opened. The Medicine Girl reentered, looking dumbstruck.

Not wanting her to find him in such a fragile state, the Goatman turned his head to dry his tears, sliding the ring back onto his finger.

"My dear, what's wrong?" he asked, once he saw her stricken

expression.

I'm b-bleeding," she stammered.

"Are you injured?" He stood up to look at her, concerned she had an unseen wound.

"No. NO!" she shouted, moving away, catching herself from overreacting. She crossed her arms. "No. I'm—I'm alright. I just need something. A rag. A towel."

"How old are you, child?"

"Thirteen colony-years on the fifth of November."

He walked over to a small cupboard, full of sheared goat wool. He grabbed a handful and pressed it into her hands. "Take this and put it in your undergarments. Keep the area clean. Replace it when needed."

"I'm sorry—" she mumbled.

"Sorry for what? There's no need to apologize."

"I just feel..." She hung her head.

"Listen to me, little one. Even the doe in the paddock has her time. Is this your first monthly cycle?"

She didn't answer. The Medicine Girl's face flushed red and hot. *She felt humiliated.*

"Listen to me," he tried again. "We are all animals. Our bodies do what they are supposed to do. These things are all natural and good."

Angry with herself, the Medicine Girl wiped hot tears from her flushed face with the backs of her hands.

He walked closer to the fire to warm himself, musing aloud. "I just wish my wife were here to help you—to talk to you at a time like this. You need a doe to talk doe-business with. Not an old buck. I wish your mother—"

The mention of her mother was far too much for the Medicine Girl. She put her face in her hands and openly wept.

The Goatman looked towards the silent heavens and patted her on the back.

"Take the goat wool. Go to sleep now." He handed her a clean rag.

She took it and blew her nose.

"I-I don't want my monthly," she gasped, starting to hiccup from her tears.

"No woman does," he frowned. "But your uterus doesn't need its thickened lining this month. And like most things we don't need, we shed."

"Men s-should have monthlies, t-too," she complained bitterly. "It's not fair."

At that, he let out a good natured belly laugh. "Oh, don't call down any more curses on men. Men have their own concerns."

"Should I sleep outside?"

"No, no. Go sleep in the loft. It's warmer up there. When you wake up, I will make you peppermint tea. It's what my wife used to make for herself when she felt out of sorts."

"All right," she replied, dejectedly. "Thank you for the wool."

"You're quite welcome. This business will pass in a few days. Then you will be as right as rain."

"All right," she repeated, as if to comfort herself. She walked to the ladder and began to climb the rungs to the loft.

The Goatman of Witt busied himself with barring the door and tidying up the cabin. He checked his meager store of foodstuffs to offer his guests in the morning. He'd send the girl out to gather eggs from the chickens.

As he worked, unbidden memories of Genevah came to him whenever the flash of gold on his left hand caught his eye, memories both delightful and heartbreaking.

Wasn't he past the age for such emotions—suffering from waves of delight and cries of lost love that threaten to drown his heart? At one time, knowing that she loved him was enough. Now he ached for the years that would never be.

"Tomorrow I will bury this ring in the paddock," he said out loud. *But tonight I will sleep with it on my finger.*

In short order, he heard the Medicine Girl snoring—*loudly for such a little thing!* He considered how exhausted she must be, wondering what awful trek these two souls had endured and where they had been.

There were just a few hours of night left. The Goatman wrapped himself in his thick goat fur coat, falling fast asleep by the warm stove.

After warming water on the stovetop, the Medicine Girl dabbed the general's face with a clean cloth.

Chapter 13

Bulls Gap, Tennessee

The Medicine Girl slept in, waking up far past the solar noon. Startled by her surroundings, she wondered why she was wrapped in woolen blankets in a cedar-scented loft.

Still dressed in the stiff United Authority pants, caked with grime and dried mud, she felt filthy. Her undershirt smelled of bitter sweat. Her hair was greasy and unkempt. She needed fresh goat wool, too.

"Are you up, girl?" called the Goatman. His voice was thin and reedy in the morning. "I made us some tea and radishes and boiled eggs."

"Yes, I'm coming down," she replied, her empty stomach rumbling at the mere mention of food. She clambered down the ladder. Taking a handcloth from the Goatman, she washed her hands and face in a small basin.

"How is my grandfa—" she stopped short when the Goatman looked at her. She rephrased the question. "How is the general?"

"A general?" The Goatman looked surprised, quickly recovering his composure. "He was restless all night. I was able to give him some warmed water this morning. He does not have a fever. There are no broken bones that I can tell."

"Good," she said, relief flooding over her face.

"I will make him some broth from goat marrow. Try to feed him some when he awakens. Wash his cuts and apply more honey to his wounds."

"Thank you for all your kindness." She hugged him, causing him to laugh, patting her on the shoulder.

"Glad to be a Good Samaritan. Now, the chickens were very generous this morning. Let's eat."

The Medicine Girl greedily set upon the food, ready to shove it all into her mouth. But when the Goatman reproached her with a disapproving look, she froze, holding two soft boiled eggs in each hand.

Reverently, the Goatman bowed his head and made the Sign of the Cross. "Bless us, O Lord, and these, Thy gifts, which we are about to receive from Thy bounty. Through Christ, our Lord. Amen."

The Medicine Girl stared at him.

"You still believe in the Christian gods?" she wondered.

"I believe in what I believe, and I will allow you to do the same," he said, smiling to take any harshness out of his words. "Now go ahead, girl. You must be starving."

The Medicine Girl didn't need to be told twice. She shelled the hard-boiled eggs and consumed each in three bites. The radishes were crisp and pungent and delicious.

"We will boil water after breakfast so you may bathe. There's a washtub in the barn."

After her long bath, the Medicine Girl towel-dried her black hair. Goat milk and lye had been combined to make a good, strong soap. She could not remember the last time she felt more refreshed.

The Medicine Girl needed to start the laborious process of washing their clothes. The Goatman lent her a long tunic to wear, which hung on her like the thick beige curtains she once saw at the Montgomery Comfort Station. Wearing the tunic restricted her movement more than she liked as she scrubbed their pants and shirts across a handmade washboard. Yet, the tunic kept her warm enough on the chilly day.

Between the laundry and the cleaning and the food preparation, the Medicine Girl was content. It suited her to be busy—it kept her mind occupied; the Goatman was grateful for a capable pair of hands and the human companionship.

Before the United Authority's invasion of Canada, he'd loved bantering with the Jesuit brothers at Marquette University. But that was before Lake Michigan became marshland, a refugee camp for those fleeing New Virginia. He shuddered to remember those days, the suffering that caused him to embrace a life of seclusion, to flee South, to learn to trust only goats.

Late in the afternoon, the Medicine Girl began to corral the chickens back into their coop to keep them safe from evening predators.

"Girl! Girl!" the Goatman called.

The Medicine Girl dropped the switch she'd been using to shoo the hens and sprinted back to the small cabin. When she opened the door, she saw the general sitting up, draining a goatskin of water.

"Medicine Girl, where the hell are we?" the general asked her as she walked in.

With a great sigh of relief, she grinned at him, eyes watering to see him chewing his bottom lip, puzzling out where he was and how he'd come to be there.

"They have a latrine around here?" The general asked, observing the room's exits, looking for weapons. "Who is this?" He motioned to a thin old man in homespun clothing.

"I am the Goatman of Witt," he replied, stirring a small copper pot on the stove top. "Here is some porridge for you when you return from the privy. Do you need help walking to the outhouse?"

The general looked at the Medicine Girl. "You may have to catch me up a little." He grimaced, attempting to stand on his own. His legs were wobbly.

"Here, let me help you," the Medicine Girl said, wrapping one of her arms around the general's waist. He exhaled noisily with each step.

"Oh my god," he groaned, taking a few more feeble steps.

"Do your ribs hurt?"

"Every single one."

While the Medicine Girl attended to the general, the Goatman wandered out to the paddock to care for the animals, securing the chickens in their enclosure as a heavy dusk fell.

I am old, he repeated to himself. His lovely goats came up to him and nuzzled his legs, bleating at him as if he understood them. Sometimes he was quite sure that he did.

If it weren't for the goats—would he continue to choose to live?

He peered up at the lunar halo, a sure sign of rain, or more likely snow. He rubbed his hands together to warm them, then returned to clean out the small barn, adding extra hay for the animals to prepare for the coming storm.

Once the general reclined back in bed, the Medicine Girl attempted to ladle thin porridge into his mouth.

"I'm not an invalid," he griped, taking the bowl and the spoon from her. Even in his weakened state, the general was an imposing figure. "Tell me how we came to be here."

The Medicine Girl recounted the seizure of the United Authority's transport and Roxy's betrayal. She described the Order of the Snake Handler's men, weapons, and hierarchy, recounting the bowmen and their savagery, how they'd slaughtered the United Authority attendants and beaten the general unconscious. She described killing who she needed to and setting the kerosene fire, dragging the general out of the truck and into a thicket, and the otherworldly appearance of the goats.

As she enumerated the Goatman's generosity and goodness towards them, the general closed his eyes, exhausted at trying to process the events of the past few days.

"Did you manage to salvage the files? The papers I had with me?" he inquired, one of his eyes open in the slim chance that she did.

"No, general. I was busy trying to keep you alive," she replied icily, rolling her eyes to punctuate her disgust. She stood up from his bedside to tidy up the Goatman's cooking area, washing out the general's bowl, making more noise than was necessary.

"That means the Armageddonists have my reports." Lieutenant General Chapman muttered this and other foul things under his breath. In frustration, he slammed his fists into the straw tick bedding, sending up a cloud of hay dust which made him sneeze.

"And *you're welcome...*" the Medicine Girl said snidely.

The general rolled over and went back to sleep.

The Medicine Girl was proficient at keeping the fire lit, chopping the necessary wood for kindling, driving the chill from the room. The Goatman was glad for the warmth, as cold seemed to easily seep into his joints as he aged.

"Goatman of Witt," called the general, his powerful voice strained by his ailments. "Thank you for taking us in. I fear what the Snake Handlers would have done to us."

"They would have crucified you," the Goatman replied. "Many MilitiaMen have a fractured take on Christianity, using scripture to justify their inhumanity, their beastliness. To crucify one's enemies like our Lord and Savior? It's blasphemous."

"It's domestic terrorism," the general amended. "And it's been going on for far too long."

"The United Authority has itself to blame," the Goatman shot back. "The lawlessness and debauchery and tribalism...Years and years of systemic corruption and wealth hoarding have one end: this modern hellscape we live in and the autocratic government we live under."

Lieutenant General Chapman recoiled at the old man's sudden burst of vitriol. "Sir, living in the south, I understand your hostility towards the government..."

"I've lived in the north, too. Before the end of electricity. Before the first cyber attack took out our antiquated powergrid. Before the first EMP bomb short-circuited every cellphone and computer. Before satellites and planes dropped out of the sky. There was plenty of hostility towards the government then—there's outright rebellion now."

The Goatman stood up and walked to refill his goatskin from a pail of spring water. After drinking deeply from it, he continued. "You remember the days before the end of electricity, General. Not only was our democracy sickened, but the land itself was dying. Fires raged. Rivers dried up. Mass animal extinctions. It was as if Oedipus needed to solve the Riddle of the Sphinx to free us from a curse. And now the curse is here, in both the body and soul of this nation."

The general crossed his arms while the Medicine Girl struggled to follow the old men's conversation.

"You are conflating a truckload of societal ills and laying blame at the United Authority's feet. We remain a government of the people, by the people, for the people—"

"Currently, you lack the *consent* of the people," the Goatman interrupted. "Unless you count the women forced into employment at your Comfort Stations and the human chattel trafficked through your Family Trading Stations as part of your constituents. But how else would you manage to collect taxes to support a centralized autocratic behemoth—one whose sole purpose is to become a law unto itself!"

"About forty years ago," the general said, trying to maintain his composure, "when I swore an oath, to a God I didn't believe in, to support and defend the Constitution against all enemies, foreign and domestic—I never imagined that most of its enemies would be *domestic*."

"About forty years ago," the Goatman rejoined, "I taught my first Comparative Politics course at Marquette University. I will remind you of John Locke's social contract."

"Don't lecture me." The general waved him off. "Let me guess— Jesuit priest. A pedantic professor, holed up in the ivory tower while men like me do the dirty work to protect your life and liberty."

"*Former* Jesuit priest, sir. God and I have had our differences."

"Was He tired of you telling Him what He did wrong?" the general replied, his voice thick with disgust.

The Goatman closed his eyes and shook his head.

"You think the government has led us to the end of the world? Well, you religious fanatics have been prophesying and rooting for that to occur for over two thousand years. Now that it's here, you think you'd be happy."

"This is not the end of the world, sir. This is not the promised Edenic millennium by any stretch of the imagination."

"How do you know," quipped the general. "Seeing how much God's promises are worth, this may be exactly what He had in mind."

The Goatman's pale face softened. "General, I, too, have cried into the empty night. I have heard my prayers sink to the ground like lead. As much as God has disappointed us both, I'm sure we are just as disappointing to Him."

General Chapman lay back, brooded in the silence.

"Look, priest. What my job has been and still is—is to maintain order and ensure public services are functioning to the best of my ability. If you are unhappy with the laws on the books or the economic policies of the United Authority, then I suggest you run for Senate. Get involved in your community. Advocate for change within the system."

"General," the Goatman addressed him in a low voice. "This isn't a town hall or a public forum. We are old men who knew how things were and how things are. You and I both know that the elections will be a charade, if they are even held this year at all. As it has always been, wealth and power are concentrated in the hands of the few. Grassroots efforts do very little but give marginalized people an illusion of hope."

"Much like religion, priest."

"Ex-Priest. I'm just the Goatman now."

"And I'm an old man with no answers and a few cracked ribs."

They sat together and watched the first flakes of the coming snowfall through the window panes.

The Goatman coughed, clearing his ancient lungs. "Maybe civilizations have lifespans, like goats and men," he speculated.

"I remember a class I had at West Point. One of the professors discussed the history of societal collapse. Who is to blame? The Mesopotamians blamed bad kings. The Romans blamed Christians. Followers of Copernicus blamed the orbits of the stars. No one really knows. Maybe it's time to die when it's time to die—for gods, kings, men, goats. And civilizations."

"Everyone looks for a scapegoat to blame," the Goatman mused. "Poor goats. Always getting held accountable for everything. And you make a good point, General. Perhaps it was just time for our civilization to end its long decay, hopefully allowing something better to be reborn in its place."

"History does tend to repeat itself."

"And you and I both know that every time history repeats itself, the price goes up."

Both men stopped talking long enough to realize the Medicine Girl had fallen asleep, soundly snoring, right at their feet.

One of the last kindnesses the Goatman of Witt performed for the Medicine Girl and the general was making them a hearty breakfast, fit for presidents and kings. He'd butchered a chicken, breaded it in oat flour and fried it up golden brown in peanut oil. He'd scrambled a half dozen eggs, adding wild onions and mustard greens from his winter garden.

Both the Medicine Girl and the general ate with delight, complimenting the Goatman on his skill and thanking him for his generosity. The Goatman nodded, offering the travelers what he could for their journey as they prepared to leave.

The Goatman finished filling up two goatskins with spring water for their long walk in the frigid air, heavy snowflakes continuing to fall.

"Follow the One Three Three. It's about fifteen colony-miles. You should be able to make it to the United Authority checkpoint by nightfall. Look for it at the intersection at Bulls Gap. Unless it's been raided, they'll get you where you need to go."

"Come with us?" begged the Medicine Girl. She hugged the Goatman around the waist, burying her face in his sunken chest.

"No, no...I'm too old for adventures. The goats need me here," he replied, patting her shoulder. "Who else could I entrust them to? Findley would bite anyone who came near him." He laughed, pushing her away. "The general will watch over you with great care."

At this, the general looked at him, wondering if that was an observation or a directive. *Either way*, the general mused, *the Goatman was right*. The Medicine Girl was as precious to him as any daughter.

The Goatman's fingers toyed with the signet ring on his left hand, reminiscent of a memory that would not fade. He had often wished that it would, that he could forget Genevah, but, now, even the painful longing in his heart was welcomed. He loved her and she loved him— time and space scarcely mattered. *Knowing she still loved him was enough.*

He decided not to bury the ring in the paddock.

"Are you ready to go, Medicine Girl?" the general called out, as she straightened up the loft.

The Medicine Girl appeared with a goatskin hat, the edges poking up like little goat ears. She wore the Golden United Authority's pants and the long tunic that drowned her frame, but kept her warm.

"You look like a little goat," the general chuckled. "With big gray eyes."

"Thank you, Chapman. I'll take that as a compliment," she replied. "I think goats are the most beautiful creatures on earth."

At this, both the Goatman and general roared with laughter.

Lieutenant General Chapman shook the Jesuit priest's hand. "I appreciate your hospitality, Goatman," the general said, shouldering the goatskin of water.

"Go with God, my son, or whoever watches over you," the Goatman amended, with a wry smile.

"That's me!" The Medicine Girl interrupted. "Go with the Medicine Girl, Chapman. I'll watch over you!"

"Thank you again," the general said, with a nod to his benefactor.

The Goatman followed them to the edge of the paddock, waving an old hand in farewell as he watched the Medicine Girl and general walk away, side by side, in the snowfall.

*Both men stopped talking long enough to realize the Medicine Girl had fallen
asleep, soundly snoring, right at their feet.*

The Medicine Girl and general walked away, side by side, in the snowfall.

Chapter 14

Richmond, Old Virginia

"Wake up, Medicine Girl. Come and see."

It was too cold and too early to be up, The Medicine Girl thought, rolling over, pretending not to hear the general.

After three weeks on a United Authority transport, she was lethargic and moody. She missed tending the Goatman's animals, collecting sweetwater from the spring, and sleeping in the privacy of the cozy loft. She missed starting a fire in the potbelly stove, hearing the bleats and tinkling of the goats' bells, trying to locate all of the eggs the chickens hid from her—a daily treasure hunt! She missed learning how to grow a winter garden and watching the roosters fight. She missed the quiet, serenity of a tiny town in Tennessee, forgotten by most. She missed the Goatman.

The cold metal of the tractor trailer chilled her blood even further, yet her goat wool tunic provided a great respite from the frigid air. Still, she felt trapped in a box on an endless highway, one she'd been traveling on for far too long.

She had grown to hate transports.

As this particular transport was a Senate Express, a score of Nonessentials were harnessed to pull the rig north on the Eight One and East on the Six Four. When the Medicine Girl went to complain to the general, he turned his world-weary eyes towards her. The senators had summoned the general to give testimony regarding the tense situation in the southern states. *There was nothing he could do about the Nonessentials.*

She brooded, guilty at her relative comfort in the trailer, while the doomed men labored under the lash.

After leaving the Goatman's home, the Medicine Girl and the general walked to the United Authority checkpoint in Bulls Gap. A very relieved attendant welcomed them. The general had been classified as missing in action, few believing he had survived the Order of the Snake Handler's attack. The checkpoint attendant was keen on collecting the reward for locating him, even if the general did walk up to the station on his own accord. After tending to their needs, the attendant sent out dispatch runners to Richmond, informing the Senate about Lieutenant General Chapman's resurrection.

The United Authority's dispatch runners had distinctive facial tattoos, they always ran in pairs. They each carried a high level universal pass, backed by the full protection of the Senate and United Authority, and a loaded weapon. As dispatch runners carried the United Authority's intelligence between officials, two bullets in their weapons were always reserved for worst case scenarios. At a minimum, they were expected to destroy sensitive information—including themselves—should insurgents capture them.

In a few days, the transport had been arranged, as well as other United Authority officials, anxious to brief the general on the continuing instability in the region, burying him in reports and gossip and bad news.

The Medicine Girl was summarily ignored, as the general spent most of his time on the transport in meetings, preparing his sobering remarks for the Senate. When he slept, he did so fitfully, his cracked and bruised ribs causing him far more discomfort and pain than he let on. The escalating pace of the deteriorating situation in the south didn't help his health much either. Most troubling, soldiers' defections were mounting by the day.

Stopping off to resupply in Fort Chiswell in Old Virginia, a medic had been attending to colony-dozens of Nonessentials when the Medicine Girl wandered out of the rig. She observed him inspecting the bedraggled men, patiently waiting for any relief the medic could give them. A few drank a thin gruel from mismatched plastic cups.

The Medicine Girl watched the medic clip off toes and fingers that had suffered from fourth-degree frostbite. She noted his slipshod wrapping of the Nonessentials' appendages in rags or cardboard or plastic scraps. He checked ears and nose, looking for signs of gangrene or chilblains. He ignored most of their other maladies.

The medic's carelessness enraged her.

"What are you doing? This man's feet need to be cleaned and dried," she protested, standing over his shoulder. "You can't bind them as they are. See how the foot is turning purple?"

The medic looked at her with utter disdain. "These men will be dead in a week."

"Well, they are alive now. You're just prolonging their suffering!"

"Listen, little girl. Either get back on the transport or I'll suture your mouth shut."

She walked away incensed, wandering back to the transport and Chapman.

From a distance, the Medicine Girl watched stoically as the miserable, exhausted Nonessentials were replaced with equally miserable, exhausted new men. *The Goatman treated his goats with more compassion*, she thought. *Even when he butchered them.*

When one of the Nonessentials balked at the medic's harsh treatment, attendants were called. They bludgeoned the recalcitrant man—not to death, but close enough. The man would spend his remaining hours in agony, laying face down in a filthy ditch by the side of the road. The attendants unceremoniously dumped his bleeding and broken body, a stark message for the others.

After Fort Chiswell, the Medicine Girl remained on the transport during the checkpoints.

She lay quietly most of the time, just within earshot of the general and the men who seemed to always surround him. The Medicine Girl noticed everything that occurred in the trailer, her sharp gray eyes keeping track of the location of the transport men, keeping a wary eye on the surrounding terrain through the small windows carved into the trailer's sides.

A thick layer of ice lay on top of the snow. The sound of the Nonessentials' bare feet punching through the ice with each step could be heard even in the far back. Heartsick, the Medicine Girl watched from the back window, as bloody footprints marked their progress towards Richmond.

She turned to the lot of military men, mulling over cold numbers and statistics. The general seemed more heavily burdened and haggard the closer they got to the capital city.

Hand drawn maps had been unfurled over a plastic crate, friendly territories outlined, annotated, changed and changed again with grease pencil whenever dispatch runners delivered news to the general.

The Medicine Girl caught fragments of the missives and conversations, some more agitated and argumentative than others. They attempted to come to a consensus of where the United Authority stood, as militias and formerly loyal groups switched allegiances in increasing numbers.

"The Carolinas cannot be trusted. Once they merged before the end of electricity, they became a law unto themselves. The tax revenue from their Comfort Stations is about 30% less of what it should be. Carolingians have always been thieves," spat a colonel.

"At this point, the northern militias stand with the United Authority. However, there have been a few white supremacist groups in Pennsylvania that lean towards the Armageddonists' movement, or theology, such as it is. No one is quite sure what unites them, except for their hatred of us," added a brigadier general.

"Sylvanians are industrious, but they don't trust anybody but ClansMen."

"We should be able to count on the individual State Defense Forces, only because of the Family Trading Stations. Very little of that revenue makes it to Richmond anyway. If we crack down on their operations in any way, they'll flip to the Armageddonists overnight," said a plain dressed man, not wearing a uniform that the Medicine Girl could discern.

"The Illuminati Pagans are still aligned with the United Authority. But they're making a push into the Florida Penal Colony, recruiting leadership from the prison gangs. Even the fringe warlords seem to be up for sale."

The Medicine Girl's ears perked up. At the mention of the Florida Penal Colony warlords, she had to bite her tongue to stop herself from asking about her father. *Was he still alive?* The black cherry flatbread she made for him and his followers seemed like a lifetime ago—in a much warmer place. She shivered, not knowing if it was the drop in temperature or the mention of her father's name.

She settled down into her tunic, letting the mens' words wash over her. Uncertain of who spoke next, she was sure that it wouldn't matter. *Things would be what they would be.*

"The Militia of the White Crosses holds sway in the Kingdom of Georgia and the Crimson Republic. Even as far as Arkansippi. We've tried to meet with their leadership, but they are hellbent on throwing in with the Armageddonists," another interjected. "They see the United Authority as a wounded animal, dying but vicious."

"The MerchantClass and the TimberLines and the RiverMen are remaining neutral, for the time being. All the pissant groups like the True Believers and the Order of the Snake Handlers have found a home with the Armageddonists, preparing for a holy war, taking down the United Authority to redraw the maps in their own image. The ultimate redistribution of wealth...and from the intel we've intercepted, these groups are promising thaneships to warlords."

"But who is the leader of the Armageddonists? Is there a star chamber we don't know about? Maybe it's an inside job, as the Armageddonists seem to know what we are doing before we do. In recent skirmishes, especially in the Carolinas, they appear to know every troop movement and supply line. These groups are not coalescing organically. Someone is pulling the strings."

"Agreed. The Armageddonists' attacks have been too calibrated and precise. The recent spate of insurrections have spread our forces as thin as possible. There may be a mole on the inside. Someone high up. A senator or even a general—"

All eyes glanced at Lieutenant General Chapman.

The cab of the truck went silent.

"You think I'm working for the insurrectionists? You can't be serious!" the general yelled, rage palpable. It startled even the Medicine Girl, who had never heard him speak in such a way.

"You survived an attack by the Snake Handlers, General. That did raise a lot of speculation," a bold-faced Colonel remarked. "Especially someone ranking so high as yourself. At a minimum, they would have used you as a bargaining chip."

The general slammed his fists on the makeshift table, upending maps, papers, reports, and grease pencils. All eyes turned towards him again, as he spoke through gritted teeth. "I have served this country in all of its many forms for the past forty years, through a third world war and a second civil war and most likely, the start of a third civil war. You want to know how I survived a murderous group of religious fanatics? That little girl over there." He pointed to the Medicine Girl. "She has more courage and intelligence and sense than all of you assholes combined. I'm going to forget you insinuated that I've been disloyal in any way to my sacred oath, Colonel. I expect a full apology from you. But know this: after my testimony to the Senate, I will resign my post. My days serving the United Authority are nearly at an end. And you can fight over my reputation when I'm gone."

"Wake up, Medicine Girl. Come and see," said the general.

She rubbed her eyes as a pink dawn cracked through leaden gray skies. It was so cold she could see her breath in the back of the transport.

As the tractor trailer lumbered into the capital city, Richmond's skyline dazzled the Medicine Girl. She had seen ruins of other cities, but through all of the chaos of the half colony-century, Richmond's infrastructure remained somewhat intact. The office buildings still stood erect, most glass panes in place, as if witnesses of better days. The muddy James River, though diminished in volume, still hugged the downtown governmental area, the place the United Authority claimed after Washington, D.C. had been burned and rendered uninhabitable.

"What are those stars in that building?" the Medicine Girl asked, wide eyed, a million questions formulating in her mind.

"Those are electric lights. The Senate has limited electrical power in their chambers."

"I thought the time of electricity was over?" She stood, mouth open, looking at the city waking up, food vendors setting up their carts, veiled women hurrying to their destinations, flocks of animals herded into open air butcher shops.

"Electricity is not over, only access to it for most of the general populace. These lights are powered by Nonessentials pedaling stationary bicycles in the basement, but they don't produce much wattage. Do you know what a bicycle is?"

She nodded. The Medicine Girl remembered her experience learning how to ride a bike, and later, how she was robbed of it on the highway. Walking seemed so much more laborious after the freedom of the bike.

"When Nonessentials pedal, their movement drives a flywheel. The flywheel turns a generator. The generator creates electricity that goes through wires to power the lights."

"We should teach this to everyone," the Medicine Girl interrupted. "My mother told me about the days before the end of electricity. Metal boxes that kept food cold. Machines that washed clothes. Boxes that played music—"

"All of those things need electricity on a scale that we cannot produce—at least, not yet," the general said, trying not to discourage her enthusiasm.

The general looked out of the window of the trailer, spotting a shop on Broad Street.

"Stop here!" he commanded the driver.

"Sir, we have the Senate's orders to bring you to the Capitol Building," replied an attendant. For its governmental center, the United Authority had taken over the Virginia Science Museum, a neoclassical building made of limestone, topped by a 100 colony-foot dome.

The general gave the young man a withering look. "I said to stop here."

The attendant called out to halt the twenty Nonessentials pulling the transport. They crumpled to the snowy streets, calling for water from the attendants, pulling meager food rations from their pockets.

The general jumped out of the back of the transport, followed by two attendants armed with weapons.

"Come, Medicine Girl. Come and see," the general said, holding out his hand to help her out of the transport.

She smiled, hopping out of the truck, landing neatly on her two feet. He grinned at her.

"Where are we going?" she asked.

"Just in here for a bit," he said, pointing to a colorful shop.

The Medicine Girl watched children her age come and go, in and out of the door with their parents, bundled up against the chill, carrying brown bags like treasured possessions.

The general opened the door, a bell tinkling to announce visitors. The Medicine Girl followed behind the general, her senses dazzled by the scene laid out in front of her.

Fragrant smells of maple syrup toffee and honey cookies wafted through the air. She watched a worker spin a thin sugar wafer into a cone, then plop down an icy scoop of creamy fruit-flavored snow inside. Cakes of a dozen different flavors—orange blossom, lemon, pumpkin—lay stacked on a counter, cut into large wedges. Peppermint sticks and candied cherries sat in pretty dishes behind the display cases. Sugar-coated nuts tucked in rich caramels were cut into lucious squares.

"Should we get a table?" the general asked.

"Will the senators be angry?"

"The senators are always angry," the general replied.

"Then it won't matter if we get a table or not, will it?"

The general nodded, motioning for the server to seat them. Noting the three-star general's uniform, the server took them back to one of the best tables in the bustling shop. Eyes followed the old general and the dark-skinned girl, wrapped in what looked and smelled like goat wool.

They sat down by a cracked picture window overlooking what had once been an elegant courtyard, now a vacant lot in need of a landscaper who would never come.

"Unroll your silverware and place your napkin on your lap," the general instructed. The Medicine Girl looked around, observing the others around her with stained, threadbare cotton napkins on their laps. She watched the general situate himself and followed his lead.

The server came by with hand-lettered menus, enumerating the specialties for the day. With each decadent description, the Medicine Girl's stomach growled as she imagined tasting the new culinary delights.

"Are you ready to order?" asked the server.

"I want—"

"I think I know what you want," the general interrupted, taking her menu and handing both of them back to the server.

"How do you know what I want?" she asked petulantly, prepared to protest.

The general ignored her. Instead, he replied to the waiter.

"Bring us one of everything."

Bring us one of everything.

The eagle looked decisively at the arrows, an implied threat to those who challenged its order.

Chapter 15

Colonial Williamsburg, Old Virginia

Glutted with sugary confections, the Medicine Girl rode in the front cab of the transport, sitting next to the general.

"I might be sick," she confided.

"I wouldn't be surprised," the general replied with a knowing grin. "We should have wrapped up the cinnamon apple tart to take with us."

"I should have eaten the tart first," she decided. "It was the best thing I've ever eaten—"

"You said that about the wedge of cake, slice of pie, and assorted cookies," he added, chuckling to himself.

She nodded in agreement then hiccoughed.

It was a short trip to the Senate down Broad Street. The Medicine Girl took in the sights of the wintry city, people bundled up, all carrying things in a hurry. Others were dressed in rags, begging in the streets, no place to go. The stark dichotomy was not lost on her. *Just like the soldiers and the Nonessentials.*

Arriving at the Capitol Building, the Medicine Girl marveled at the architecture, asking the general question after question. She was curious about the massive black granite sphere, marking the entrance of the building, impressive even in its worn state.

"That's a kugel," the general explained. "Back in the days of electricity, a water fountain would burble up under it, causing that entire nine colony-foot slab of granite to rotate in all directions."

"It's enormous. How much does it weigh?"

"Maybe thirty colony-tons," mused the general, remembering a distant childhood memory. *As a boy, he had held his father's hand and asked the same question.*

The Medicine Girl and the general climbed out of the rig, trailing the armed Senate attendants. Frost blanketed the grounds, as the Medicine Girl held onto the general so his footfalls were sure. She didn't need him slipping on the ice, cracking more ribs or breaking a hip on the rough-cut brick walkways.

"Medicine Girl," the general said.

"Yes, Chapman?"

"After we are done here, I've made arrangements for you to see your mother."

The Medicine Girl stopped short, her gray eyes wide.

"Today? I will see my mother today?"

"Soon, but not today." The general patted her shoulder. "I have sent dispatch runners to the Old Virginia Tidewater warlord. His compound is down the Six Four, near the ocean."

The Medicine Girl's mind raced. *She would see her mother.*

"I have retained two attendants who will take you to her in a small transport. Not a truck, but a small pedal-car."

"How many weeks will it take to get there, Chapman?" she asked.

"Not weeks, Medicine Girl. Colonial Williamsburg is a two-day trip. You could walk there yourself, but I want you to be safe and go with the escort."

"You mean safe from people like Roxy?" The Medicine Girl raised an eyebrow, then shook her head. "I'd rather you just give me a flint steel, a machete, and maybe—"

"Maybe another slab of peanut butter pie?" he interrupted with a wry smile.

She pretended to retch.

"Or walnut clusters? Candied raspberries? Orange cream cookies?"

"I may never eat again!" she cried aloud, holding her stomach, still full from their confectionery feast.

They both laughed companionably as they made their way through the heavy doors to the old planetarium's theater.

The entire Senate awaited the general's testimony.

As their eyes adjusted to the darkened chamber, small tea lights lit their way to the front row of seats. In the orchestra pit, a few rows of Nonessentials pedaled stationary bikes, wires leading to contraptions for a purpose she could only guess. The Medicine Girl wandered over to the lights and observed them, touching the bulbs with her fingers.

"They are warm, but they don't burn!" She turned to the general and demonstrated by tapping the light. He smiled at her, indulging her curiosity.

While they waited, he told the Medicine Girl how entire cities were lit up with much bigger lights, all the colors she could imagine. She looked skeptical, losing interest. *Why would anyone need that much light? Night was for sleeping.*

She watched the senators mill about the room, freely conversing with one another from their plush theater seats. An occasional chair was missing from a row or two. All seats faced the empty stage, save for a single lectern, which prominently boasted the seal of the United Authority firmly affixed to the front.

The Medicine Girl noted the eagle on the seal held arrows in one clawed fist and an olive branch in the other. The eagle looked decisively at the arrows, an implied threat to those who challenged its order.

"What does the banner say in the eagle's mouth, Chapman?" The Medicine Girl motioned to the podium.

"It's Latin for *Authority Strong*," the general whispered as an attendant escorted them to their seats.

The Medicine Girl looked around at the hundred odd men, so old, dressed in richly spun fabrics, thickly woven and brightly dyed. *The senators looked like candies in the sweets shop*, she thought. None of the men seemed to take notice of her. She eavesdropped, overhearing their spirited conversations, their blustering and badgering, their inappropriate comments about women and dogs.

One corpulent man made his way to the stage. He wore a pendant of some kind on his lapel, its meaning lost on the Medicine Girl. It was like the colored ribbons on the general's uniform, but this man did not look like any kind of soldier.

"He's so big," the Medicine Girl remarked to the general, as she had never seen someone so large. "He must eat—"

The general gave her a sharp look to let her know to keep her thoughts to herself. She folded her hands and wondered if all capital cities had such quantities of food for their leaders.

"Gentlemen, a quorum being present, the select committee to investigate the insurrections in the southern quadrant of the United Authority will now come to order. The select committee is meeting today to receive testimony from Lieutenant General David Lee Chapman—"

"David Lee?" the Medicine Girl whispered, elbowing the general. She snickered, repeating. "*David Lee.*"

He motioned for her to be quiet.

The senator continued. "As the princeps senatus, I declare without objection that I am authorized to call a recess or an adjournment at any time. I now recognize myself for an opening statement. Let me say a few words at the outset, how I plan to run this proceeding. Gentlemen, we will be guided by the facts, the facts on the ground told to us by a person knowledgeable of the states in question, the political landscape in general, and the understanding of the people who populate the areas under extreme duress. I will remind the senate that we are one body, with no place for political grandstanding or partisan tirades in this investigation."

At this, bitter laughter and sidetalk shattered the silence. A few men jeered, the Medicine Girl not quite making out what they were saying.

"Order. Order, you rogue's gallery! I will remind my 99 brethren that our history as a Senate and as a country has been far from perfect. We've been torn apart yet brought back together. Time and time again. From the days of the United States of America to the United Regional Authorities to the United Authority, we are the last bastion of democracy. Pay heed to our honored guest, my friends. For if we do not act or if we act wrongly, the bright light spread in the Hellenistic Age will be extinguished on our watch."

The Medicine Girl noted that half of the men in the chamber applauded; the rest looked bored.

"So lend your ears to one who has a wealth of knowledge of the challenges of our times, Lieutenant General Chapman."

A smattering of applause. The Medicine Girl imitated the clapping audience members, unsure of how to respond. The general gave her a thin smile, walking ramrod straight to the stage, up a few stairs, and directly to the podium.

"Senators, I will be brief." The room went silent, as senators leaned forward to listen to the old general, his words measured and firm. "The south has fallen into the Armageddonist's hands further and faster than you or I could have imagined so many months ago. Even as I speak, many of the southern warlords we've empowered from the Carolinas to the Texas border have coalesced against us. State defense forces seemed to have melted away and joined any number of militias, from the White Crosses to the Brotherhood of Men to God knows what else is fomenting in the hills and wastelands. We have received intelligence reports that a few northern militias are following the same course."

The general paused, looking around the room at familiar faces. Most senators had spent the majority of their lives in the halls of government, removed from understanding what their citizens faced in their daily struggles. At this somber news, a few shifted uncomfortably in their seats.

"The young, the poor, the disaffected don't look at our blue and gold uniforms as legitimate or helpful or welcome, and rightly so. We enslave or kill our citizens for minor infractions. We require them to toil in heavy labor, with no meaningful support and no hope for change. We sell their children or marry off their daughters one night at a time."

"I object—" yelled one senator. "You are attacking legal institutions upheld by our court system."

"This is not a liberal bastion, general! Tax revenue and order must be maintained—" screeched a voice from the rear of the auditorium.

"Point of order, gentleman," another crowed. "I motion all of the general's testimony be stricken from the record!"

The general looked down at his scuffed boots until the melee of voices quieted down around him. He cleared his throat, overcome with emotion.

Lost. We have completely lost our way.

"There is no authority here, senators. Just power. And the power is shifting. The warlords have always allied with the strongest leader to protect themselves. And now, the United Authority is neither united nor an authority to them. Nor should it be."

"Treason!" called a voice.

"Arrest that man—" cried another.

The general raised his voice above the din. "I am a military man, sworn to protect the Constitution. I serve this country. I know my duty. I do my duty to the best of my ability. You, gentlemen, should be honored to focus your time and effort and concerns on the lives and liberties and properties of our people. You are supposed to maintain the internal order, ensure life and liberty and the prosperity of the State—not to line your pockets with what you can skim. How have you done nothing of value for the people? We cannot expect loyalty from our citizens when we exploit them, use them, injure them—and sometime *murder* them for what amounts to pure personal gain."

"Patently untrue—"

"You lie!"

"Resign, General!"

"I have offered my resignation to General Bingington as well as the chairman of the Joint Chiefs of Staff. My final duty is to inform you of the situation on the ground. Suffice it to say that our government's years of malignant neglect have reaped the whirlwind. It's here now. The southern enemies are at the gate, no doubt followed by others once they see how hollowed out the United Authority has become. Instead of debating pet projects or gerrymandering political maps or figuring out how to extract more tax revenue from our citizenry, I would suggest you work on fortifying and defending Richmond. For war and death are coming here. May God have mercy on the United Authority."

The general walked down the stairs from the dias, making his way directly to the Medicine Girl.

"Let's go," he barked.

The room again was electrified, a sea of voices swirling around the room. She took one last look, old men with red faces now up in arms, now angry at the general's blunt words, leaning over, shouting at one another.

Nothing would change here, she thought. She turned and followed the general out into the foyer of the Capitol Building.

"The transport leaves at dusk for Colonial Williamsburg," he explained to the Medicine Girl, ushering her down a back corridor. "Do you still have my universal pass—the medallion?"

The Medicine Girl nodded, pulling the medallion out of her right pants pocket.

"Good," he replied.

"Are you coming with me?" she asked. "You don't work for them anymore, right? You just resigned. You quit. You can come with me."

He ignored her question, biting his lower lip as if puzzling something out.

"I want to show you something before you go," the general said. Walking quickly for a man still healing, the Medicine Girl matched him stride for stride.

Armed attendants saluted him as the general opened a heavy door to a paddock behind the museum. The Medicine Girl exited the building, her eyes adjusting to the bright winter sunlight.

Two large mammals with muscular deep torsos trotted on their four slender legs in circles around the snowy field, led by a high ranking United Authority officer and two attendants. As the Medicine Girl's gray eyes blinked in wonder, she marveled at the animals' long, thick necks and elongated heads, their shiny brown coats, their oval hooves.

"Those are horses, Medicine Girl. The military industrial complex is importing them from Calgary, far north in New Virginia," the general informed her, as if he were addressing a colleague. "They hope to buy hundreds of them for our soldiers."

"They're beautiful..."

"They are," he agreed. "But war is coming, which means the war profiteers are selling the latest military weaponry. And these animals are it."

She didn't hear what he was saying, wholly enamored by the animals. She ran to the fence, leaning over to get a better look at the beasts.

"My mother told me about dinosaurs and elephants and giraffes," the Medicine Girl said. "She spoke of horses, too, but she said they were all killed for food or died from disease."

"Many of them died from neglect, too. And parasites." The general joined her at the fence, crossing his arms and hanging over the fence next to her.

"That's sad that so many died," she replied. "Horses are so beautiful."

"And smart. Horses are very smart," he added. As if on cue, two horses walked over to the Medicine Girl and the general, the HorseMen following behind, saluting him.

"You have something for the horses?" the general called out to them, motioning to the Medicine Girl. A HorseMan trotted over to give the young girl standing next to the lieutenant general a couple of small apples and a few scraggly carrots.

"Hold the food out on your palm," the general advised. "Like this," he demonstrated.

She fed the horses treats, smiling as the horses' wet noses and mouths tickled her hand. She stroked their long graceful necks, laughing with delight at their chomping apples, core, seeds, and all.

"Are there more horses?" she wondered aloud.

"More are coming. These are just the start. The military's plan is to reintroduce them into secure areas and build up herds. They'll be used for transportation and battle."

"They shouldn't be used at all," the Medicine Girl said. "Who cares for them?"

"The HorseMen. They'll train others. Maybe you can learn? These two horses are going to an encampment near your mother's place near Colonial Williamsburg."

"My mother will love to see the horses," the Medicine Girl responded brightly.

"Maybe you can take her there—with the warlord's permission, of course. It's a shame Assateague and Chincoteague have been reclaimed by the sea. When I was your age, hundreds of wild horses lived there. Not too long ago...but I guess I'm an old man," he sighed, patting the horse's strong neck. The horse nuzzled him in return.

They spent a long while out in the paddock, watching the HorseMen put the graceful creatures through their paces.

"It's time, Medicine Girl."

The general led her through the Capitol Building to the front portico where a pedal-car awaited. Two armed United Authority officers stepped out, greeting the general by name. He introduced them.

"Medicine Girl, this is Captain Danes and Captain McElroy. They will take you to your mother. I trust these men with my life."

"Just like Roxy?" she said, failing to get a rise out of him. The general ignored her, taking a drawstring canvas bag from the men and handing it to her.

"This will protect you if these men can't."

She took the bag, rummaged through it, holding up a flint steel and a small machete and a few prepackaged meals. *There was even an entire tube of Neo!*

"You must come with me. Please," the Medicine Girl pleaded with him.

"I cannot." He tousled her hair. "There is so much to do here before I leave."

"Where are you going? Should I come back to see you with my mother?"

The general stooped down to her level, looking her straight in the eye. "I want you to promise me that you will never return to Richmond, Medicine Girl. The capital is a live target." He swallowed, continuing in a low voice. "In the coming weeks, this entire city may be rubble. Do *not* return to Richmond under any circumstances. Do I make myself clear? Shelter in place until the worst of what's coming is over."

"Richmond will be gone?" she asked, incredulously.

"It looks more and more likely."

"Even the sweets shop?" she said, crestfallen.

The general could only offer a grim smile. "I hope not, Medicine Girl. I hope not."

"Where will you go?" she asked again in a small voice, cinching the canvas bag tight. She threw it over her shoulder.

He sighed, looking up at the darkening sky. Night fell hard in the late winter afternoons.

"I don't know yet," he replied.

"You did like the goats," the Medicine Girl suggested.

"I did like the goats," he mused.

"I'm sure the Goatman could use some company. Every morning, you could find the eggs the chickens like to hide."

"I'll think about that," he promised. "One day, I hope looking for eggs is all I have to worry about. Now get in the pedal-car, young lady. There are blankets in the back to keep you warm."

The Medicine Girl started to get into the vehicle, as the attendants took their seats at the controls in the front. Quick as a fox, she turned to the general and threw her arms around him, catching him off guard.

"Goodbye, David Lee," she whispered, hugging him tight. "I will miss you my entire life."

"Farewell, Medicine Girl. I have never had a braver or more useful soldier. God bless your journey. I wish you and your mother peace in this troubled world."

With that, the general kissed the top of her head, leading her into the cab, tucking a thick cotton blanket around her, and securing the door.

From his pocket he pulled out another brown paper bag full of candies from the sweets shop. The Medicine Girl took the bag, opened it up, and popped colored rock candy into her mouth. As she pulled away, she waved and smiled at the general, calling out his full name.

Lieutenant General David Lee Chapman watched the two captains pedal the Medicine Girl down Broad Street, watching until he could no longer see them, standing in the street until the sun fully set.

Nothing would change here, she thought. She turned and followed the general out into the foyer of the Capitol Building.

Chapter 16

Shirley Plantation, Old Virginia

The attendants to the warlord in Colonial Williamsburg were the first ones to notice the stark change in Lincoln. Of course there were rumors, but as usual, they proved to be completely true. Lincoln, their stoic warlord, had fallen in love with another warlord's concubine. *One from the Florida Penal Colony.*

Lincoln had first met her at a gathering in Western Savannah in the Kingdom of Georgia. It was, of all things, a political meeting of like-minded warlords. All the heads of southern militia groups and regional warlords were in attendance; all voiced their disaffection and displeasure with the United Authority's way of doing things. From as far away as western Tennessee they came to discuss their concerns and plot out future strategies, the Memphis contingent proving especially adept at unifying the disparate group under a common goal.

"We will bring about the end of the United Authority's boot stamping on our face—forever. We will usher in the final battle of good and evil in this country. We will unite! We will join together as Armageddonists!" Xerxes had cried to a receptive crowd. His dutiful minion Darius jotted down notes from the proceedings, those who seemed amenable to their cause and, more importantly, those who did not.

"You feed off the United Authority's trough," spat the leader of the White Crosses. "Illuminati Pagans are MilitiaMen in name only! Federal swine!"

Voices clamored, as Xerxes fought to control the narrative.

"True, we serve the United Authority," Xerxes conceded. "But that is for now—a ruse to cover our growing strength. For our power steadily grows, gentlemen. Those who despise the United Authority and its endemic corruption are unifying under the Armaggedonists' banner. When we are strong—and when it is time, we will work together to end the United Authority for good, as it should have ended after the second Civil War—in defeat and ignominy and disgrace!"

Cheers sounded from the four corners of the room.

"And where will the new capital be—Memphis?" one man near the fire called out. Side chatter and muttering voices grew louder, the fractious group united as a bag of feral cats.

Lincoln said nothing, reserved as always. He was content in his realm, self-sufficient and independent. He'd come to meet with his peers only to understand the changing tides. Lincoln had his own plan and had cultivated his own alliances. He simply observed his compatriots, keeping abreast of the political landscape out of necessity. Lincoln ruled the Tidewater region well, regarded by most as a fair man who exiled his problematic citizenry instead of murdering them. A fair number of men and women worked in his fields just for that reason alone, devoted to him almost to a fault.

Lincoln observed the Warlord of Tallahassee, a brutish man with stupid pig eyes. The warlord had brought several of his Floridian women, faces painted thick in garish colors, half naked in their tropical attire. The Florida women fawned over him in feigned delight, eyes dead and smiles too wide.

Lincoln noticed one who stood apart, one with gray eyes and long black hair, wearing a simple muslin tunic, her feet shod in moccasins. This particular woman radiated intelligence. He watched her taking a moment to change the bandages of a serving boy. She cleaned his jagged wound on his shin and applied a layer of Neo on his abraded forearms before tearing off the bottom of her tunic for a makeshift bandage. Relief washed over the young boy's face. He voiced his thanks to her. She patted his shoulder and whispered something to make the boy laugh.

Lincoln remembered being a serving boy in a cruel household, having no one around who seemed to care for him when he was hurt or, more often, frightened and lonely. *Was there anyone who cared for this snaggle-toothed, pockmarked boy as she did? This was a boy who could be kicked or killed on a whim.* Lincoln watched as she used the remnants from a wine glass to clean his wounds, impressing Lincoln with her resourcefulness. In contrast to the garish others, he was moved by her kindness and unadorned beauty.

He decided at that moment to have the gray-eyed woman—not as his concubine—but as his wife. The only concern was negotiating a fair price with her current warlord.

As in all matters in which he was decided and resolute, Lincoln acted at once. Unarmed, he walked over to the Warlord of Tallahassee's entourage, waving off his own personal attendants. Unsettled, they watched Lincoln, ready to defend or protect him as needed.

Surely the Warlord of Tallahassee was a lout, an ox of a man with no refining graces or much to offer but brute force and poor leadership. After a brisk discussion, the Warlord of Tallahassee seemed more than willing to be rid of his least-favorite concubine.

For a modest fee, the Warlord of Tallahassee quipped, he would throw in her young daughter. He said this to hurt her mother, who hung her head in despair. But the Warlord of Tallahassee was not serious about the offer. He'd made other plans for the Medicine Girl.

When the Medicine Girl's mother first arrived in Colonial Williamsburg, Lincoln had his attendants show her to her own cottage, replete with a bathtub full of hot water, special soaps and ointments and lotions, a closet full of clothing, and a pantry full of delicacies. He instructed the kitchen to make a dozen different dishes for her arrival since he didn't know what she liked to eat. Restless, he bothered the cooks in the longhouse, coming in to see how preparations were going. The kitchen staff gave each other knowing looks; Lincoln never cared about these types of household matters before.

After surveying the lavish spread in her well-appointed quarters, the Medicine Girl's mother stepped outside, calling others to share in her good fortune. There was far too much food for her alone to eat. Curious older women and young children appeared from the narrow streets or from tending the small gardens. They shared the ham steaks and cold potato salad and sugar cookies. Soon, the Medicine Girl's mother was a fixture in the community, making friendships easily, helping where she could.

She would later learn that Lincoln had dismissed all of his concubines before her arrival. Like a young man in spring, he'd been heartsick from the moment he had first laid eyes on her at the warlord's assembly.

Lincoln had not slept well until she arrived safely from Florida. He was furious that she had been tied behind the transport wagon, her feet blistered and worn after walking the hundreds of miles. The Warlord of Tallahassee meant it as an insult, which Lincoln repaid by ordering her chaperones to be punished for their mistreatment of her. What remained of them afterwards was delivered to the penal colony in a small box.

Now that she was on his plantation, he could scarcely be in her presence.

Odd, his attendants thought, *that a man six colony-feet and five colony-inches tall, weighing close to three hundred colony-pounds could be felled by a single arrow from Cupid's quiver.* They whispered behind his back.

Lincoln knew they talked about him in this way, but he did not care. He avoided the Medicine Girl's mother for several weeks. The idea of talking with her distracted him so much that he stopped considering it. Instead, he busied himself running his plantation, working on a few lucrative projects, especially the one no one was permitted to speak of outside the Shirley Plantation.

At first, the Medicine Girl's mother awaited Lincoln in her appointed cottage, resigned to the fact that she had been purchased as a bride. The Warlord of Tallahassee made that crudely clear before she left.

After a day or two, she grew tired of waiting for an official greeting from her new warlord. Leaving the claustrophobic parlor, she freely walked the cobblestone streets, inspecting the grounds of the historic areas, greeting the families and attendants who labored in Lincoln's shops and fields. There was a blacksmith, a carpenter's guild, a cooper's building, and weaving looms, all in use. Decades prior, artisans demonstrated their skills for wide-eyed tourists. Now they served Lincoln and the people he protected.

After the wars, Lincoln and his men settled in Colonial Williamsburg, damaged from the wars yet mostly intact. It proved the perfect venue for a new world without the conveniences of the modern age, as it had been constructed in the 18th century and rebuilt in the 20th century with Rockerfeller money. The Tidewater area had proven to be safer than most. And although Lincoln was a stern warlord, he was effective and fair. The community thrived under his leadership, loyal and territorial.

Outsiders were rarely welcomed.

On her walks through the streets, the Medicine Girl's mother greeted workers and attendants, taking time to learn their names and remember whose children were whose. She pulled ticks off the boys who ran through the woods, helped deliver babies, offered comfort to the sick and relief to the dying.

Most welcome were the pain remedies she provided, treating infections with ointments she concocted from nearby greenery. Soon, she couldn't leave her cottage without assorted children running towards her, hugging her legs and showing her something they'd collected—a pretty stone, an old bottle cap, a bug. As was her nature, she took time to kneel down on their level, thoughtfully examining each treasure to the children's delight.

The Medicine Girl's mother taught the older children what to gather from the wetlands and fields, how to find a specific berry or leaf, and why the ingredient was needed for a tonic or tea. As Lincoln's people suffered less, the community began to trust her.

After several months, she returned to the old apothecary shop, where she preferred to live, carrying some prized meadow rue.

To her surprise, she found Lincoln sitting in the front room.

"Lincoln," she addressed him, nodding her head in deference. She was surprised at how tall he was, as she had only seen him from afar.

"Welcome to Colonial Williamsburg. I hope you are finding things to your liking," he greeted her, a small covered plate in his enormous hands. His large frame was perched on the edge of an overstuffed couch. "Cook made some extra pastries this afternoon. I thought you might like some," he paused, putting the plate on a small wooden table. The silence was heavy between them. "W—what name should I call you?"

"You may call me Medicine Woman," she replied.

"Do you have a given name?"

"I do," she answered.

He waited, expectantly.

"Will you tell me?" he asked.

"Will you build two more wells in town, one near the children's lodge and another by the old women's quarters?"

"Are you negotiating with me?"

"Do I have to negotiate with you?"

"Are you going to question me until you get what you want?"

"Are you going to improve the living conditions of your people, people who serve you and live under your protection?"

Rising to his full height, he put his hands on his hips, an imposing figure. He jutted out his chin, stubborn and petulant.

She, a fraction of his size, crossed her arms, attempting to repress a smile, but couldn't, not fully. His attempt at intimidation reminded her of a little boy flexing his skinny arms. Her smile turned into a snicker, the snicker turned into a full-throated chuckle.

"Are you laughing at me?" he asked, incredulous and a little hurt.

"Just a little," she confessed.

He offered her a shy grin.

"Are you going to build me two wells?" she repeated firmly, regaining her composure.

"I will build you *four* wells," he replied. "Anywhere you wish."

"Well, then," she said, hands on her hips. "My name is Mika."

Mika gave birth to Lincoln's child the following year, Lina, a chubby little girl with ebony skin, flawless like her father.

The three of them often took dinner outside, letting the baby roll on a thick quilt under a gentle sky. Lincoln and Mika marveled at her.

Mika's teenage daughter arrived in a pedal-car from Richmond, alongside two grim-faced United Authority captains who escorted her to Lincoln's office in the Governor's Palace.

After General Chapman's surprising letter, the Medicine Girl's arrival had been greatly anticipated.

The Medicine Girl felt her mother's presence before she saw her. As the captains talked with Lincoln, exchanging papers and words about the state of affairs in low tones, the Medicine Girl paced in front of his desk.

Two years without her. The last image she had of her mother was of being bound, pulled behind a wagon, cursed at by filthy men. She had been silent, mute with shock at seeing her beautiful mother in despair.

Would her own mother recognize her?

Hearing footfalls down the long corridor, she turned to see her mother rushing towards her, arms outstretched. The Medicine Girl did not wait, running to meet her midway.

Wordlessly, mother and daughter embraced, both weeping, clinging to each other, sinking to the floor. The two held each other, Mika rocking the Medicine Girl as if she were a young child, her lanky frame curling up on her lap.

Mika pulled back to look at her girl, two years gone, now grown into a young woman. The Medicine Girl had her gray eyes, darker, more somber than those in Tallahassee.

"Oh my love. You are well?" Mika asked, looking her over, feeling her daughter's arms, pulse, throat. She stroked her daughter's black hair.

The Medicine Girl did not respond, falling back into her mother's arms. Her mother kissed the top of her head. They held each other that way for a long time.

Lincoln broke from his meeting, briefly peering down the corridor, to witness the tender scene. Smiling to himself, he imagined being reunited with his Lina, his own baby girl that had too much of his heart.

Mika had been overjoyed with the news of her daughter in Old Virginia. Lincoln had worked closely with Chapman to give his wife her deepest desire.

He was pleased.

Returning to his business with the government, Lincoln moved the United Authority captains into the portico to finish discussing their multi-year joint project. It was coming to a close. The United Authority needed a strict timetable as to when the product would be ready for delivery.

The United Authority's need for Lincoln's product was becoming dire. Many of the generals had pinned their remaining hopes on his efforts.

Late in the spring, Mika was heavily pregnant, the birth of her third child yet a month away. Her two-year-old daughter slept in a restored antique crib in the same room as the Medicine Girl. The toddler often woke her up in the morning, ready to play much earlier than the sleepy-eyed teen.

"What does the baby feel like, Mika?" the Medicine Girl inquired, both of her hands on her mother's stomach. "It feels like a vat of eels to me."

"This baby wrestles with himself," her mother complained, calming down the outline of an errant elbow. "He cannot wait to make his arrival. He will come within the week, and you will help me deliver it."

The Medicine Girl beamed. She had attended many births with Mika over the months, gaining a wealth of knowledge with each one, successful or not.

"Was I as restless as this little brother?" the Medicine Girl wondered.

"Both you and Lina were as calm as the morning."

"Mika, why didn't you give me a name?" asked the Medicine Girl, sitting up in her bed. It was quite late when her mother returned from Lincoln's office at The Governor's Palace. He had been keeping later and later hours as United Authority men and dispatch runners made more frequent visits.

"The Warlord of Tallahassee decided your future husband would name you...like a dog," she added bitterly.

"Would you give me a name now?"

"Is it important to you that I do? At your age, you could name yourself." When her mother looked at her, the Medicine Girl's gray eyes were downcast. "Oh, I see that it is important to you," she remarked, holding her daughter as close as she could with her distended belly. "Let me think about a name for you, very carefully. I want you to have the perfect name. We will name both you and your brother at the same time."

This pleased the Medicine Girl, who snuggled into her cozy straw bed, the cotton-spun sheets fresh and crisp, dried in the April sun.

"Lincoln wants to take you with him to the Shirley Plantation tomorrow. He has something important to show you—something you can help him with."

"Do you know what it is?"

"I do," her mother teased. "And you will find out sooner if you go to sleep right now."

As usual, Lina's cooing and babbling awoke the Medicine Girl from a deep sleep. She rolled over and greeted her little sister, letting the toddler grasp her long fingers in her strong little fists.

"They are waiting for you!" her mother exclaimed, coming into the girls' room, thrusting a small woven bag into the Medicine Girl's hands. Lina heard her mother's voice and began to fuss. Mika reached into the crib to pick her up while calling out orders to the Medicine Girl. "Wash your face and clean your teeth. There is no time for breakfast. Dress in layers and remember the spring rains often cause flooding, so pack an extra pair of boots. Please hurry before Lincoln changes his mind. Oh, maybe you aren't responsible enough to do what he needs you to after all—"

Interrupting her packing, the Medicine Girl threw her mother a sharp look.

"I'm sorry," her mother apologized, rubbing her temples. "Your little brother decided to dance on my bladder all night. He will be a wildman, indeed," she decided, rubbing her stomach. She sat down on the edge of the Medicine Girl's bed. "I shouldn't have said those things to you. You can take care of yourself."

"I should have awoken earlier," the Medicine Girl replied. "And I should have packed last night. I'm sorry, too."

"It will be fine, my love," her mother gave her a hug, kissing her cheek. "Just hurry."

Lincoln's wagon was drawn by oxen, animals who moved steadily, but they were slow and ponderous. Forty men and a few women accompanied the wagon, pulling handcarts and pushing wheelbarrows full of supplies.

Traveling on the Five, the trip to the Shirley Plantation would take a day, the longest the Medicine Girl had ever spent in Lincoln's presence by herself. The two sat side-by-side behind the drivers, Lincoln telling the Medicine Girl all he knew about the Tidewater area, before and after the last wars.

"Now the Lower Virginia peninsula is relatively peaceful. The York and James Rivers are toxic...even before the bombing of the Air Force bases," Lincoln explained.

"I'm used to boiling water," the Medicine Girl replied. "It feels odd when I don't."

"I guess people can get used to anything," he mused. "In the fall, we will take Mika and the babies down near the place where Jamestown used to be. It's underwater now, the first white man's settlement, built almost five hundred years ago..."

The Medicine Girl quit listening. Adults seemed to get lost in the past, jabbering about things that couldn't be anymore. It didn't matter to her that they drove those rusty rectangular husks by the millions on the roadways and listened to music in wires stuck in their ears or asked a machine to make weather predictions. She could tell the weather by looking at the clouds. She could sing her own songs, but preferred the quiet, anyway. The wreckage of cars that still littered the sides of the highways looked ugly and pathetic in the overgrowth. She was grateful to be able to walk wherever she wanted, not be reliant on a metal box.

The past didn't seem any better. It just seemed past. The faraway look in adults' eyes whenever they spoke of the days before the end of electricity unnerved her. *What matter did any of those distant memories make? Now was now. Let the dead bury the dead.*

In an enthusiastic monotone, Lincoln spoke to her throughout the dozen colony-hours or so about endless things, as if he were teaching her to become her own warlord. He spoke of the best way to govern and handle uprisings, dropping names like John Locke and Thomas Hobbes. He used the term *Machiavellian* and explained how it was better to be feared than loved.

The Medicine Girl didn't want to interrupt him, but she knew Lincoln's people loved him far more than they feared him. His innate fairness and good nature had grown gentler and kinder after the arrival of Mika and the birth of Lina.

His enemies knew it, too.

As the wagon and following throng rounded the final bend to the entrance of the Shirley Plantation, the Medicine Girl noted that armed guards monitored the perimeter. They were stationed at watch towers. They held military grade weaponry.

"What crops are worth guarding this well?" she asked Lincoln.

"You'll see," he promised.

As they entered, the gates were secured behind them. As the handcarts full of supplies and other goods were offloaded into the store houses, the overseer strode over to update Lincoln of the goings on of the plantation since his previous visit.

"What is the count?" asked Lincoln.

"As of this morning? One thousand and forty-two."

Lincoln's eyes widened. "That many?"

"It's been a bountiful spring," the overseer remarked. A rickshaw-carriage had been prepared for them, pulled by two young men who stood abreast of each other. There was room for all three of them on the elongated seat. The overseer, Lincoln, and the Medicine Girl climbed in.

"Pay close attention, Medicine Girl," Lincoln instructed. "I will need your assistance with this project—one General Chapman has a keen interest in."

She ceased glancing around the main square and looked forward. In short order, the rickshaw pulled past the few bustling outbuildings and large gardens, dark soil mounded and seeded for the first crops of the season.

Around the bend, a wide expanse came into the Medicine Girl's view, a large verdant field, covered in tender grasses, sprouting through the rich soil, fertile with the spring rains.

Eating the sea of greens were horses as far as the Medicine Girl could see. Hundreds and hundreds of foals, mares, colts, fillies and stallions.

She began to laugh with unfettered glee.

She began to laugh with unfettered glee.

Chapter 17

Charles City, Old Virginia

Throughout the week, the Medicine Girl rarely left the fields, and then, only for a quick meal or an occasional change of clothing. Otherwise, she stayed with the horses from sunrise to sunset. Often, the Medicine Girl slept in the stables.

Lincoln often joked the horses smelled better than she did. If he needed to find her, the Medicine Girl was somewhere among the sprawling green where a thousand horses roamed. Tall wooden fences encased the colony-acreage, keeping the product out of view. An outer fence with slats covered in rows of double-stranded barbed wire, punctuated by guard towers, kept the product safe.

To the Medicine Girl, the animals were perfect from mane to tail, their beauty dazzling her as she acquired animal husbandry skills. She had named a few of the animals, giving them a sobriquet alluding to a certain physical feature. She named a brown and white pony *Patches*. Another was called *Bright Star,* for the distinctive white marking on its muzzle. *Midnight* was for a black mare and *Cloudy* for a gentle ivory colt. Each horse, she found, had a distinctive personality, unique peccadilloes, and, surprisingly, a keen sense of humor.

Unlike the debacle with the bicycle, the Medicine Girl took to riding horses. She had three favorite steeds, ones who seemed to know her well from the very start, becoming increasingly affectionate after she fed them special treats on her outstretched hand. The HorseMen marveled at her natural ability, as she used neither crop nor whip. Those who did earned her wrath and sharp tongue. The Medicine Girl could not abide anyone hitting one of *her* horses.

For the preceding five years, the United Authority cultivated HorseMen to maximize product breeding. The product flourished in Calgary, cultivated now for the United Authority's general purposes.

Lincoln was one of a few warlords profiting from the public-private contract, still classified as a top secret operation. Certainly, the horses would aid United Authority troop movements, if only to increase communication between outpost and command. There were just so many tattooed dispatch runners, bested by the slowest of horses.

Used primarily in the west, horses were now being farmed in several undisclosed locations in the south under strict military control. There were concerns about the project being discovered, but the generals believed, however, that most southern MilitiaMen would more likely eat a horse than master it.

At first, one of the HorseMen attempted to teach the Medicine Girl to ride sidesaddle, but she complained and importuned Lincoln to let her ride properly. Lincoln could deny her nothing and ordered the HorseMen to let her ride as she wished. *It was bad enough that his stepdaughter walked among the men*, some of the HorseMen groused. *Now she rode like a man, too.*

After helping her learn how to groom the animals, the HorseMen showed the Medicine Girl how to disseminate sweet hay, how to take care of the paddock, how to collect droppings from the main areas for fertilizer, and how to dig up ragwort and other poisonous plants that the horses might unintentionally eat.

One of the HorseMen whistled for the horses using his fingers, startling her.

"How did you make that noise?" she asked, inquisitively.

"I'll show you," the man walked over to her. "First, use your index and middle fingers to make an A-shape…cover your teeth with your lips. Curl your tongue back. Then blow."

It took her a few times, but soon the Medicine Girl had the loudest whistle in the paddock, proving an effective way to call over her favorite horse for a treat.

After a few days, the Medicine Girl took to wearing a broad-brimmed hat, one left behind in the stables by a United Authority HorseMan.

Lincoln watched her from the main gate. *The hat suited her.*

The spring evening was warmer than most, and Lincoln and several of his attendants took their suppers and ate at tables with the other HorseMen. Great pots of seasoned beans and slabs of cornbread were laid out, dripping with rich butter from Lincoln's dairy in Colonial Williamsburg. The Medicine Girl helped herself to extra field greens, putting several oatmeal cakes into the pocket of her trousers for later.

"The HorseMen say you show great promise," remarked Lincoln, between mouthfuls. "You seem to have natural equestrian talents."

"The HorseMen aren't half bad either," the Medicine Girl replied, adding an impish grin.

"Would you like to stay here a few days longer?" Lincoln asked. "A couple of the mares are expecting foals any moment now."

"Could we stay?"

"We could," he teased, watching her frown. "But maybe it's lonely here for you. We could send for Mika and Lina…?"

"Yes! I would like that very much!" The Medicine Girl nodded, clapping her hands.

She imagined Lina's eyes growing wide at the sight of the horses. *Their beauty defied description*, she thought. Even if Lina were old enough to comprehend, what could the Medicine Girl compare the horses to? *Large beautiful dogs?* Lina was still so little that most of life's everyday wonders were dazzling. *And a little brother would be the biggest wonder of all*, the Medicine Girl smiled to herself.

"We were scheduled to return home on Sunday," Lincoln reminded the Medicine Girl. "But I'm sure Mika has already anticipated our delay. She knows how you are."

"Mika could have her lying-in here," the Medicine Girl suggested. "We could all stay here until the baby is born."

Lincoln looked out across the bucolic fields, away from the hectic heart of Colonial Williamsburg. He trusted men to run things there for a little while. It would be good to have his family together, before the United Authority planned to take delivery of the product before colony-months' end.

There would be other herds, but this first group had proved especially satisfying to foster. Lincoln felt a strong yearning to share this moment with Mika.

"I like the sound of that," he nodded. "I'll send dispatch runners tonight to ask Mika and Lina to join us."

"What if she doesn't want to come?" the Medicine Girl pouted.

"Then you and I will return to Colonial Williamsburg as planned," Lincoln stated, noticing the Medicine Girl rolling her eyes. He frowned at her. "Mika is the mother of my children, Medicine Girl. I'll go where she is."

"Fine," the Medicine Girl agreed, but secretly hoped her mother was curious enough about the horses to come and see for herself.

Dispatch runners ran in pairs, as sometimes they ran themselves to death. Cardiac arrest struck them like lightning—the heart can only take so much. The microtears from running were not the only stressors on their hearts. The messages they carried had their own heavy burdens.

The runner who arrived just before dawn on Monday morning was drenched in sweat, his breathing labored, his eyes red and bloodshot. Alarmed that he arrived alone, the guards at the Shirley Plantation carried him into the compound, laying him down on the packed earth, just outside the main sleeping quarters.

The Medicine Girl heard the commotion in the yard, just outside her window. She rolled over in her comfortable bunk, used to the dogs' barking and the attendants' footfalls. Due to the product's worth, Lincoln and his closest advisors were protected around the clock by a heavier guard than in Colonial Williamsburg.

When the Medicine Girl heard Lincoln's voice in the foyer, she sat up, wrapping herself in a flannel sheet, making her way to the door.

She listened to the strange voices, speaking low and quick. When the men followed Lincoln out into the receiving area, the Medicine Girl padded behind them, hoping for a word or a glance from Lincoln.

The men encircled a thin, emaciated figure, lying supine on the ground. The Medicine Girl made her way to the front, covering the shivering man with the sheet. All stood in silence in the cool spring air, waiting for the man to catch his breath.

"Lincoln," the dispatch runner gasped. "Lincoln," he repeated over again. His breath came hard. "Now. Now." There was little life in the man, his feet bleeding and raw.

The Medicine Girl continued to attend to the man, ascertaining what his major ailments were. She felt the man's heartbeat and pulse, both rapid and erratic.

His eyes were wild.

"Lincoln—" the man whispered.

"I am here," Lincoln said, standing over the tattooed man.

"S-send the others away. What I have to say is for you only," the man muttered in labored, ragged breaths. "Lincoln…"

"Leave us," Lincoln ordered his attendants to stand away. The Medicine Girl did not move from Lincoln's side.

Lincoln kneeled down beside the man, as the others dissipated, standing apart. He spoke to the runner in a quiet voice, ordering him to continue.

"Lincoln," the dispatch runner murmured, putting a thin hand on Lincoln's forearm. "The Illuminati Pagans were in Williamsburg."

"Impossible!" Lincoln barked. "They are too far west. Why would they come?"

No response.

Lincoln wanted to shake the man, slap him, make him take back his words.

The dispatch runner opened his eyes, looking pained when his vision focused on Lincoln's face. He suffered from the news he carried, not his own dying body.

"It was a raid."

"Surely they were stopped!" Lincoln yelled. "We have garrisons at every point. We have scouts. We have—"

"We have been betrayed," the dispatch runner whispered with his remaining strength, half arising, placing a hand on Lincoln's chest. He faded back to the earth, his few remaining breaths ugly rasps.

The Medicine Girl's eyes shut, tears streaming down her face. She did not make a sound.

"Do not die until you tell me all," Lincoln grabbed the man by his shoulders. Through gritted teeth, Lincoln demanded the dispatch runner to tell him everything.

"The Pagans wanted the horses."

"Their own scouts should have known they weren't there—"

"They tortured your attendants for the location. One by one. For the location," he spoke in a hesitant voice, now a faint whisper.

"Did they talk—"

The dispatch runner shook his head, attempting to gain enough strength to continue. "No one said a word. No one confessed anything... not even Mika," the dispatch runner's voice cracked.

Lincoln stood up. His breathing was erratic, hands shaking. "Tell me Mika lives. Do not lie to me. Tell me Mika and my children still live."

The dispatch runner shook his head, too weak to verbally respond.

Lincoln's head rocked back. He fell to his knees, grasping his hands together. He gave one long anguished cry, silencing every man and woman on the plantation.

The Medicine Girl collapsed where she stood, curling up, weakened, overcome by loss.

Several horses standing along the fence sensed something amiss. They whinnied, breaking into a run to the main fields as the sun's first light came over the horizon.

Without another sound, Lincoln took one last look at the dispatch runner and the Medicine Girl, both splayed on the ground. *How much she resembles Mika*, he thought.

He knew he would have to send the Medicine Girl away. Mika's death already threatened to undo him, and he knew very well what happened to weak warlords.

Lincoln walked away from the two prostate forms, towards the cadre of his personal attendants.

There were plans to be made.

A day later, the Medicine Girl awoke from a dark restless pit. Her dreams were dark, claustrophobic, terrifying. She felt more exhausted than she'd ever felt before, her mind and body aching to return back to the night.

Someone had laid her back in her bunk. *She must have fainted after the dispatch runner had said...after he had said...* She couldn't complete the thought. Instead, she put the dark memory in the furthest recesses of her mind. She would think about her mother and Lina and her baby brother later.

For now? Her lips were parched, her eyes gritty. A plastic tumbler of water, a sliced green apple, dried meats, and a large wedge of cheese on a covered plate had been set out for her on a small table.

She forced herself to eat, although nothing had any taste. The food felt like stones in her belly.

I will go to my mother.

She stood up and scanned the room for something she could take with her. She wrapped the remaining food and placed it in her jacket pocket. She would walk through the kitchen and lift several knives and a flint.

The beauty of the spring day was lost on a girl running by herself at a rapid pace down the Five. Small streams now were enlarged with the spring rains, renewing the countryside with blue wildflowers and yellow daffodils. Animals emerged from burrows, anxious to provide for their offspring while hawks eyed them overhead.

The Medicine Girl kept off the main roads, her eyes peeled for MilitiaMen. She wanted a man to kill with her own hands.

The dispatch runner had said...he had said...

She was tormented, now running as fast as she could towards Colonial

Williamsburg. She ran to her mother and sister and the baby brother she would never meet. The Medicine Girl ran to make her mother proud, using the skills that she had taught her. She ran harder because Lina would love the horses, her big dark eyes would light up with wonder!

The dispatch runner had said...he had said...

She was weeping as her pace slowed. Her heart hammered in her chest. Her mouth was full of coppery spit.

Her mother was going to give her a name—the same time when she named her little brother. Lincoln would take her back to the horse plantation, and she would learn how to run the entire operation, besting the HorseMen with her skills. She was such a quick learner! Her mother had to tell her things once and she remembered them. Nettle fibers made natural cordage. Use a charcoal slurry for stomach ailments. Find jewelweed to cure skin rashes.

Rivulets streamed from her face in the midday sun. Blinded by an ocean of tears, she choked, breathing hard, her vision tunneling, her heart racing.

The dispatch runner had said...he had said...

"My mother is dead!" she cried aloud as she passed an ancient sawtooth oak, tall and majestic, its verdant leaves bursting forth, creating a dappled canopy.

She stopped and considered the tree, wandering closer to it, pressing her face against its rough bark.

I cannot go any further, she realized, feeling the tree with both hands. She slunk to the ground, ignoring the bark's abrasions to her face. She curled up against the oak, covering her head with both arms.

There she wept for hours unabated, until she weakened, falling into a dreamless sleep.

Bleary eyed, she touched her own face, blood clotted where she had raked it against the tree.

Chapter 18

Four Colony-Mile Creek Park, Old Virginia

"Wake up, Medicine Girl," a meaty hand shook her shoulder. Bleary eyed, she touched her own face, blood clotted where she had raked it against the tree. Her head throbbed. Her empty stomach growled, adding to the nausea she felt when she sat up.

It was very dark and she was cold, having laid on her side in the mud. The stars were hidden; dense dark clouds threatened rain. A low rumbling of thunder sounded far off in the distance.

"We're here to take you home," a voice said. She didn't recognize the voice. Too apathetic to care, she nodded and let them help her stand.

Kill me, she thought. *How much easier would it be to die?*

"I need to get to Colonial Williamsburg," she mumbled. "My mother is there—"

"Colonial Williamsburg is no more. It has been razed to the ground."

"No! No! You are wrong. My sister Lina is coming to see the horses," she tried to explain. "I need to get her."

The two men stood in silence watching the teenage girl talk wildly, frantically, refusing to accept the reality of things. She looked at them, desperately trying to get them to understand.

"Come with us, Medicine Girl," one of the men said as tenderly as he could. "Climb into the wagon. Here are some warm blankets. The cook packed your favorites…"

"I'm not hungry," she said. She couldn't imagine ever wanting to eat again.

One of the men shrugged, then unceremoniously hoisted the Medicine Girl into the back, meeting with little resistance. She collapsed like a sack of potatoes.

As the men repositioned themselves to pull the cart, she wrapped herself in a blanket, pulling it over her feverish head, lying supine under a pitch black sky.

Mika. Lina. Catalina.

The men's plodding footsteps jostled the wagon, lulling the Medicine Girl into a wretched trance, then a sleep, though an unsettled and troubled one.

"Is she well enough to speak with me?" Lincoln asked the female attendant, the one who had bathed and dressed the Medicine Girl upon her return.

The attendant had washed the Medicine Girl's wounds and treated her blistered feet with Neo, using small dabs from the last of the yellow tubes on the Shirley Plantation. *Antibiotic ointments were becoming impossible to get, even off the black market.*

"She is much better now. Her fever has broken," the attendant answered. "She is eating a little more."

"Send her to me when she is ready," Lincoln ordered. The attendant nodded and left him to his own thoughts.

Alone in the small office, Lincoln's demeanor crumbled. He put his head in his hands, allowing himself a few moments to feel profound loss.

Mika.

He allowed himself to weep for a while, but if he lost himself in his grief for her, then hundreds more would die. *The Medicine Girl would die.* He steeled himself, cauterizing the secret places in his heart.

There would be a time for retribution.

Since the news of Colonial Williamsburg, the United Authority's HorseMen sensed a fundamental change in him. Lincoln's eyes narrowed, his tone grew sharp, his commands more succinct and brutal.

He sent dispatch runners to Richmond regarding the status of the horses, asking for more attendants and guards. He needed a directive on the status of the product delivery, as every day he felt targeted, wolves circling.

He sent dispatch runners to the leader of the White Crosses in the Kingdom of Georgia, too. Those particular messages were coded and sealed. Should Lincoln's missives be discovered, they would bring him a slow painful death.

In truth, he despised working with militias, all about as trustworthy as snakes in a garden. And now it seemed they were turning on themselves.

It was no secret the White Crosses despised the Illuminati Pagans the most, seeing them as degenerate atheists, wrapping themselves in the Armageddonists' flag for financial gain. However, the Pagans were ready to die for their nebulous cause. Their end goal was to amass power. Keeping it seemed to be their raison d'être. In ruthlessly doing so, they had earned a reputation of maintaining it by any means necessary.

Occasionally, Lincoln gazed out of the small office's window onto the horse fields. The guards now monitored the perimeter in double shifts, as spies for the Pagans were being caught by the handfuls. It was foolish to think there weren't more. It was also foolish to think they'd extracted any quality intelligence from the Pagan spies by flaying them. Torture seldom elicited useful information.

But Lincoln needed to hear the Pagan's screams, the men he held responsible for his wife and children's deaths. He stayed and watched the entire process, a skilled KnifeMan artfully making all the necessary incisions needed to peel off a man's skin in one clean pull.

"Lincoln?" a voice asked. Everyone tread lightly around him these days, as his temper flared white hot at intermittent intervals.

"What," he snapped, being brought back to his untenable situation. *The papers on his desk were hopeless. He could not think of how to resolve any of the plantation's problems.*

"Dispatch runners from Richmond are here."

"Send them in," Lincoln muttered, weary of hearing what any dispatch runner had to say.

A thin, gangly man walked in, clasping a plastic container from which he downed great gulps of water. Sweat poured down his face and back.

"Is your communication oral or written?"

"Oral, sir," replied the dispatch runner, upending the water container.

"The codeword is Lina."

"Thank you, sir. The United Authority has received your dispatch about the raid on Colonial Williamsburg. United Authority troops will be repositioned to complete a civil-oriented reconnaissance assessment. The United Authority sends its condolences to you for the loss of your family."

"Where are the Pagans?" Lincoln asked evenly.

"Unknown at the present. The Carolingians have been alerted to give no quarter to the Illuminati Pagans. It is thought they are headed west to Knoxville."

"Knoxville?"

"Darius now leads the Western Armageddonists, repositioning his militias and factions from Memphis. He is moving the Family Trading Stations and Comfort Stations to the Carolina border as well. They've begun making offensive strikes from defensive positions in the Blue Ridge. The mountainous terrain has made it hard to detect the Armageddonists movements."

"Has there been an official split?"

"Recent intel believes so, with the White Crosses reconvening in Atlanta. As it stands, there is a détente among the factions until Richmond is burned. The militias will stand together until the United Authority is toppled, then they'll fight over the scraps."

Lincoln rubbed his head with both of his palms. *Wars and rumors of wars.*

He looked out again to the peaceful horse paddocks. The animals whinnied and trotted in the sun, helping themselves to mounds of oats, nuzzling one another in greeting.

How simple life could be, he thought wistfully.

The Medicine Girl looked at the bowl of warm oatmeal mixed with crushed walnuts and dried fruit. Honey had been poured on top to entice her to eat.

Instead, she lay back down and closed her eyes.

Finish your breakfast. Wash your face. Lincoln would like to see you this morning, the female attendant informed her.

The Medicine Girl didn't even know the attendant's name and had never seen her before the raid. Now this woman acted like her mother, minus any of Mika's grace and easy charm. She pretended to care for the Medicine Girl without caring for her at all.

The loss of her mother created an emptiness even greater than when she had buried Catalina. Leaving Tallahassee, the Medicine Girl had hoped that she would find her mother. Now, there was nothing left to hope for. She felt as hollow as a cicada shell.

And now Lincoln wanted to see her.

What would she even say to this stepfather?

It had been a privilege for Mika not to be just a common law consort or worse, a concubine, to him. Lincoln had married Mika, and her mother seemed to love him. They had been a real family, if only for a little while.

That's what you get in this world for hoping beyond the end of the day, she concluded. She vowed never to forget that. Believing in anything more than seeing the day's end was foolish. *Hope was dangerous.*

Bitter tears welled up in her swollen eyes. The oatmeal was now cold and congealed. *Strength*, she thought. *She would need her full strength and faculties.* She reluctantly spooned the porridge into her mouth, feeling like she would gag on every pasty bite.

In a sudden fit, she threw the bowl against the wall, shattering, oatmeal splattered across the floor.

A waste. A waste of food.

She felt guilty, then a surge of anger flared up into a rage. Looking left and looking right for an escape route from the claustrophobic room, she felt the walls closing in around her. Perspiration dripped from her armpits; her heart pounded in her chest as if she'd run all the way from Richmond.

Above all, Medicine Girl, be patient.

She breathed, slowly in and slowly out, as her mother had shown her. She wrested control of herself. She threw herself facedown on the thin mattress, covering her head with a blanket, blocking out the light.

Mika, I am lost, she whispered. *Where are you?*

In time, the Medicine Girl's sobbing ceased. A quiet calm washed over her. It was not a feeling of peace, but something far more useful. *Clarity.*

She had recalled her mother's favorite question: *What can you do now to alleviate suffering?*

The Medicine Girl bitterly laughed. She didn't want to *alleviate* suffering. She wanted to *cause* suffering—a lot of it. Decided and full of purpose, she pushed away the last of her breakfast. She rifled through a basket of clothing, finding a pair of baggy trousers and a long-sleeved shirt.

Surely Lincoln wouldn't let the deaths of his wife and children go unavenged. He would need her, as she could do things he couldn't.

And she would gladly find whomever was behind the Colonial Williamsburg raid and vivisect their own children in front of them.

"Send her in."

The Medicine Girl walked into Lincoln's office near the horse paddock with her face devoid of emotion. She stood before him, on the other side of a small table. The table was stacked with papers that Lincoln had been reading in a vain attempt to make order out of chaos.

When Lincoln looked up to see her approach, he again was struck at how much she resembled her mother. He leaned back in his wooden chair.

"Are you well?"

"I am," she said, eyes level with his.

He paused before responding. "We are moving the horses in a few days. I will need your help."

"What do you need my help with?"

"The United Authority needs the horses positioned just outside of Richmond, say a colony-dozen miles southeast. They have built a compound specifically for the horses in Four Colony-Mile Creek Park. Between our men and the United Authority's HorseMen, we will need a few more for the drive."

"And?"

"And, if you are ready, I'll need you to drive a thousand heads with the team. I've seen you in the paddocks. You are very good with them."

"Is there a water source on the property?"

"There is," Lincoln replied. "The United Authority is preparing a holding pen as we speak. Other horse proprietors are bringing their product in as well."

"Is the military using horses for defense or offense?"

"The military is taking possession of the product in preparation for war. What they decide to do with them is up to the generals."

"You mean the military is preparing for the MilitiaMen's siege on Richmond."

He looked at her with renewed respect and a little caution. *How much has this child overheard?*

"I have no knowledge of what they've planned, but I need to deliver the product," he stated firmly. "I am a man of my word and we have been paid for our services. Can I count on you to bring the horses to Richmond or not?"

"No," the Medicine Girl said, with a gravitas that made her seem Lincoln's equal. *General Chapman had warned her about returning to Richmond.*

"No? Explain."

"I mean *no*—do not take all of the horses to Richmond. The ones that you bring will be seized by MilitiaMen or slaughtered for food by starving men surrounding Richmond."

"Where have you heard—"

"The United Authority has very few days in power." She crossed her arms, giving him a withering look. *Try to deny it*, she seemed to say.

"Where are you getting your information from?"

"You and I both know the kitchen attendants and plantation's wives traffic in gossip—information that is far more accurate than all of those dead papers on your desk."

Lincoln leaned forward. "What do you suggest?"

"Gather all your trusted men who escaped the Williamsburg raid. Have them take half of the horses to the White Crosses."

"Are you out of your mind?" Lincoln was shocked.

"No, I pay attention. It's your only move."

"Explain."

"The White Crosses are pushing north out of the Kingdom of Georgia. They will have to confront the Illuminati Pagans, who grow in number with each passing day."

Lincoln wondered if she had read his dispatch, then shook his head. *Impossible.* "Let me ask you this: where is the best place to position the horses to help the White Crosses fight the Pagans? Raleigh? Charlotte?"

"Not the Carolinas. Those people will be in perpetual warfare until the last Carolingian is dead."

"Show me on this map," Lincoln said, unfurling a hand drawn map on yellow vellum. "Here is Knoxville. Here is Richmond. And we are... here." He pointed with a long forefinger.

The Medicine Girl peered at the different towns and cities.

"So, little general," Lincoln teased her. "Where do we position five hundred horses for battle?"

"Abingdon."

"Show me where."

"Near the Old Virginia-Tennessee-Carolina border. I've seen it off of the Eight One. There's plenty of spring-fed streams and endless fields for grazing. Not many locals. Area seems all but abandoned."

Lincoln leaned back again, considering her suggestion.

"I'll send the HorseMen to Richmond with what I will call 'the first installment,' explaining how we are sending the product in increments for protection of the United Authority's assets. This is more truthful than fabrication. It's a good plan."

"We could stage a false raid," the Medicine Girl added. "That way, you might avoid getting crucified if this goes awry."

He gave her a small smile. "I'll need to send some messages out," he said, dismissively. She turned to leave.

"Oh, Medicine Girl?"

"Yes, Lincoln."

"Get some rest. It's going to be a challenging week—for the both of us."

"You, too, Lincoln," she said, walking out of the small room, without once turning around.

The Four Colony-Mile Creek Park was nothing more than a shoddy campsite surrounded with double loops of razor wire, less than a dozen colony-miles from the Shirley Plantation.

Lincoln and the Medicine Girl turned over the first installment of the product—200 horses—to some very nervous United Authority HorseMen and their cautious attendants. No one higher than a sergeant was at the site, a curious state of affairs that put Lincoln on edge. *Where was the leadership?*

Per their agreement, Lincoln planned to return in two days with another 200 horses; however, the quartermaster and Lincoln had a difference of opinion on the delivery timetable.

"It's imperative we have all the horses—now!" screamed the man, sweating profusely, looking unkempt and distracted.

"I have an arrangement with one of your generals, sir. Perhaps you would like to take it up with him?"

"I would, but he's most likely dead," the quartermaster shot back.

The Medicine Girl waited outside the canvas tent while the two men berated one another.

Lincoln stormed out of the tent, motioning his men to fall in behind him. They rode the few hours back to the Shirley Plantation, saying very little.

Lincoln rode his steed, holding the reins far too tightly. The Medicine Girl chastised him, but he had yet to become as comfortable with the animals as she was.

She had selected Patches to ride back, the horse with a temperament most suitable to her own. She clung to his neck, feeling his healing warmth in her arms. His smooth canter lulled her into a peaceful reverie.

Just before the second installment of 200 horses was prepared for transport, dispatch runners arrived at the Shirley Plantation. One had a filthy bandage wrapped around his head, keeping his fractured eye socket from losing the bloodshot orb. Speaking was becoming increasingly difficult for him. His partner was in worse shape.

One of the dispatch runners was shown into Lincoln's office.

"Is your communication oral or written?"

"Oral, sir," replied the dispatch runner, holding himself upright by leaning on a chair.

"The codeword is Medicine Girl."

"Thank you, sir," the dispatch runner mechanically replied. "I regret to inform you that Richmond has fallen."

Occasionally, Lincoln gazed out of the small office's window onto the horse fields.

Chapter 19

Henrico County, Old Virginia

"I am going," the Medicine Girl decided, her arms hanging loose by her sides, her chin jutting out. She'd already packed a small canvas bag with the essentials, including a flint steel.

"You are not going to Richmond," Lincoln replied, an edge to his voice that would have given anyone else pause. "You are needed here. We are preparing for the southwest move. Now that the HorseMen have gone, I'll need you to train the White Crosses. None of those men have ever seen a horse!"

"I'll be back in time to take care of everything."

"You'll be back in pieces. The final dispatches coming out of Richmond are unspeakable, Medicine Girl. Assuming the White Crosses coming from Richmond don't get delayed by the spring floods, they'll be here late tomorrow."

"White Crosses were in Richmond?"

"All the militias were in Richmond. Everything is up for grabs," he muttered. "Allegiances and alliances are off."

She grit her teeth together until her jaw ached. *She needed to get to Chapman.*

"I need you to help organize the drive to Abingdon. Our advance parties are setting up now. We need to leave. This place is no longer safe."

"Is any place safe?" the Medicine Girl wondered aloud.

Lincoln stood and put a large hand on her quivering shoulder. "Yes. There are safer places. But being this close to Richmond isn't one of them. Splinter groups will raid us in days. We have to go. There isn't any time for your side business."

She bristled at his flippant remark. "Chapman isn't *side business*. I'm getting him out of Richmond. I will bring him here. He will be useful to us." She turned to leave, slinging the bag over her shoulder.

"Chapman is most likely captured or dead. If he's captured, he'll soon wish he were dead. The Pagans are fond of making examples out of the brass. You'll find him gibbeted, hanging in some iron cage alongside the Two Nine Five."

"How are you so sure he's captured?"

"How are you so sure he's alive?" Lincoln countered. "He's an old man no longer in service to the United Authority. He resigned before you arrived in Colonial Williamsburg, before Mika—" He paused, closing his eyes. He inhaled sharply. "He resigned before you reunited with your mother. For all you know the general is tending goats in Witt with that priest you kept talking about."

"The Goatman of Witt," she corrected him. "The Goatman would be useful to you in Abingdon. He's smart and resourceful and—"

"Medicine Girl," Lincoln said, rubbing his eyes. "Old men want to be useful to a point. Then they just want to be left alone."

"And what do old women want?"

"From what I can tell, old women just want other old women to complain to."

"That's not funny," she muttered.

"It wasn't meant to be. Now put your things down. You aren't going anywhere."

"I'll be back before the White Crosses arrive. And I'm taking Patches."

"The White Crosses may have your general in chains," Lincoln warned. "Or his head on a pike. What will you do then?"

"I will eat their hearts," the Medicine Girl replied without hesitation. She gave him an icy grin, raising her eyebrow as if daring Lincoln to challenge her.

He shook his head and sat back down at the small desk, defeated by her petulance, watching her leave without another word.

After the FerryMen helped her cross the James River, Patches trotted the few hours up the Nine Five to the outskirts of Richmond without faltering. Patches was becoming her most trusted ally, a solid horse she was beginning to cherish like a sibling.

As she rode closer to Richmond, she smelled the acrid smoke burning from different sections of the city. The stretch of highway she was on was empty, unusual for that time of day. She kept to the edge of the road, ready to gallop off into the brush at a moment's notice.

I should have left at night, she thought, criticizing her foolishness. Mika had called her stubborn—said it would be the end of her. It seemed more than possible this fool's errand would be her last act of defiance— *but against whom? God? Lincoln? Herself?*

She felt she had no choice, led on by forces greater than herself. *She had to get to General Chapman.*

At the intersection of the Nine Five and the Eight Nine Five, she saw a United Authority checkpoint. She fumbled into her canvas bag for the general's universal pass, as if that still stood for something.

The Medicine Girl failed to see any attendants at the gate. A Family Trading Station loomed behind the main checkpoint building, its smashed front doors ajar.

It appeared vacant.

Curious, she dismounted, walking Patches at his left shoulder, her right hand holding the folded lead. She scanned the area for any movement, any sign of life.

She glimpsed inside the unguarded checkpoint building, now a mess of cracked plexiglass and sodden papers. A small fire had been set. With nothing worth confiscating, she continued her exploration of the Family Trading Station, its structure a retrofitted cinder block hotel with chains affixed to the walls. She couldn't be certain, but hair and teeth seemed to cover various parts of the filthy floor.

The smell was intolerable.

She entered the lobby, Patches close at hand, whinnying on occasion to protest the stench. The Medicine Girl rubbed his neck to soothe him in the strange place with too many disturbing smells amid the heavy silence.

As the Medicine Girl's eyes adjusted to the gloom, she saw a young man in a sodden military jacket, its purple trim hanging loose from numerous tears in the once white wool. The youth held a rifle as if protecting the desperate people behind him.

In truth, Jasper had been left behind to guard the checkpoint, his militia captain knowing he would be an impediment to their directive in taking down the United Authority. *One-legged soldiers were not useful in battle, no matter how brave they were.*

"I am PFC Jasper Crimson-Atlanta, service number 9380577. State your name and your business." The small group behind the young man cowered.

The Medicine Girl came into full view and stared at him, hands on her hips. She noted his missing leg, his war-weary face, his bowed back. His crutches were far too short for his tall lanky frame. The people behind him looked worse off than he, if that were possible.

"State your name and your business," Jasper shouted, "or I'll shoot you where you stand." His lips were dry and cracked.

She walked over to the emaciated boy and plucked the rifle out of his hands. She moved the bolt handle up and to the rear, cycling through the chambers to kick out empty casings.

"You've been out of ammunition for days," she said.

"Tell me who you are," Jasper repeated.

"I am the Medicine Girl. You're alive because I removed your gangrenous leg when you lay near death on a scrapping field in the Kingdom of Georgia," she replied with little emotion. "Who are these people you guard?"

"You are the girl—"

"I am," she said. "Who are these people?"

"They are Nonessentials. I am to keep them—"

"You are to keep no one," the Medicine Girl interrupted. "The United Authority has ceased to exist. I cannot imagine every checkpoint or Family Trading Station or Comfort Station hasn't been abandoned at this point."

"I am to stay here until the White Crosses return," he stated, straightening, attempting to rise up to his full height.

"The White Crosses are heading south and west without you," she said. "Richmond burns."

"And I helped burn it," Jasper bragged.

The Medicine Girl walked over to him and stood inches from his face.

"Tell me, Jasper Crimson-Atlanta, burner of capitals...where are the United Authority's generals?"

Jasper sealed his lips together.

A middle aged man with an eye infection called out to her from behind Jasper's back. "The brass were taken to the chopping blocks after they hanged each senator," he reported. "One by one. All senators and generals are dead. All of them that could be found. Their bodies feed the fish in the James River!"

"Not all are dead," she said.

"Any United Authority military leader in the Capitol Building is safely dead. Summary executions," another man confirmed.

"By whose authority?" the Medicine Girl asked.

"The Armageddonists," Jasper muttered.

"And where are they now, Jasper? Who is the leader of our country now? What have your anarchists brought to this land, besides more chaos and bloodshed?" She spat.

His eyes wouldn't meet hers. Jasper staggered on his one leg, folded up onto the floor, overcome with exhaustion.

"We are starving," complained a middle aged man, eyeing the horse. *They'd almost forgotten the taste of fresh meat.* "Do you have anything to eat? Hardtack? Crackers? Jerky?"

The Medicine Girl grew silent, stroking Patches' long nose. The horse nuzzled her.

"How many of you are there?" she asked.

"Eighteen. But there are women left in the Comfort Station nearby. They've barricaded themselves in. A dozen or so. My sister—"

"You have fifteen colony-minutes. Gather who and what you can. Have the temporary wives and their attendants bring anything useful— anything of value. Do not bring me MilitiaMen. Do not bring me soldiers. If you see any of the United Authority generals, you will bring them to me."

"How about dispatch runners?"

"Of course," the Medicine Girl agreed. "Any civilians you see, bring them as well. But we leave very soon. There is no time."

"Where are we going?" a man asked, a shred of hope wavering in his voice.

"Ten miles away. There's a place with plenty of food. Meat Oats. Water. Wild berries. A place where I will show you how to ride a horse. A place that is better than this horror," she replied, looking around the barren space. "This is a bad place."

"What if we see soldiers or MilitiaMen?" a thin voice asked.

"Kill them," she replied.

"And you will kill me, too, Medicine Girl?" asked Jasper, blank-eyed, mildly interested in her response.

She leaned down to his level. "If I wanted you dead, Jasper Crimson-Atlanta, you'd have already been buried with both of your legs missing."

Thirty-seven of us, the Medicine Girl counted, standing outside the checkpoint, preparing to cross the Chippenham Bridge. The Comfort Station women were overburdened with anything they could carry, but they brought precious little food and fewer water bottles.

Jasper negotiated and reasoned with the individual parties to share what little they had. The Medicine Girl watched the boy graciously thanking those who shared and reminding them how generous others had been.

Within a few minutes, Jasper had diplomatically coalesced the ragtag group of misfits into a fairly cohesive whole, one infused with the spirit of goodwill. *Perhaps they are tired of being afraid*, the Medicine Girl mused.

She watched as the young walked side by side with the old, the healthy helping the ill.

As with most empires, the United Authority's collapse came faster than anyone was prepared for.

The Medicine Girl knew that Jasper's group was well aware of the power vacuum left in the United Authority's wake, now filled with competing forces who were turning on each other. Loyalties dissolved. Order vanished. All this tiny group had were each other.

"Jasper, get on this horse."

"No," he said stubbornly. "I'll walk like a man."

"Get on the horse."

"You get on the horse," he shot back.

"For whatever reason, Jasper, you seem to have an air of authority over these people," the Medicine Girl whispered low to him. "We need to get out of here. You need to lead them. Get on this horse or I will slit your throat and bathe in your blood."

"Say please," Jasper replied.

"Please get on this horse or I will slit your throat and bathe in your blood."

He frowned at her, but let her help him straddle the horse, awkwardly positioning himself until he settled in.

"It's a quick ten colony-mile walk, people," Jasper called out. "We can rest well once we get there."

A small cheer went up, the hopeful mood of the group brightening as they headed over the ramshackle bridge to Four Colony-Mile Creek Park.

For a moment, a flicker of concern crossed the Medicine Girl's face. She chose not to dwell on it.

The Medicine Girl was shocked to see just fifty or so of the two hundred horses remaining in the temporary paddock.

"We cannot stay here very long, Jasper," the Medicine Girl warned.

"We must eat," Jasper stated. "These people are starving."

"There are oats in the storage bins."

"They will want meat," he replied.

The Medicine Girl pointed at a horse with a limp. Jasper relayed her instructions to a few of the men, gobsmacked at seeing so much available food.

By afternoon, the women had fried slices of horse meat in oil on low fires. Several pots of oats steamed on coalbeds. Several men drew water from a well while the younger Comfort Station girls discovered berries along the marsh.

"How far is the walk south to Lincoln?" one of the older men asked.

"We won't walk there. We will ride," Jasper said. "And we will have to learn very quickly," Jasper added, as the famished people savored their meal.

The Medicine Girl noted how friendships had sprung up like wildflowers, as if they'd been starved for authentic companionship as well as food. There were sounds of genuine laughter, as people began to share their colorful histories.

"Could we stay here—at least for the night?" asked one of the Comfort Station women.

"What is your name, ma'am?" Jasper asked.

"I am Ursula."

"Ursula, it isn't safe here. We need to gather and pack whatever we can, learn to ride these animals, and head to—" Jasper looked at the Medicine Girl. "Where are we going?"

She rolled her eyes. She *hated* talking to people! The Medicine Girl cleared her throat. "Tonight we will be going to the Shirley Plantation to meet Lincoln, your new warlord. We will sleep there. Tomorrow we will travel to Abingdon, under the authority of the White Crosses."

"Is Lincoln a good warlord?" came a small voice in the crowd.

"Is there such a thing as a good warlord?" yelled a male voice from the back. *Laughter.*

"He is neither good nor bad," the Medicine Girl replied truthfully. "But he is fair."

"So, are we Armaggedonists now?" Ursula asked, a murmur arising from the group. Jasper and the Medicine Girl looked at each other to formulate a clear response. The Medicine Girl shrugged.

"We are ourselves, for now," Jasper explained. "Would you all agree to that for the time being...could we all just take care of one another? When we get settled, we can decide who we are or if we still want to be together. But for now, time is short and there is much to do."

A sea of voices started talking, discussing, entreating, looking to Jasper for direction.

"There is a Family Trading Station near Woodvale. It's on the way. I had a nephew sent there last month. Could we see if he's still there?"

"I worked at the Comfort Station in Petersburg. There are some good women there. Excellent cooks. They do wonders with herbal teas!" a woman chimed in.

"I know the next checkpoint. The Nonessentials were treated worse than diseased cattle. I'm sure if they are still there, they would be glad to join the warlord Lincoln in Abingdon."

Jasper held up his hands to quiet the commotion.

"All of your concerns are valid. I want to hear them all. But let's move systematically before we are surprised by hostile forces who'd happily kill us and take the horses for themselves."

The small band settled down, well fed and ready for further instruction.

"The Medicine Girl will take half the women to the horses," Jasper continued. "The men and I will scavenge what we can and pack everything useful to take with us. Our lives depend upon it. So move quickly. When we rejoin you, each woman will train one or two of the men on how to ride."

There were nods and no objections. Each seemed to know their duty.

"We should depart within the colony-hour. Agreed?"

"Agreed," came dozens of voices.

The Medicine Girl looked over at Jasper and gave him a thin smile. She walked to her own horse, Patches, who was happily eating clover on the clear spring day.

The ladies from the Comfort Station, in all stages of makeup and dress, followed after her into the paddock, their high heels making odd indentations in the earth and mud.

The horses, curious about the new visitors, trotted over to greet them, eating the berries they held out flat in their outstretched hands.

As the Medicine Girl's eyes adjusted to the gloom, she saw a young man in a sodden military jacket.

Chapter 20

Granville, Old Virginia

Lincoln had waited as long as he could, breaking his stare out of the office's window which faced Richmond. He put his head in his hands.

Mika, Mika, he whispered to himself. *I am so sorry. But how much longer can I wait?*

In truth, he was certain the Medicine Girl was dead, if any of the gossip were true. After the United Authority's fall, chaos and brutality reigned in the streets, the highways, the hills.

The militias had united for a brief time, just long enough to decapitate the federal leadership. They'd struck fear in any residual supporters, making them think twice about resisting the coalition of MilitiaMen, now united under the Armageddonists' flag.

It was, indeed, a terrible dawning, one where power shifted from moment to moment. The thinly held alliances between the United Authority and the powerful regional warlords unraveled in the wind. People scrambled to affiliate with any group offering a modicum of safety or normalcy or something to eat.

As usual in desperate times, women and children suffered disproportionately.

Horror vacui, Lincoln thought. *Nature abhors a vacuum.* The void would be filled by something. *Surely one of the southern militias would struggle their way to dominance in the region,* Lincoln thought. *Hopefully sooner than later.*

Anarchy was bad for business. With his newfound horse trade, Lincoln found it satisfactory to pay off a stronger warlord to keep some semblance of law and order. He just needed to know which one to trust and which one to be wary of—the need for duplicity made everything twice as hard.

But among his people, the absence of the Medicine Girl was keenly felt. She was well liked by the attendants, their families, and their younger children, who scrambled after her in the paddock, learning from her how to care for the horses.

She had been extraordinary, taking advantage of the HorseMen's expertise and adding her own. For a Floridian, the Medicine Girl understood the southern terrain well, having traipsed through the thoroughfares in her recent years on foot.

Lincoln found himself listening to her advice on a myriad of matters, surprised at her grasp of nuance, her simple stratagems, her practical ideas. She'd been a good shadow counselor to him, offering a unique perspective, sometimes opposing the personal attendants who too often agreed with him.

The move to Abingdon? He feared he needed her more than even he knew.

Where are you, Medicine Girl? He frowned, turning to watch the last minute packing and frantic loading at the main gate. He'd given a directive to his people that they would abandon the Shirley Plantation within hours.

There were no more dispatch runners coming from the United Authority, which had ceased bureaucratic functioning. Rumors swirled over riots at the Family Trading Stations and kidnapping of women at the Comfort Stations. Worse crimes were hinted at, since lawlessness reigned in the United Authority's wake.

Lincoln had few men to spare for reconnaissance missions; it was a futile effort to see which group was coming over the rolling hills to raid him. He felt as if his exodus was moving too slowly, as if fire and brimstone were burning the back of his heels.

Lincoln's knack for organizing a thriving community with potable water, meticulous sanitation, and a fair division of labor earned him his people's fierce loyalty. They'd follow him, as it was only a matter of time before the PadsFoots and thieves banded together and raided the Shirley Plantation, well known for being stocked with plentiful gardens. The possibility of fresh horse meat would invite marauders in droves.

When raiders would inevitably come, Lincoln knew there were few weapons to protect themselves with. They would have to use farm implements, axes, and hatchets. So many men and their weaponry had been lost when Colonial Williamsburg was sacked.

He drifted off in thought of his former home for far too long, lost in the memory of walking cobblestone streets in relative peace and prosperity. *How quickly everything could change.*

Every minute seemed to become more fraught with possible violence, as Lincoln turned the final plans for evacuation over to his chief attendants—all good men, battle tested, and loyal as brothers. He had precious few wranglers to manage the horses, their most valuable asset, ones that would prove vital in the coming days.

Lincoln had taken efforts to ensure all of his remaining attendants and their older children learned to ride. Some handled the horses better than others, but the majority were capable enough to transport them south and west. A week in the saddle would be taxing on all of them, but the de facto leader of the White Crosses had agreed to Lincoln's passage through the southern part of Old Virginia. The White Crosses were anxious to integrate the horses into their military campaigns.

It was time to go to Abingdon.

The Medicine Girl knew their plans, he comforted himself. *Perhaps she was already en route?*

He had waited far too long to leave.

"Lincoln?" inquired his chief of staff.

"Yes, Rucker."

"Everything is attended to. Are we waiting any longer?"

Lincoln looked at Rucker's face, lined with worry, just like everyone else's since Richmond's fall. *You'd think we'd be used to living in a state of constant fear by now*, he thought.

"No, Rucker," Lincoln replied. "We cannot wait. We need to move out now."

"We've retrofitted the wagons to the horses, sir. It'll make carrying the water barrels and other supplies much easier instead of overloading the horses. And the children and their caregivers will have an easier journey riding in—"

"Thank you, Rucker. I'll be out by the main gate in a few moments." Lincoln busied himself by putting some papers and personal items into a satchel.

Rucker flushed, seeing Lincoln's face fall when he mentioned the attendants' children. Rucker retreated from the room, watching Lincoln give one last look out of the window, almost willing himself to see the Medicine Girl appear on the horizon.

"Jasper!" Ursula called out.

Jasper pulled up on the reins to stop, his horse complied, both turning towards the frantic voice.

"What is it, Ursula?"

"That man is harassing Miranda again!" she screamed. "He put his hands on her!" Ursula's face was a smear of heavy makeup. Her gaudy dress made riding a challenge.

Jasper awkwardly dismounted from his horse, using both of his crutches for support.

From up ahead, the Medicine Girl heard Ursula's plaintive cry, yet she did not dismount. Instead, she circled back on her steed to where the Comfort Station women were watering their horses at Bailey Creek. Ursula had voiced her concerns about various and sundry things since the beginning of their trek, but now three of the women each held a knife, surrounding a miserable looking man sporting a few new gashes. A chunk of his cheek was missing.

Jasper approached the group on foot, while the Medicine Girl sat stoically on Patches. She looked annoyed by the turn of events.

"We don't have time for this idiocy," the Medicine Girl remarked.

"We aren't going to be party to this group if molesters go unchecked," Ursula countered. The Medicine Girl narrowed her eyes at her, then turned to the man in question.

"What is your name?" she demanded.

"Freddy," the man mumbled, his speech difficult to understand as he was missing most of his teeth. The few still in his gums were fractured and broken. "I'm a Nonessential worker from the Nine Five."

"You are nothing now," the Medicine Girl declared. "Were you planning to rape this girl?"

The three women circled him more closely, the point of a paring knife at his neck.

"They are Comfort Station girls. Even Nonessentials are entitled to—"

Jasper approached the group, hobbling on his crutches faster than most men could run.

"Freddy!" he called out. "You'd been warned."

"We should kill him," the Medicine Girl decided, waving Jasper off. "Let these three have at him, and let's be done with it. We need to get to the Shirley Plantation before nightfall. This person is taking our daylight. I should kill him just for that."

"No, we should not," Jasper contradicted her in front of the others.

"No?" the Medicine Girl replied. *Was Jasper correcting her?* It took every colony-ounce of patience for her not to spur Patches onward and leave the fractious group in the dust. *To hell with these people.*

Instead, the Medicine Girl rode close enough to Jasper so her horse's belly brushed him back, threatening to knock him over.

"No," Jasper repeated, moving to avoid the Medicine Girl's horse from stepping on him. "No, we will not kill him."

"This Freddy isn't going to change, Jasper. Let's end him."

The three other women looked hopeful, ready to gut Freddy, awaiting Jasper's consent.

"This isn't right," Jasper said.

"Neither is attempted rape," Ursula replied sarcastically.

"Then what would you do with him, Jasper?" The Medicine Girl asked, ready to object to whatever he said out of spite.

"Banishment," Jasper stated. "Freddy will be exiled. Strip him of everything of value. Have him start walking back the way we came. He may survive a day or two. He may not. Regardless, he isn't our problem."

The three women looked at the Medicine Girl, who gave them a nod. Disappointed, they backed away from the man, now bleeding on his face and neck.

"Get out of here, Freddy," said Jasper. "You will never be part of us again. Don't ask for mercy. Don't beg for supplies. You are alone."

Freddy looked at the small group, gathered together, in complete disgust.

"We are all dead anyways. Today. Tomorrow. It doesn't matter," Freddy spat. "Now who's to say you won't stab me in the back while I'm walking away? Who's going to keep these bitches off of me?"

"No one will touch you. Start walking north now. If you glance backwards, I will kill you myself," Jasper warned.

The man needed no further encouragement. Holding a torn rag against his cheek and neck to staunch the bleeding, Freddy scrambled up the road, taking great care not to look back.

The Medicine Girl looked at Jasper, impressed with his decisiveness. In hindsight, if they had killed Freddy, the small group would have been traumatized on some level. Violence begets violence. *She'd seen it in Tallahassee too many times to count.*

The assault on the Comfort Station woman had to be addressed in a serious and meaningful way, an example to the other men who may have conjured up similar notions for women outside the gates of the Comfort Stations. A bright line had been established.

Lincoln will find Jasper useful, she concluded.

The group reassembled for the short journey to the Shirley Plantation. The aggrieved party had her revenge, knowing that Freddy would not last long on his own. It was quite a warning to those who rode that if they were uncivil, they would be shunned by their immediate society—a society who welcomed all who adhered to their basic rules. *No murder. No stealing. No raping.*

Freddy's departure united the disparate group, as it saw the offender dealt with swiftly. The Medicine Girl watched the other women embrace the assaulted woman, as an older man tended to her facial contusions. *They are alleviating one another's suffering,* she thought. *Mika would be pleased.*

Soon, the women mounted their horses, calling out to each other, making good natured jokes. The men rode to the rear, looking over their shoulders for Richmond refugees, stragglers or loners desperate enough to attack a small retinue, even one on horseback.

For now, the gentle spring evening was breezy and warm, their stomachs were full, and the Medicine Girl was content in the knowledge that she was bringing good people who would be useful to Lincoln's plantation.

The Medicine Girl's company arrived at the Shirley Plantation, its gates wide open and unguarded.

Lincoln had left.

The group of thirty-six riders dismounted, letting their horses roam in the familiar paddocks, eating the sweet grass. The Medicine Girl instructed two men to fill the watering troughs from the nearby spring.

"Check the kitchen for any provisions. I have a feeling we'll be hunting for squirrels and rabbits for dinner tonight." The Medicine Girl instructed some of the Comfort Women to glean the small gardens just outside the paddocks. *Maybe a few potatoes could be found?*

Several from their group devised a systematic scouting party, ensuring that every section of the camp would be scoured for anything of value. They were a scrappy, hard working lot—falling in line together, enjoying the relative freedom of being outside the United Authority's strictures.

Former dispatch runners laughed with Comfort Station Women. A Family Trading Station boy and an older woman discovered a berry bush, delighting in picking off the fragrant fruit and placing them in a wicker basket.

Jasper busied himself with making a small fire. The Medicine Girl looked worried, wondering if the smoke would draw unwanted visitors. But there was water to boil and some sort of stew to cobble together. She sat by him while he used flint steel to light the tinder, blowing the sparks into a small flame.

"How far away is Abingdon?" Jasper asked.

"Roughly 350 colony-miles," the Medicine Girl replied. "It'll take us a week or so, depending on the weather."

"Will Lincoln welcome us? We have a lot of mouths to feed."

"Lincoln needs people whom he can trust," the Medicine Girl explained. "He lost so many when Colonial Williamsburg was taken—taken by your murderous MilitiaMen." She gave him a disgusted sidelong glance.

"What are you saying, Medicine Girl?" Jasper asked. "The White Crosses had nothing to do with Colonial Williamsburg."

"Your colleagues—the Illuminati Pagans—did. They killed a lot of Lincoln's people. And my mother. And my sister. And my unborn baby brother." She stood up to walk away.

"That's not what happened," Jasper replied, shaking his head, reaching out to touch her arm.

She paused. "You know what happened?" The Medicine Girl's eyes grew wide. She sat back down by his side. "Tell me, Jasper. Tell me what happened in Colonial Williamsburg."

"I can tell you what I've heard. Rumors. Gossip..."

"Jasper, you and I both know that dispatch runners know more of the truth than generals," she said fervently. "And you and I both know attendants know more than any warlord."

"True," Jasper conceded.

"Tell me everything. Leave nothing out!" she cried.

"It was a raiding party," Jasper said, looking disgusted. "They asked permission from the Board of Southern Militias to take Lincoln out, since he was working with the United Authority. They said he couldn't be trusted. It was known Lincoln was raising livestock for the United Authority. No one thought of horses. Most people didn't think horses could live this far south."

"Go on."

"The Board declined the raiding party. They said that Lincoln was a free agent, able to contract with whomever he pleased. Lincoln paid the Board its dues, so they protected him. But some warlords don't abide by anyone else's council."

"Jasper, who raided Colonial Williamsburg?" The Medicine Girl grew impatient.

"The militia groups behind the raiding party were unknown, but well financed. At least half were mercenaries. Godless men. Murderers, all. They came up the Nine Five fast, right out of the Florida Penal Colony—"

The Medicine Girl's mouth pressed hard into a thin line.

Jasper looked at her, noticing her eyes narrowing, her jaw clenching and unclenching.

"I'm going to need you to say that again," she said in an unnerving, calm voice.

"The Colonial Williamsburg raiders came from the Florida Penal Colony. From what I understand, the Warlord of Tallahassee wanted his concubine back."

Deidra Whitt Lovegren

"This Freddy isn't going to change, Jasper. Let's end him." The three other women looked hopeful, ready to gut Freddy, awaiting Jasper's consent.

Chapter 21

Roanoke, Old Virginia

Word traveled down the Eight One. *The United Authority had fallen.*

Jalen took the news in stride. She had held back on her federal payments for several months, anticipating such an event. *Death and taxes, my ass,* she thought while she took inventory of the Black CatHouse's provisions, determining what was needed to ride out the latest political storm. In her short life, even the worst of times seem to be over in six months or so.

She ordered the attendants to double the garden plantings in the rich Old Virginian soil and to lay up dried meats and root vegetables in the cold cellar. She even pilfered half a case of Neo from a retreating Illuminati Pagan warlord.

Jalen knew how to survive.

No one in Jalen's Black CatHouse was surprised about Richmond's fall. Militiamen had been telling tales and spilling secrets about "the cause" since Xerxes' death.

It was no surprise to anyone that Darius usurped Xerxes's position either, making bold moves to control the Armageddonists. Turned out, he'd always been the power behind the throne, though a disloyal power. Darius was still not to be trusted, especially now that he was becoming a major force in the south.

Granted, the speed of the United Authority's implosion was startling, but Jalen knew the cancerous rot had eaten it from the inside. Like the husk of a dead tree, the slightest kick was all that was needed to splinter the shell into pieces.

That's what prompted Jalen to disassociate herself from the United Authority's Comfort Stations altogether. Besides, Tennessee was becoming increasingly restrictive as the Armageddonists consolidated power. She needed to move east, where someone with her talents could have more autonomy.

Jalen liked Roanoke, though, tucked in the Ridge-and-Valley section of the Appalachian mountains. Roanoke had been known as the Star City before the end of electricity. The people were tolerant, kept to themselves, and let her do business without much fuss. A few Christers looked askance at her on the sidewalks, but she learned to pay them no mind. There were fewer and fewer True Believers as time went by, most of whom formed their own societies or MilitiaCults, like the Order of the Snake Handlers. That group in particular came to the Temporary Wives with the most distasteful of requests.

She yawned, stretched, thinking of her move from Nashville to Roanoke with all of its initial complications. Yet now, her Black CatHouse ran smoothly, its profits shared equitably, her working wives empowered and content.

As usual, Jalen met with her crew just after ClockOut, a good time to discuss pressing issues and to address any of her girls' complaints. ClockOut had evolved into a GroupShare time, as pillow talk proved a more accurate intelligence gathering service than a phalanx of dispatch runners. The day's traffic of men was much lighter, another harbinger of disorder and portent of bad days to come.

Jalen worried if she should be more worried.

"Are we boarding up, Jalen?" asked Mitzi in her thick southern accent. "We can head south if need be. I have people in the Tricorner area who will take us in. We could jump between three states to avoid who we need to until we see how this all shakes out." Mitzi, her business partner and lover, still lounged late in the evening, dressed in a thick green robe. A bit threadbare, the robe had an embroidered logo from a famous Nashville hotel, one popular in the days before the end of electricity.

"I don't know how this will go, Mitzi," Jalen sighed, too weary to worry. "Let's see what tomorrow brings."

Mitzi flashed her a concerned look. Jalen knew that Mitzi would stay up most the night working on additional exit scenarios should they be needed, if Roanoke became more unsafe. Though she was off the beds, Jalen helped out the girls on occasion, in an attempt to keep the per diem numbers equitable. Truth was, Jalen liked being a temporary wife on occasion. It was exciting to be desired, especially when she sold herself on her own terms. The payment was hers, a change from the days when she earned a pittance, most of her money turned over to the United Authority or some grubby warlord.

For Mitzi? She was happier in management, handling the procurement and accounting functions. Mitzi had a knack for hiring attendants and temporary wives, deftly interviewing ex-Comfort Station runaways or displaced Family Trading Station orphans who routinely showed up on their stoop. The majority of the women were sent on their way due to disease or mental illness or moral turpitude. There were other CatHouses that catered to more deviant desires.

Jalen and Mitzi hired women who were content being subcontractors, choosing their own work schedules and advertising their own special services, within acceptable parameters. It was easier to run a CatHouse when the girls felt they had control of their work product, Mitzi concluded. Jalen, as usual, agreed.

The cook Mitzi hired was a marvel, and ex-United Authority mess hall steward. How Mama June managed to produce quantities of tasty meals from a paucity of ingredients baffled both Mitzi and Jalen to no end.

"Thought you'd like a midnight treat," Mama June walked into the main parlor, holding out a tray of peanut butter cookies. The working girls giggled with delight, helping themselves to three or four, fighting over every one. Jalen and Mitzi exchanged a knowing look, while the girls stuffed as many treats as they could into their mouths, laughing and teasing one another.

But after the girls went off to bed, Jalen and Mitzi stayed awake, with Mitzi proposing various contingency plans long into the night.

There were worse places to be in this godforsaken country than in the Middle Appalachians, Lincoln thought.

In the end, Abingdon proved to be less desirable than Saltville, a deserted town twenty colony-miles northeast, nestled in the valley of the Appalachian Mountains. His scouts found that Saltville's creeks ran clear and the mountainous region had plenty of game in the woods and thick hardwood trees for firewood and weapons.

The decision to jettison Abingdon had come quickly, when Lincoln's scouts saw firsthand how it had become a haven for unaligned religious zealots. This concerned Lincoln, as apocalyptic cults created disorder. MilitiaCults were unpredictable. Now that the United Authority had collapsed, Lincoln had thrown in with the White Crosses. At least for the time being. His mind worked out possible scenarios as he knew his horses could sway the balance of power in the south for any of the militias. Lincoln needed to be careful with whom he aligned himself.

Lincoln gathered his men to discuss monetizing the inland saline marshes, as salt was always in great demand. Rucker had already suggested leading a special task force, ready to make Lincoln's salt production a reality.

Lincoln's scouts did well, securing Saltville's decrepit nine-hole golf course, cordoning it off with fencing from before the wars. Though rusty and missing sections of chain links, it was a far easier paddock to repair than building one from scratch.

Lincoln heard cheers outside the sprawling cinderblock high school he'd commandeered for his offices and living quarters.

"What are the celebrations for?" Lincoln asked. Rucker entered the former principal's office, grinning from ear to ear.

"One of the attendants ran down a 12-point buck on horseback," Rucker replied, gleefully. "Looks like venison stew for a few nights!"

Lincoln grinned. It was a good omen.

The Medicine Girl broke a rabbit's neck with one firm twist. She laid its carcass on a flat rock near the stream where the others watered their horses. They had stopped just outside of Lynchburg off of the Four Six Zero.

She cut off the rabbit's head, feet, and tail, removing its fur in one swift movement. She then gutted the animal, ensuring all of its innards remained intact, avoiding contaminating the meat with fecal matter. She inspected the liver in the twilight, looking for muddled spots or discoloration. As the rabbit's liver was a deep red, the Medicine Girl put the meat on a spit, roasting it over a fire.

Jasper stopped, dismounted, encouraged the weary travelers to stretch their aching limbs. Their horses were exhausted from the long trek, and it was tacitly decided they would break camp and start fresh for Abingdon in the morning.

Assuming all had gone to plan, Lincoln would have the new plantation and horse paddocks up and running in Abingdon, the Medicine Girl thought. Her plan was to leave these people to his good use, each member proving to be stalwart and trustworthy so far, especially after Freddy's banishment.

Lincoln would be glad to see her, glad for the capable hands she brought to work with the horses and attend to the endless needs of the plantation. These were skilled people with her, in a variety of areas, and their knowledge in their current surroundings surprised even her.

The Medicine Girl had spent the past few days planning her own trip much farther south—to settle personal matters. What she would do and how she would murder her father consumed her waking thoughts, from the very moment Jasper connected him to the Colonial Williamsburg massacre and her mother's death.

Was it possible that her mother was still alive? Was sweet little Lina alive? Had her baby brother been born—or had he died as Mika was tortured to death?

Patches instinctively felt the Medicine Girl was distracted, fussing at her when she gripped the reins too hard or led him off road into the mud. She found herself chewing her bottom lip like the general, running over endless scenarios in her mind.

The Medicine Girl longed to speak with General Chapman— especially on this particular night. There were so many things that she needed to discuss with him, wondering if he were dead alongside the others.

She could imagine Richmond in ruin, especially the Capitol Building, even the sweets shop. She'd been raised on watching things be brutalized, broken, and burned. *Why did she think anything she loved would remain alive or intact?*

She dismissed her dark thoughts, focusing on preparing meat for their dinner. She began to skin another rabbit, still tending the other one on the spit.

Jasper dropped two more dead animals by her side. They'd learned to work together without much communication, an unspoken arrangement they both preferred.

She remained lost in thought, snapping, gutting, skinning the rabbits while others made small fires to boil water. Ursula and another temporary wife patted out ground oat flour to boil into dumplings. Others looked to the horses, inspecting hooves and tending to their individual needs as the Medicine Girl had shown them.

There was much she knew that she patiently taught them, but there was much she did not know. She had not delivered a foal; the HorseMen hadn't time to teach her everything before being called back to Richmond. She tried her best, learning lessons the hard way, such as the impossibility of splinting a horse's broken leg and the difficulty of putting a horse down without it suffering.

But there were many things she did know. She knew she would take Jasper's people to Lincoln. She knew she would rest Patches and pack what she needed. She knew she would make her way down the Seven Five to Tallahassee. She knew she would determine if her mother still lived.

When all that was done, she would disembowel her father and set his intestines on fire.

In the morning, the Medicine Girl arose, counting the horses and sleeping bodies in their groupings. As usual, Jasper had been up, discussing concerns with the 3rd watchman.

"I heard something on the Four Six Zero, but farther west," the watchman reported.

"What, specifically?" Jasper inquired.

"It sounded like people running, feet moving at a clip. No voices, though. Quiet. Disciplined."

"Did you see anything? Smell any fires?"

"Not really. Just shadows in the distance."

This concerned Jasper as the horses could not be kept quiet. *Certainly this passing group had heard them.* Jasper had taken precautions by setting up camp far from the main thoroughfare, but horses were noisy beasts, whinnying randomly, chuffing loudly when finding a good bit of clover.

He wondered if his group of thirty-six were safe under his care. His eyes scanned the horizon. He would tell the Medicine Girl about the watchman's concerns. She would know what to do. With luck, they'd make it to Roanoke in a few days. After that, it might be a week until they reached sanctuary in Abingdon.

Jasper's second greatest act of faith was believing the Medicine Girl's stepfather would welcome him, a cripple, along with thirty-six refugees.

His greatest act of faith had been letting the Medicine Girl take off his leg on a battlefield in the Kingdom of Georgia, so long ago. He had trusted her then, too.

Jalen and Mitzi dozed on the front parlor's couch in the Black CatHouse, a bottle of spirits sitting empty alongside two glasses on a rickety coffee table.

Business had been dismal the entire week, and the girls were restless and grumbling. A pair of refurbished high heels lay by the front door. Jalen had sent the girls to bed early, but even Mama June's cooking couldn't soothe their discontent. The girls fought over the same tricks, trying to make any money during a disappointing month. The ledger Mitzi tried to explain to Jalen was opened to a gloomy page, showing negative numbers in long columns.

They were too deeply asleep to awake to the sounds of breaking glass. The fire started in the kitchen, plastic bottles full of accelerent bursting into flames, igniting threadbare curtains and thickly matted carpets. From the kitchen, the flames licked across the ceiling and quickly up the stairs, effectively cutting off an exit from the second floor.

In the front room parlor, Mitzi awoke first, coughing and sputtering.

"Jalen!" she yelled, shaking the inebriated woman next to her.

"What's burning—" Jalen mumbled. "You aren't cooking are you, Mitzi? You aren't very good…"

"Everything is burning!" Mitzi cried. She watched in horror as the flames engulfed the back of the Black CatHouse. Panicked cries for help came from the bedrooms on the second floor, where Mitzi and Jalen themselves would have been if they hadn't opened up another bottle.

"Come—!" Mitzi grabbed Jalen around her waist and dragged her out into the street. Both shrieked into the night, tears streaming down their faces. From the house, muffled screams were cut short, drowned out by a black, inky smoke.

Both Jalen and Mitzi fell to their knees, watching the Black CatHouse fully ablaze, white clapboard walls falling in on themselves.

Their girls were dying, Jalen wept in Mitzi's arms.

"Well brethren, we missed these two Whores of Babylon," calmly remarked a man missing a chunk of his nose. A large ill-formed scar bisected his face.

"Who the fuck are you?" screamed Jalen, looking at a half colony-dozen, oddly dressed men.

"I am Frances Zebulun," the leader declared. "We are from the Order of the Snake Handlers, and God has decreed that Roanoke needs to be purged of sin."

"You killed nine women!" Mitzi yelled, her anger making her apoplectic, eyes bulging with an intense desire to strangle the man.

"Correction," he offered her a sickly smile. "In a minute, I will have killed eleven jezebels for our Lord."

He pulled out a Bowie knife and slowly walked towards them.

For a midsize trading town, the streets leading into Roanoke were empty, unusual even this late into the night. Jasper determined they would look for a secluded spot to feed and water the horses. A few of the riders stifled yawns, more than ready to tuck in for the night.

The Medicine Girl and Jasper looked at each other as their group wearily rode horses down the Eight One. The clip-clops of the horses' hooves echoed more loudly than either of them would have liked. *They needed to get off the highway, away from the larger population centers.*

Both Jasper and the Medicine Girl scanned the area.

"Fire!" someone called out from the back.

Jasper looked up in time to see a large wooden house ablaze, just off the main road. Hearing women's screams, Jasper kicked his horse and sped over the crest towards the burning house, the Medicine Girl right on his heels.

Rounding the front, the Medicine Girl spied two women on the ground, kneeling before a small group of men, one of whom held a menacing knife. The other men's call-and-response chants sent chills down the Medicine Girl's spine. *I know this tribe*, she thought. *Snake Handlers!*

She led her horse forward, Patches leery at the sight of flames and the smell of burning flesh. Removing a length of thin-gauged wire from her shirt pocket, the Medicine Girl rode up on the men, trampling one and causing the others to scatter.

The man with the knife looked stunned, having never seen a horse before in his life. His brief delay was long enough for the Medicine Girl to loop a length of wire about his neck. Patches rode on, yanking the man off his feet, the wire cutting sharply into his neck, sharp enough to snap it clean.

"Eve!"

The Medicine Girl pulled up on the reigns, looking wildly back at the women. She circled around, allowing Patches to trample the dead man, his face purpled, his hands losing their grip on his Bowie knife.

Jasper had dismounted, tending to the women as best he could.

"Eve!" Jalen called out again.

"Jalen?" the Medicine Girl replied. "Jalen!"

She halted Patches, dismounted without hesitation. The Medicine Girl flung herself into Jalen's arms, as both grasped each other tightly.

"Oh Eve," Jalen wept. "We lost the girls. The girls are dead!" Jalen pulled back to look at her. "Eve, are you well? Where have you been? Where did you get horses? Who is this man? Eve!" Jalen held on to the

Medicine Girl tightly.

"Eve?" Jasper said out loud. "Your name is *Eve?*"

As Mitzi walked over to the burning wreckage of the house, the second floor collapsed inward. Overcome with loss, Mitzi put her head in her hands and sobbed.

Jasper put his hands on Mitzi's heaving shoulders in an attempt to comfort her as best he could. "What can we do? What happened?"

"What always happens," Mitzi said bitterly, shaking her head. "What always happens..."

"You saved our lives," Jalen said to both the Medicine Girl and Jasper. "Thank you. Thank you, both."

"Jalen, what are we to do?" Mitzi despaired, looking at everything they had built, now ash and rubble before them.

"You will come with us," the Medicine Girl said. "We're going to a horse plantation. You will be welcome in Abingdon."

"Eve, there aren't any horses in Abingdon," Jalen replied, puzzled at her words.

The Medicine Girl looked crestfallen. *Was Lincoln dead, too?*

"Are you sure there are no horse plantations in the region?"

"Not in Abingdon. Rumor has it there is a new one in Saltville, run by a Virginian warlord. Someone named after one of the old-Colony Presidents. Washington or Madison—"

"Lincoln?" the Medicine Girl interrupted.

"Yes, that's it—Lincoln. But this Lincoln is not in Abingdon. He's in Saltville."

"Then you will come with us to Saltville," the Medicine Girl replied.

Patches rode on, yanking the man off his feet, the wire cutting sharply into his neck, sharp enough to snap it clean.

Chapter 22

Saltville, Old Virginia

The last of the frosts usually came at the end of March, but Old Virginia's soil had thawed even earlier in the season, as the earth continued to warm.

In the days before the wars, Lincoln knew that the planting season for potatoes, corn, turnips, and beets had been late in April. As a little boy, he had watched machines do what colony-dozens of men now had to do by hand—back breaking work, the kind of repetitive movement that machines were good at. But after the end of electricity, the fragile infrastructure and supply chains shuttered into a dysfunctional heap that bred more chaos, more hunger, more carnage.

Once the food riots began, people were too frightened, willingly trading personal freedoms for a modicum of security. *We are only civilized because we are comfortable*, he'd heard the Medicine Girl say, quoting her beautiful mother.

Lincoln wondered if the Medicine Girl still lived.

He also worried about the spring planting. Getting enough laborers wasn't the problem; there were plenty of stragglers all over the countryside looking to align with warlords, trading their servitude for a mess of proverbial pottage.

Lincoln's approval was required by anyone who appeared on the plantation requesting sanctuary. The newcomers were thin and desperate, holding a sick child or assisting an elderly relative, approaching the edges of the burgeoning plantation with hands outstretched.

Lincoln had built up thriving communities before, hoping this one would outlast him. He was growing both older and more weary, especially after the loss of Mika and the children. *Some days, getting out of bed seemed like an act of bravery.*

The collapse of the United Authority hadn't been unexpected, but Lincoln had not fully considered the long term implications of its loss. With the power structure holding the fragmented country together gone, its former citizenry would embrace tribalism.

Perhaps things would not change that much? Lincoln himself would not miss paying taxes or navigating through the multiple levels of bureaucracy to get anything done. Dealing with militias was far easier, assuming the warlord proved somewhat stable and reliable. Still, Lincoln felt a definitive layer of order had been removed along with the federal government.

He had capable people working the land and knowledgeable attendants bustling in the kitchens and clinics and makeshift schools for the community's few children. Even in the worst of times, he felt the children needed to learn the basics of literacy and mathematics. Whatever civilization they had left needed to be transmitted, or it would be lost in a generation. Chores were assigned and expected at all ages; there was far too much work to do to indulge layabouts. Everyone needed to contribute. Of all the sins, Lincoln punished slothfulness the most severely.

On Lincoln's plantations, rulebreakers were as rare as the punishments were harsh. Seldom did scofflaws get a second chance, as Lincoln felt examples needed to be made in keeping order. He was keen on making punishments public.

Lincoln's chief concern was the potable water supply, as the rains often came too heavy or too late during the planting seasons. He taught his people to sprout seedlings by hand, demonstrating how to dig trenches between the mounds, building up mulch around the tiny plants, tending to them until they firmly took root.

He would start mass producing chickens and rabbits in earnest, since they were easy to maintain and provided a steady source of protein.

Lincoln was reluctant to slaughter good horses to feed his people, as the horses themselves were becoming a precious commodity, especially since the militias had learned how much of an advantage they would be in battle.

At dawn, Lincoln arose from his bedchamber, located in the principal's office of the former high school, washing his face with warm water in a clean plastic tub.

In Colonial Williamsburg, the Medicine Girl had demonstrated the ease of setting up small scale desalination plants, a skillset she learned from her father, the Warlord of Tallahassee. Lincoln had his workers reserve the residual salt for the plantation's use, stockpiling extra stores for eventual sale to other plantations and communities. Fortunately, Saltville had an unpolluted water source, making the task less arduous.

Rucker proved an excellent chief of staff, organizing Lincoln's people into cohesive units, overseeing and handling personal concerns and with a fairness that rivaled Lincoln's own. At first, a few upstarts had to be put to death for stealing food from the high school's reconstructed cafeteria, but the public display of the men's gruesome executions ensured a quick return to regular order.

Lincoln kept his favorite horses tethered behind the high school, within sight of his bedchamber. He enjoyed watching them graze on the former high school's football field. The chainlink fencing had been adequate, further bolstered in part by wooden slats. Having the horses nearby proved convenient for Lincoln to ride his favorite steed whenever he wished, often patrolling the plantation's perimeter himself.

He approached a large gray mare, gray as Mika's eyes had been. Grabbing a handful of the horse's mane, he deftly used his muscular arms to pull himself up, throwing a leg over the horse, one whom he found exceptionally patient. *Perhaps this particular mare had remembered the one horse who had bucked Lincoln en route to Saltville, ending up as horse stew for the entire camp?*

He gave the mare a sharp kick to gallop towards the main paddock on the nine-hole golf course, where the majority of the horses were kept.

Lee, one of Lincoln's chief HorseMen, greeted him at the former clubhouse, a ruin of what had been a serviceable facility decades prior. A few padded chairs, glass display cases with trophies from a distant age, and broken banquet tables still remained. Lee sported a green blazer he found buried deep in a linen closet, nattily emblazoned with the golf course's crest. He'd even found a pair of men's beige leather golf gloves, which Lee wore with pride—even during mealtimes.

Lee called out to attendants milling about, preparing for Lincoln's inspection of the horses. He had divided them into quadrants for ease of administration.

At the expected time, Lincoln rode into the golf course's parking lot, chunks of asphalt punctuated by roots and other greenery pushing through the dilapidated lot.

"Lincoln!" Lee greeted the warlord, watching him dismount from a particularly large horse. An attendant led the mare away to water.

"Lee, always a pleasure—" Lincoln shook Lee's hand, patting him on the shoulder. Lincoln looked around, admiring the continual improvements to the paddock. A new watering trough, a section of the barn expanded.

"What's today's count?"

"After last night's successful birth, we have four hundred and seventy three horses in total. One hundred and fifty-two stallions. Twenty-seven colts. Two hundred and three mares. Ninety-one fillies."

"Any more pregnancies?"

"Hard to tell at this point."

"Any illnesses?"

"Not this week. There were four we had to put down last week due to injury, but we checked with Cook who salvaged them. He's come up with interesting horse jerky recipes. Quite handy for the winter months."

"Good, all good," Lincoln replied. "Do you have enough attendants to expand this operation? I'm meeting with the White Crosses in Abingdon later this week. They are looking to buy fifty horses to start up a cavalry division."

"We could always use more hands, preferably household attendants. We need to get the lodging up to par, so to speak," Lee laughed at his own joke. Lincoln favored him with a smile.

"Are we looking for comfort wives or just general housekeeping?"

"Both, if you can spare a dozen or so from the main compound."

"I'll talk to Mamacita," Lincoln promised. *Mamacita was even more efficient than Rucker, if that were possible.*

"And maybe send us some female attendants who know basic first aid—and we could use more Neo. There are lots of puncture wounds in working with the fencing...and we need it to treat a few horse bites, too. They can be feisty bastards," he laughed.

"Trust me, I understand," Lincoln replied, grinning as well. "I'll talk to Mamacita and see what she can do."

Darius held on to the door frame, waiting for the tremors to subside. Knoxvillians were used to the ground shaking, locals taking the earths' rumblings all in stride. *After all, there were worse things.*

Even after the fracking industry had gone bankrupt before the wars, eastern Tennessee suffered from the occasional earthquake. After the end of electricity, the tremors did not abate, growing more persistent if not stronger. *However,* Darius thought, *at least they weren't as bad as the ones that carved up post-California into grotesque slabs—a few that now resided at the bottom of the Pacific.*

An attendant came in with an armful of uniform samples for his approval, various designs in white and purple, the purple dye obtained from the boiled roots of the local cherry trees.

"I do like this one," Darius cooed, fingering the rough spun tunics. "They'll look smart on a regiment coming over the crest of a hill. Almost regal, in a way..."

"How many should we order from the textile makers?"

For a moment, Darius was lost in thought, thinking of his miserable childhood among the looms, interweaving the weft through the warp. He could still feel the tightly held threads under tension while his small fingers did the weaving, so much more efficient than large adult ones. He unconsciously felt his hands for the calluses long since healed, the ones he earned working twelve hours a day. The marks from the beatings and whippings were still evident on his back.

"Sir?"

"Three hundred," Darius replied, blinking back to the present. "That's the minimum to start. Tell them to expedite the order. Come to an agreement. I trust your negotiating skills," he added, a bold-faced lie. Darius trusted no one, especially when it came to money.

He flipped through the assortment of styles, some bold and imposing, some clownish. Darius wondered if fashion would ever be important to the populace again, the cut of a pair of trousers or the heel of a boot. But he supposed when most people had trouble feeding themselves and their families, fripperies like leather coats and natty hats weren't a priority.

Shame, really.

Regardless, Darius had plans for moving his forces east, and the purple and white of his coalescing army would strike fear into the scoundrels and wastrels along the way. Certainly some would join his Armageddonist cause simply for clothing and a hot daily meal. Yet the moment for bold action was at hand. While the Carolinas were still in flux and various ragtag militia groups vied for power among the United Authority's ashes, it was the perfect time for Darius to act. Otherwise, the White Crosses would become even more entrenched in the southeast, making them harder to eradicate. Of all the militias, Darius knew the White Crosses would never yield to him peaceably.

He tried on one of the tunics, failing to button it over his protruding belly. *The downside of being in charge,* he frowned at his girth. *Eating too well, eating too often.*

As a child, he'd had so little to eat. Now, his starving body held onto every calorie. With a word, he could order any meal he wanted, and a comely serving attendant would bring it to him. He took full advantage of both.

But he still felt eyes on him, at all times. Even in a position of great and growing power, Darius felt unsatisfied. He took the tunic off and threw it at the attendant. "Three hundred of these. In two weeks."

Scurrying out before Darius' notorious temper flashed into a rage, the attendant picked up all the clothing, retreating through the doorway. Guards had been doubled, standing stoically with an assortment of weapons.

Darius walked to the door and closed it. *Were his guards watching him? Were they reporting his actions to someone else who meant him harm?*

Darius remembered the gray eyes of a little girl who could appear next to him as if she were a phantasm. He remembered the jimson weed. He also remembered the promise he made to himself. He would kill the little gray eyed girl with his own dagger, the one that still had Xerxes' dried blood on the hilt.

Darius shifted on the overstuffed stool by his vanity table, applying a thick, ruddy foundation that he felt made him look more youthful. He drew heavy black lines around his eyes, making them look enigmatic in a way.

Yet somehow, Darius failed to look as magnificent as Xerxes did on his worst day. *That was the problem with being short.* Height garnered immediate respectability—a virility—that he felt he did not convey. He would look into wearing elevated shoes.

Another slight tremor from a small earthquake made his jars of cosmetics and facial paint rattle, each vibrating and shaking in a discordant tune.

Darius grinned at himself in the mirror. *It was a sign,* he felt. The earth moved. *He would move.* The time was right and the omens were good for pushing east.

"Colonel Fortinbras?" a young second lieutenant asked, standing outside the canvas tent. "Is Colonel Fortinbras available?"

Fortinbras muttered, opening his eyes. He needed just a few more minutes of peace before another harrowing day. The previous night's burning of Kingsport, Tennessee and the subsequent crucifictions of the small band of stray Armaggedonists had taxed him.

It was too early to be awake, the sky still blue-black before dawn. Fortinbras's stomach grumbled.

He stood up in the cramped tent and stretched. The scrapping field leader of the Militia of the White Crosses ached in every joint and bone.

For a man not yet fifty colony-years old, he felt twice that age on most mornings.

"The sergeants are preparing the men to move out. Do we have orders, sir?"

"We do, lieutenant," Colonel Fortinbras rubbed his eyes. *Another hour of sleep. He'd give his soul for one more hour.*

"Where are we headed, sir? Another scrapping field?"

"No, lieutenant. We've been selected for a special mission."

"Where to, sir?"

"Abingdon."

"Where are we headed, sir? Another scrapping field?"
"No, lieutenant. We've been selected for a special mission."

Chapter 23

Abingdon, Old Virginia

Mamacita worried about Lincoln.

"You need to eat," she tried again, handing him a plateful of her corn tortillas stuffed with scrambled eggs.

Thanks to hybrid seed engineering, stalks of corn sprouted throughout Old Virginia's territory, regardless of the season. Mamacita sent the little ones out to scavenge for corn cobs, bringing back dozens of ears to shuck. They stripped off the corn kernels, soaking them in lime. Once the kernels were dry, she and her attendants ground them to make *masa harina*.

"I'm not hungry right now," Lincoln replied, pouring over a few drawings of a small-scale desalination plant. Rucker's team debated whether thermal distillation or reverse osmosis was the best way forward. After hearing from both sides, Lincoln was perplexed on how to proceed. His gut, which held him in good stead, told him to wait.

Lincoln did what he always did when considering what would be best for his people: he used paper scraps to flesh out a decision matrix, untangling his mind by diagramming all of the possible consequences. The fine charcoal nubs he used to scribble on cardboard or waste paper or a wall were a far cry from the printed and bound architectural plans he'd studied many decades prior.

At some point when his future plantation became established, Lincoln would focus on making paper in greater quantities. He'd experiment with crafting more sophisticated pens and ink. *Perhaps a modified printing press would follow close behind?*

A half dozen of his attendants awaited, bringing him a myriad of business concerns and personal problems. He still needed to ride out to the golf course and receive his update on the horses in preparation for the Abingdon meeting.

He'd planned to take Lee with him, his best HorseMan on staff. Letting his men who were experts in their field finalize the sale of commodities tended to yield the best results, and Lincoln was more than happy to share the burdens of decision-making. This bonded his men to him more tightly, as Lincoln used larger carrots alongside his larger sticks to ensure his people worked at capacity.

Across the old high school's main hallway, Rucker was bogged down in management decisions, organizing the transport of the horses to the White Crosses as well as vetting transients who seemed to arrive in fits and starts on a daily basis. Some of the people who appeared on the plantation's borders had specialized talents. They were invited to stay. More often than not, deserters or suspected miscreants were shown the way out of town at the point of a knife.

On occasion, entire families wandered onto the property, bringing rumors and gossip, begging for work on the plantation and a respite from the road. Cagey orphans appeared in small feral packs, pledging to dig ditches and boil water and wash clothing. Battered temporary wives showed up, alone, asking for kitchen or domestic work.

Rucker questioned each and every person before Lincoln vetted them himself. Rucker marveled at how uncanny Lincoln was in spotting fraudsters and would-be troublemakers.

Lincoln sighed. There was an exhausting array of matters that required his immediate attention.

"I am not leaving until you eat all of this," tiny Mamacita insisted, placing one of the golf course's fine china plates, full of her mouthwatering food, directly in front of him. It was no longer piping hot, but the tortillas smelled delicious. "I made this myself, just for you. I went out to the chicken coops and gathered four eggs, just for you. I added some goat's milk and some wild onion and some salt from your own plantation, just for you. And now, you will eat it all—just for me."

Lincoln pursed his lips. "If I eat this, Mamacita, will you leave me alone?" he inquired, one of his eyebrows arched.

She frowned at him. "I will leave you alone until supper. Then I will bring you *two* plates of food!"

Not breaking his eye contact with her, Lincoln picked up the first tortilla, consuming it all in three large bites. He continued to stare at her while polishing off the second one immediately thereafter.

"Are you satisfied?" he asked, wiping his mouth on the sleeve of his threadbare gray sweatshirt.

"*Eres un animal,*" she muttered, taking the plate, turning to leave.

Rucker inadvertently blocked her path, walking into Lincoln's chambers, eyes lit, accompanied by a broad grin across his face.

"Lincoln! Come to the main gate!" Rucker called, waving for them both to follow. Mamacita had never seen Rucker so animated. The man hardly ever showed any emotion on his face, let alone a smile. She trailed on Lincoln's heels as they made their way down the wide hallways, still dotted with rusty beige lockers in various states of disrepair. The small group exited through the old high school's entrance, through its thick metal doors.

Standing in front of the school's circular driveway, wide enough for school buses that hadn't run for decades, Lincoln saw that a large group of attendants and their families had spontaneously gathered. Cheers and whistles came from the crowd, celebrating an oncoming procession of several colony-dozen travelers, either riding on horseback or traveling in makeshift horse-drawn wagons.

"Medicine Girl!" someone called out as the group neared. Lincoln stopped short, scanning the group, seeing her in the front, riding Patches alongside a tall blonde youth who was dressed in a shabby United Authority tunic.

On the Medicine Girl's other side were who appeared to be Temporary Wives, dressed in their finest. They waved back at the attendants and their families, responding good-naturedly to the catcalling from a few of the men.

Seeing Lincoln, The Medicine Girl urged Patches forward, making her way to the front of the old high school. Several feet from him, the Medicine Girl pulled up on Patches' reins, stopping the horse while dismounting in one fluid movement.

Wordlessly, Lincoln gathered her up into his arms, burying his face in her hair. She hugged him with all her remaining strength, until the rest of her companions arrived, dismounting as well.

"You brought all of Richmond with you?" Lincoln said to her.

The Medicine Girl looked up, her eyes brimming with watery tears, red-rimmed with fatigue. "Can they stay?"

"If you want them to stay," Lincoln assured her, taking a quick inventory of the eclectic group. He looked at the Medicine Girl, trying to ascertain as if she were injured. "Are you safe? Are you hungry?"

"I'm always hungry," the Medicine Girl said, leaning into him. "It's been a very long ride, Lincoln. We are all so tired."

Jasper rode up on his steed, awkwardly dismounting the best he could on one leg. He retrieved his crutches and approached Lincoln, who had the Medicine Girl tucked under his arm.

"Sir, I am Jasper Crimson-Atlanta of the Militia of the White Crosses, outsourced for special detail to the United Authority."

"Stand down, Crimson-Atlanta. Let's get you all fed and cleaned up a bit, then we will talk at length. Rucker? Could you see to the Medicine Girl's guests?"

Lincoln looked up in time to see two women approaching him with a singularity of purpose. One of the women was strikingly beautiful; the other appeared fiercely determined. Rucker mumbled something to Lincoln as they approached.

"Where's this Rucker? Are you Rucker?," the tall blonde inquired. Rucker looked at her full in the face, hearing his name called. Jalen sauntered over to him, wearing a dirty jade green frock, her beauty still apparent under the dust and road weariness.

"I am Rucker."

"Well, Eve said you handle logistics around here. I'll need a bath and a bed and a huge glass of lime water at your earliest convenience." She paused and rifled through her oversized bag. "And send someone over with sandwiches. We haven't eaten well in days!"

"You could be more diplomatic, Jalen. They don't have to take us in," Mitzi whispered. Identifying Lincoln as the person in charge, Mitzi turned to him with a dazzling smile and extended her hand. "Pleased to meet you, Mr. Lincoln. I am Mitzi, Jalen's business partner. Have you considered a CatHouse for your plantation?"

Not to be outdone, Ursula rounded the curb after handing off her horse to a HorseMan to tend. Catching the end of Mitzi's remarks, she intruded on the conversation, touting her expertise to anyone who would listen.

Others began to talk to whomever seemed most amenable to their cause, pleading their own particular case to stay, requesting assistance, inquiring about the plantation and the warlord's treatment of his people.

Trafficking in gossip was necessary in chaotic times such as these. The clamor of conversations added to the chaos.

Lincoln raised his hands, greeting them while quelling the chatter. "People, we will need to get all of your horses tended to. Rucker and his team will process you as soon as possible." He nodded to his attendants, who were already putting plans into motion. "Mamacita, see that they're fed. These people will need access to the bathing facilities and help finding appropriate sleeping accommodations."

"Yes, Lincoln," Mamacita said.

Rucker nodded in compliance, calling a few of his own subordinates to sort out the newcomers. Some seemed qualified and useful. As for others in the newly arrived group? He wasn't so sure.

"And Mamacita, take these two ladies over to the golf course later to meet with Lee," Lincoln instructed, motioning to Jalen and Mitzi. *Lee would either thank him for the CatHousers or quit on the spot.*

As the horses were taken out to the pasture, the weary travelers followed directions as they were given. Attendants looked at their cuts, burns, and other ailments from the long journey. They were checked for lice and other communicable diseases. Lime water was brought in and received with much gratitude.

Lincoln knew that Mamacita would churn out enough food within a colony-hour to sate their hungry bellies.

What a wide array of people, Lincoln thought. There would be much to learn from each of them. He decided to have Rucker send them to him, one by one, so he could interview and extract whatever information they had—and he would start with the Cathousers.

"Medicine Girl, where did you find all these people?" he asked, noticing the girl tucked under his arm was fast asleep, still standing on her feet. She was held up only by Lincoln's strong arm about her waist.

Smiling softly, Lincoln lifted the Medicine Girl into his arms and carried her inside the old high school.

It was a five colony-hour journey to Abingdon. Lee drove the horses, his capable HorseMen on both sides of the herd. Lincoln and Rucker took up the rear, accompanied by heavily armed attendants. By noon the day had grown hot, summer seeping into spring, bringing its heat and humidity much earlier than usual.

The Old Virginian countryside was verdant, quiet, almost peaceful as the horses whinnied and clopped along, south and west on the Eight One. The meeting place was just outside Abingdon.

Colonel Fortinbras had arrived with a colony-dozen or so of his own men, battle-hardened, prepared to drive the horses as best they could to the White Crosses' stronghold in Atlanta. Fortinbras had known Lincoln before his Colonial Williamsburg days, trusting Lincoln more than his own men, and definitely more than his generals. Those fools were hellbent on reclaiming the southeast, including the Carolinas. *A suicide mission*, Fortinbras thought. *Attempting to bring civility to the Carolinas was utter folly.*

Word had it that a viral hemorrhagic fever ravaged the Carolinas' remaining cities, but any information coming out of the region was suspect. Even so, the situation changed daily as religious factions and smaller militias merged and split at will. In his last official brief, Fortinbras had been informed that the Carolinas' militias had united in part. They had been in talks with Darius and the Armageddonists about joining their cause. If that were the case, the White Crosses needed a robust cavalry, sooner rather than later.

Fortinbras arranged the delivery with Lincoln in the early afternoon. Held in a dilapidated Old Virginian winery, the tasting room at the entrance still boasted stained glass windows, miraculously intact, giving the room a rustic charm and quiet elegance. A large rectangular oak table took up the majority of the space, with assorted chairs and mismatched stools dotting the perimeter of the room.

Lincoln knew the place well. His group arrived promptly, Lee and his men corralling the horses inside a makeshift paddock near the winery's former loading dock.

Lincoln and Rucker dismounted, watching the HorseMen coordinate with Fortinbras' MilitiaMen, who stood wide eyed and slack jawed at their first look at the horses. They approached, bringing buckets of water and fresh hay, watching Lincoln's men stroke the horses' long necks and muscular shoulders, scratching their ears, talking to the horses as if they understood.

A few other of Lincoln's attendants followed him into the winery.

"Lincoln," Colonel Fortinbras stood, hand outstretched.

Looking leaner and older than his Colonial Williamsburg days, Lincoln shook Fortinbras' hand, taking a seat near the door. His attendants sat directly behind him.

"My lieutenant tells me your herd looks very strong—very healthy!"

"Agreed," Lincoln said. "You have a fine selection. We've included several good breeders. Lee is my chief Horseman, down from Calgary. He worked with the United Authority's men before Richmond fell. He knows what he is doing." Both men walked to the windows and peered outside to see Fortinbras' men take their first steps in animal husbandry.

"As discussed, we will need you to educate my men in the care and feeding of the animals. The generals are working on training HorseMen for the militias, but I'm afraid the Carolinas have bogged them down."

"Of course," Lincoln agreed. "Lee is the right person for the job. I'm sure your men will be fast learners."

As if on cue, there was a loud thud and the sounds of commotion. Several horses whinnied before a flurry of screams and angry cursing.

Both men looked at each other and laughed.

"I've been bucked off a few times," Lincoln admitted. "It takes a little while to get your sea legs."

"I can imagine," Fortinbras agreed.

"So, how do you want to proceed?" Lincoln asked.

"Well, first teach us the basics. Tacking up. Grooming. I'm sure there are other things I'm not aware of. The southern generals are committed to investing in cavalries. With the United Authority down, there is no dependable transportation or communication. Horses are inevitable. They'll make moving troops and supplies far easier than the transports. There is talk of using them in battle, too."

"I presumed as much," Lincoln said, his voice somber.

"In any event, I'm glad to see you." Colonel Fortinbras shook his hand again, putting an arm around his shoulder. "The Colonial Williamsburg business was regrettable. I was sorry to hear—"

Lincoln interrupted him. "We've planned to stay a few days until your MilitiaMen have a good grasp of things. We've brought bridles, halters, and reins to spare."

"What about saddles?"

"We are working with our LeatherMen, but it's a process. We're still a new plantation. Things take time."

"This herd will be sufficient for our current needs. I'm sure the generals will put in future orders once they see what we can do with a trained cavalry, small as it is," Fortinbras replied, folding his hands in front of him. "Are we agreed about a hard colony-currency price?"

Lincoln grew silent.

"I think we need to talk," Lincoln said, crossing his legs. A young boy dressed in a White Crosses uniform poured Lincoln lime water before disappearing through a door.

Fortinbras leaned back. "I'm here. Let's talk."

"No," said Lincoln. "*We* need to talk."

Fortinbras looked around the room at his Chief of Staff. With a simple nod, the room was cleared of all White Crosses.

"Rucker, take the men out and have them help with the instruction," Lincoln ordered. "Take everyone out."

Rucker gave him a puzzled look. Lincoln gave him a curt nod, and Rucker disappeared without a backward glance.

Lincoln stood and walked over to Fortinbras, sitting down on his right side.

"What is it, Lincoln?" Fortinbras said. The two older men studied each other.

"How many men are under your command?" Lincoln asked.

"Roughly a thousand."

"Are they loyal to you?"

"More so than to the generals. But I will tell you this, Lincoln. These men are tired of fighting endless skirmishes on bloody scrapping fields without pay, without seeing their families, without any clear direction. It's just battle after battle, for very little reward. And recently, we've led some of our best brigades into bloodbaths. Frankly, I'm tired of seeing my men be grist for the mill."

Lincoln looked down, feeling the weight of the Colonel's words, trying to discern whether he should proceed in the direction his gut was heading.

"Tell me, Lincoln. What's on your mind?" Fortinbras asked.

"My stepdaughter arrived with an assortment of stragglers out of Richmond. Nonessentials. FieldHands. Several Temporary Wives, a couple of free Cathousers. And let me tell you, these Cathousers are smart. They've heard enough rumblings from southern MilitiaMen to ascertain what's happening in this region. I've checked with several other of my sources and it rings true."

"What is it?"

"Unaligned militias are coalescing behind the Illuminati Pagans. In droves."

"Pagans...uniting behind Darius?" Fortinbras chuckled. "Who'd follow that sawed off little—"

"Apparently, the Carolinas."

"You can't mean—"

"I'm afraid so. By the end of summer, Darius plans to push east into Old Virginia while the Carolingians push west. White Crosses are embroiled on too many fronts. When both groups meet in the middle—

sacking and burning and looting whatever they can—they'll head south to Atlanta. In one Grande Armée."

"Atlanta? They'd be foolish to take on the entirety of the White Crosses." Fortinbras looked sickened.

"The White Crosses are spread too thin, Colonel. Darius knows this, instigating skirmishes to thin your lines."

"Darius! That little shit!" Fortinbras put his head in his hands.

"And worse?" Lincoln said. "Apparently two of your generals are going to flip. Mayfair and Buchanan."

Fortinbras hit the table with both of his fists.

The men sat in silence for a bit, calculating the human cost of the south run by the Illuminati Pagans.

"Saltville is in the crosshairs," Lincoln said wistfully. "Especially now that the horses are a known commodity…"

"It's worse than you think, Lincoln. The White Crosses won't hold together. Division is already rife throughout the ranks. My men are on half rations. If Mayfair and Buchanan turn their coats, the confidence of the men will break. Even now—" He didn't finish.

Fortinbras tapped his fingers on the table, considering his options. They were few. And he knew very well what Pagans did to captured military leaders.

"We are both in precarious situations," Lincoln pronounced, eyeing Fortinbras.

"I know you, Lincoln," Fortinbras said. "You won't let another Colonial Williamsburg happen again. What is your plan?"

"We join forces. You have the MilitiaMen. I have ample support services. We will follow behind your army with provisions, medical personnel, HorseMen, Comfort Station women, family services attendants—whatever you need. Your men's families will travel with us in a military/civilian joint campaign to somewhere safe. Somewhere out of the way until these next waves of wars are over."

Fortinbras felt the gravity of Lincoln's proposal, but also the weight of the truth of what he had said. Inventorying the events of the past month, there had been disturbing and worrying signs. *He should have suspected Mayfair and Buchanan!* Their recent behavior had been so far out of character.

Fortinbras, a man given to caution, ventured one question. "Where's *safe* these days, Lincoln?"

"A place located three weeks south. A place we'll need to clean out a bit, but it shouldn't be too hard. The warlord there is violent, but stupid."

"You don't mean—"

"I do. The Penal Colony of Florida."

"More specifically?" asked the Colonel.

"Tallahassee."

She hugged him with all her remaining strength, until the rest of her companions arrived.

Chapter 24

Macon, The Kingdom of Georgia

The Medicine Girl retrieved her knives from the wooden target, pleased with her improvement. She still missed her old machete, taken away from her long ago, but she'd become friendly with a smaller one she'd acquired.

The day was warm; perspiration trickled down her neck in rivulets. She wiped her brow with her forearm. As she prepared to throw again, she spotted Jasper hobbling around the corner of the makeshift stable, the one housing Lincoln's finest horses.

The Medicine Girl did a double take, as Jasper approached, standing upright, not hampered with his ever present crutches.

"Jasper!" she called out, putting her knives down on a tree stump. She scurried over towards him, eyes wide in amazement. "Jasper, where are your crutches?"

As he turned towards her, he smiled, hesitantly walking down a small embankment. Though he wobbled a bit, he steadied himself, holding out his hands for balance.

"How did I do?" he asked, as she took his hand. He laughed as he attempted to turn too quickly and stumbled.

"You walk like a newborn deer!"

He looked a little hurt, ducking his head so she couldn't see him flush red.

"How'd—how did you..." she didn't finish her question before he pulled up his trousers to reveal a carved wooden leg, its end tucked neatly into a matching boot.

"It's pine," he explained, knocking on the leg. "Frank the WoodMan made this one for me out of pine. I'll have another one made out of oak one day. Oak is stronger, but heavier to haul around." Jasper grinned, for the first time looking boyish and hopeful.

"How did they stick it on?" The Medicine Girl asked, coming closer, touching the wooden leg and admiring its craftsmanship.

"It's strapped to my upper thigh," he explained. "There's a cap made of horse leather attached to my stump. It's lined with sheepskin to make it less painful."

"Does it hurt?" she asked. "Does the stump hurt when you walk on it?"

"I'll get used to it," he stoically replied, taking a seat on a weathered metal bench.

"Are you still working with the horses?" she asked, curious as to how he spent his days.

He gave a heavy sigh, followed by a shrug. "No, I don't think I am. They need someone...someone different than me," he mumbled. "I'm better with the smaller animals anyways. Rabbit hutches. The chicken coops."

"I talked to Lincoln about us raising goats. Maybe you and I could get that started? Goats are remarkable animals." She was speaking too fast, tucking a long black strand of hair behind her ear. "And goat milk is delicious. You can make soap out of it. Cheese, too. And goat fur is very soft. I have a goat fur blanket—and it's amazing. Goats are really, really useful."

"You said as much on the way from Roanoke. Your friend is the Goatman of Witt, if I remember, right?"

"Yes. He is a good man," she said, looking off to the west. "You'd like him, Jasper. The Goatman is very patient, very practical. He would be useful here."

Jasper nodded and looked down at his wooden leg.

"Maybe I'll ask Lincoln to send for him," she added. "He could become the Goatman of Saltville."

"Probably so," Jasper agreed, standing up gingerly. "Well, I need to get back to the pens."

"Okay," the Medicine Girl agreed, reluctant to see him leave. "I'm in the clinic most days. Come by if some chicken pecks you."

He nodded, turned on his good leg and made his way back to the field path.

The Medicine Girl watched him go, picking up her knives again and holding them for a long while before continuing to practice.

Late into the night after he returned from Abingdon, Lincoln knocked on the classroom door of the Medicine Girl's living quarters, surprised to see her up as late, reading a tattered high school science textbook by candlelight.

"Learning anything new?" he asked.

"Not really," she replied, adding, "I wish I had a microscope."

"I wish you had a lot of things," Lincoln replied.

"How did it go with the White Crosses?" she asked, without looking up. She turned a page.

"They were amenable to your suggestion," Lincoln reported matter-of-factly.

The Medicine Girl nodded in reply. She put the book down and looked squarely at him. "So, when do we move out?"

"One week. Rucker is getting started on the arrangements now."

"Have you sent out your advance team yet?"

"They were gone before we left for Abingdon."

"We could use goats in Tallahassee, Lincoln. Witt is only a four or five day round trip. It's faster if I take Patches..."

"Do you think the Goatman would come with us?"

"Does he have a choice? The newcomers who arrived today told Ursula horror stories of what's happening in the west. There's no check on the Pagans, Lincoln. They're eating up Tennessee and moving east. If they get horses..." she trailed off.

"I know, Medicine Girl," he rubbed his red-rimmed eyes. *He knew what would happen.*

"Darius will eventually control all of the south," she said assuredly. "People want a strong man to lead them, no matter what they have to give up."

"Darius is mad."

"What will we do when he comes this far east? Maybe even to the penal colony?"

"We'll fight or head far north or far west," Lincoln attempted to reassure her. "We'll survive one way or another." He wandered over to her knives and inspected each one.

"I'm tired of fighting," she mumbled. "I want to raise goats."

He gave her a small grin, imagining the years of her feeding her goats and shearing fur and milking nanny goats and delivering kids. *The life of a Goatwoman didn't suit her one bit*, he thought.

"I hope we all are tired of war," Lincoln replied. "I'm sure there will be a meeting of the minds at some point to carve up the country. It's been done several times before us and will be done until the end of man on this continent. Eventually, cooler heads will prevail, Medicine Girl. War does not last forever."

"Yes, but terror does," she whispered low, an uncharacteristic flicker of fear in her voice.

Lincoln had wished the Medicine Girl hadn't heard what was happening in the hills and hamlets as the Illuminati Pagans expanded their territory at an alarming rate. At the Abingdon winery, Colonel Fortinbras had told Lincoln in graphic detail about the blood rituals Darius had instituted before, during, and after each raid. The colonel shuddered at the unspeakable things they'd found at some of the scrapping fields—the trophies and keepsakes the pagans had taken. Their barbarism had increased with their burgeoning power.

"The Goatman will come. Let me ride down to Witt with a few HorseMen. We'll take the animal wagon for the goats. I'll explain the whole situation to him. I can be very convincing."

"Of this I know," Lincoln chuckled before growing serious. "I'm not sure if I can spare the HorseMen at the moment, but there are others who might go. There is just so much to do to prepare to leave."

"I will go."

"You are not going to go."

"Lincoln, I am leaving tomorrow morning to get the Goatman of Witt." The Medicine Girl stared at him, jutting out her chin.

"Then I will find attendants to escort you to ensure you are not captured, beaten, assaulted, or crucified. Is that all right?"

She rolled her eyes and returned to her outdated science book. She pretended to mull over a chapter on cell division.

"And don't sneak off in the middle of the night, Medicine Girl. Things are more dangerous than when Richmond fell. Nothing is stable."

She sighed. "I can take care of myself."

"I'm sure you can," Lincoln muttered. "But I'm not willing to risk losing you, too."

At that, the Medicine Girl looked up at him, to see if he was sincere.

"All right, I won't sneak off in the middle of the night," she agreed. "But I am leaving tomorrow to get the Goatman. Where do we meet up with the White Crosses, in case you leave me again?"

"I didn't leave you. You ran off and I assumed you were dead."

She rolled her eyes again. "If we get held up, where are we meeting the White Crosses?"

"Macon."

"You need to avoid Atlanta," she warned.

"You'd make a good general," Lincoln noted, only half kidding. "Yes, Atlanta is problematic. The White Crosses' command post is the last place we want to be. When Fortinbras takes his men offline, they will be classified as deserters, and the White Crosses do not take kindly to deserters...The exodus to Florida must be very fast," Lincoln leaned against the door frame, fatigue having caught up with him.

"I'd make a great general," she replied.

He massaged his neck, stiff since the long trail ride. "I worry about moving the families. We have to move a great number of people through a very difficult part of the country. And there won't be time to wait for stragglers. Even those coming from Witt," he added, looking pointedly at her.

"Do you think my father knows we are coming?"

"If he did, we would already be dead," Lincoln mused. "You know there are spies everywhere. Rucker had two beheaded in the paddock today—Snake Handlers disguised as former dispatch runners. Darius rewards those with any information. So little is known about what is going on out there." Lincoln walked over to the classroom's windows. "I think the Illuminati Pagans thrive on rumor and innuendo."

"And ignorance," the Medicine Girl offered.

"Yes, indeed. Ignorance, too."

The Medicine Girl grew quiet. *Two spies caught on the plantation?* She was certain Lincoln blamed himself for their presence. The idea of bringing any possible harm to his community sickened him. *So much could go wrong so quickly in this world.*

"Is it really too dangerous to go to Witt?" she asked in a small voice.

"It is. I'd prefer you not go. You are too valuable to me to lose," he stated firmly. "Let me send a few men down to the Goatman. A smaller party may be better on foot. Write him a letter and convince him to come. Okay?"

"Okay," she agreed, worried now about the noises that came from the nearby paddock or farther off into the darkened distance. She was torn between being pleased Lincoln was talking to her like an advisor and being afraid of the unseen things that surrounded them.

Lincoln noticed her discomfort. "We are safe tonight, Medicine Girl. No worries."

"Okay," she said again, looking at the top of the old school desk where she had laid her various knives. They'd just been sharpened on a whet stone and gleamed in the candlelight.

"You won't be needing those to defend yourself or anyone else tonight, I promise you. There are good men attending this whole corridor. Besides, do you think Mamacita would let anything happen to you?" He gave her a wry smile. "Be at peace."

"Okay," she repeated a third time, eyelids heavy. Lincoln walked over to her and pulled up a thin coverlet to tuck her in on the moldy gym mats she laid on.

He looked around the classroom, remembering a time when students sat in desks with laptops and textbooks, learning all that man had discovered, hoped for, and imagined. At an earlier time, bells rang, students fell in love in the hallways, families attended football games on Friday nights—all rooting for their team to score. *Now, MilitiaMen chanted on the scrapping fields, celebrating death.*

Those gentler memories seemed to belong to another race of men. Lincoln had to now worry about moving a few thousand people south through hostile territory, running into rabid quasi-religious militias, and breaking into a penal colony to find a safer place to start over yet again. The enormity of it all threatened to overwhelm him.

He looked at the Medicine Girl's knives, all within arm's reach. Seeing her adapt so artfully to the awful normalcy of the world disheartened him, making him miss her genial mother even more.

He shut the door as he left. The Medicine Girl could hear him talking with a few men down the hall. She thought she heard him say her name.

In the dark, the Medicine Girl reached over and grabbed two of her favorite knives and placed them under her pillow. Regardless of Lincoln's assurances, she knew that bad men always seem to find a way. Her own father had taught her that.

In her restless dreams, her subconscious conjured up images of Mika, but she chose not to entertain thoughts of her mother. Instead, she dreamed of putting one of the knives that lay under her pillow into her father's heart.

Jalen and Mitzi lay sprawled out on a rough spun straw mattress, making plans to set up their smaller CatHouse by the nine-hole golf course. It was far enough away from the main plantation, where wives and children held sway.

"Lee said they expect three dozen HorseMen and just as many attendants by the end of summer," Mitzi figured. "I'm guessing we need two or three girls, depending if I work, and even more if Saltville becomes a stop on the way to Abingdon." Mitzi scratched out numbers with a piece of charcoal on the floor.

"Ursula could prove useful," Jalen suggested.

"I don't like her," Mitzi said. "But if we don't invite her in, she could set up her own place and drive prices down. I'd rather keep a watchful eye on her from the inside, rather than compete with her on the outside."

"You're kind of a badass," Jalen cooed, kissing Mitzi on the lips. Mitzi stood up to pour both of them a plastic mug of boiled water.

Jalen stared at the floor to puzzle the numbers out, wondering if she could hire a tailor or seamstress from Abingdon on credit. As for other finery? It would be hard to come by for quite a while. She'd talked to the WoodMen about carving her high heeled shoes, but she couldn't imagine they would be very comfortable.

There was a slight knock at the door. Without waiting for a response, the Medicine Girl poked her head inside.

"Eve!" Jalen cried. "Come in, my love."

The Medicine Girl smiled sheepishly and climbed onto the mattress next to her. Jalen gave her a rib-cracking hug.

"What are these numbers?" The Medicine Girl pointed at Mitzi's markings.

"We're setting up a CatHouse at the main horse paddock, right next to the golf course. This is just a little number crunching to determine personnel and other expenses."

The Medicine Girl shook her head.

"What's wrong?" Jalen asked.

"Don't waste your time."

"What do you mean?" Mitzi looked offended.

"Saltville is being vacated. Lincoln's calling a meeting tomorrow to discuss it with everyone. We're heading south to Macon in a week."

"Dammit, we just got here!" complained Mitzi. Jalen stood up and put her hand on Mitzi's shoulder. "I hate the Kingdom of Georgia... there's nothing but sorrow in the south."

"We'll be fine," Jalen said soothingly, a large smile spreading across her face. "I'm sure wherever we go, there will be opportunities—Eve, where are we really going?"

The Medicine Girl hesitated. "The Penal Colony of Florida."

Jalen looked dumbfounded. "Say again?"

"The Penal Colony of Florida."

"You have to be fucking kidding me," Jalen replied, her smile still wide, but turned brittle and cold.

Mitzi threw her hands up. "Convicts? Prisoners? Prisoners are violent and don't have any money! We can't go to the penal colony. Surely there is some town along the way we could..."

"Lincoln will explain it all tomorrow," said the Medicine Girl. "The violence is getting worse now that the Illuminati Pagans are taking over the south."

"The pagans don't like independent Cathouses," Mitzi added. "They saw how much the United Authority raked in. I'm sure they think they can run comfort stations as well as the United Authority did for twice the price." She shook her head in disgust.

The two women stewed in silence, upset over this unwanted bit of information. The Medicine Girl walked over and sat on the floor before Jalen's large cosmetics box.

"Do men really like this stuff?"

Mitzi and Jalen looked at each other.

"Some do," Jalen offered.

"Can you show me how to use it? The black eye stuff and the red cheek powder..." The Medicine Girl took the lid off a small jar, smelled it, and put it back. She held up a few brushes and sponges, not having any idea what to do with them.

"Who do you want to get pretty for, Eve?" Jalen coyly asked.

"No one," the Medicine Girl replied. "No one of any consequence."

Mitzi and Jalen made eye contact again, suppressing snorts of laughter.

"Well," Jalen said, sitting down next to her. "Let's start at the beginning. In this jar," she took off the lid and dabbed a little beige cream on her forearm, "is foundation. It covers up all the blemishes and imperfections on your face, but it's not your skin tone at all." Jalen demonstrated by dabbing some of the foundation on the Medicine Girl's forearm. "You are too young to need foundation anyway."

"Is there a brown color?" she wondered.

"There are all sorts of colors, but I just have this one. And you don't need foundation."

"I don't?" the Medicine Girl asked.

Jalen held up a hand mirror. "See? Your complexion is a light mocha, not pasty white like mine. And your skin is flawless, except for a few scars, but that just gives your face character. Maybe just a little blush on your cheekbones..." Jalen swished some of the powder on her cheeks with a small paintbrush.

The Medicine Girl frowned at her reddened cheeks. "I look like I have a fever."

Jalen took a small sponge and started to blend the powder.

"Is that better?"

The Medicine Girl turned her head from side to side, knitting her eyebrows, scrutinizing her face. She nodded.

"What's the black stuff?"

"Mascara."

"Do we put that on next?" the Medicine Girl asked.

"Not yet." Jalen rummaged around in the box to find her dark gray eyeshadow. It would offset the Medicine Girl's smokey eyes, accompanied with a little black eyeliner.

"Could I try some lipstick, too?" the Medicine Girl asked.

"It depends," Jalen teased, holding out two tubes. "Do you think Jasper likes pink or red better?"

"It depends," Jalen teased, holding out two tubes. "Do you think Jasper likes pink or red better?"

Chapter 25

Thomasville, The Kingdom of Georgia

Vacating Saltville proved far easier than traversing the four hundred colony-miles through the South to Macon. The early summer heat gave no quarter, punishing both man and beast, making the quest for water more of a necessity than it should have been.

What remained of the roads oozed asphalt. More than a few horses needed to be put down for breaking their legs on the uneven terrain. Morale wavered from day to day, causing several families and a few individuals to divest themselves of Lincoln's caravan, preferring to take their chances elsewhere.

Lincoln declared mandatory siestas during the hottest noontime hours, preferring to move his people at dawn or very late at night. Like his men, Lincoln's eyes scanned the horizon, his unease heightened by seeing a random scrapping field, now and again, on either side of the sprawling roadways.

He allowed his people to scavenge the dead, but little remained. More bodies hung from trees, spanning a wide variety of ages, most bearing the markings of the Illuminati Pagans, silent witnesses of their increasing brutality.

While Mamacita organized the women into efficient cooperatives, the Medicine Girl took note of all that was happening. Her careful attention to detail proved useful in stopping minor concerns before they became major problems. She noted the children who needed to be tended, the pregnant women who required special care, and the ones who suffered with stomach ailments or broken arms or infected wounds.

Alleviate suffering, her mother had always said. There always seemed plenty to alleviate.

On the road, there was always wood to be gathered, water to boil, game to be hunted, fish to be netted. There were always roots, flowers, bark, and leaves to be gathered for tonics and purgatives and pain relief. There were always people, thirsty, hungry, tired, hurt, and afraid.

At times the Medicine Girl looked out on the caravan and despaired. *There are too many of us.*

Lee and a number of HorseMen rode ahead of the main party, helping to ensure the way was clear for the families to follow, an assembly of horse-drawn wagons and handcarts. There were many who walked barefoot, leaving tracks in the red clay, soft and pliable after the summer rains.

Man, woman, child—everyone was armed with some sort of weapon, ready to use at a moment's notice. From sharpened knives of all sizes to deadly slingshots to crude maces, all took Lincoln's counsel to be prepared and alert, especially until they united with Fortinbras' MilitiaMen and their respective families. Lee, himself, brandished an old shotgun, refurbished, just as threatening as it had ever been in decades past. He had precious few cartridges left, hoping just the sight of the weapon would instill fear in any bold HighwayMan.

We're averaging twenty-five colony-miles a day, the Medicine Girl fretted. She wondered how the addition of three thousand more individuals would tax their journey. All around her, she felt the prickly paranoia creep into side conversations.

She watched as spies for the Illuminati Pagans were captured, Lincoln's men extracting what little information they could before dispatching them. However, those men didn't concern the Medicine Girl. It was the ones who weren't caught that kept her up at night.

Outside Macon at the Griswoldville Historic Battlefield, Lincoln dismounted, surveying the mass of people before him, all busied in the chaos of bivouacking, tying down belongings for the 150 colony-miles south to Thomasville. The families were to wait there until Tallahassee was secured.

Colonel Fortinbras had, indeed, managed to bring the majority of his MilitiaMen and their families along, joining Lincoln's people—all of whom needed clean water, food, transportation, and shelter during the warm nights and scorching days.

The Medicine Girl stole up behind Lincoln as he surveyed the scene.

"I need you to stay with the families in Thomasville," he said without acknowledging her presence.

"Not a chance," she stated.

"I'll take care of your father," Lincoln insisted.

"You can bury what's left of him when I'm through." The Medicine Girl spat. "But there won't be enough to feed a crow."

They stood companionably, side by side, watching the intermingling of Fortinbras' people with their own. Colonel Fortinbras spotted Lincoln and waved a greeting from across the field, walking towards him. Several of Fortinbras' men fell in line behind him.

"Do you trust that man?" The Medicine Girl spoke in a low voice.

"With my life," Lincoln replied just as softly. "And yours."

In short order, Colonel Fortinbras joined them, shaking Lincoln's hand, nodding to the Medicine Girl.

"Does the Warlord of Tallahassee know we're coming?" inquired Lincoln.

"Our scouts believe so. Prisoners are amassing by the border, but that could just be for safety. Two storms are advancing on both sides of the peninsula. From what I hear, the barometric pressure has dropped under 1000 colony-millibars."

"We're a week out. Maybe Mother Nature will do most of our work for us?" Lincoln looked at Fortinbras. Fortinbras shrugged.

"We can talk about timing later, Lincoln. The storms will eventually pass, preferably not in our general direction. For contingencies, we'll need to find an adequate shelter if either storm heads due north."

"You think we should continue south, regardless?"

"I'm less concerned about a natural disaster than Darius' unnatural one. His Eastern assault? That storm just continues to wreak havoc," Fortinbras muttered. "Pagans are taking over town by town and not meeting a lot of resistance. White Crosses are defecting in droves. When I left Atlanta, it was a shitshow, Lincoln. The brass were accusing one another of selling out, of colluding with the enemy. I don't think there is one general I can trust anymore. The leadership is crumbling."

"Darius likes his spies to plant misinformation with his bribes and lies. He knows fear mongering dissolves trust faster than anything else... and without trust, no leadership can stand for long."

"Darius is the devil," Fortinbras agreed. "And a smart, conniving, tactical one at that."

"I am going to kill Darius," the Medicine Girl said, standing between the two men. "And this time with my bare hands." The Medicine Girl pantomimed snapping a neck.

Colonel Fortinbras gave Lincoln a startled look.

"There is some history there, and she probably could," Lincoln said, nodding at her.

The Medicine Girl looked at them both, then left the old men to their decisions. Unnoticed, she slipped away from Lincoln's side.

Lincoln and Fortinbras watched their people settle in for the night. Out of necessity, the two groups coalesced, de facto leaders emerging and calling out commands. From somewhere, they heard laughter. They heard singing.

Weary as he was, Lincoln couldn't help feeling an *esprit de corps* being established among the thousands of people in front of him, a feeling that gave Lincoln a modicum of hope.

As the hot sun cooled and prepared to set, women sent young children to gather wood or haul water to the impromptu cooking sites. Older teens dug latrines or took their slingshots out to hunt for rabbits or squirrels or raccoons to add to the stewpots. Men assembled canvas tents and makeshift sleeping quarters. The horses, their whinnys and chuffings echoing through camp, were tended to by Lee's men and fed tiny crabapples and shriveled carrots by young children.

Lincoln and Fortinbras supervised it all, tacitly feeling that perhaps some good would come from all of their efforts, hoping against hope that Darius would turn north and leave them alone.

The Medicine Girl spotted Jasper hobbling towards the roosters and chickens in wooden crates, neatly stacked on the back of a horse drawn wagon. Jasper sighed. Much to his chagrin, the chicken coops needed to be attended to. Jasper wondered how much of a chicken was fecal matter, as he had just cleaned out their cages at the previous stop.

He unrolled a spool of wire fencing in a closed circle to pen in the chickens while he washed out cages and laid down fresh straw. He took care to place several low bowls of boiled water along the sides of the pen; if the chickens didn't drink enough water, especially in the blistering heat, they wouldn't lay eggs. Any foodstuffs were far too important not to take every precaution in producing, so Jasper did his duty as he always had, with dedication and precision. If Jasper had to squeeze the eggs from the chickens himself, they would lay.

Jasper stood up to find the Medicine Girl inches away from him.

"Oh, sorry," he said, stumbling a bit, finding his footing. "I didn't see you there."

"Are you in charge of the chickens?" she asked.

"I'm in charge of *these* chickens," he corrected her. "There's a lot of chickens in this caravan."

"There's worse work," the Medicine Girl replied. "You could be digging latrines." She watched as Jasper removed chickens, one-by-one, from the crate and placed them into the pen.

Jasper laughed. "Well, at least I'm not over the pigs. They do not like to be transported—and those bastards bite!" He continued placing the chickens on the ground, watching them peck the dirt for bugs and worms.

"Have you ever been with a temporary wife?"

"Excuse me?" Jasper turned, looking at the Medicine Girl. His face turned red as he squeezed the chicken he was holding a little too tightly. The chicken squawked in protest, its wings flapping to show its discomfort. Jasper put it down.

"I said," the Medicine Girl repeated more loudly, "have you ever been with a temporary wife?"

Jasper looked at his feet. "That's a very personal question."

"So, you have."

"I didn't say that."

"Well, you didn't say you hadn't."

Jasper exhaled and looked at her. "Some of the White Crosses took me to a Comfort Station once. They filled out the temporary marriage certificate for me, but nothing came of it. I just left and waited outside until they were ready to go."

"Why did you leave?"

He shrugged.

"Do you like girls?"

"I like girls who don't ask a lot of embarrassing questions," he said, turning his back on her.

In silence, Jasper finished his tasks, all but ignoring the Medicine Girl.

After a time, she sensed he wasn't going to talk with her anymore and left.

Six days later, Fortinbras and Lincoln rode into Pebble Hill Plantation, southwest of Thomasville. Dotted with live oaks and red brick walkways, the advance team had taken over the stable structures on the abandoned 3,000 colony-acres, securing a paddock for the hundreds of horses accompanying Fortinbras' MilitiaMen, Lincoln's attendants, and their extended families.

"What happened here?" Lincoln said, surveying the grounds with numerous intact outbuildings, untended gardens with fertile soil, and clear running streams. "Why hasn't this area been resettled?"

"No one from the outside knows it's here," Fortinbras replied. "That's why it is perfect for us. And the locals believe this land is cursed."

"How so?"

"Right after the end of electricity, there was a series of cholera outbreaks. Killed scores. A few of the residents turned to voodoo or Santeria for relief. There was talk of animal sacrifices and worse."

"It just looks like an overgrown plantation, Fortinbras. You could grow anything here. Cotton. Sugarcane. Corn."

"And tobacco. This soil is well-drained. It would be easy to grow. It's a short-cycle crop."

"Surely there are more beneficial crops to grow." Lincoln raised an eyebrow at his old friend.

"I hear you, Lincoln. But tobacco is profitable."

Rucker came up to greet both men.

"Lincoln, we're setting up a command center in the Main House."

"Fortinbras and I will share an office for now, Rucker. When is the rest of the caravan expected?"

"Tomorrow afternoon."

"Any more incidents that I should know about?"

"Nothing that lower level attendants haven't been able to handle. You'll have to address the camp to settle everyone's nerves. Rumors about the aftermath of the hurricanes hitting the penal colony are running rampant. Some are saying there is no drinking water within a hundred colony-miles. Others are saying the storms turned towards Texas."

"When's the next briefing?" Lincoln asked, turning to Fortinbras.

"I have a dozen men returning from Tallahassee," he said somberly. "They're supposed to be here by morning. We should have the latest information and a better idea about logistics then."

"Good," Lincoln replied. "Rucker, how are preparations for the caravan's arrival?"

"All is well in hand. The spring appears to have potable water, but I've had a water crew boiling all afternoon. We'll have the stewpots ready. Oddly there is a tremendous number of possums in the area."

"Good, Rucker. Better safe than sorry, especially with this plantation's history of cholera." He glanced at Fortinbras. "And again, Rucker, thank you. And thank your men. Once again, you've done fantastic work."

"Can I get you anything, sir?" Rucker asked.

"Any chance I can get a hot meal and a clean bed?"

"I'll second that," Fortinbras heaved an exhausted sigh. "I'm getting a little old for this world-building, Lincoln."

"Amen, brother," Lincoln chuckled.

They followed Rucker onto the plantation's main grounds.

The sky was red in the morning, a sure sign of bad weather. Lincoln worried about the caravan, as just a few groupings had arrived throughout the night. He and Fortinbras had marginally underestimated how challenging moving both families and horses would be; MilitiaMen were used to hardship and deprivation. The organized body had metastasized along a hundred colony-mile stretch. Lincoln couldn't protect them all, but knew keeping them in lockstep would prove impossible.

Fortinbras and Lincoln took breakfast in their joint quarters, sorting out a number of concerns and complaints in preparation for the arrival of the main body of their assemblage.

A baker must have been attached to Rucker's advance team, as a pile of boiled bagels sat on a tin plate in front of them, alongside thick raspberry preserves. Both men were on their third bagel when Rucker entered.

"Your Tallahassee men are back, Fortinbras." Rucker informed him. "Should I send them in now?"

"Absolutely," Fortinbras barked. "And bring them plenty to eat and drink. And Rucker?"

"Yes, sir?"

"How many men are there?"

"Two."

Rucker disappeared while Fortinbras looked at Lincoln and put his head in his hands. "Another ten men dead."

"I'm sorry, Fortinbras."

"Good men. Trustworthy. Brave." Fortinbras eyes watered.

"I'm sure they were."

"Those men have families arriving tonight or tomorrow. Dammit, Lincoln. What do I say to them that I haven't said to a hundred other wives and children? I'm so tired of—"

A knock at the door interrupted him. Two very dirty, very spent men entered, collapsing onto a bench nearest the door.

Fortinbras walked over to shake his men's hands. "Frank. Taylor. So good to see you."

"Good to be seen, sir," Taylor whispered, his voice hoarse and grating.

"Can I get you anything—anything at all?"

"Rucker took good care of us, sir," Frank replied.

"I'm sorry about the others..." Fortinbras said weakly, struggling to find adequate words.

"They suffered, sir," Frank rasped. "Exceedingly."

Fortinbras put his hands on Frank's shoulders. "I am so sorry for their suffering."

They sat in silence for a moment.

Lincoln cleared his voice. "Do you have any knowledge about the hurricanes' path? Did Tallahassee see any damage?"

"None," Taylor replied. "But the area just south of Orlando has been decimated. Now the Warlord of Tallahassee's position is more entrenched. Civilians from the central penal colony have moved northward. Tallahassee has doubled in population in the past week. All are under the warlord's aegis. The influx is taxing the water and food supplies. There is unrest."

"So options for an incursion are good?"

"Expect a lot of collateral damage," Frank said. "There are many women and children..."

"What do you recommend?" Lincoln asked.

"The Warlord of Tallahassee is universally hated," Taylor said bluntly. "There is no love lost between him and those he purports to rule over. He doesn't do anything for his people. Even his own attendants serve him more out of fear than loyalty. The warlord wouldn't be hard to dispatch. Three or four companies could take him out—and all of his sycophants."

"Would the colonists fight for him?"

"The colonists want clean water and something to fill their bellies. Most of all, they want order and protection. The warlord is providing neither."

"Thank you, gentlemen," Lincoln said, anxious to discuss the matter in depth with Fortinbras. "You've given us a lot to think about."

"One more thing, sir?" Frank said, his voice low.

"Yes?" Lincoln replied, one eyebrow raised.

"Your wife Mika," he said. "Mika is alive."

Chapter 26

Tallahassee, The Florida Penal Colony

The Three One Nine was seldom used, quiet, empty in the midnight hours. The Medicine Girl road Patches hard, covering the 35 colony-miles from Thomasville to Tallahassee before sunrise, even though a few squalls and rainbands blinded both horse and rider.

Having overheard Fortinbras' men give their report, only three words mattered to her: *Mika is alive.* At once, the Medicine Girl had grabbed her knives and a waterskin, mounting Patches within minutes of hearing her mother's name.

She marveled that her mother may have survived the Colonial Williamsburg massacre, wondering about her siblings, hoping they were all safe, too. On some level, she wondered if all she had heard was false information, a ruse to distract Lincoln, make him careless in the coming battle for Tallahassee.

Let Lincoln and Fortinbras draw their maps, plot their stratagems, prepare their men for battle. She couldn't be bothered with begging Lincoln for permission to leave. He would never have let her join Fortinbras' companies of MilitiaMen; instead, he would have relegated her to domestic work, brewing herbs and wrapping twisted ankles and applying salve. He'd never willingly let her go into harm's way, as if he had any control over what she did or did not do.

She decided Lincoln was irrelevant. For the Medicine Girl, there was only one person who lived that mattered and only one throat that needed to be cut.

Over time, Patches' hooves on pavement slowed. She knew her horse needed to rest, his mouth frothing and eyes rolling, although he would have carried the Medicine Girl to the gates of heaven or hell until he dropped. Knowing this, she pulled up a bit on the reins. She slid off of his back before Patches came to a halt.

There was an old shelter by the side of the road, roofless, abandoned. Spidery St. Augustine grass grew between the cracks in the pavement.

She and Patches could refresh themselves a bit at this outpost, as rainwater had collected in crevices and puddles.

As usual, she was hungry. She needed something to eat, needed to clear her head.

The Medicine Girl tied the reins to an old gas pump, then drew a small machete from her thigh holster. As Lincoln had taught her, she circled the building to ensure she was, indeed, alone.

Behind the dilapidated structure, she noticed a cluster of sabal palmettos. She plucked several flowers and chewed on them, plucking a few purplish-black berries, thinly fleshed but sweet.

She remembered her mother's words: *When you feel weak in your body, you need protein. If you cannot find any meat, find nuts. Find beans. If necessary, kill the palm and take its heart.*

And so she did.

This would be a long day, she thought, hacking the woody base. She hoped the heart of the palm was large. The Medicine Girl would need all of her strength.

The Warlord of Tallahassee awoke in his straw tick bed, then slapped a wide-eyed young woman next to him. Half-dressed, she recoiled, a slap the least she feared from him. She gathered her few belongings and scuttled out of the room.

"Come here!" he yelled. A serving attendant entered, carrying a heavily ladened breakfast tray. The warlord grunted, nodding to the round table next to his bed. The attendant set the tray down, placing an assortment of serving dishes before him. The warlord demanded silence, his attendants knowing full well the punishment for interrupting the warlord's thoughts.

His portions of food were huge. The tray held a heaping bowl of scrambled eggs, freshly cut persimmons and figs, sweet nuts, and various dried meats. The serving attendant waited, as the warlord demanded all dishes and uneaten food be taken away the moment he finished.

Lazily, the warlord reached over and grabbed a handful of seasoned alligator meat, shoving it into his mouth. There was a savory flatbread of some sort, a delicacy one of his concubines made that kept her in his favor for the time being. Into his maw, he popped rings of fried dough, slathered in honey butter.

While eating, the warlord brooded in the quietude of his chamber. Soon, he would arise to see what fresh hell awaited him in the main meeting room in his cinder block lair. The old home had changed little over the years. Its few rooms seemed full of gibbering sycophants, who feared the Warlord of Tallahassee and his temper, even more so since the destructive storms sent an influx of refugees from the center of the peninsula.

Although potable water was still available to most, the warlord's food reserves were being depleted. Since the unwelcome immigrants had arrived, the new throngs of beggars offered little to the citizens of Tallahassee but outstretched arms and empty palms. The markets and trade had been hampered; there were simply too many people with too many unmet needs and too little means to buy anything.

Worse, the Kingdom of Georgia hadn't engaged in any Family Trading for weeks, even though he assured them by messenger that all was well in the former penal colony. Rumors of plague and cataclysmic damage from the storms scared any who could buy those selling themselves or their children. So many women had set up impromptu CatHouses that the price for a temporary wife was hardly a colony-dollar, even though few took old currency anymore.

Facing empty stores and emptier stomachs, the warlord's people waded deeper into the swamps to hunt whatever they could, often becoming hunted in turn. In recent weeks, the Tallahassee alligators feasted, the boars attacked, and the coral snakes sunk their fangs into unsuspecting hunter-gatherers. The newcomers, with little knowledge of the plants in the region, also grew sick eating stalks and flowers of flora they knew precious little about.

Business was bad and getting worse. What the warlord really needed to avoid were scores of people dying from hunger and disease. Thus, he kept order the way he always had: unchecked brutality.

It had been easier before, when he had the United Authority's backing.

The strands of razor wire that had cowed the inmates to stay within the borders in the penal colony before the United Authority's fall was always pure theater: the Warlord of Tallahassee came and went as he pleased, as long as he funneled the appropriate taxes into the Richmond coffers and operated as a United Authority stooge.

The Warlord of Tallahassee had always been willing to sell his fealty to the highest bidder. But now that the United Authority was gone, so was the legitimacy and unflagging support for his rule, incompetent as it was.

The Warlord of Tallahassee had never been a statesman; he had no idea or desire how to organize people into a functioning whole, harnessing others' talents and resources to better the community. That was something Mika blathered about, when he used to talk to her.

A cold sickness clenched the warlord's belly. He felt the power shifting, knowing full well that he needed a strong backer to maintain any semblance of power. He had reached out to Darius, pledging his loyalty to the Illuminati Pagans, such as it was. But none of his messengers arrived back in Tallahassee in one piece, a great sign of disrespect.

But it was worse than that. The mutilation of his messengers wasn't just a rejection of an alliance. It seemed to be a promise of what was to come.

The warlord looked at the breakfast tray, still quite full. Petulantly, he took one bite out of each item and spit it back on the tray, one by one.

"Take this to that thing in the shed," he ordered the attendant, who had not moved a muscle during the warlord's repast. "Bring me a jug of blueberry wine," he muttered. "And bring me another girl. Someone new."

The attendant nodded, gathered the bowls and plates onto the tray, and scurried away.

The Warlord of Tallahassee rolled over in bed and gazed at the ceiling, troubled, discontent.

The Medicine Girl recognized the familiar trails leading to her father's lair, slightly changed over the years by the punishing elements.

As a young girl, she'd always observed, paying attention to her father's movements, how he set up men on the perimeter, where he'd position the guards.

Things hadn't changed much.

By midmorning, she was on the outskirts of the warlord's property, a half-colony mile from the cinder block house. She could easily run that far, do what she needed to do, and be back within a colony-hour or two. She was certain how to find her father. She was less certain of where to find her mother, assuming she was even alive.

In a thicket, she loosely tied Patches to a thin tree near a clear stream and a swath of St. Augustine grass. Patches would stay, obedient animal that he was, her clove hitch knot easy enough for the animal to dislodge, if needed. She inspected her knives, drank from her waterskin, and talked to her horse.

"I will be back, Patches. Wait for me here. If I don't come back by nightfall..."

The horse nuzzled her before returning to an especially dense cluster of crimson clover. She wondered if she would ever see him again, but there would be time for reflection later. With a final embrace of her horse's neck, the Medicine Girl set off, running at a steady, brisk pace towards the heart of Tallahassee.

She kept off the main paths and padded through the woods, her leather clad footfalls light on the sodden ground.

The serving attendant knew better than to rearrange the food on the tray before he took it to the shed. The Warlord of Tallahassee took great pleasure in finding ways to humiliate others, but especially *her*. It had been two days since he had brought her anything at all.

As the serving attendant walked to the small enclosure directly behind the cinder block lair, he wondered if she still lived. Mika had been so ill when she first arrived, burned, grief-stricken, exhausted. Mentally, her mind had been too taxed to understand her predicament.

He could hear her sing, on some days.

During those first few weeks that she had been imprisoned in Tallahassee, she would rock on the floor, calling out for her lost children. The warlord had taken great pleasure in exacerbating her injuries and pains, taunting her, kicking her repeatedly until he grew bored. He could be heard screaming at her, terrible things that made the blood run cold.

You think you are more than a slave? I didn't sell you off to have you lord yourself over an entire plantation. Lincoln bought my trash and tried to make you a countess. You are nothing! You have been and will always be nothing!

You think Lincoln loved you? Why would anyone care for you, worthless whore? You only bore me a girl, and a surly little bitch at that. I had them rip your unborn child from your womb to see if you could produce a son. Turns out, you could have— if you had only tried!

You were beautiful once. When you bewitched everyone here with your simpering and fawning. You conjured everything but the poisons I asked you for. Why do you think I bought you? You are so ugly now—no longer useful for anything!

These days, the warlord never talked to or about Mika, merely sending his food scraps to her when he felt like it. On more than one occasion, the serving attendant had smuggled in enough sustenance to keep Mika alive. She was always grateful for the smallest of kindnesses.

The serving attendant knocked on the sliding door to the rusty shed.

"Yes?" her voice replied, pleasant and clear.

"I'm here, ma'am," he said, placing the tray with the remnants from the warlord's breakfast on a rough hewn wood bench. "I'm going to unlatch the door now."

"Thank you."

Thank you, he repeated to himself, sighing. All this time, she never failed to be gracious. *How his heart ached for her and her suffering!* Her gentleness and concern for him personally grieved him. Sometimes he wished she would curse and scream at him—it would make him feel less complicit in her terrible treatment.

The serving attendant hadn't reported the hole she made in the roof, the one she used to collect rainwater. He failed to mention a plastic tumbler missing from a tray either, one she secreted away. It was so easy for one to dehydrate in the stifling Florida heat.

"Are you well?" the serving attendant whispered. "I can find more wild lettuce for your pain."

"Don't take the risk," she replied. "I'll be alright. You must be careful, son."

The serving attendant dislodged the wooden slat that kept the door closed. As the door swung open, Mika crawled to the opening, breathing in fresh air with great pleasure.

Her face was radiant, still beautiful, though scarred on one side from the inferno. Her legs were now useless, the results of a recent savage beating to her lower back. In a way, her paralysis was a blessing, since she often had wept from the chronic pain in her legs, the results from her lengthy torture during the sacking of Colonial Williamsburg.

But Mika's hands and arms were still strong and useful. She grasped the serving attendant's hands in greeting, giving him a dazzling smile.

"I'm so glad you've come." In a self-conscious moment, she struggled to set out the waste bucket she used for a toilet, and her face reddened with embarrassment.

She was used to being the caregiver to others. On some level she felt ashamed for being a burden.

"I'll bring you a clean bucket," the serving attendant said. "There is a lot of food today," he added, attempting to sound cheerful, turning to the wooden bench to pick up the tray.

Instead, he saw a young girl with cold gray eyes standing in front of him, holding a machete.

"I'll take it from here," she said in a low voice.

The blueberry wine had been potent.

The Warlord of Tallahassee opened the patio's steel doors from his bedroom, pissing an impressive arc to empty his bladder. He left the doors open as the day was fair and his bedroom smelled foul. The light breeze was welcome as the storms had moved north, laying waste to those who planned to unseat him from controlling the former penal colony, if the rumors were to be believed. *But in such dark times, who believed in anything anymore?*

He threw himself on his bed, exhaling in frustration.

"Come here!" The Warlord of Tallahassee called out, tired of waiting for the serving attendant to bring him what he wanted. There were so many refugees who would have been delighted with the prospect of pleasing him. *How hard could it be to find him someone new?* He threw an empty plastic glass against the door in protest.

"Come here!" he shouted again, an edge to his voice.

No one came.

This incensed the warlord, who fumbled out of his bed, half dressed, half inebriated.

He stepped out into the hallway.

Empty.

The guards he'd doubled were gone.

He'd have their scalps.

Just as he was determining whom to excoriate, a hideous cry echoed from down the hallway, signaling a discovery of something too awful for words.

The Warlord of Tallahassee hadn't lived as long as he had not to understand that danger was now inside his own lair. He slammed his bedroom door, flicking a long line of latches shut to secure it.

Near the entrance, a thick heavy plank lay, used to solidly bar the door. He hefted it, wobbly in his hands, and slid it into its metal groves.

He felt a brief moment of relief. *It would take a small army to breach his bedroom door*, he thought with satisfaction. That would be enough time to—

The patio door, he remembered, as a greasy coldness washed over him. Turning towards the other side of his bedroom, he sobered up.

Two very angry gray eyes, much like Mika's, seemed to pierce him. The Medicine Girl stood on the other side of his bed, just inside the patio door.

"This place is no longer safe for you," she muttered, seething through clenched teeth. The small machete glinted malevolently in her fist.

The warlord dropped to his knees, rolling near the bed frame, feeling for the weapons he'd secreted there.

Gone.

"Guards!" he screamed, still impotently feeling around the bed frame. He came into a crouch. He kept his eyes on his daughter, watching her every move, her every breath. He knew full well what she was capable of—*he had trained her himself.*

"Your guards are gone. Your weapons are gone," she said in a monotone, toying with the bloodied machete in her hands. "And now I am going to slit your throat."

"You can't kill me," the Warlord of Tallahassee replied, giving a dismissive laugh.

"I'm going to kill you right now."

"I am your *father*. Daughters do not kill their fathers." The warlord needed a weapon, anything to batter her with, but his movements were heavy, his body bloated with food, his mind slowed by blueberry wine.

"You are no father. You aren't even a man."

"I am your father. I am *your father*," he emphasized. "And you and I can rule this colony together. You and I. Together." He held his arms out, offering her a rare smile, showing his rotted and missing teeth.

"Declare your allegiance to no one," the Medicine Girl said. "That was the best advice you ever gave me." She advanced towards him.

"Stay away from me," he said, moving towards the bedroom door, fumbling with the numerous locks. He attempted to lift the heavy plank to free himself, but his hands fumbled, fear appearing to cause his grip to slip. He sank to his knees.

The Medicine Girl rushed him then, poised to strike, her machete high over her head in preparation for a death blow.

By the time she realized her father's ploy, the warlord had grabbed her elbow with his left hand, wrenching it painfully until she dropped her weapon. Then he pulled her arm hard, effectively dislocating it. With his right hand, he jammed two of his filthy fingers, the fingernails jagged and uneven, into her left eye socket. He dug deep.

Recoiling, the Medicine Girl gave an unnatural shriek, covering her damaged eye socket with her right hand. The warlord stood, with almost a friendly grin on his face, pleased with himself. He wiped his fingers on his trousers.

Returning to the bedroom door, the warlord laughed, lifting the wooden bar with ease. He prepared to call out for a guard, an attendant, anyone who must have noticed the commotion in the cinder block lair.

Before leaving the bedroom, he turned to gloat, to take one more glance of the little bitch who attempted to assault him, who threatened to murder him.

Before he could register her movement, the Medicine Girl nimbly jumped on top of his enseamed bed. With her right hand, she pulled a blade-heavy throwing knife from her thigh holster, shifting her weight forward as she let the knife fly.

With a sickening thud, she pinned her father's skull to the wooden door, the blade of the knife cleanly slicing through his left eye socket.

The Warlord of Tallahassee's hands reached for her knife, his hands bloody from attempting to grasp the two-edged blade. He howled loudly in pain and terror, but another knife, thrown just as well, ceased his cries entirely.

"What are they doing?" Lincoln asked.

Fortinbras returned from conversing with his returning scouts. A sea of MilitiaMen and Lincoln's able-bodied attendants were poised, ready to ride down and seize Tallahassee at a moment's notice.

"Apparently, the city is in shambles," Fortinbras replied. "The warlord is dead. There is no leadership in place. The scouts said the locals are infighting. They know we're coming, Lincoln. We'll be walking into a buzzsaw."

"Nature abhors a vacuum, Fortinbras. This might work out well for us, assuming we can contain the situation, assuming we can make order out of chaos. And quickly," Lincoln mused.

"There is a tide in the affairs of men…"

"Which, taken at the flood, leads on to fortune." Lincoln finished the quote and the two men fell to a companionable silence.

"These penal colonists, Lincoln. Brutality is their byword. Now is the time. I say we go. Fortune favors the bold."

"Then we go," Lincoln agreed. "Rucker? Tell the men that—" Lincoln stopped, seeing a solitary horse with two riders heading north on the Three One Nine. He squinted, as the shapes came more clearly into view.

"Stragglers?" Fortinbras asked, but Lincoln had already left, his own horse riding south at a full gallop.

The Medicine Girl had her head down, riding north, seeing the assembled mass of MilitiaMen fanning out before her. She'd wrapped the left side of her face, balling up cotton over her eye until she could clean her wound with garlic and honey and ginger.

Her mother, legs useless, was fastened to her daughter's waist. Mika rode silently, her arms around her daughter.

A lone rider on a steed approached them. The Medicine Girl peering into the afternoon light to see Lincoln, grim-faced and determined.

In no time, both riders converged, both simultaneously slowing their horses to a halt. Lincoln slid off his steed in a heartbeat, walking quickly over to Patches, untying Mika from the lash about the Medicine Girl's waist.

"I know you," Mika smiled, as Lincoln took her in his arms. Mika wove her arms about his neck.

"She can't walk," the Medicine Girl stated, but Lincoln paid her no mind. The Medicine Girl called out to her mother, hoping she wouldn't be afraid. "Mika, this is Lincoln. He is a friend."

"I know Lincoln," Mika said, touching Lincoln's face. "I know Lincoln."

Lincoln buried his face into Mika's neck and sobbed.

"Who is this little girl, Lincoln?" Mika said, her voice carefree and kind. "She reminds me of someone who used to play around here."

At that moment, both Rucker and Jasper rode up, accompanied by a few of Fortinbras' men. Lincoln carried Mika off to the side of the highway, placing her under a shade tree, both of them lost in a private conversation no one wanted to disturb.

The Medicine Girl stood by Patches, who'd found a juicy bit of grass growing through the cracks in the crumbling asphalt. She held her bloodied makeshift bandages, wincing, her feet unsteady. She bent over and vomited.

Jasper approached her.

"I'm glad you're alive."

"I was never in danger," the Medicine Girl answered. "I can handle myself."

"Are you hurt?"

"Probably."

"Should I get the MilitiaMan's medics?"

"I may need all of them," she nodded, her voice thick with pain.

Jasper called out, sending men to summon the field medics.

The Medicine Girl walked a few steps to the road's shoulder, finding a shady spot under a leafy tree. As the adrenalin left her body, the pain flared up in earnest. She knew she needed to clean out her eye socket and administer some type of ointment. *Preferably Neo.* But something was better than nothing.

"Are you coming with us to Tallahassee?"

"Oh, I think I'll wait for you in Thomasville," the Medicine Girl mumbled. "I think I'm going to take up gardening or maybe raising goats..."

"You know, I think goats—"

Several of Fortinbras' men approached. The medic unwrapped the Medicine Girl's bandages without making a sound. *He had seen much worse.* As Jasper watched in horror as the medic cleaned the eye socket with clean water and administered a salve from a small black jar.

The Medicine Girl winced, conscious during the procedure, but keeping stone silent. She let the professional she trained work without asking him too many questions. Her silence let Jasper know she was gravely injured.

Jasper now stood over her, asking her if she needed water, asking her anything to keep her talking. Anything to keep her from going into shock.

He was heartsick at seeing the extent of her injuries.

Another MilitiaMan interrupted Jasper's thoughts. "Excuse me, Jasper, please—but I need to report back to the Colonel."

"Of course, sir." Jasper replied. "How can I help?"

He turned and pointed to the Medicine Girl. "Well, I know who she is. But who is the woman with Lincoln?"

The Medicine Girl now lay motionless.

"Who is the woman with Lincoln?" the scout inquired again, a little more gently.

Jasper crouched down to sit next to the Medicine Girl, putting his arm around her shoulders.

"That woman is—" her voice caught, heavy with emotion. "She's—"

"She is Lincoln's wife," Jasper said, grasping the Medicine Girl's hand. She held onto his, her grip weak and cold.

Tears from her remaining gray eye streamed down the Medicine Girl's face as she wept. Choked with emotion, she tried again to explain who it was that Lincoln held in his arms.

"That is the woman who taught me how to heal, who taught me how to alleviate suffering. Her name is Mika, and she is my mother."

"This place is no longer safe for you," she muttered, seething through clenched teeth. The small machete glinted malevolently in her fist.

Acknowledgements

This feisty little girl would not have come to life without the tender care and nurturing of Russell Norman, who unexpectedly sent me a rendering of the Medicine Girl after reading a short story I'd written. Who knew that one email would lead to the founding of Blue Marble Publishing, two podcasts, a couple of novels, and an enduring friendship? Russell's indefatigable spirit, good nature, creativity, and work ethic inspired me to write my best. His cheerleading made this a labor of love instead of one of futility. No one likes writing into the void, and I am grateful for "the Aussie" who spurred each chapter on, his illustrations capturing exactly what I failed to communicate by words. I am grateful for his ability to read my mind, for his dedication to quality, and for the joy in working on a rewarding project with an equal partner.

A very special thanks to my loving husband, Jim, who took over far too many household chores and domestic duties while I immersed myself in a dystopian world. His keen eye and thoughtful remarks made this a much better book with every revision. His broad knowledge of historical events made my writing about the future much easier, as he could effortlessly explain why mankind repeats—and often amplifies—its failings. Jim's meticulous attention to detail as an attorney caught inconsistencies and errors that no mortal could. For his many kindnesses and unflagging support and love, Jim has all my heart. Thanks for being my companion through the decades and being a wonderful father to Robert, Thomas, and Jack.

To my editors, Scott Pack, Eric Bowles, and Jon Casper—what can I say, gents? You were spot on with your commentary, suggestions, and critiques. I applaud your endless talents and abilities in helping hacks become authors.

Thanks to Reedsy Prompts, especially for Contest #98, where writers were asked to write a story involving a character who cannot return home. The Medicine Girl appreciates your conjuring her into existence.

Most importantly, a lifelong thank you to my beautiful and kind mother, Eva Ann Decker Whitt.

No daughter had a better mother.

The Medicine Girl Saga
The Medicine Woman

Book Two in the Series

In the aftermath of the United Authority's fall—war, pestilence, and famine continue to ravage the land. Nation-states, already reeling from societal and environmental collapse, fail to provide the basic necessities. Bloodshed brings strife to a land born after the end of electricity, as MilitiaMen coalesce around the banners of ambitious warlords.

After five years of relative peace, the Medicine Woman is kidnapped, becoming enmeshed in a brutal conflict between those who love her and those who want to weaponize her.

In the sequel to *The Medicine Girl*, the Medicine Woman struggles to maintain her humanity. Her mother's mandate to "alleviate suffering" proves almost impossible to fulfill as she makes her way through an amoral world—one hell-bent on making her an instrument of destruction.

Scheduled for publication in 2023

Please Check

www.deidrawhittlovegren.com

for updates.